CATCH MY

Breath

The Breathe Series: Book Two

WENDY L. WILSON

Printed in the United States of America
ISBN: 978-0-9962379-2-5

Cover Design by *Cover to Cover Designs*
Cover Photo by *MH Photography*/Female Cover Model, Male Cover
Model, *Julio Elving*,
Author Photo by *Ashleigh Pettis*
Editor, *Jeremy Thompson*
Formatting by *Champagne Formats*

Dedicated to the two most important women in my life ...

Mom and Grandma

You believe in me without hesitation, love me unconditionally and support me whole heartedly through every step of my life. I love you both more than I could ever put into words and am blessed beyond measure for having you in my life.

Finally Moving Forward

9:06 AM ... COME ON. Each tick of the hand thunders through my body as I stare at the large round clock above the doorway to the cafeteria. Click ... another minute passes by in slow motion, deliberately holding me back from moving on to the next chapter of my life.

"And the best dressed this year is ..."

Still watching the clock, I tune out all the chatter of my class-mates seated around me and the ramblings of our class president, busy announcing the most outgoing guy, the shyest girl, the best dancer and most improved student during our senior year. I could really care less. Honestly, I would have preferred to skip out on the whole senior breakfast.

"Wow, best dancer my ass ..." Evan chuckles beside me as I look up to see Grayson Hanners trip over his own feet and barely catch himself before face planting into the food table. "Smooth, real smooth," he whispers in his usual sarcastic tone. I can't help but laugh myself.

Glancing back over to the wall, my body starts to vibrate with excitement. *Ten minutes; only ten minutes left.* Then I will be on my own headed off to California for college and leaving all the painful memories that are associated with this place behind. I'm just ready to move forward; to make my own path in life and leave the one that was chosen for me behind.

"What?!" Evan exclaims, scooting his chair back with a high pitched screech as it grinds against the hard ceramic floor tiles.

The entire class roars as he makes his way to the head of the room. After grabbing his certificate, which is basically nothing but a piece of paper that shows that other students knew who you were, he makes a spectacle of strutting slowly back to our table. Bouncing back down in his seat, he tosses his large white rectangle certificate down beside my award entitled Most Athletic.

"Class Clown," I read aloud and belt out a genuine laugh. *Definitely fitting.* "That didn't actually surprise you did it?" I whisper as a few people around the table look my way.

Evan rolls his eyes as they begin to call out another name. "I was really hoping for Most Witty or Excellence in Sarcasm, maybe even …"

"Most Non-Filtered Student, Socially Challenged or Student Body Smart-ass," I say with a smirk, looking his way.

"Pshhhh …" he huffs out as his lips quirk up at the corners. "I am not socially challenged by any means. You, my friend, are socially challenged. You spend all your time between studying, football and working out. Seriously dude, the monkey-cracker is going to dry up if you're not careful."

Spitting out a cough and nearly choking, I snap my head around to see how many ears caught that comment. Tyler spits out a laugh to the side of me and Nick casually slaps Evan's hand in a congratulatory gesture.

"Hey, it is not going to dry up …" I huff out as Evan barely holds in a burst of chuckles. My stomach starts to ache with impending laughter. Shaking my head, I give up. "I don't care about that shit."

The bell finally rings and I breathe a sigh of relief, however I'm not sure what I'm more thankful about; all the dirty looks we got as Evan made each of us crack up, the fact that the most boring hour of my life is over or that we are done, out of here. Only one more day until graduation, two months of enjoying summer and then I'm off to California; I can't wait.

While a steady stream of bodies flood the room heading for the exit, Evan and I slowly stand up, him with a cheesy smile on his face and me wanting to bolt for the door.

"We did it! We're now adults, ready for the world!" He rolls his eyes and I have to smile at his sarcasm.

"I've been ready for a while," I say more to myself than to anyone else.

"Yes, but now it's official … well … it will be once we get handed that little rolled up diploma. I guess it's rolled up … it always is in the movies. Why the hell do they roll it up if it's so life-altering? I don't want a paper. I want a damn trophy or a medallion to wear around my neck."

An arm falls around my shoulder and I crane my neck to see Tyler with his arm draped over Evan's shoulder as well.

"We all need a damn medal for putting up with your ass for all these years," he laughs.

I chuckle as we join the flow of people rushing out into the hall and pass room after room of freshman, sophomores and juniors, still stuck in class. They all look pissed; I remember that feeling. I always envied the senior's freedom on that last day of school.

"Yeah, right. You guys would be a mess without me around."

Snickering at Evan's confidence in himself, I nod my head agreeing with the irony of his statement. He may have meant it as a joke, but given we met shortly after my mom died, he's pretty on point. I would be a disaster without his smartass comments and bullshit pranks that always have a way of keeping me in the present rather than allowing me to sink into the bottomless pit of my past.

"Hey, Evan … so what's this summer job you're doing?" Matt's voice calls out as he and Nick join us on our way out of the main building and to the parking lot.

"Oh yeah, it's out on my grandfather's property at the lake about five hours from here. He has a slew of cabins that need renovations. Judd and I are heading out the day after tomorrow." He nudges me in the arm as we stop a few yards from my truck. "It's about six to eight weeks of work, twelve hour days, lodging provided, all the sunshine and swimming you can handle and of course, my company to keep everything interesting."

We all laugh, exchanging looks that mock Evan's enthusiasm about being the main attraction.

"You better pitch a better proposal than that," Tyler jokes.

3

Matt clears his throat to the right of me. "Ahh yeah, kinda like how much are we going to get paid for roasting under the hot sun every day and having to listen to your mouth for a whole twelve hours each … and … every … day," he draws out his words for dramatics.

Evan stands tall and presses his lips together in a humorless expression that is hard to take serious. "Does fifteen an hour sound good?"

I swing my head around and make eye contact with him as he winks, code for keep my mouth shut. His grandfather approached me last week about a temporary job at his construction company, that's when we went over the particulars of this job. However, I was offered $18 an hour, so I don't say a word.

"Sounds good to me," Nick says excitedly. "Who all is going?"

"So far, I think it is both of my brothers, Jake and Tristan, Evan's brother, Mitch, then Evan and me," I answer, looking to Evan for confirmation.

"Yep," he agrees.

"What all will we be doing?" Tyler jumps back into the conversation.

"Probably a whole lot of chasing ass with both your older brothers out there." No doubt Matt and the others have heard all about my brothers escapades.

"No way, no how," Evan snaps. "You guys are not going to have time for chicks. So just get that out of your head." He looks around to make sure he has our full attention. "I'm hoping for two teams of four guys so we can split the workload. Grandpa wants a total revamp so we will be doing it all: roofing, painting, new fixtures and awnings, new decks, fixing the docks and whatever else we can dream up." Evan looks around to each of us. "So you guys in?

"Hell yeah, man," Tyler speaks up clearly pumped about the offer.

"I'm in. Some of us aren't getting full ride scholarships to college," Matt laughs shoving me in the arm.

I look at him and grin, proud of the fact that I'm getting a scholarship to the college I want. While these guys were out partying, going to school dances and chasing girls, I was working my ass off for it.

"Yeah, I can't pass up those wages either. Count me in," Nick chimes in putting the crew up to eight guys.

Evan mouths the word "Yes," and then points back and forth between us. "Ok, so tomorrow night … drink, have fun, drop some panties, but … you make damn sure, hangover or not, that you are at the lake by one or two, at the latest. Got it?"

We all nod in agreement, ready to disperse when Matt raises one last question. "So wait, wait, wait. Let me get this straight … so there isn't going to be any girls on the crew," he says, trying to ruffle Evan's feathers.

"No there isn't going to be any girls on the crew. Damn man, do you think we would get anything done?" Evan points out again. "That would be a disaster waiting to happen with Tristan and Mitch out there."

I chuckle. It would be an occupational hazard for my brother to be on a roof with women nearby. *No way would he get anything done.*

"Speaking of chicks!" Matt hollers in a warning tone as I look over my shoulder.

Turning my head, I am met with full lips hell bent on swallowing my mouth whole. *What the hell! Really?!*

"Whoa!"

"Nice!"

"Hell yeah!"

All the guys call out comments and whistle only egging her on further as I pull my head back, severing our contact.

"Hey," I snap with a bad attempt at trying to conceal my annoyance.

Tiffany, a girl I have hooked up with on more than one occasion in the past two years stands only inches from my body with one hand on her hip and the other gracefully pawing at my chest.

Flipping her brown hair over her shoulder, she looks at me through deep dark brown eyes that have lived most of their life under the veil of pain and abandonment. *I really don't want to hurt her feelings. She knows as well as I do that we are not a couple.*

"What? Are you not happy to see me?"

I look down at her hand, slowly trailing back and forth across my chest like I'm a damn dog that she's petting as aggravation bolts through me at her stubbornness and not so subtle need to claim me.

"You weren't this annoyed to see me this past Saturday night," she whispers a little louder than I'd like.

She knows it isn't like that at all.

"Ohhh … burn," Matt calls out, obviously listening in on everything. *Great.*

"Ahhh … I was …" I trail off, not sure what to say as my mouth remains gaped open. I stare over at the guys with a look that is more than likely sending out a distress signal.

Evan shakes his head with his signature smirk in place, before realizing that I am in dire need for help. "Oh yeah hey guys, let's go nail down the game plan for the graduation party." He corrals them away, but quickly leans in towards my ear. "So I see the monkey-cracker isn't being starved after all."

Tiffany lets out a quiet squeal and snakes her arms around my waist. I keep my hands slack at my sides, embarrassed from the public display of affection.

"Hush, Evan," she bats her eyes. "He just doesn't kiss and tell, like you."

"Ha!" Evan blurts out dramatically holding his stomach. "Kiss and tell … honey, I am the master at keeping that shit to myself."

The guys all burst out laughing.

"Man, you would be on the rooftop, air humping and announcing it to the world that you got laid," Tyler belts out as they all start to walk off.

Evan gives me one last look, pointing over his shoulder to the guys. "They don't believe me. They actually think I'm a virgin," he chuckles and then panic takes over his features as he darts after them. "Whoa, wait … do you think I've never …." His voice trails off as I'm left alone to deal with Tiffany.

Pulling her towards the parking lot as I head to my truck, I speak to her gently, not wanting to hurt her feelings, "Tiffany, what are you doing?"

It's not like I don't care about her. She's a sweet girl, attractive as hell and 100% crazy about me, but I don't feel the same about her as she does for me.

She folds her arms across her chest and sticks out her lower lip. I shake my head and laugh.

"I was hoping I could come over tonight," she whines.

"That's not what I meant and you know it," I say in a stern voice letting her know I'm serious.

"Oh come on Judd. We're graduating and never going to see half of these people again. Who cares what they think about us?"

A frustrated sigh spills from my mouth and my head spins with the impending topic of rehashing what we are to each other. This subject seems to rear its ugly head every few months.

She moves in toward me, once again stroking my chest. *I'm going to have to sever whatever this is between us once and for all.* I open my mouth to speak, but luckily get saved just in time by a couple of her friends.

"Tiff, hey … we are going out to Miller's Creek in a bit. You want to come?" one of them yells out, pausing a few feet from us.

"Yeah, wait for me."

My chest remains idle on a breath I didn't realize I was holding as she pushes off my chest and walks away, only to spin around and face me again.

"I'll see you tomorrow night?" The suggestion in her tone rings loud and clear, but I'm sure to any listening ears, they would assume she is talking about graduation and the party. I know she means sneaking in my window later that night. Smiling in reply, I hop in my truck to head home.

Twenty minutes later I'm enjoying the rare pleasure of relaxing; I'm not at the gym, not on the field and not racing off to the farm where I have worked since I was thirteen. I blow out a sigh, sinking my head back into the soft cushion of the couch and close my eyes when the front door swings open.

"Hey," Jake says excitedly, throwing his bag to the floor and slouching down beside me.

Opening one eye, I level him with a stern you're-messing-with-my-quiet-time glare.

Clueless, he looks at me with a wide smile. "You wanna play chess?"

The vibrations of a chuckle move up my throat and out of my mouth as I take in his excitement, so I nod. In no time, he has the board set up on the bar in the kitchen. We both totally suck at this game and we know it, but its quality time together plus we get a kick out of teasing one another at how bad we are.

Crinkling my brows, I stare down at the small tan and black squares. *I hate this game.*

"I saw you walk by my class after breakfast this morning. Everyone in class was moaning and groaning about how it wasn't fair that the seniors get out a whole week early."

I laugh, "It will be your guys turn soon enough. I thought the same thing last year. I was so pissed." Pinching the marble texture of one of my knights between my index finger and thumb, I move one space. "I thought you were hitting the gym today?"

Jake looks down at the board with a puzzled expression.

"That's a check mate, right?" He quickly grabs the instructions booklet and starts silently reading as I clear my throat to bring his attention back to my question. "Oh right ... no. I've got weeks of laying shingles and whatever else Evan will have us doing, so I think I'm good." He looks up and his face falls when he sees me staring him down more than likely the same way Mom used to when we didn't do our chores. "What?" he tosses the box. "Screw the directions."

The door swings open and we both snap our head as Tristan strides in and back to his bedroom without a word. Jake and I remain quiet as the muffled sounds of drawers opening and shutting, fabric swishing together followed by the metal sliding against metal fills the air and already has my irritation peaked. Coming back out of his room and down the hall, he finally makes eye contact, but it takes all the courage I have not to snap when I see the bag clutched in his hand.

"Well, I'm heading out. You two heading that way Saturday morning?"

I grit my teeth, a surge of anger bolting through me with the realization that he is not even willing to stick around for my graduation. Jake immediately swings his head around to look at me. He knows exactly what is going through my head. He was there only a few weeks after Mom's death when Tristan had to walk up on that stage and grab his diploma, knowing Mom wouldn't be there. How could he not be there after that happened to him?

"Yeah, we'll be there," I spit out, my mouth tight and jaw tensed.

Jake looks from Tristan to me and back again. I know he's itching to say something, but I'd prefer to let it lie. I'm not going to beg him to come.

"Wait, Tristan," Jake pipes up as I glare at the back of Tristan's head just before the door closes. "Tomorrow night is Judd's ..."

"I'll see you guys Saturday," Tristan interrupts, glancing over his shoulder and quickly darting his eyes past mine like a scared animal. He knows I'm pissed. "Don't be late and ahhh ..." He pauses at the door, gripping the door knob and for a second, just a millisecond, my heart pounds in my chest thinking he may be the adult in the family for once. "Be careful driving through the hills." He slams the door shut and the room falls silent.

Leaning back in my chair, I fold my arms over my chest, draw my eyebrows down, clamp my jaw and stare at the table, fuming that he is skipping out on it. *What an asshole!* Ever since Mom passed away he has completely checked out of our lives. If you're not sporting a set of double D's then he's not going to waste any time on you.

"He's just caught up in his own world, you know?" Jake says as he stares at me, clearly reading my thoughts or my face for that matter.

I shake my head slowly and fling a chess piece across the board, pissed off that I even let it get to me. This is Tristan and this is what he does.

"No, he doesn't give a damn just like Dad!" I spit out, shoving myself away from the table.

"You know that's not true. He's just screwed up."

Jake is always the first to jump to our older brother's defense. It's in his nature to be optimistic. Don't ask me where he got that from; maybe Mom, who knows. Me on the other hand, I completely butt heads with Tristan. To say I'm not his biggest fan is an understatement. I love my brother, but I'm sick of his selfishness and irresponsibility.

"Well, I've had enough of his bullshit! It's time for him to grow up," I say in a harsh tone. "Seriously, man ... what is it going to take for him to act his age? Mom dies and he decides to throw us on the back burner? We all lost her! All of us!" I let out a sigh and start to pace. "You don't see either of us running around getting plastered every night and going through women like it's a damn contest."

As soon as the words leave my mouth I know they're going to bite me in the ass. My eyes flicker to Jake as he stands up folding his arms with a smirk on his face. My anger quickly dissolves as I take in

9

his amusement as my hand flies up to stop him, but it's too late.

He throws his head back on a laugh. "Wait, wait … I seem to re-call someone else taking part in that contest." His laughter gets louder and it completely breaks through the bitter mood that Tristan has cre-ated in me.

"Shut up," I join in on his laughter, my shoulders shuddering and stomach dancing.

Jake's eyes well up with tears from laughter as he recreates the image he saw the morning after Mom died back when I was only fif-teen.

"You came stumbling in the door at the crack of dawn and I seri-ously thought you had seen someone murdered with the look on your face. Oh my gosh … I can still hear you and Tristan's conversation …"

Quietly pulling the front door shut behind me, I grit my teeth and hold tightly to my shirt and shoes. My feet hurt from the two mile hike home and my head is about to explode.

"Judd, where have you been?" Tristan's voice is like nails down a chalk board. My shoulders tense up as I turn slowly to face his wrath. "I've been worried sick." His face is pinched into a snarl with his nos-trils flared and a deep crease between his brows. He looks like Mom, and instantly guilt rises into the back of my throat.

"I ahh … I …" I don't even know what to say. How do I explain that only seconds ago I woke up in Tyler's pool house with a head full of blonde hair draped across my chest, absolutely no recollection of what happened only hours before and my bare body flush up against another much more curvy body that is also stark-ass naked.

"Spit it out, Judd. Why didn't you come home? Do you think I don't have enough on my plate right now? I cannot … cannot handle you going off and disappearing right now!" he hollers, sounding more like a parent rather than my brother. "No call, nothing."

He folds his arms over his chest and gives me an intense glare; not quite angry and not hurt, more like confused and overwhelmed, waiting for answers that I don't have.

"I'm sorry," I sniffle, my chest quickly heaving with the threat of an emotional overload. "I don't know what to tell you." Tears well in my eyes, instantly rolling down my face and gathering at my chin.

Tristan's expression softens as he takes a seat at a bar stool in the kitchen. "Just start from the beginning, then," he says calmly as if our mother did not die less than twenty-four hours ago.

So that's just what I do. I start from the beginning, from the second I got home and found Mom's bed empty, to the next minute when I was at Tyler's house for a small party he was having since his parents were out of town.

"I didn't think it would hurt. I just thought if I drank, I might forget about it all." Tristan's eyes look vacant as I talk about losing Mom and for some reason that breaks something inside of me. It makes me feel distant and fractured from any connection with him. "The next thing I know, I was waking up this morning in bed with a girl and condoms on the floor beside us."

At last Tristan's face changes and emotion takes resident, only not the kind I was expecting. "So what happened with this girl?" he snickers.

Shooting him a glare for laughing at a time like this, I ball my hands at my side and yell, "It's not funny, Tristan. She was naked and so was I." I pause, taking in how he presses his lips together to hide his widening grin. "Do you know what this means?!"

"Umm ... yeah, I think I can figure it out," he stumbles over his words as he suppresses a laugh.

What the hell is funny about this? "She could be pregnant!" I shout out with tears streaming down my face one after another.

He breathes out a quiet chuckle and tilts his head as if he pity's me. "Judd, condoms were created to prevent that one thing so I'm thinking you're ok. Actually, I'm impressed."

My eyes widen and I drop my mouth open in disbelief. "Impressed?! That I got drunk and slept with some girl I don't even know? I don't even know what we did or who she is."

Tristan puts his hand out to calm me down, "No, I'm impressed that you were so drunk you don't remember and still thought to use a condom. That's a plus and you know what, this sort of thing happens. You're not the first kid to do something like this."

This is most definitely not something Mom would have said. She would have tanned my hide and asked questions later. Screw the condom. She would have banned me from any store that even carried

11

them until I was thirty if she were here; she would be so disappointed in me.

My mouth is agape, but he continues to laugh, covering his huge grin with both his hands. It's no use, two deep dimples dip into each of his cheeks as his eyes glimmer with amusement. Just what the hell is so funny about this? I am mortified, confused, no longer a virgin, curious as hell on who this girl was and about to break into a fit of sobs that have no end in sight. But just as my confusion hits an all time high, it's quickly amplified when my brother gets up from the bar stool and throws his arms around my shoulders.

"Judd, don't worry. You're a responsible kid and it happened ... it may suck how it happened, but eventually it happens to all of us. I'm just shocked you beat me to the punch." I laugh and look up at him, embarrassed yet comforted by his words and affection. "Listen, let's get all Mom's craft supplies together and go out to the wishing well. I have an idea, something I want to do to pay tribute to her. I think she would love it and we need to do this." He holds me at arm's length, looking into my eyes. Deep down, facing anything that has to do with knowing she is gone will more than likely tear me apart, but with the viewing, followed by her funeral, I know it will leave all three of us reeling with grief and unable to focus on anything.

Just as we have all of Mom's mosaic supplies gathered and while I am frantically searching for my wallet, a knock sounds at the door, immediately putting a knot in my stomach. Tristan swings the door open and a flash of bright blonde hair greets us. My mouth drops. I cannot say a word.

"Hi, ummm ... I wanted to return this to ummm, Judd." The girl stands on our front porch, in a short sleeve tee and slim fitting jeans, much more than I saw her in last. She has a sweet smile, but I can immediately tell she is older than me. Silence fills the room and suddenly it seems deafening as Tristan glances back with a smirk and she continues to bat her eyelashes in my direction. What do I do?

"Ahhhh ..." I try to speak, but my tongue folds in on me and decides no way, not going to do it.

Tristan clears his throat and looks back at the girl, wiping the shitty grin off his face. "Yeah, that's my little brother. Umm, here," he says, pulling the wallet out of her hand and handing it back to me before stepping outside. "Let's go outside to talk."

After he pulls the door closed behind him, I'm so stunned that I could swear my brain just shut down. Still, like a magnet my ear is pulled along with the door and glued to the hard wood surface instantly.

"Do you know he is only fifteen? He's just a kid. What were you thinking?" His voice is muffled but I can still make out every word.

"Geez, I didn't know," she snaps back. "Relax, it's not like I'm going to expect him to marry me or anything. We both just drank too much and one thing led to another. It didn't dawn on me that he was your brother."

"Well he is going through a lot right now so I really doubt ..." my brother starts, but her pleading tone cuts him off.

"I know, I know. I heard what happened and I didn't put two and two together until I woke up this morning and saw his wallet. I saw his name and address and realized that he is your younger brother." She pauses and I crush my ear to the door harder to strain to hear. "I'm so sorry to hear. Will you still be at graduation?"

"Yeah, I'll be there. My mom would have ...." His voice trails and I hear an emptiness in his words as if he is holding back so much more than he is putting on. Taking an immediate detour, his voice kicks up a notch, "Judd tells me he used condoms? So I assume I can tell him you are not carrying his child."

"Oh my gosh, don't say that. I am graduating in just a few weeks. We were safe ... don't worry. He had some in his wallet."

"Well, he was a virgin up until last night, so I guess he was just prepared," my brother chuckles and I want to die from the amount of information he is giving out. "So, if he asks what all happened, what should I tell him?"

I want to vomit.

"Weeeellll, here," she draws out the first part of the comment in a flirtatious tone, "Give him this and tell him I had a really good time."

Laughter followed by the door knob turning has me lunging away from the door and clear to the other side of the room. I shove my hands in my pockets and try my best to look bored all while my insides are jumping.

I look up as Tristan makes his way to me with a sneaky smirk on his face and a small square of paper in his hand.

"Here you go," he holds the paper out and I grab it hesitantly, my thumb sliding across the smooth crisp edges before I hold it up to see what is on it. "Congratulations stud, apparently you must have rocked her world," he spits out a laugh as I look the note over.

Judd,
I had fun! Give me a call over the summer and maybe we can hang out.
Jess
(555-2346) Call me!! ♡

Friday night comes in a blink of an eye and I am more than ready. I stroll into the gymnasium to grab my cap and gown and am immediately greeted with Evan's sarcastic mouth.

"Man, let's ditch this. Who needs to graduate, anyways? There's a street corner that looks highly profitable that I had my eye on. There are plenty of women that would pay good money for this body."

Laughing, I slip my gown over my shoulders and start heading to the football field. Everyone is already lining up in rows and calmly waiting for the music to start, although inside surely they are all bouncing around like me.

A while later my entire body is wound tight with anxiety and anticipation, music finally belts out over the sound system. A teacher motions for the first person in each line to slowly walk to their designated seat and I let out a relieved breath. My feet begin to follow along with the person in front of me, but walking slowly is a challenge. What I really want to do is hightail it up front, grab my diploma and toss my cap out my truck window as I drive away. However, that's not going to happen so I do as the teacher instructs and stroll to the second row of seats.

Once I'm in my seat, my eyes wander to the sea of people filling up the bleachers. It's not likely that he changed his mind and even more doubtful that I would be able to spot him in the crowd, but I look for Tristan anyways. Of course, disappointment fills my heart once again as I find no trace of him.

The last four people take their seat and the principal steps up to the podium. Minutes stretch by with speech after speech, although it's all garbled words as my mind swims through thoughts. *Tristan's not here. Mom's not here and Dad's not here.* I look around again at all the faces in the crowd, some old, some young and nearly all of them with a huge smile portraying just how proud they are to watch someone they love graduate into life.

"Judd Michaels to the University of California."

My head snaps to attention and I stare at my peers before noticing a couple bodies here and there standing. *Oh shit!* I bolt to my feet and smile; my face flamed with embarrassment for being caught in a daydream while they were announcing scholarships. Loud cheers arise, but the loudest of them all is my obnoxious best friend.

"Judd the stud!" he belts out with a loud whistle as all the members of the football team join in with whoops and hollers.

I lower my head, grateful that no one seemed to notice my lack of attention on one of the biggest days of my life.

The seconds draw out in slow motion until one by one each of the kids that I have spent years growing up with heads to the stage. My row stands and forms a line. I take this moment to make eye contact with Evan standing six bodies in front of me. He flashes me a huge grin and a bit of nerves takes hold, leaving my hands jittery and my stomach flipping in excitement.

"Justice Allen Whithers," the first name in my row is called out. I anxiously watch as each person shakes hands with our superintendent then proudly grasps their diploma; that tiny certificate that signifies over a decade of learning, staying awake for eight hours a day and anxiously waiting for this day to come.

"Evan Dane Jansen."

The superintendent of the school waits while he casually struts up, making a complete spectacle as usual. Evan comes to a stop and sticks his hand out, crossing it over to grab his diploma. Of course with Evan you can never expect to be serious. He slaps his hand sideways against the superintendants hand, grabs hold of his forearm then moves his hand down into a fist grip before grabbing his certificate.

Our superintendent seems taken aback at first, but when a loud cry of laughter moves over the entire student body, he soon joins in. Nodding his head, he says something to Evan and they resign to a normal serious hand shake. I cheer on my friend as he pumps his fist in the air and hops off the stage. A few more names are called and then the moment I've been waiting for is upon me.

"Anthony Judd Michaels" the voice rings in my ears, beckoning me forward.

One-by-one, I step up the stairs and outstretch my hand. It falls down on the smooth rolled form and a huge breath escapes me. My name is shouted out in several directions from my classmates, but my mind is so loud it all fades out as I shake the superintendent's hand. *Finally, I'm moving forward.*

The After Party

AFTER TEN MINUTES OF scurrying around to reclaim my cap, forty five minutes of mingling and a whole lot of pictures with classmates, we're on our way.

"So Tyler's parent's said it's cool?"

Evan laughs as we wind along a dirt road out in the middle of nowhere, behind a line of cars all heading to our graduation party.

"Yeah," Evan keeps his eyes on the road as we turn past a huge metal gate onto a private lane that leads up to Tyler's parent's 52 acres of farm land. "They only have one rule and that is for everyone to turn their keys in at the door."

I laugh as we pull into a field where all the cars are parking side-by-side. A worn looking barn sits to the right side of the field with loads of people slowly trickling in, all carrying coolers while some lug in band equipment.

"Evan, keys?" Tyler hollers from behind us as we hop out of the jeep.

"Yeah," he yells back, tossing them in the air. Tyler catches them and makes his way around, gathering more from others that are hopping out of their cars. "I'm the sober tonight though, so I'll need them back around midnight. We have too much shit to do tomorrow for me to be hitting the bottle," he calls out loud enough that myself, Tyler, Matt and Nick get his drift.

We join up with a couple of our classmates as we walk inside the dilapidated barn. A band is setting up in the corner, several people are milling about with drinks in their hands and the party is already underway. I grab the nozzle of the keg sunk into a pile of dirt in the corner and watch my cup slowly rise to the rim with a thick layer of sudsy froth nearly spilling over the edge.

Evan hangs back, talking to a group of guys that he played baseball with.

It doesn't take long for warmth to settle in my chest and the misty effects of the alcohol to begin to cloud my judgment. When you spend all your time working out, playing football and training, it leaves little time for drinking so my tolerance sucks.

Comfortably lounging in a pile of hay that I hope no horse has pissed in, I lean back and close my eyes as soft hands comb through my hair. Casey, our head cheerleader, gracefully sits on a hay bale behind me straddling her legs on either side of my head while a couple of my teammates along with a few other girls go on and on about their summer plans. I can't concentrate on a single word, though. My mind and body are centered on the hand that keeps dipping into the back of my shirt.

All of my thoughts are getting hazy and the more I drink the better her hands feel on my skin. *I need to cut myself off and find Evan before I have a replay of the first time I got drunk.* I hit several firsts that night in my drunken stupor and have regretted it ever since.

"Hey guys, I'm gonna take off," I speak up, careful to pronounce each syllable of each word.

I pull myself up to stand, stumbling then quickly catching my balance. My legs are heavy as weights as I step through the hay back to the main area of the party where everyone is dancing and listening to the band that is playing at an ear-splintering volume. I sweep the room, everything blurring together, but my eyes quickly fall on Evan, slumped on a speaker in the corner with a bottle of water in his hand and a smirk ticking at the corner of his lips as he watches me walk up.

"Man, I have never noticed how ignorant people act when they are drunk. Did you see that chick over there?" He tells me pointing out in the crowd to a girl that is swinging her shirt above her head.

Someone needs to cut her off. I laugh and turn my head back to him.

Evan jumps off the speaker, pursing his lips as he nods his head. "You're drunk off your ass, aren't you?"

I bust up laughing, but stop abruptly when I see Tiffany in the distance making a beeline for me.

"Can we get out of here before I'm too hammered to stand?"

Evan follows my line of sight. "Yeah, leaving isn't going to stop her, Dude. You know that."

I'm already staggering away towards his vehicle, keeping my eyes pinned on her. Luckily, after grabbing his keys from the warden, we both reach the jeep. I jump in, immediately pressing my head into the hard headrest and close my eyes with my mind light and hazy with the weight of sleep setting in.

"Wake up because there is no way I am carrying your ass inside," Evan says as his hand shoves at my shoulder.

"What the …." barely coherent. I stop talking, shake my head and clutch onto the doorframe for support before pushing his hand off and sliding out. "I've got this."

His laughter fills the air and I don't even have to look back to see the smart-ass expression on his face. "Don't forget to get your butt up and out to the lake as early as you can tomorrow."

I raise my hand in a salute, too sleepy to form words.

Inside, I stagger back to my bedroom, stumble to my bed and throw myself into my hard mattress. With my face buried into the security of my pillow, I slide my hand over my denim jeans, into my pocket and pull out my phone. Not concerned with where it will land, I toss it onto my nightstand with a quick look at the time. *1:11*; at least I'll get a solid six hours of sleep before we hit the road.

A lead weight pulls at my eyelids as I flip onto my back, encompassed with the serene sensations of sleep as I drift off.

A loud thud erupts in my dark room, ripping me out of my dreamless slumber and has me on high alert. I snap my head up. "What the hell?"

Tiffany lays flat on her belly on the floor below my window with my nightstand knocked over beside her.

"What are you doing?" I ask in an annoyed tone, rising up to stand. *So much for a solid few hours of sleep.*

I help her up then reposition my furniture, scooping up my phone and checking the time. Only two hours have passed since I got home.

Tiffany's body falls in bed behind me, curling up under the sheets and nuzzling her head to my pillow as if it is the most natural thing in the world. *Great!*

"Tiffany, how did you get here? You didn't drive, did you?"

She shrugs her shoulders from under the covers and that automatically tells me she probably did. *Damn it, she's going to kill herself one of these days.* I scoot in beside her, restlessness and the spiraling remnants of a buzz has me dismissing any thoughts of what we should and shouldn't be doing right now. Her soft breaths grow steady beside me so I close my eyes as her body nuzzles against me. There is no need for conversation tonight. We can talk in the morning. My eyes seal shut once again and sleep takes over.

A tickling sensation across my chest and the rustling of sheets wakes me. Glancing down, I notice I lost my shirt somewhere in the middle of the night and Tiffany is slowly trailing wet kisses over my abdomen with her chestnut brown hair cascading around her face and soft suckling noises every time her mouth meets my skin. *This is going in the exact direction that neither of us needs it to go.* With it being morning and her hand grazing the top of my thigh, not all of my body is in agreement though. Ignoring my body's desire, I firmly grab her shoulder to stop her from the seductive mission she always seems to be on.

"Hey, you can't keep doing this to yourself. You know it's not going to work."

She places her elbows on my chest and looks into my eyes with a pouty expression. If it weren't for my throbbing headache, I might even fall for it; I always have before.

"Judd, we can do the long distance thing, you know. We could try at least," she says in an innocent voice that she usually uses to break through my defenses.

"It's not going to work this time so you can quit with the act."

She huffs out a breath and crooks her eyebrows into a pissed off frown. *I really don't want to hurt her feelings. I never do, but she always seems to leave crying. I hate that.* The one thing I've always had a hard time handling is seeing a woman cry. It makes something break apart inside of me and I'm willing to do anything to take their pain away. A single tear and I am reminded of all the times Mom would cry. She would cry every single time she came home from the doctor's office, for months after Dad left and every time she thought no one was watching. Eventually, when she had no more tears to give this Earth, it was our turn to cry with the knowledge that she was never coming back.

Taking a deep deliberate breath of courage, I gulp down my hesitation of discussing this yet again, and open my mouth, "No we can't try. You know I don't feel the same and that wouldn't be fair to you." I speak as gently as possible while sitting up against my headboard.

Rising up to face me with her body softly draped over mine, she looks at me with fluttering eyelashes and an impending storm brewing within her.

Desperate to nip this in the bud, I grasp her hand in mine and give it a caring heart-felt squeeze.

"Tiffany, I know you have this void inside you that you keep trying to fill. I understand … I have that same void, you know. We've discussed that a million times. Not having a Mom and Dad growing up has just left you empty and desperate for love, but this isn't the way to fill it. I care about you … I really do. I just don't feel what I should if we were going to have a relationship."

We've had numerous conversations about our pasts and although I've never shared with her everything about my Mom and Dad, she does know that neither of them are in the picture; a common factor of life that we share.

Unlike me though, she has bounced around from foster home to foster home since she could remember and every time a foster parent is ready to pass her on to the next, it takes a chunk out of her. Those tattered, broken pieces of her heart have left her with non-existent self-esteem and a deep need for love.

That is exactly what led us to each other. When I first met her it was through hearsay in the locker room. I'd overheard a lot of guys saying that she was easy. I'm not the type to take advantage of that, but her name stuck with me. After a football game, I caught her behind the bleachers with one of my teammates that had just been talking shit about her, calling her a slut and making a bet with a couple of guys.

It made my stomach turn. My ass would be black and blue had I ever talked about a woman like that; Mom would not have stood for that. That single memory had me slamming my fist into his face for the disrespect he was showing Tiffany. Since then, she has been convinced that she loves me as if I'm some type of Prince Charming ready to carry her off into the sunset. The one mistake we made after that is falling into a pattern of leaning on each other for companionship and comfort, so the lines between friendship and a relationship have become blurred.

I slip my shirt back on as we continue our conversation, "I know this is a lot of my fault. We should have never crossed the lines." I put my best effort forward while trying to spare her feelings. "I truly think the world of you, I hope you know that, but when we are together, it should feel different … I mean I should …" I pause and watch as her eyes well up with tears. "I mean, just think …" My heart aches watching her hurt from my words and now I just want to stop talking, push it aside and discuss it some other time. This is what always happens.

Before I know it she is in my lap with her arms around my shoulders. I place my hands at her waist to hopefully ease the pain I am causing by letting her down.

"We just can't …" my words are clipped off as her mouth falls back to mine and now my sense of remorse switches to anger. *Why the hell does she keep doing this to herself? It's like she is not hearing me!*

Annoyance festers inside of me at her persistence. "Tiffany, no, I mean it. Please, don't make this harder than it already is," I beg her, nudging her away.

"But I love you and I know you would love me if you tried."

Oh shit, she had to say that. Why does she have to say she loves me?

"No, I won't … I don't," I snap and immediately regret putting it that way. "But that doesn't mean I want to lose you. I like hanging out with you, but being together like this has to stop. This isn't good for either of us. It's like we are just using each other to fill that void and it just leads you on and it only confuses me. You deserve so much more than you know, Tiffany."

She leans back to look at me, hanging onto my neck. I keep a firm grip on her. *Wait, I actually have her complete attention. She isn't arguing with me this time. She isn't trying to talk over me. She is listening.*

I go on, "You're gorgeous and you have such a big heart. Some guy is going to be so lucky to have your love." Her eyes sparkle with unshed tears and my heart tightens at the sight, but I push on, "Please don't cry. It's just ... don't you want to have a life with someone that knows exactly what they want; someone that isn't going away and will be here any second you need them?"

She studies my face as if I'm telling her the secrets of life before finally speaking. "But I want it to be you," she whispers and it is nearly my undoing.

It's not my love in particular that she desires it's just love in general. I guess when you're deprived of it your whole life, you become desperate, almost frantic for it. I've always been clear with her that I'm only interested in being friends but then we'll get caught up in the moment and one thing leads to the next. Afterwards, I feel like an asshole and I'm sick of feeling like an asshole.

"No you don't, because before me there was always someone. You deserve to find someone that really loves you and I know you will find it someday, just don't sell yourself short, ok?"

Nodding, she slowly slides off my lap to sit beside me. Once her hand reaches to wipe away a few fallen tears, I bounce up and in two steps I'm at my desk, ripping a tissue out of a blue cardboard container. I step back over to her and crouch down offering up the tissue as I look into her eyes. We've been here on more than one occasion and I'd really like to know that this conversation did in fact stick. *Time for this merry-go-round to stop.*

After blotting her deep dark eyes, she lifts her lips into a small smile that brings me hope. I don't want to hurt her; that's never been my intention.

Just as I'm about to wrap up the subject, a loud thud breaks the comfortable silence of my bedroom and makes us both jump as the door swings open.

"Hey, did you want to grab something to eat on our ..." Jake's voice trails off as he looks from Tiffany to me and back again. "Sorry, I didn't know you had company." He immediately spins on his heels.

"Jake, it's not ..." No sooner than the words are out of my mouth, the door swings shut and he darts away.

"Well," she says in a cheerful tone that is much different than just moments ago. "I better go and let you be on your way." She stands up and wraps me in a monstrous hug. "I guess this is goodbye? Will you be back before it's time to leave for college?"

I pull away enough to look into her eyes.

"I'll be working about five hours from here for the next month and half or so then I'll just have three weeks back home before I leave for California."

She doesn't say a word, but as her soft lips place a gentle kiss against mine, her goodbye is felt like a whisper in my ear. She's been such a big part of my life in the last few years. There have been times that I thought I wouldn't survive the night as I grieved over my mother, but her being there, even in silence helped ease the heaviness in my heart.

"Bye," I whisper, knowing I'll keep in touch with her and always be here if she needs me. "Promise me, you'll be good." She smiles and nods her head, completely understanding my meaning.

After walking her out to her car, Jake and I hit the road. We are running about an hour behind so we make the decision to grab a quick bite to eat at home rather than stopping. The ride there is boring to say the least, so I close my eyes for a few extra hours of sleep.

Scrunching up my face as my eyes peel open, I'm greeted by blinding sunlight and a blur of trees passing by the passenger window.

"Where are we?" I say, pressing my arms to the roof of the truck and bowing my back to stretch.

"Almost there. About thirty more minutes."

I sit up straight and look around, everything beginning to familiarize. Jake and I have come out here on several occasions since Evan and I first met. Glancing over, I notice Jake shifting uncomfortably in his seat.

"You want me to take over?" He quickly shrugs and I decide I best discuss other things before we get to the lake. "Hey, what you walked in on this morning was nothing. We were just talking, that's it."

He laughs and gives me a sneaky almost embarrassed grin over his shoulder. "You really don't need to explain. I've seen her over more than once, Judd. Besides, I didn't think another thing about it. I just didn't mean to bust in like I did."

"Yeah, I just wanted to clarify that it was not what it looked like." He has seen her leaving my room before, I know that, but the last thing I want him to think is that I am anything like Tristan. Walking in on strange girls in his room is a common thing in our house. He really needs to use some sort of code for when someone is in there keeping him company.

"It's ok," he chuckles, his chest shaking and vibrating with amusement. "I had hoped you would relax, unwind and enjoy the after party. I just figured you took my advice and brought the party home."

We both erupt in laughter as I shake my head in complete disagreement with his assumptions.

All Work and No Play

GRAVEL CRUNCHES BENEATH OUR tires as we pull into the lot between two cabins. Water stretches out in front of us with a dock and a small convenience shop to the right and a quiet, sandy beach to the left.

My brother and Mitch both stand to the left near Evan's grandfather's cabin, both with their arms folded over their chest as Evan points to a mass of shingles that have been stacked against the cabin.

More crunching sounds rise into the air behind us as a red truck pulls into the lot. *I guess we are not the only ones running late.*

"Whoo, you boys ready for this?" Tyler hollers, looking much livelier than I feel.

"I'm ready," Jake says. "I think Judd's just ready to pack up and get to California." He settles up beside me, nudging me with his elbow.

He throws his door open and jumps out, Nick and Tyler soon following his lead.

"Are you in a hurry to leave us all behind?" Matt laughs.

Matt slaps me on the shoulder and I narrow my eyes at Jake, with a sliver of a smile. "I am not in a hurry to leave."

Jake laughs, seeing right through me. He knows very well that I am anxious to leave, but what I haven't found the courage to tell him yet is just how hard leaving him will be. He's my baby brother, one of my best friends, the one person that I stood side-by-side with the day I found out Mom died and the same person that cried with me each day as we waited for Dad to come back.

"I'm just in a hurry to play football again." Shame tugs at me as I try to explain myself while waging a silent conversation with Jake. *I need to talk with him soon.*

Nick and Tyler join us and we all make a ceremony out of slapping hands and shoving each other in a cave-man like greeting.

"I hear ya," Tyler looks around, glancing over to Tristan and Mitch, both which also played football back in high school. "We practically have a team gathered now."

"With the exception of Evan's baseball-loving ass," Nick adds, igniting laughter from us all as the others walk up.

"Hey, no hating on baseball; it's un-American dammit. Show some respect." Evan smirks as we all laugh.

"Man, this is impressive," Tyler glances around at the view. "So all this is your grandfather's land?" He points around at an endless row of rustic cottage-like cabins that run along the water's edge.

"Only the ones on the west side of the lake. Oh and that one he sold to an old friend years ago. Their son owns it now and used to come out with his family but it hasn't been occupied in a couple years." Evan's face etches into a frown for a second as he points to the parallel cabin then out to the opposite side of the lake. "All those belong to some big shot that sunk a shit load of money into amping his side up. It was like a war between my grandfather and him at one point, fighting to appeal to the summer vacationers," he chuckles as we all glance over across the steel blue waters to the bigger, pricier cabins.

The rest of the afternoon, we walk the entire property, sweating our asses off and finding out what needs to be done and who will be doing the work. We're each assigned specific duties and a crew to work with. Luckily, and as expected, I work side-by-side with Evan.

He hangs onto a clip board as we go from cabin to cabin and stays in a totally serious tone while talking with us. This is a side he rarely shows, but when his grandfather puts him in charge of something he definitely takes it to heart, abandoning his usual sarcastic-everything's-a-joke demeanor for an all-work-and-no-play attitude.

So far the local store called The Snack Shack is about the only building that is not in bad need of a makeover. It's hard to believe that we can get it all done in a little over a month.

When the sun begins to set, we all disperse back to our cabins and call it a day. Grabbing my bag, I roam down to the shower house to get cleaned up. Running late this morning left me with no time for a shower, and considering I was laying in hay for half of the previous evening, I have no doubt that the other's probably think I smell like a barn.

Inside the shower house I look around and laugh. *This one is going to be fun.* The dark dreary atmosphere meshed with crud and grime caked in every crevice reminds me of a rest stop that you would see in a horror flick.

Dropping my bag onto a bench in one of the shower stalls, I pull the curtain shut and quickly slide out of my clothes. The water comes out cold at first but with the hangover I have had all day, I welcome the shock to my system. After turning the knob to slightly tweak the temperature of the water, it washes over me while I stare down at the mini cyclone of water swirling around the corroded metal drain. With a deep breath, I imagine all my worries, all my pains of the past being swept away with it. *This is going to be a good summer. I'm going to get along with my brother. I'm going to have fun. No distractions; no girls sneaking in my window and we are five hours away from every horrible memory I have had in my life.*

Thankfully, the next few weeks fly by with busy days and relaxing evenings. For the most part we start working on one cabin at a time until it is completed before moving on. There are a total of eighteen cabins on his grandfather's property and numerous out buildings so it has required some pretty long hours. Each day we work from sun up to sun down and then lug our equipment back to the tool shed. Our down time consists of hitting the beach afterwards, even though half the time none of us have the energy or motivation to do anything but lay around.

"Ok, that's it. I can't do it anymore," Tristan announces as he scoops up a towel and heads towards the door. "Screw swimming at the beach with a bunch of guys I've had to look at for nearly four weeks straight. I'm going nuts."

He holds his hands out as if this will emphasize the level of frustration he is getting at. We all hear him loud and clear. Evan chuckles while we all grab our stuff. Tonight Evan, Jake and I decided to skip out of the swim and take the boat out for some night fishing.

"I'm sure you'll find a large supply of skimpy swimwear across the lake, man … just don't get too carried away and end up missing work. We are making good progress and I'd like to get all of it done before schedule."

"Don't worry … depending on what we find over there, we'll be back," Tristan laughs.

"Wait. Are you all headed over there?"

"Why not? Seriously, a four week dry spell is about all we can stand. We have to go find some action. You guys wanna join?"

Evan looks at me and Jake with a warning in his eyes. Jake smirks at me and shakes his head slowly, almost as if he is gauging what I want to do before answering.

"No, we're not going catting around with you," Evan says before either me or Jake can answer. "… and you better not be late in the morning, Tristan … I'm serious."

I laugh at Evan's serious tone as Tristan lets the screen door slam shut. He knows as well as I do that work will take a backseat for my brother if women are involved.

With a wide grin, Tristan sticks his head back inside between the screen and door frame. "You sure you don't want to join us."

Evan frowns and Tristan laughs harder, allowing the door to fall closed as he jets off towards his car.

"He's not going to be back by morning, is he?"

I shake my head and look at Jake who also has an all-knowing smile. "Definitely not," I inform him without a doubt in my mind.

"No way," Jake adds, grabbing his pole and tackle box. "We'll deal with it tomorrow. Let's go catch some fish."

The next morning, and as expected, Evan, Jake and I get started at the crack of dawn and the rest of the gang strolls into the parking lot about an hour later, amplifying the bad mood that Evan already seemed to be in. Stationed on the roof of the first cabin, which is Evan and Mitch's grandfather's personal cabin, we stay busy replacing the decking, throwing down new tar paper and then laying new shingles one-by-one.

The sun is high overhead reflecting off the surface of the lake and calling out to us like a tall glass of water that we want desperately, yet can't quite reach. I shed my shirt hours ago hoping for a bit of relief from the heat, but the kicked up temps seem to be sautéing my skin as sweat rolls down my forehead, arms, neck and back.

"Did you see that one chick? She could not get enough of this." Tristan stands tall, flipping his hand down the length of his body as if he's a luxury menu item.

Matt cracks up, "Which one? I saw a couple disappear with you."

"Don't give him that much credit, boys ... they just knew I was waiting over by the dock," Mitch adds in a cocky tone just as annoying as Tristan's.

"Shhhhhitttt ... you wish!" Tristan arches his brows. "Anyways, the only one I was wanting to join me is the owner's daughter dressed in that skimpy little number that's staying in the huge front cabin with all her uppity friends. She is a serious freak," he shrugs. "Figured that'd be fun."

"Oh we could hear the freak coming out of her all the way over at the beach." Tyler chuckles with his eyes widened.

Tristan nods with a grin.

Wiping at his forehead, Tyler swings his head over to Evan. "I think we should call it a day, don't you Evan?" Tyler pipes up.

"Sounds like a plan to reconvene across the lake." Tristan snickers igniting a dirty look from Evan. I shake my head at his ridiculously obnoxious comments.

"No way, man! We need to at least get half of this roof laid before the end of the day! Get your lazy ass back to work! It's only mid morning!" Evan snaps.

Hours at it and his pissy mood only seems to deepen. *Maybe the heat is getting to him.*

"Hey are you going to bite my head off if I jump down to get a drink?" I ask fairly certain he is going to tell me to get back to work.

Evan nods his head and then yells out. "If you need a drink, have to take a piss or need to cool off that's fine as usual, but we're on a time-crunch today. Do what you need to do, and get your butt back to work so we can get this done."

He flashes a bit of smirk and I laugh. It's in his nature to goof off just like the rest of us, but he is determined to make this summer job go off without a hitch, so he can take over his grandfather's company when he steps down.

Hopping off the roof, I make my way over to my truck for a drink. Right now, throwing the jug of water over my head sounds more appealing than drinking it. My feet ache and my back is shouting out in pain as I walk across the lot. My hand falls on the door handle of my truck and I make sure to grab my hat first. My hair keeps sticking to my forehead and the sting in my scalp tells me it is bright red by now. After weeks in the sun, my back resembles a sheet of leather more than flesh, but for some reason my head keeps burning and peeling.

I slide my hat on backwards so that the bill doesn't get in my line of view the remainder of the day while I work. Gravel crunches behind me as I grab my jug and put it to my mouth, closing my eyes in relief as the still cool liquid glides down my throat and quenches my thirst.

From the corner of my eye, I make out a gray van pulling up and parking a couple yards away. It strikes me as odd, since these cabins were supposed to be vacant up until the Fourth of July.

Several girls hop out of the van and quickly notice my friends up on the roof. The guys also take in the sight of our company prompting whistles, cat-calls and a level of foolishness that only woman can invoke in a man.

Of course Tristan stands up demanding attention. "Hell yeah … it's about damn time we get company."

I glance to Evan, who has halted in his hammering with a deep frown etched across his face. Snapping my head back in the direction of the van, I search for what has his crappy mood going further south. Looking from one face to the next in the lineup of girls, I nearly dismiss it as unexpected guests that he'll have to get rid of until one face looks familiar. I swear I've seen a picture of her in Evan's camper. She and another girl take turns returning his angry glare.

Just when I'm about to write it off as drama I do not need, I come to a mind-blowing, heart-pounding stop when my eyes land on a blonde in a tight pink tank top. *Holy shit!* I stand up straighter, squint-

31

ing to get a better look. *Wow!* My breath catches in my throat and the water jug nearly falls from my hand. She stands solo at the side of the van, taking in the tension between Evan and the dark haired girl much like I've been.

Gripping my water tighter, I slam the truck door hoping she might look my way so I can see her face better. *Evan's all work and no play rule is going right out the window, because I have to know who she is.*

On a Mission

THE SOUND OF MY door slamming alerts her to my attention, but instead of making eye contact with her, I hastily covered my face with my water bottle. *I'm definitely not smooth. I have no idea how to do these things.* After watching Tristan in action for the last few years, it should be easy to catch a girl's attention.

Watching her through the corner of my eye, I swipe my forearm over my forehead to wipe away beads of sweat while taking a couple more guzzles. She watches my every move, sending a wave of confidence through me.

"I think Alyssa sees something she likes," a female voice says farther away.

The blonde's expression shifts from curiosity to panic in two seconds flat and if I wasn't so awe-struck, I'd laugh.

Lowering my jug slowly, I keep a steady eye on her as she stares back my way. Our eyes collide and a small smile sneaks onto my face.

Fumbling around, I carefully place my water in the back of my truck, but I cannot look away. Her long blonde hair flows over her shoulder and down to the center of her chest framing her small oval shaped face. She has a porcelain skin tone that is definitely not intended for a day out at the lake, but I can't help but wish I was the one that could smooth tanning lotion all over it. Trying not to be obvious, I continue to watch her. Her eyes sparkle under the sun and nearly look as pale blue as the sky with pouty lips that have my heart drumming. That's not what has me so transfixed on her though. It's also not the way her tight top and short blue jean shorts hug every inch of her small frame, although that does have my pulse quickening. The look in her eyes is what has me ready to surrender.

At first glance, I catch a hint of sadness to them. It's almost as if she is emotionally beat down and I totally get that. It's a look I can sympathize with, but then again, maybe it was a long, tiring ride and I'm reading her all wrong. Regardless, every fiber in my body wants to race to her side and sweep her away. Her eyes stay on me, so I give her a small smile.

"Are you joining us up here anytime soon?" Evan yells out, breaking our eye contact and the trance she has me under.

Hesitantly, I turn and walk back to the ladder but cannot shake the grin that is tugging at my lips. I climb to the roof quickly, almost desperate to look back at her, but as soon as I gather my tools and crouch back down, each girl trails into the adjoining cabin with luggage gripped in their hands. *I guess they are staying for a while.* Sighing, with a tad bit of excitement, I get back to work.

"You know anything about that?" Mitch asks, looking towards Evan.

Evan glares at him, making us all aware that our neighbor's arrival has only deepened his foul mood. I'm not sure what has pushed his mood further south but I've got a sneaky suspicion that it's the dark-haired girl.

Tyler speaks up in Evan's place, "He talked to someone about them coming yesterday. I had to move several cots from the storage shed over there earlier this morning. I wasn't sure what all it was for, but it's looking good from what I can see now," he chuckles.

Mitch laughs, but all amusement has left Evan's face as he casts a dirty look in Tyler's direction …

"So are they staying for a while?" I ask quietly and nonchalantly, not wanting to be too obvious.

"Got a little crush, do ya?" Evan teases.

My eyes snap over his shoulder to the other guys. Giving Tristan something to pester me about this summer is the last thing I want. I chuckle at his choice of words. *Crush? I don't even know her, but I sure as hell would like to.*

"Don't answer me, but I saw the whole googly-eyed shit going on down there. The blonde, huh?"

Just hearing the word blonde brings a smile to my face. I nod my head, but leave it at that for now.

A couple hours of pounding nail after nail into the roof go by and we are over halfway done with our day. Just when I'm prepared to give up on seeing the bright-eyed blonde again, giggles and squeals rise into the air, grabbing our attention like dogs to a fire hydrant.

"Alright," Tristan says as the girls one-by-one strip down to their swimsuits.

The first girl, a petite brunette along with a slender blonde and Evan's dark-haired obsession all jump in, igniting whistles and hollers around me.

"Great! We're never going to get this done with this kind of distraction," Evan mutters while joining the others as they watch the girls swim out towards the floating dock. *Yeah, that is definitely the girl that did a number on him years ago.* I don't know the whole story, but I know something happened between them and he says she hates him now.

Lodging a nail into the gritty gray shingle, I swing the hammer clasped in my other hand just as I sneak a quick glance at the gorgeous blonde.

"Damn it!" I yell as it slams into my thumb.

Without thought, the hammer is abandoned on the roof and the tip of my thumb is in my mouth like I'm a toddler trying to comfort myself. As the warmth of my tongue soothes the throbbing sensation in my finger, my eyes divert back to her. She flings off her shirt and steps onto the towel she has draped across the sand. My mouth drops open when I take in her perfect silhouette covered with only two tiny triangles being held together by a string. *Whoa!*

"Are you going to work today?" Evan says from behind me, making my heart drop into my stomach.

I swing my attention to him and nod, hoping to fend off any further comments. "I'm working!" I snap back, grabbing a few more nails and my hammer.

A couple more swings and a few glances later, renders my thumb damn near crippled. *This girl has me hypnotized.* Fortunately, I get the next nail in, but the guys have all seemed to notice my interest.

"Oh shit, Judd … she's topless now," Tyler cries out beside me.

My chin catapults up so fast it nearly gives me whiplash and my heart is racing a hundred miles an hour, but all I'm met with is laughter all around. She's still lounging on her stomach across a bright yellow towel with a book in her hand.

"Oh man, I thought your head was going to pop off," Matt cracks up, pointing at me as I turn back and give him a withering look.

"Ha … Ha, Matt."

"Oh dude, she's on the move," Nick loudly whispers, throwing a nail to get my attention.

I breathe out an insincere chuckle and go on with my work. "Whatever, guys. It's not going to work this time." I continue to slam my hammer down until my nail is flush.

Discretely casting my eyes to the side without moving my head, I try to check her out but it's no use; I can't see her from this angle. *What if he's telling the truth and she is leaving? Shit! No, they're just screwing with me.* I'm dying to look, but refuse to give in to the game they've had going the past hour. Staring down blankly at the nail I just drove in, a tap on my shoulder brings me back to reality.

"They're actually being serious," Jake's words have me snapping my head around to look. *Him, I believe.*

Her book now lies on the towel with her feet planted a few inches away. Her shorts slide down her legs, suddenly making my throat dry and in desperate need of something wet. I gulp and study the curves of her hips. She darts off towards the water, bouncing over the shimmery sand and the whole thing plays out in my mind in slow motion to some sexy ass music.

I snap my mouth shut, once her head falls below the water. *The guys are definitely going to give me shit for this.* Without looking, I reach in my belt for another nail and one finds me. A sharp, piercing pain jabs the tender flesh right beneath my fingernail.

"Shit!!" I holler, rising onto my feet. *What the hell is wrong with me?*

The guys laugh in unison, clearly enjoying my frustration as entertainment for the day.

I settle back down on the roof fully intent on staying busy and not looking out at the water, but it takes all of five minutes for my will power to falter.

At last, the sun goes down, signaling the end of our work day. After helping Evan lock up the tool shed, I high tail it to the shower house to wash off. I'm determined to run into that girl if I can pull it off.

I'm twenty feet away from the shower house when my wish is nearly granted. The girls round the corner and hop off of the dock directly in front of me. I stop dead in my tracks, my mind racing with paranoia of whether she'll think I'm a creep if she sees me. One at a time they walk off the dock heavy in a discussion and girly giggles that I cannot even focus on through my own loud thoughts. *Where is she?*

"… skinny dipping later tonight. What do you guys think?"

My ears perk up and I am fully listening now. *Skinny-dipping? Do girls really do that?* I sidestep to stand amidst a couple trees hoping to go on unnoticed as I watch for her. *Creep is right. This is insane!*

"Alyssa, are you going to join us?" one of the girls calls out, kicking my memory into gear. *I think that was her name.* My heartbeat speeds up as I wait to hear her reply. *Say yes ... say yes!* Right then, she crosses over the edge of the dock into view.

"I guess, but I think I need to drink quite a bit more to catch up."

The girls laugh and a smile forms on my face. Their voices quickly fade out of ear shot, but I don't move. I don't even bother to approach her instead I remain still, watching as she walks away. *Damn, I'm such a chicken.*

"Hey man, what are you doing?" Evan calls out from behind me, making me jump and heat up from embarrassment.

I swing my attention to him and smile. "Being a coward," I chuckle.

He looks at me in confusion, so I fill him in, "Ok, this may very well make me sound like a creep, but I kind of accidently may have eavesdropped on all those girls conversation," I admit, ducking my head and raising my shoulder as if I'm delivering this news to my mom and waiting for a scolding.

He grabs his waist and belts out a laugh. "Kinda, my ass."

I stare at him, clueless on whether to laugh with him or go on the defense.

"Crushin' hard on blondie, are we?"

"Whatever … anyways, one of the girls mentioned that they may go swimming later." I look over at him as we near the shower house, but he looks bored with the topic already. "Skinny-dipping," I add with my brows drawn up.

This gets his attention. Snapping his head towards me, he shares the same expression I'm sure I had on my face a few moments ago when I first heard the topic mentioned.

"Seriously? They said they were skinny dipping later?" He asks with a shitty grin.

"Who's skinny dipping?" Tristan's voice calls out from behind as I step onto the dock.

Great. That's all I need. I zip my lips and walk in so I can quickly wash off. We each disperse into separate stalls and in between water in my ears and the subtle sounds of my fingers scouring shampoo into my scalp, I catch clips of Tristan and Evan talking.

"… that's what Judd said he heard."

What the hell, Evan?!

"Are you shitting me? Hell yeah, this summer job keeps getting better and better," Tristan hollers two stalls away.

If I had to bet money on it, I'd say he was going back to make lake plans with the rest of the gang. *Now I almost wish I hadn't heard them. I'll just have to get to her first. No way am I letting any of the other guys slide in there before me.*

I shower off as quickly as possible in cool water to steer off the way she affected me, throw on some board shorts and grab my stuff, but just as I am coming out of the stall, the entrance door creaks.

"Later," Tristan yells before I catch sight of the door closing.

Evan walks out of the shower next to mine as I'm reaching for the door to exit and sprint up to the cabin before Tristan can get all the guys on board for crashing the girl's party.

"Wait up," he hollers as I'm preparing to flee.

With an antsy rap of my foot on the floor, I resist racing out and hold back, keeping the door held open as if it will quicken the leaving process.

"Why did you tell Tristan that?"

Evan laughs, "Are you afraid he's going to dip into your plate of sushi before you can? Besides, I figured that was right up his alley. Come on, I mean … skinny-dipping?" he chuckles a little harder, but all I can do is stare over at him wondering if he realizes that Tristan will be aiming for any of the girls, not just the one I'm interested in. Smirking back at him as he pokes along behind me, I bring him up to speed on the big picture.

"He won't just be diving into my plate so to speak. I think my brother would be happier sampling a little bit of everything on the buffet," a knot settles in my stomach for joking about something that my mother would consider so disrespectful, but then I catch Evan's changed expression.

His smile falls and he speeds up to walk beside me. "Yeah, no way, man. I know her and her clothes will stay on," he says confident-ly.

"Ok," I give up, "Either way, you joining me?"

He nods in agreement as we fly through the cabin door. My eyes instantly dance to the clock above the fireplace, surprised that it is only a little past 9:00.

"Judd, just the man we wanted to see," Mitch says before the door even has a chance to swing shut behind me.

I look over at Evan and he shrugs.

"So did you hear what time this event is taking place?" Mitch asks with all the others eagerly listening.

Sighing, I relent; they're going to go down there anyways. I'll just leave a little early and hope to catch her before the other guys come barging onto the beach.

"All I heard is one of the girls mention a midnight swim. So I'm assuming midnight," I say without looking at him; I'm not a huge fan of Mitch. He treats Evan like shit and he is exactly the type of friend that Tristan needs to stay away from.

Reaching into the fridge, I grab a container of meat and a couple slices of cheese and then slam the door shut.

"So let me get this straight, all those girls are planning to strip down to their birthday suits and go for a group swim?!" Nick asks in amazement.

"Do girls actually do that shit?" Tyler pipes up with an equally excited tone to his voice.

"Lucky for us, this group of girls does," Tristan speaks up, already changing into his trunks.

Like he will actually keep those on tonight; the only attire he'll need later is a condom. I'd laugh my ass off if these girls are sensible enough to not fall for his tricks. However, it looks like most of the ladies were tipping back drinks pretty hard on the lake earlier so more than likely most of them will be plowed by midnight, if they keep going like that.

"Holy shit! I think I've died and gone to heaven," Tyler jumps into the conversation and then the discussion amps up to a whole new level of sleaze.

I scarf down two sandwiches and a handful of chips while the rest of the guys start hitting the beer. *I'll wait to drink. I'd like to keep my wits about me tonight.*

The minutes drag by, and the familiar urgency that I felt watching the clock tick by on the last day of school rises within me. It reminds me of the nervousness and anxiety that took root inside of me each day that was marked off of the calendar after my mom got sick. At least this time it is exciting. Glancing back at the clock, I come to one conclusion. *I can't wait any longer.*

"Come on let's go. I'm sick of waiting," I say, gripping the handle of the door.

"Well ... well, someone has an eagerection about getting down to the beach," Evan sarcastically comes back at me, immediately pushing a spit of laughter out of me.

"Where you guys going?" Matt's question turns all eyes on us.

"We're just going down to the vending machine before we head to the beach."

Lying to my friends is ridiculous especially since we will potentially be walking in on a handful of naked girls swimming after dark, but I really don't want anyone to mess up my plan.

"We'll see you in a bit." I wave over my shoulder.

"Hhhmhuh ..." Tristan murmurs as Evan and I head out.

The skeptical look I get from Tristan tells me that they will soon be following.

We head straight forward towards my truck and stop when the sound of female voices fill the air in the direction of the beach. Fortunately, there are no overhead lights so we are able to move in closer, undetected. *This girl is going to write me off as a total pervert if she catches me spying on her friends while they strip down.*

Stopping at the edge of the beach, I desperately scan the area for her blonde hair. Evan looks around as well, but I don't see either of the girls we're searching for.

"You going to tell me what's going on with this girl?" I whisper to him. He has always remained pretty closed off about what happened summers ago with her.

He snaps his head around and frowns. "I figured you could use a wing man. You're not smooth enough to pull this off and not get caught."

I laugh. *He's right about that.* The last thing I am is smooth at scoping out girls; that's my brother's department.

"Besides, come on … a bunch of naked girls, of course I'm going to be willing to join you." He laughs quietly, his eyes roaming the beach.

"Yeah, sure … a wingman, huh? You're just worried about what I …" her voice pulls me from my train of thought and dead-ends everything I was saying. I already know that voice like I've heard it my whole life.

"I think I am going to take a walk and finish off my drinks. You all are way ahead of me. Maybe the alcohol will help me loosen up. I'll be back in a bit," her soft gentle voice sings as several girls throw their suits down to the ground and race into the water without a second thought.

When I see the two girls she is talking to fling their tops off, I have to focus to see if Alyssa is actually dressed. *I cannot believe I am doing this. I'm a freaking peeping tom.* I can barely make it out, but I see the small outlines of a swimsuit on her small figure as she walks down the water's edge.

"Holy Shit! Did you see that?!" I look at Evan and then back to where he is looking. "No don't actually look, damn it!"

Snapping my head back around to him, then over to where Alyssa is walking, I'm at a loss of what he is talking about, but I do not want to lose my chance.

"Hey man, I'm going to go catch her …" I start.

Evan interrupts me, his face twisted in shock. "She took off her damn top! I can't believe she took it off! What the hell?!"

I look back trying to figure out what he is so aggravated over.

"Don't look, man!" he whisper-shouts without taking his eyes off the water.

I shake my head. *I really don't want to blow this.*

"I'll catch you later. I'm going after her," I try to get his attention, but I assume he is no longer listening; he's too busy fuming about that dark haired girl taking off her top.

"What the hell! Do you know how long it took before she let me see …" Evan's words are cut off by shouts and hollers in the distance as the guys finally decide to bust up the quiet, peaceful night setting.

Damn, I have to go. Last thing I want is for Tyler or Nick or especially Tristan to find her all alone in the woods and start hitting on her; t*hat's my plan. I'll just unintentionally run into her and think of a smooth way to explain how I knew she would be down here.* My heart speeds up with expectancy of finally being face-to-face with her. *I'm on a mission to find her and I'm not wasting another second.*

Make her Mine

"I'LL SEE YOU LATER man," As soon as the words leave my mouth, I am already treading sand.

I catch all the others joining up with the girls and hear all the excitement arising with their arrival; they waste no time with the whole "clothing optional" party.

"Holy, son of a …"

I crane my neck back for a second at the sound of Evan's voice then twist around so I can focus on the task of running along the dark shoreline. Suddenly, a head of silky blonde hair along with a small framed body only covered by a few pieces of fabric slams right into me. My arms fall around her instantly as we both tumble to the ground. *Yeah, smooth; real smooth.* This is not exactly what I had in mind when I thought about running into her, but then her soft, perfect body wrenches beneath me and I do not want to move.

Noticing movement beside our heads, I sneak a glance as she wiggles a wine cooler in her hand. I have to suppress a laugh at her not-so-subtle-spill-check. Pulling my head back just enough to look at her face, I'm hit with the unbelievable fragrance of her skin or hair. *Geez, she smells incredibly good, like strawberries.* Looking closer at her blank expression, it dawns on me that I may be crushing her while the vibrations of my heart clarify that I am indeed crushing on her hard.

"Are you ok?" I whisper, lifting up only a few inches above her to alleviate the full weight of my body on hers.

Her stomach is flush up against mine and with both of us only sporting swim attire, the smooth, soft feeling of her skin has me breathing heavier than normal. Finally her eyes open and she looks up at me. *Damn, she's beautiful.*

Her hand makes contact with my skin and a smoldering heat splinters out from her fingertips and moves through me. My lips lift into a wide grin and my pulse races as her fingers run over my chest. She hasn't said a word yet. If I didn't know better I would actually think she is mute. Using one hand to hold my body above hers and with my knee buried in the sand between her legs, I lift my other hand to wave it in front of her face, making sure she registers my presence. Grains of sand cling to my skin and feel half embedded under the bandages I had placed on my cracked open thumb.

"Did I knock you out or knock the breath out of you?"

Her deep and heavy breaths that match my own, reach my ears, but she still says nothing.

Finally she shakes her head and mumbles "Yes … I mean no …" in a confused tone.

I laugh at her answer and then decide to tease her, "I did knock you out?"

She stumbles around with her words, appearing more nervous than me. *Maybe I'm not the only one feeling a connection.*

Just as I am fully enjoying this playful banter we have going on and the fact that she is nervous around me as well, a total buzz kill sounds from behind me.

"Dude, are you doing her already?" Tyler yells out from only a few feet away. *Great!*

"Way to go, Judd!" My older brother calls out from further down the beach.

"Hey, need a condom? I think we have some back at the cabin!" That sounds like Matt and I'm sure she's ready to get the hell away from me after all that.

"Piss off guys," I mutter under my breath, venting my frustrations.

Rising up and away from her, I immediately feel as if something's missing. I reach my hand out to help her up, eager to touch her again in any way possible. A sigh of relief slips over my lips when she places her hand in mine.

"Sorry … my friends stumbled upon a discovery and were getting a bit too frisky for my taste. I figured I would head in the opposite direction."

The wildness at the beach picks up with the sounds of girls screaming and loud splashing through the water. *Time to find some place more private.*

"You wanna join me?" I ask, praying that she says yes, just as she gives me a gentle nod.

I stare at her, taking in all her delicate features. Her hair falls around her face in soft waves continuing down to the center of her back. Although it is dark, her high cheek bones seem blushed, possibly from embarrassment due to my friends comments and her lips; *Oh, her lips … damn!* They are plump, moist and look like they need to be kissed. My eyes proceed to study her as they travel down her neck, but her hand clutched around a bottle suddenly blocks the view I'm so desperate to see. It startles me out of my daze, until I realize she is offering me one of her drinks.

"A peace offering?"

I smile and gladly take it, hoping it will push away the apprehension that she seems to bring out in me.

"I'm Judd by the way," I inform her as our feet start to lead the way down the shoreline.

She bursts out in a jittery laugh that matches my shaky hands and drumming heart.

"I'm Alyssa. I'm sorry …"

Zoning out, I watch how she throws her head back as she laughs and how her hair dips further down, past the center of her back. After craning my neck to check her out, we make eye contact and I try to focus in on what she's saying, but it's no use. Once she finishes speaking, all hesitation flies away.

Strolling beside her in absolutely no hurry at all, a sudden surge of confidence hits me and I want to know everything about her. "So, I've never seen you out here. Have you been here before?"

Looking up at me, she answers my question, "Actually, my parents used to bring me and my sisters out here when we were little, but gosh … it's been at least …" My attention flickers in and out of what she is saying like satellite reception during a thunder storm as my eyes continue to drop down lower, watching her chest rise and fall with each word she says. "What about you?"

Oh shit! Quickly snapping my head back to look at her, my body starts to vibrate with nervousness. I clear my throat to shake off the feeling and hope that I didn't miss anything she was saying.

"You know, I'm not sure if I came here when I was little, but I've been coming out here regularly for a few years now. This summer I'm giving my best friend a hand on some renovations. His grandfather owns the land and the cabins over here," I stop speaking for a second and look for a suitable place so we can sit. "Well except for the cabin you're staying in," I say, as a nice clearing comes into view.

Smiling, I automatically think of all those cheesy quizzes on my newsfeed about the 'best date places' or those goofy surveys girls would pass around in class about 'what's your dream date'. *This is perfect.*

I let her sit first, gently placing my hand near her lower back, close enough to touch but not quite. She slides down, settling into a small patch of dirt with no hesitation at all. Quirking my brows, I smile and sit down beside her.

"Do you go to school out this way?"

"Nahh," I answer back and take a swig of the drink she gave me. The bitterness of tequila mixed with the sour tang of lime nips at my tongue, making it numb as if I've been sucking on a saltlick. "I actually live about five hours away in Rosemore. I graduated from there just last month."

She blows out a small laugh and for a second I wonder if I said something stupid or stumbled over my words.

"That's crazy. I actually graduated from Fairview High last week."

I join her laughter, knowing had I ran into her back in high school, this would totally be considered fraternizing with the enemy. Our schools were extremely competitive against one another and the winning school always earned major bragging rights for kicking the other's ass. Our schools loathed each other and football games with Fairview were especially brutal.

"Did you ever go to any of the Fairview-Rosemore football games?"

"I went to every single one. I was a cheerleader, so I cheered at all the football games. What about you?"

My eyebrows bolt up in surprise and my chest rises with pride.

"I played. I was the quarterback. Wow! I'm sure we crossed paths a time or two."

"I'm sure …"

Silently, I start going over each Fairview-Rosemore game in my head. Other than a quick glance when they would do the whole leg kick, I really don't remember checking out many of the cheerleaders from any of the schools; I was too focused in on winning the game and gaining a scholarship.

"So are you going to the local college in Rosemore?"

Suddenly, an awareness comes to me with this question. Here I am hitting on and tripping all over myself with this girl and I'm leaving in a little over a month.

"No … I have a scholarship to play out in California, so the end of July I will be headed to UCLA."

An unexpected quiet falls over us and I cannot even find the words to speak. Here I've been in such a hurry to leave and right when everything is headed in the right direction, someone that totally captures me like no one else ever has decides to walk into my life. *Timing is definitely not everything.*

Leaning closer to her, I nudge her shoulder with mine just as an excuse to touch her again.

"What about you? Do you have any plans for the future?"

Scooting my hand closer her way, I glance down and see her fingers only inches away, laying in the midst of pebbles, sand and dirt.

"I got accepted to Purdue. I leave in August."

Well that's just great. Where is that … Indiana? "Oh, I see. Do you know your major yet?" I ask, staring at how her skin lights up under the moon light and how every now and again she'll lick her lips, making them glisten. I suck in a deep breath and try not to think; just listen.

"You know, I have no idea," she laughs as I tip my bottle back for another drink, but quickly find that it's empty. Swapping the drink into my other hand, I then place my free one back down between us, making sure it is just a tad bit closer.

I nervously laugh, grazing my fingers along the side of her hand and flames automatically ignite.

"What's funny?"

Holy shit, I'm a dork. Did I just laugh at absolutely nothing?

"I was just trying to figure out how I never noticed you at a game," I say the first thing that pops into my mind. *Smooth ... real smooth. Make her seem like I didn't notice her now.* Had I looked her way, ever, I would without a doubt remember seeing her in a short skirt on the side line of a football field.

A crazy beautiful smile breaks loose on her face and my whole body heats up as I slowly inch my fingers to feel her skin again. I notice her glance down, but I don't move away one bit.

"When's your birthday?" She throws out giddily.

It catches me off guard and seems out of context, but I smile, nearly embarrassed by such a simple question and excited that I see the same amount of nervousness in her as she searches for anything to talk to me about. I'm prepared to talk about the puppy I got for Christmas when I was five if I have to.

"September ... 8th."

"No way ... " she gasps.

"What? Is yours that same day?" The smile on my face cannot get any bigger.

She throws her head forward, laughing. "Oh no ... mine is in September though."

I look at her, waiting.

"Oh ... it's September 25th."

I nod my head, a strange sense of satisfaction coming over me from knowing the tiniest bit of information about her.

Our conversation flows like beer at a frat party and before too long our friends are calling us in the distance. I could talk to her all night, but moreover, I am completely hypnotized by her lips. I do plan to kiss her. I'm not sure if it will be here or possibly when I walk her back to her cabin, but I will kiss her.

My empty drink is still clutched in my hand with a grip that is certain to break it in half if I don't calm down, but it is offering a nice excuse to move around and reposition my hand just a little closer to hers. *I'm half tempted to just grab her hand up in mine.*

"Judd!" Evan's voice calls out, closer now, and our time alone has come to an end.

Of course, when I want to be left alone it doesn't happen, but on a job site if I need help there's never a soul in sight. Every fiber of my body is screaming for us to stay put, but I stand up with my hand held out.

"We better go before our friends call the rescue dogs out."

With a solid grip, she pulls my hand and stands in front of me, falling forward before catching her balance. I place my hands as gently as possible at her hips to steady her; maybe she has caught up with her friends now.

Gulping down this ball of nerves that has been wound up in my stomach all night, I pull her in and swear she is drawing closer to me as well. My heartbeat pounds up into my throat and although words are coming out of my mouth, I'm not quite certain what the hell I'm saying until she pulls back a bit.

"I just think the alcohol rushed to my head or something …"

I look down at her and a small smile emerges on her face.

"I really like your smile, Alyssa."

I don't even think; the words just tumble out of my mouth. *God, I want to kiss her.* Goose bumps form across her waist where my hands are located and her body shivers beneath my touch. For a second I think she may be cold, but as I move my hand a fraction of an inch across her bare skin, another shiver ignites. My confidence explodes with this.

She keeps her eyes glued on my mouth and at this point it would be so easy to pull her flush against me and wrap my arms around her. A part of me already feels so comfortable with her that it is telling me to go for it. Instead I lean closer and ask.

"Alyssa?" I barely hear her muffled murmur, but it sounded like a green light so I move forward hardly able to control my hunger.

"Can I kiss you?" I say only a breath away from her lips.

Her lips crash into mine and it's abundantly clear that she wanted this as much as me.

At first I go slow, unsure of her rhythm. Her bottom lip falls between mine like two puzzle pieces interlocking with one another. Our mouths move in sync, although as her chest grazes over my skin I have to focus on something other than kissing her. *Don't get turned on, don't get turned on. Think of work. Think of ...*

My head swims with visions of her skin as I slowly open my mouth. She follows my lead and I dip my tongue in on a soft, moist caress and taste the sweetness of her breath; nothing has ever felt this good.

Although I want to run my hands down the length of her body, I hold back. However, when her hands roam over my chest in a soft wispy motion, I take in a sharp breath and my body reacts. *I no longer have this situation under control.* My thoughts race with the things I want to do to her and for a moment I'm confused. *Has Tristan hijacked my mind?* Visions of our bodies on the ground, in the water, on the dock, in my cabin, in my bed; they fog my head. *What the hell.*

"Oh shit, I'm sorry," Evan's impeccable timing comes through. "I didn't mean to interrupt." The amusement in his tone sounds out loud and clear despite his words.

"Sure you didn't," I mutter, even though I'm thankful for his shitty timing. Normally I would want to kill him for interrupting such an intense moment, but something about Alyssa makes me want to slow down yet speed up at the same time. Up until a few minutes ago all we did was talk tonight, however I already feel completely at ease with her, as if I've known her my whole life. Last thing I want to do is screw that up by moving too fast. I'm not sure what is going on here, but I'm determined to make her mine.

My New Favorite Thing

"GETTIN' IT ON IN the woods, huh?" Evan sneaks an obnoxious look my way as we walk away from Alyssa's cabin, but damned if I can't get that kiss out of my mind.

"It wasn't like that," I laugh, refusing to let him antagonize me over this.

No longer able to resist the overwhelming urge to turn, I swing my head around, but instead of seeing her beautiful silhouette, I'm met by her captivating blue eyes watching me walk away. She looks right at me and her smile tells me everything I need to know; there is definitely something here. A huge grin emerges across my face like a dorky school boy with my first crush as I stare back.

"And here I thought I had it bad…" Evan trails off and I snap my head back to look at him.

"So what is the deal with you and her, anyways?" I ask, knowing I'll more than likely get the same information that he's told me before; she liked me, I liked her and now she hates me … end of story. He's never been a big talker about his personal life, then again, we don't sit around and share our feelings.

His body jolts upright and he spits out a sarcastic no-way-in-hell-am-I-talking-about-this chuckle.

"Not important," he pauses, kicking at the ground as we walk. "So you and blondie?"

Raising my eyebrows in amusement of him quickly changing the subject, I press my lips together to contain the silly ass grin that I've had glued to my face all night.

"What time is it anyways," I lamely counter his subject-change with my own.

"Ha … you're not going to tell me what went on out in the deep dark woods with your little dream girl, are you?" he pauses, but I keep my face free of emotion, carefully watching my feet tread along the pathway while still holding back a laugh. "Were you sucking face all night?"

I remain blank, not giving in, but practically staring past the ground now and envisioning my lips on hers once again. *Holy geez.*

Moving closer, Evan jabs me in the side with his elbow and I flinch, scrunching up my face at the jolt. From the corner of my eye, I see him raise his hands, cupping them both in claw-like manner as if he is squeezing something pliable.

"Did you go in for the ole' cup-check?" he pesters.

A flash of her black bikini top spins through my mind and the way her chest rose with each breath she took, each word she spoke. I blow out a frustrated breath and shake off the thought. That's an image that is sure to stick with me. I turn my head to look at Evan, noticing that the position of his hands has changed. A grin sneaks onto my face as he begins to slap his hand through the air in front of him.

"… or did you slap that ass and make her scre …"

"Ok..ok," I snap with a chuckle as we near the cabin. "We just talked."

He spits out an exasperated snicker, "Ahh yeah, because from where I stood, it really looked like talking."

I roll my eyes, "Then we kissed, or well … she actually kissed me," I say a little dumbfounded myself with that fact.

"Wait, she kissed you? Whoa … and then what happened?"

I crack up at his excitement, a bubbling sensation of laughter rising within me. "Then you interrupted us, you jerk-off."

"Oh yeah … sorry about that. The girls started asking about blondie and then her sister, Abby came and asked me to go find you two," he drops his voice a couple octaves, trying his best to sound like a girl. "Oh.my.God, I need to find my sister. I don't even know that guy she's with." He laughs. "Like you're some serial killer or some shit like that. So basically, I had no choice in going to search you out. I was trying to steer off an angry mob of women."

Holding up my hand to stop his ramblings, I assure him that the interruption was needed, "Seriously don't sweat it. My thoughts were moving us from vertical to horizontal real quick so I was thankful for the bucket of cold water, so to speak."

We step onto the porch of the cabin, silence all around us and only the dim lights from the shower house in the distance in front of us.

"Why the hell would you be happy that I broke that up?"

"You know I'm not like that. I could care less about putting notches in my belt. I actually like her." I glance up to see if he is going to laugh, but all he does is nod, listening to what I have to say. With a grin, I add, "I did tell her where I would be working later today."

I look around, quickly noting the stillness of the water, the sounds of frogs croaking and crickets chirping in the night along with the soft swish of leaves and limbs brushing together right above our heads. I'm assuming it's early morning and that means, I'll be running on empty all damn day.

"Ahhh, gonna get it on in the shower house, then?" He yells out a little louder than I'd prefer with his hand held up in the air as if he's waiting for me to reward his smart-ass comment with a high five.

Looking at his hand, then giving him a put-your-damn-hand down look, I quickly make him aware of the volume of his voice, "Quiet down … last thing I want is for Tristan to be giving me shit for this the next few weeks." I crack the door open slowly, not wanting to wake Jake or Tristan.

Lowering his hand with a chuckle, he shrugs as we walk inside. My eyes immediately swoop to the clock which just looks like a dark hole in the wall at this hour. As soon as I reach my bed, I grab my phone and hit the main button to light it up. *2:33 … shit.*

The annoying buzz of my phone alarm sounds less than a few hours after my head hits the pillow and I'm already dreading the exhaustion this day will bring. Mentally checking off each to-do through a sleepy fog, I grab a cup of coffee, pack a shitty excuse for a lunch, drag all the supplies from the work shed and gear up for a full day ahead.

By mid-morning, adrenaline overpowers my sleep deprivation and I am running full-speed, ready for my work day to be over so I can find Alyssa.

I manage to tear down all the old mirrors, paint the vaulted ceiling and walls and scrub down all the sinks. Rushing through, I check off one task at a time. Moving on to attaching the new mirrors, the entrance door that is also in bad need of replacing, creaks open behind me. *Great!* All I need now is to have to sit out a half hour of my work so someone can shower up. For some reason, campers from nearby grounds seem to have gotten wind that this side is temporarily closed down and have been showing up to use our shower houses. *Today is not the day for this.*

Sighing, I put my best effort forth to hide my irritation, "Hang on a sec and I'll get out of your way," I call out as I strain to lift the new mirror into its updated bracket. *These damn things are heavier than I had anticipated.*

I get it positioned in front of me and nearly drop it when my eyes land on an unexpected reflection dressed in a small animal print swimsuit and nothing else.

"Hey," I say with a ridiculous smile on my face. *Geez, she looks amazing!*

"Hey back." Her voice sends a shock wave through my body.

For a minute I contemplate throwing the mirror to the floor and wrapping her up in my arms. That would probably get me fired; it'd be worth it though. She must read my mind on the whole dropping the mirror thought because within a second she is by my side snatching the screwdriver out of my hand.

"I'll screw, you hold the mirror."

I raise my eyebrows up, half turned on by her "I'll screw" comment and half impressed that she knows how to use tools. My lips rise into a smile like there is a magnet constantly pulling them in an upward motion when she is near. I settle the mirror into the cradle of the bracket and we get to work.

Now the day goes fast.

"So what can I do?" she asks as I toss aside papers listing the job duties for each site.

I gulp and look around, nervous about giving her any of the tasks

I have to complete. This shower house is pretty well as disgusting as they come. At this point, I have the choices of painting, which is a two person job as it is, putting the new fans up, *no way am I letting her do that* and then there is scrubbing the shower and putting up new curtains. *That one is a definite hell no.* Those showers are so crudded up with grime that I dread doing it.

"I think I'll put up the fans next, but I don't have two ladders and honestly they are really heavy." I say, half gritting my teeth and hoping I don't offend her. Then an idea sparks to mind as I remember how easily she screwed in the brackets as I held the mirrors just a bit ago. "Can you hand me tools up, while I take down the old fans," I ask, thankful that I left my tool belt back at the cabin.

"Sure." She gives me an easy, extremely contagious smile.

Standing high up on the ladder, I loosen each tiny bolt and compile a small group on the top step. I carefully balance the fan with one hand which is hanging by a few wires, while glancing down when I hear the sharp yet quiet sounds of metal hitting a solid surface.

"I got it."

I look down at the sound of her voice and see her bent down to the ground. My eyes flick to the top of the ladder, seeing a vacancy where the bolts and screwdriver were laying. Teetering back and forth on this ladder must have knocked them off.

"Thanks," I say, guilt crashing through my conscious until I see her bend over to grab up another run-away bolt.

She pops up with a smile, a flaming red glow to her face and a bolt held up in her hand. "I think I got them all. Do you need them up there?"

I shake my head, unable to summon any words at the moment. The weight of the fan knocks me out of my daze as my muscles begin to seize and fire up from the strain of the fan motor. She watches my every move as I twist the wire caps off and lower them to the ladder, instantly feeling a bit of a shuffle beneath me. Looking down, I'm greeted with her face, just below me, standing on the bottom step of the ladder with her hand reached up grabbing a hold of all the caps. A sense of excitement races through me, possibly from the brush of her chest against my pant leg or maybe even from the fact that she is so eager to help me out. I'm not sure, but it automatically has my mouth tugged into a grin as I hang onto the fan motor and slowly step off the ladder behind her. One step down and she instantly grabs the edge of it, so that it is steady.

"I'll be right back."

I exit the shower house and open the door to a small supply closet, located to the left of the entrance door. Evan had mentioned to place excess parts and supplies here in case something would go haywire, although these fans look as though they were on their last leg.

Hurrying back inside, I get busy on the next fan and am pleasantly surprised that she knows her tools. Phillips screwdriver, pliers, tin snips, it doesn't matter; she never asks for a description or questions what I'm asking for, she just hands it up confidently.

Halfway into getting the second fan up and well into a great rhythm of getting it done, I watch as she slips on a pair of gloves. Bent onto all fours, she scours the first shower stall floor, her whole body wobbling and shaking with each scrub motion. *Man that has to be nasty to her.* I really do not want her to turn around and leave, but then again I'm unable to look away.

After fumbling around as I hand-screw a bolt onto the blade, I reach into my pocket for another one.

My mouth drops open as I get ready to ask for the socket wrench, but I stop, my body heat intensifying and my lower extremities thinking on their own. *Holy shit.* Her ass is sticking up in the air and her back glistens with sweat. *The socket wrench can wait.* Last thing I want to do is interrupt her work. Reaching to grab the next fan blade and rearrange the order of my work for the sake of preserving this moment, I clip my hand along the edge of the two other blades that I have wedged on the step, nearly knocking them to the ground.

"Shit," I say under my breath with another quick look in her direction.

Oh hell! This time, her back is bowed and her ass is stuck out even more, making me think some very x-rated thoughts. She looks up and completely catches me staring. I quickly grab the next fan blade and make out that I am inspecting its construction, looking from the sculpted edge to each of the three screw holes that are predrilled in it. *I don't think she fell for that.*

A small smirk slowly sneaks across my face, but I force it down and continue on with my work. No doubt this would go faster if I didn't have the distraction of her bent over below me, but I am perfectly fine with that.

Finally, I get the last fan set in place and I turn them all on high before we dive into painting the floors. Only a few more items to check off the list and we will have nothing but a fun day ahead. It doesn't take long to get a coat of paint down on the floor. The only complaint I have is that she is across the room from me. However, considering she is edging around the sinks, I have a great view again. *I really owe whoever invented bikinis a huge thanks!*

After a quick lunch that I now wish I would have put more thought into, we set down our painting equipment as I carry the ladder out. My foot catches on something and I glance down seeing a mess of paint. *Dammit.* I grit my teeth and clamp my jaw tightly at the added time it will take for me to clean up the mess. Setting the ladder down in front of the door long ways, I reposition the wet paint sign so that it is visible from the shoreline. Hopefully that will deter any outside campers from coming in and undoing all our hard word.

Spinning around, I make my way back inside just in time to see Alyssa's feet fly into the air. My eyes widen and my heart trips up, sending me sprinting over the floor to catch her fall. Her head lands in my hands and my whole body falls forward with her, forcing me to push the weight of our tumble towards my hands so that my body weight doesn't crash on top of her. My knuckles take a hard hit, a sharp pain rushing through my fingers and up to my wrist. I've been working with my hands for a straight month with very little wear and tear to them, but this week, I have managed to slam them with a hammer, jab them with nails and now use them as a shield.

She lets out a small whine and my heart sinks with the thought of her being hurt.

After searching her face for any sign of distress, she teasingly moans out, "Ouch, my butt!" and my chest rises with a sigh of relief.

We both laugh at the clumsy turn our day has taken. I had one hell of a view of that area of her body earlier so I'd hate for it to be damaged in any way; I let her know, too. As our laughter dies down, a heart pounding silence forms between us and I literally cannot take my eyes off her. Our chests are pressed together and I'm trying hard not to put my full weight on her, but my arms are fairly exhausted from a lack of sleep and countless minutes holding the heavy ass weight of three fans in the air.

I pull one of my hands out from behind her back and run it along the contours of her face while keeping the other pinned behind her head as a cushion. My eyes snap down to her mouth for a second and I cannot get the images of last night out of my head. Gravity tugs at me and I'm not even sure my mind is functioning anymore. My lips find hers and with slow tender movements, we relive the highlight of our moonlight walk. Once again, my whole body responds, but this time, having my body against hers.

Pulling back, I lick my lips fully intent on going in for another kiss, but another subtle stinging sensation in my hand has me holding off. I drag my hand out from behind her head so that I can get repositioned and am shocked to see a mess of blonde hair mixed with sticky gray paint all tangled up and stuck to my hand. For a minute, I have no clue how to even tell her; I don't even know if she'll be able to get it out.

"Shit … your hair. There's paint in it," gushes from my mouth in a distressed tone that I'm sure will have her bolting to her feet and knocking me to the ground.

I push back to kneel across her, sparking a quiet whimper from her. All the girls I've ever known would be going ballistic right about now. I carefully pry each strand from my hand, dread engulfing me. *Damn! How is she going to get this out?* Looking down to assess her panic in this situation, I'm floored to see that not only is she not freaking out, she is calmly watching every move I make with very little concern in her eyes. I can't even read the look on her face.

At first, she nearly looks disappointed, not at the situation but at the u-turn our day took with this venture. That's what I'm feeling, because paint or no paint I am getting extremely turned on from being this close to her.

I pull the last hair from my hands and grin, leaning down to suggest something that I hope she is up for. Her breathing picks up and I can't help myself from swooping in to capture one more kiss.

I graze my lips against hers in a teasing quick kiss then move my mouth to her ear.

"You're beautiful," I whisper, a bit embarrassed by my boldness, but also knowing she's beyond that.

Staring her right in the eyes, I take in her reaction to my words and get the sneaking suspicion that she is equally affected by me as I am by her. *I can't believe I'm going to suggest this.*

Moving back to her skin, with my lips close enough to take a nibble, I go for it, "We have paint all over us. Do you want me to help you clean up?" My heart is about to fly out of my chest and jet down the road at warp speed.

Although, those are the only words that come out of my mouth, they are not at all what I am thinking, because right now I want nothing more than to remove this tiny bikini, lay her down and run my tongue down her body until she is screaming for me. However, it's been a while so once her bikini is off, it may be a show-stopper for me. Either way, I'd still make sure we both enjoyed it.

After she gets up and takes in the extent of paint covering her, we both laugh. Pressing my lips together to control my hunger, I put my hand out and silently pray that she'll take it in her own. Her eyes go straight from my hand to my face, but I don't relent; I don't even feel in control of my actions anymore. With no words spoken between the both of us, she takes my hand and I lead her to the last shower stall. My head spins and I squeeze my eyes shut to ward off all the images and possibilities that are cropping up in my head as I crank the water on full blast.

Stepping aside, I nervously motion for her to pass by me, "Get in … I'll help you wash it out of your hair." *Holy shit, did I really just say that.* Blood swishes through my veins at high speed, my pulse throbs in my wrist as if it may break free and my chest clamps around my heart as I struggle to breathe through each second that passes.

Panic finally sets in and blankets every feature on her face, but all I can do is laugh at what she must be thinking. Honestly, it's what I'm hoping for.

"You can shower with it on," I suggest with a snicker. Her mouth snaps shut, but I have to tease her a little more. "Unless you want to strip down." A smile twitches at my lips as I slowly but surely feel my cheeks rise in amusement of her nervousness.

I didn't expect for this to be a legitimate shower complete with no clothes, however I won't stand in the way if she suddenly drops her clothes to the ground. Her worry eases some with my joke and she moves past me to get in, still in her swimsuit.

Once her body is under the spray of water, she turns to face me and closes her eyes while the water glide over her head and down her chest. When she opens her eyes and looks at me, I force myself to snap my mouth closed before my entire chest is soaked through with my own saliva. She may actually see drool dripping from the corner of my mouth at this point. *Holy hell, I think showers are my new favorite thing!*

Something is starting

"WAIT!"

I stop and stare at her. She doesn't sound mad; she doesn't even sound concerned that I am going to join her. I've never showered with a girl before, but I'd have to admit that it does make the top five on my bucket list.

She points to my jeans in question. "What about your jeans?"

Hell, if she wants them off, I can handle that. I'm confident enough.

"Should you maybe ..." she hesitates, trailing her eyes down my body, "... take them off or ..."

A surge of excitement rockets through me and I move my hand to the snap of my jeans, looking at her to make sure she's comfortable with this. *I can't believe I'm doing this.*

Her eyes open as wide as saucers as she watches my hands with the same hungry look that is plastered on my face. She mumbles something, but my mind has already zoned off in anticipation of being under the water with her. My heart is about to hammer its way out of my chest plus my pants are already tighter.

I did bring a pair of swimming trunks with me this morning so I could quickly change and go find her later, but no way in hell do I want to interrupt the intensity of this moment to go change now.

I ease the zipper down, nervously expecting her to stop me. After sliding them off, I stand there in only a pair of black boxer briefs,

61

wishing I could read her mind. Keeping my eyes pinned on her, I watch her mouth drop open as she stares, definitely not focused on anything above my waist. Fidgeting nervously, I look down and know I can't hide the fact that she has turned me on. Embarrassment flushes my skin, so I quickly jump in behind her.

She instantly turns to face me, taking in my state as the streams of water wash across my boxers, soaking them down and allowing all of my anatomy to rise to the occasion for a prolonged "Hello". Maybe I should be humiliated, but I'm too excited that I spilled that tray of paint. I'm also extremely grateful that we just happened to be working in the shower house. *Thank you fate.*

Without a single word spoken, I reach up to wash the gooey mess from her hair. She moves in closer, her slick wet skin pressed to my body and the sounds of our breath is so heavy that it nearly drowns out the spray of water aimed at us. I massage my fingertips gently through her hair with a steady pattern of soft scrubs, tender touches, and a truck load of caution so that I don't rip her hair out in the process; it's matted in there pretty good.

Her head falls against my chest and although it should be driving me crazy, I'm 150% focused in on the sticky paint that seems to be cemented to each strand of hair. Breathing out discretely through my nose, I take a minute to calm my breaths, heartbeat and areas down below that refuse to listen to my brain. A quick smooth warmth hits my chest through the water and even though it could be anything, I know without a doubt that her tongue just grazed my body.

I don't think. My brain is no longer steering this vessel. A new captain has taken control and it is raring to go. In two seconds flat I have her up in my arms and pressed against the wall.

I claim her mouth as the heat from her body presses up against me, making slow rubbing motions that drive me insane. This is without a doubt moving way too fast, but I am like a runaway train, unable to put the brakes on. It's so tempting to move these two tiny scraps of fabric that stand between us; to slide her suit aside and to feel everything that I so desperately want to feel, but I hold back.

Looking down at her chest heaving up and down, the need within me is overpowering. I take a deep breath and focus on her, prepared to stop if I get any indication from her what so ever.

My hand sits just below her swimsuit top and I want so badly to
Feel her …
See her …
Taste her …
To slide it to the side … or just remove it all.

If all of her is as sweet as her lips, I may not be able to contain
myself. She nods her head, clearly reading the question in my eyes
and my whole sense of control falters. I dive in, pushing my hand beneath the wet fabric and take a full handful of her beautiful body while
my tongue dances with hers.

I should put the brakes on, but holy shit, she feels so good. She
urges me on giving me permission to remove her top with another nod
and I don't hesitate to untie the small strings that hold her garment
intact. The water pushes the fabric down her body which is still tightly against mine, offering very little room between us, but I manage
to take in the full sight of her bare chest, unable to resist going in for
more.

"Oh thank you," I mutter under my breath more to myself.

My mouth descends on her plump, voluptuous breast, pushing a
low whimper from her mouth. I shift her downward against my body;
the urgent need that seems to be burning within her is raging inside
of me as well. We grind and rub against one another in a rhythm that
makes my mind run away with what everything else would feel like
with her. I have no control anymore; my mind has packed up and left,
leaving one thing to lead me forward and it definitely does.

With an insatiable hunger, I wildly taste and lick at her lips and
neck until the most intense feeling I've ever felt begins to build and
build and build within me. Throwing my head back in an eruption of
sheer ecstasy, a loud groan escapes my mouth. A soft moan comes
from her as I fling my head forward into her neck unable to think,
speak or move. All I can do is squeeze my arms around her tightly
while the aftershocks of our momentum spark through me.

The wave subsides and an overwhelming exhaustion sets in. My
arms and legs may very well give out so I tighten my grip on her with
one hand cupping her ass and the other around her waist. It takes extreme effort to catch my breath but this is a feeling I can live with.

As soon as my heart rate returns to a non-heart attack state, I search her face to see if there is any level of regret in her eyes, but all I am met with is her beautiful smile. That makes me take a deep breath as I slowly lower my gaze to where our chests are sealed together. Her wet, bare breasts are perfectly crushed against my skin and my restraint is barely hanging on from wanting to throw her down for round two.

Instead, I hold back as we come down from our high … slowly.

"Can you stand ok?" It's a simple question, but as soon as I say it, I regret it. *That sounded so cocky … it seemed like she was as into it as me, but what if she wasn't?*

She nods, so I set her down, my arms feeling a bit of relief from being free of any weight.

"I really didn't mean that in a cocky way as If I rocked your world or something," I tell her awkwardly, my voice jumping in pitch and tone from our activities as if I'm spastic and juiced up on caffeine. "It's just … I about fell to my knees myself, there at the end," I say sheepishly, my chest expanding on a deep breath as I wait nervously for her to say anything.

"Well, just to be clear you did rock my world …"

Pride swells in my chest with her words and I seriously do not want to leave this stall. Instead I kiss her again. Afterwards, she nonchalantly covers her chest with one arm and suddenly looks a bit shy, so I concede to give her a little privacy.

Looking down, my mind freefalls along with my gaze, carefully going over everything that took place. *Wow … did that really happen?*

"Ummm … I'll be right back," I say, still staring at the floor so she doesn't feel any more vulnerable.

I give her a smile that probably says a thousand words, two of which are 'hell yeah' and then I excuse myself so she can fix her suit. Once around the corner and out of sight, I rush into the stall, tear off my soaked briefs and slide on my trunks faster than I've ever moved. I don't even think I opened Christmas presents this fast as a kid. I'm hoping to catch her before her top is fully affixed. I already got several good looks, but one more definitely wouldn't hurt. Who knows, maybe she could use some help.

I tip toe back into the shower she is in and chuckle. She's standing in front of the stall, holding her swimsuit against her while trying to tie it at the back, but that's not what's funny. The confusion that coats her entire face as she sees me in clean trunks is down-right hilarious.

"What?" she mouths, pointing at them.

"What…" I counter right back, cracking up, "Did you really think I'd stop in the middle of all that and say excuse me while I go get my swim trunks on." I laugh harder, watching her expression as she joins in on my amusement. "No way was I going to chance you leaving," I tell her completely honestly, probably sounding like your typical sex-crazed and one-goal-in-mind sort of guy. *Could I have ran over and changed before jumping in? Absolutely. Would it have lead in the same direction if I had? That I do not know, and that is why I continued in the direction we were heading.* Showers are definitely my new favorite pastime.

Taking in the pull-tug and fumble war she has going on with her swimsuit strings, I slide back to the stall behind her to help out. *Wish granted … again.* Intentionally brushing my hand over her shoulders as I take my time tying it back together, I stare at her delicate skin with a hunger inside of me that is so strong it may very well leap out of my body and take on a life of its own.

I pull the string taut, my chest tightening along with it. If I had it my way, we would have just left it off. I'd really like to turn her around and have her naked chest pressed against mine again.

Blowing out a breath to steer off the arousal that is rushing up on me, I lean in closer to her.

"Do you want to go down to the lake and swim? We could join up with the guys," I suggest, feeling greedy and hoping she will say no because I really don't want to share her company. "Honestly, I don't care. I just want to spend the afternoon with you." I tell her the absolute truth.

For all I care we could hole up in the shower house for the rest of the day, especially since we have firsthand experience of what potentially lies beyond those doors now. I run both my hands over her shoulders and down her arms until my hands are woven around her waist in an embrace. She quickly flips around in my arms to face me, her eyes falling on the ridiculous smile that has been carved across my face since she walked in today. Sliding her arms around my neck, she pulls herself against me with a playful gleam in her eyes.

"Me too." It's the only words she says, but it is enough assurance to rocket my ego to the moon.

After a prolonged moment of looking into her eyes, a couple stray nibbles to her neck and so many swipes of my hands across her bare skin, my heart is on the verge of exploding and my fingertips and lips have become addicted to the satin texture of her skin. Reluctantly, we separate and go about finishing up my workload that truly could not have gotten done without her help. *Where the hell did this girl come from,* is all that keeps buzzing through my head.

"So … " I pause before speaking. So far, neither one of us have said much. It's almost as if both of us are wondering the same thing, yet too afraid to speak. *Was that too fast?!* However, there is still so much I want to know about her. "I never asked before … how long are you staying?"

She unravels each curtain and carefully places them on their new shiny brass curtain rod before moving onto the next. Meanwhile, I busy myself wiping up the spilled paint with the roller until it is nice and smooth.

"One week." She glances over at me as I stop rolling and stare at her. *Damn … that's one week less than me.* "You?"

Shaking my head to knock myself out of my thoughts, I continue rolling in the last of the paint mess that I literally could kiss to show my appreciation for.

"Up until the fifth."

She looks at me with an equal amount of disappointment as I'm sure is clouding my own eyes.

"I can get the last one."

I grab the last vinyl curtain and snap each ring into place while Alyssa stands beside me working on the opposite end. After it is up, we gather all the supplies and put them near the door. The storage shed is a bit of a hike so having everything easily accessible and not scattered helps aid in the clean up process, plus I'm in a hurry to just have a lazy afternoon with her.

But no sooner than we step outside to get the ladder, we find Evan sitting idly by the edge of the dock. As soon as he turns his smartass face our way, I know he is going to embarrass her. One glance at me with a quick getting-busy-in-the-shower-house smirk on his face and

I'm ready to grab her and race off. Luckily, she stands her ground as he pesters her. We all end up laughing and I take the opportunity to hold onto her as tight as possible. The feeling of her small hand in mine does something crazy to my heart and stirs feeling inside of me that I've never felt before.

With two extra arms, we load up all the supplies and head up to the storage shed together.

"So just to clear everything up so I know exactly what to tell all the other guys … you guys did or did not steam up the mirrors in the …"

"Evan!" My eyes go wide and I look over at Alyssa who has a silly smile on her face as if she is preparing to bust up laughing.

"You tell us, because I'm sure you came in. Admit it," she says, looking all sorts of sassy and in control of this conversation. If she did not have a crate loaded down with rollers, brushes and other paint supplies, I would expect for her to have her arms defiantly crossed over her chest.

Evan sneaks a look my way and anxiety shoots through me. *Don't you dare tell her that I told you she may come here today. I had no way of knowing she would show up; that was just plain luck.* I'm about to pipe up to change the subject, but Evan does a good job at deterring the flow of the conversation himself.

"Nahh, I didn't come in. I'm not into that shit," he laughs and they carry on back and forth with friendly chatter. I'm glad too.

So far, my tongue seems to have crawled down my throat and given into retirement, because I cannot muster up a single syllable. My head is throbbing with questions and worries. *Is this too fast? Did I initiate that back in the shower or did she move first? Did she want it as bad as I did or did I urge it on? Shit, she didn't want to stop, did she?* I dismiss that thought quickly, banishing it from my mind with the memory of her whimpers and moans. I look over at Evan who is currently talking her ear off about who knows what. *God, I hope I didn't move too fast. I do not want to scare her off. Why the hell am I analyzing everything?*

On the return back to the Snack Shack, I manage to flip my brain off for a second, but still don't say a word. Instead, all I do is concentrate on the rhythm of my heart, the way it speeds up when I look over at her. I focus in on the softness of her skin against mine as I trace small circles on her hand with my thumb.

While completely caught up in Alyssa and what just happened between us, Evan's loud sigh and pissy tone smacks me out of my reminiscing.

"Ok, that's it. I have no clue what is taking this long. They should have already shut it down for the day. I bet they screwed something up." He storms off, shaking his head. "See ya in a bit."

My eyes follow him until he's out of sight. That's the only signal I need to steal her away and unload my mind.

Pulling her around to the other side of the dock's convenience store, I brace her body against the wall, my body heavy with exhaustion yet burning with adrenaline and the need to make sure this is all going in the right direction.

But before that ... I need to taste her sweet lips again. I pull her to me, our lips welding together in a slow intimate dance that leaves us both needing to catch our breath.

"Am I moving too fast for you? I mean, is this too fast or am I making you uncomfortable or scaring you off At ALL??" I ask her feeling pretty confident that she feels the same as me.

It's as if we went from zero to a hundred in one afternoon, but geez, it feels amazing. Does it even matter how fast we take it, because there is something here; something intense and strong; like a magnet or a pull and even if I had it in me to resist, I know I would still end up back in this exact spot.

"I don't think this could go fast enough for me."

Her answer lifts me off the ground. I want to break dance; I want to pump my fist in the air; I want to celebrate. Touchdown, graduation, scholarship ... those have nothing on what that simple phrase did for me.

"Good gosh, woman, I...I am crazy about you. This is all kinds of new for me. I mean I'm not usually like this and I definitely don't move this fast *ever*," I trip over my words for a second nearly saying something that I know is too soon to feel.

I've never wanted something like this before and for a moment my stomach sinks. This may be exactly how Tiffany felt for me or how my mom felt for my dad and neither one of them got what they wanted; they lost it. Squeezing my eyes shut, I shove those ideas away and focus on Alyssa rather than the crushing weight that has held my heart down for years.

I'm not sure what this is and where it will lead us. From my experience something this perfect doesn't exist. What I do know is that something is beginning here and for the first time in my life, I am so ready for this ride.

The Craziest Week of My Life

LATER THAT NIGHT WE end up falling asleep in the back of my truck. All through the night her soft touch would skim over my skin and she would clutch onto me with a strong sense of need and desire in her grasp. Each and every time, my eyes would open and I'd have to steady my breaths.

The next morning, her hair tickles across my neck and I know without a doubt that she stayed in my arms the whole night. That made me feel on top of the world until I got a face full of water from Evan. Remembering my comment about the bucket of water; he thought it would be cute to douse my fire by pouring ice cold water on me. Considering the state I woke up in, it was probably for the best. At least the water put that flame out before she had time to notice.

The next few days seem to go in fast forward and the end of the week is sitting there like a ghost. She is only staying seven days, so the more time that goes by I get a sick feeling in the pit of my stomach just thinking about us going separate ways. It's silly to dread it because Fairview is just a hop, skip and a jump from Rosemore, but we've been fairly inseparable since day one and I've gotten used to lying beside her each and every night.

I've never imagined enjoying sleeping the night away with a girl. With Tiffany, it always seemed too committed and like I was leading her on further, but then again, a lot of times, I didn't have the heart to tell her to leave. The following mornings, it would get awkward with me searching for an excuse to escape, regretting us getting carried away and her practically planning our wedding.

With Alyssa it's not like that at all. I'm the one pilfering through ways to prolong the night so we can suck up every ounce of time together. Of course, she and I haven't gone that far, but I'd be lying if I said that every soft kiss of her lips doesn't have my body coming unhinged with desire. I literally have to focus on anything other than her or showers or strawberries or swimsuits … basically, I just have to not think and work excruciatingly hard to push away the massive blood flow rushing beneath my shorts when we're together. It's always like waving a red flag … "Yep … this girl does it for me!"

With Alyssa, no amount of time together is long enough; I can't seem to pull myself away from her. That is one thing life has taught me: Time is valuable and every second should be cherished whether it seems to suck at the moment or not. It's a blessing, because tomorrow doesn't come for everyone.

Meeting Alyssa has truly had me wandering through so many memories and possibilities of what could have been done differently. One thing I know I would have done so much differently is spend hours, days and weeks with my mom, assuring her how much she was loved. Instead of locking myself in my room the day after my dad left, feeling sorry for myself, maybe I should have thought of Mom and went and hugged her. After all, he left us all. He left her with three kids and a diagnosis that she knew would ultimately end with her leaving us parentless. Time is precious, and if these last few days have taught me anything, it's that when instances that make your heart pound uncontrollably come along you should stand back, take a deep breath and realize that God has thrown a touchdown pass directly to you. Those are the moments you should never let slip by.

Today is one of those days.

A cool breeze sweeps through the air and thankfully the cabin we are working on today is blanketed by a canopy of trees, offering a surplus of shade and a bit cooler temps. Looking up in between getting a few more shingles down, I'm surprised to see Alyssa strolling up beside Jake.

"Ahhh, shit …" Evan spits out jokingly as I toss the air gun down and sprint to the ladder.

I don't even bother to take each step; instead I leap off half way down and fly to her in a matter of seconds.

What I thought was just a simple visit, quickly turns into her hoisting a board up on her shoulder and working right alongside of us, just like one of the guys. Talk about thrilling the hell out of me. I felt like one of those cartoons, mouth drawn open, eyes wide and drool puddling at my feet as I watched her in amazement.

"You gonna stare or come help," she teases, oblivious to the fact that I am impressed

After lifting my mouth off the ground, I race to help.

"Here, I can get that for you," I throw a 2x6 on my shoulder, much like she did, but I make damn sure to flex a bit so she can be equally awestruck by me.

Keeping my eyes on her bent over silhouette, I walk back towards her and the half built porch frame.

"Oh, no … no … no! You were helping up here," Evan announces above us as I drop the board onto the frame to her side.

"I can help you finish this and he can help with the porch," my little brother comes to my rescue, making himself at home on the roof with the air gun already in his hand.

"What! No …"

I look up, watching Jake and Evan in amusement, but still not moving a muscle to hop up there. *I'm good here.*

"You need to head back over to the other cabin and finish up there. I'd like to get all of this done with the next few days."

"They're finishing up … that's why I came over … to find out what was left." Jake automatically starts throwing shingles down and getting to work."

"Really? Alright! Well, this is all. We have this cabin left and we are done," Evan exclaims with a proud, disbelieving tone as the rest of us smile in celebration of all our hard work nearing the end.

"Are you guys really almost done?" Alyssa swings a hammer at the board she has held in front of her, looking more like a pro than most of us.

"Yeah, I guess so." I grin and watch her work for a second before getting back to it myself. "Where did you learn to work with tools?"

She keeps busy, not pausing in the slightest, but as I look at her profile I see a small smile crop up on her face as she slides the next board a couple centimeters from the next.

"Here," I whisper in her ear as I lean across her back to place a t-square between the two boards as a spacer. Once again she shivers and the corners of my mouth rise. It must be 99 degrees in the shade today … no way is she cold; it's definitely me.

"Oh no … hey, they'll be none of that going on while we're working." Evan breaks through my solitary bubble that surrounds Alyssa and me.

Pulling back, I give him a smart-ass look. Lowering my eyebrows and pressing my lips together to contain a laugh.

"You do not see Jake and me up here all …" he arches himself over Jake, with a goofy look on his face while Jake innocently places a shingle in place. "Oh, let me help…"

"Get off me, man," Jake pipes up instantly, shoving Evan away with his free arm.

"Exactly …" Evan points down at us with his brows raised and eyes widened. "We work … no smooching … no giggling and flirting … no making out …"

"Ok," I cut him off, embarrassment crawling to the surface of my skin as I glance over to her.

She looks back with a quick what-did-we-do smile and then up at Evan. "Got it."

"Making out … I'm in." Tristan walks up, casually leaning against the corner of the porch. "I'm not sure I'd go that far with this group of ugly faces, but I do see something I like." He looks right at Alyssa, slapping me on the back.

Annoyance surges through my fists as I clamp down on the board I'm holding. "Yeah, no way, Tristan." I know he's teasing, just like Evan does, he loves getting under my skin, but he and I don't exactly see eye-to-eye.

Call me crazy but when your mom dies and weeks later rather than being able to grieve, you find yourself having to spend every second working so that your guardian can go out and party, chase girls and get drunk every night, that tends to put a damper on your relationship. Last I checked I wasn't appointed guardianship of two teenagers that desperately needed their older brother to hold them together. He was the man of the family growing up after Dad left; he was who we turned to for advice and help with homework when Mom was getting sicker and sicker. If I did something stupid or got in trouble for a bad choice, he was the one that chewed my ass because by my freshman year, Mom was completely bed ridden and the ALS had already robbed her of any sort of life she would want to live. After she passed and when we needed him the most, he checked out. If I hadn't given up on my brother ever returning, the last straw would have definitely been him skipping out on my graduation.

The afternoon rolls on with all of the guys pulling together to bring this last job to a close.

"You know how driftwood has all those holes and ridges embedded in it from hours in the water … that's about how the porch is gonna look by the end of the day from Judd slobbering all over himself." Evan and the others go on and on all afternoon with comment after comment that has me ready to dig a hole and crawl in.

When the last nail is tapped into place, I blow out a sigh of relief that the day is done. Alyssa gets a kick out of it all, smiling and laughing quietly as she works. Once in a while, I get a glimpse of pink across her cheeks and my level of embarrassment lessens and twists into rifling back a comment at them. Needless to say, we high tail it back to my cabin, restless, eager to be alone and somewhat turned on.

No sooner than we get inside, she curls up on my bed and I have one choice and one choice alone, I'm getting in that bed with her. As the warmth of her body presses back against me, my hands think on their own, venturing to places they've never explored on her body. I proceed with even more caution than I did in the shower, but once my hand is all the way beneath her swimsuit bottom, it is truly the most electrifying experience of my life. I've never touched someone in a way that I touch her, with feeling behind each kiss, each trembling stroke of my fingers or caress of my hand. I've touched someone in a drunken haze that I never remembered and I've gone all the way with someone in a time of weakness when we needed a mutual comfort, but never like this.

My chest rises and falls rapidly with each small sound that moves across her lips, urging me on as my fingers slide over her silky soft skin. I'm nervous as hell and each time her breathing picks up, I get even more excited. I move my fingers back and forth, in and out, watching, studying her to see what she likes the most. It's as if I'm a virgin all of sudden, lead by my heart into each movement for the first time. She leans back hard towards my body the more I touch her, even turning her neck so I can taste her mouth and even though it takes a minute for me to work out the coordination of my hand and tongue in two separate places, it has me about to lose it.

She lets out a loud whimper as she jolts forward then quickly retracts back against me, almost melting against me; there's no doubt, I remember that sound. I smile with confidence, yet almost wanting to ask her if she did, but I don't.

After that, she suggests touching me back. *Holy shit!* I want to roll over and give her complete access to anything she wants to do to me, but I actually stop her. This isn't a marathon; I'm hoping we have time for all that. She falls to sleep fast, and so do I after my body relaxes from the intensity of her movement and an extreme case of needing some sort of relief.

Upon waking, we decide on fishing for the rest of the day. I truly want to kneel on my hands and knees and thank the Lord for sending me this gorgeous angel that knows how to handle tools and that likes to fish. *Wow ... jackpot.*

Racing along behind her as we head to Evan's grandfather's private dock where he keeps all his water toys, I stare at the way her hips sashay from side to side, the way a single drop of sweat gradually rolls down her back and the way the sunlight bounces off each strand of her blonde hair. Looking my way with an all-knowing smile as she shimmies her hips, she totally catches me checking out her ass ... hard.

"Arrgghh ..." I smack my hand through the air towards her butt, barely grazing it as she squeals and darts away.

She stops just ahead of me and glances over her shoulder, overlapping her feet on a slow, graceful and sensual walk that has my eyes falling straight to her ass ... again. It's drawing me in.

She laughs and I let out another groan, "Arhhh ..." but this time

I grab her into my arms.

Her eyes sparkle with mischief and giddiness as she breaks free of my hold with a smile. As soon as she speeds off, I race after her only to tackle her to the ground about five feet up. My chest fills with an explosive flood of contentment as I look at her squirming happily within my grasp and retreating into my arms.

"Ok, I give up, I give up," she gasps, right as my fingertips attack her stomach.

My mouth opens and I smile; really smile and watch her as if I'm seeing her for the first time. I take a deep breath and pull her arms above her head playfully with my knees to each side of her waist. I'm careful to not bear any weight onto her as I kneel with pebbles and dirt scratching my shins and portions of my feet not covered by my sandals.

I keep my eyes on her as she stares back, suddenly we are completely alone and silence engulfs us. It's as if we're stranded on an island, just her and I. Maybe we've even been there for years, because right now the raw emotion that is overcoming my heart should be something you feel after decades with someone, yet we've only known each other for a week. *A week; is this too soon?*

"Alyssa …" I whisper, my smile falling and my mind swimming with all that I want to say to her; none of which I plan to.

How is it that this is happening?

Is this real?

Do you feel what I feel?

I feel like I've known you my whole life; have we met before?

Alyssa … I think I love you.

She looks alarmed for a second. "What's wrong?"

I can't say a word though. My tongue is knotted into a bundle of confusion on whether I am interpreting correctly what my heartbeat is telling me. *Am I in love with her?* I've never felt any of this before, yet with her, I felt it the second I saw her step onto that gravel lot; the moment my eyes fell on her. It was like I was looking into a crystal ball, staring right at my future.

A bird whistles in the trees above me, practically beckoning me on.

"I …" is all I manage to get out, but should I say the rest?

A blink of her eyes as she watches me in suspense throws me off my high-wire and makes me lose my courage. I shake my head then reopen them with her still watching me.

"I just wanted to say this is the best summer of my life." If I had to choose a whole life without her and this past week with her, I'd choose just the one week. It doesn't consist of my entire summer, but from where I'm sitting, this is the part that matters. "Come on, let's go."

I jump up and help her to her feet, knowing I'm a chicken once again. We gather our stuff and in no time we're out on the lake, enjoying a rare escape from everyone else; completely and utterly alone. I veer the boat south to a place Evan showed me a couple summers back. It's somewhere he came a lot and from how he told it, I'm thinking he didn't come here alone.

As soon as we are settled in for some fishing, we start talking. Imagine my surprise when the first sentence out of my mouth is asking about her family. *Why'd I do that? I never do that!* I close my eyes and look up to the sky for a second, pleading that I did not open up a line of future questions that I'm not yet prepared to answer, but her reply surprises me.

"My family is close. You know what … there's another reason for this trip …"

I perk up to her comment, remembering how one night she had told me that one of the reasons she came out here this summer is to get her mind off of a cheating ex; an ex that she had just broke up with recently. That fact made me extremely uneasy, knowing she could very well be on the rebound, but then I told myself to trust my instincts.

"My father is waiting on test results to see if his cancer has returned. A few summers ago he battled cancer, but he got past it. Then last week, I came home and found out that we may possibly have to relive that same heartbreaking experience. I just don't know what to do if …" she trails off and my heart falls into my stomach. I want to lunge across the small fishing boat and wrap her in my arms so tight that she will never feel the same anguish I did.

A slicing pain rips across my chest, infiltrating my heart. I've sat in that chair; I remember that discussion, that agonizing wait on test results. It kills you.

"Ok boys ..." my mom's hands shake as she lowers them to the kitchen table where she has gathered all of us.

Jake and I sit across from her with Tristan to her right. He looks nervous too, biting the inside of his lip and occasionally placing his hand on hers to steady her nerves.

"So I know you have probably noticed that I've been getting clumsier lately ... falling and needing some help from time to time, but ..." she looks to my brother and he nods. It's apparent that he has already been told whatever news she is about to deliver. "I finally got answers from the doctor."

I stare at my mom, threading my brows together, scrunching my nose and curling my lips. I don't understand what is going on. Jake remains silent too, fidgeting his fingers in front of him. A tear slips from Mom's eyes and my mouth falls and my face tenses.

"Mom ..." I say quietly, wanting to leap over the table and hug her. I hate seeing her cry. She's done it a lot lately, while washing dishes, listening to music, alone in her bedroom. I even caught her sitting in the driveway in her car the other day with her head hung forward and a river of tears that I never thought would stop.

She takes a deep breath and sucks it all in, all the emotion, as Tristan pulls her closer to his side.

A sense of courage, strength and determination takes over her face as she goes on. "The doctors say I have a disease called ALS," she pauses. For a second, I wonder if I'm supposed to ask questions. What's ALS? I know what disease means and it's never good.

"Do you have cancer?" I ask, knowing that is a disease that I learned about in health class.

"No honey," she smiles and reaches across to squeeze my hand. "I have something called ALS. It's got a longer name ... a medical name, but ALS is the shortened version. It ummm ..." her voice trembles and she looks to Tristan, a silent request for help.

He jumps in, finishing for her as tears start to fall from her face one at a time, an endless parade.

"It means she'll start losing function of normal things like walk-

ing, moving ... things like that ..." *my brother stops and his gloomy expression and watery eyes have me on high alert. This is bad. "Ummm ... she may eventually have to stay in bed, but it's ok ... I'm going to take care of her and we'll just carry on, ok?" He looks at me and Jake with an encouraging smile, but I'm not convinced. I'm ten and I've never seen my brother cry, but as he wipes away a fallen tear, I know he's not telling me everything.*

"Mom, will you be ok? Is there medicine you can take to make it go away?"

Her and Tristan share a look and she huffs out a breath with more tears. My brother pulls her to his side.

"She'll be ok ... I'll take care of her," he answers and my shoulders relax.

Mom quickly interrupts my sigh of relief, "No ... no, Tristan ... I can do this." She turns and faces Jake and I. "Sweeties, everyone goes to heaven eventually, you know? I am on medication, but it doesn't do much for this disease."

"Are you gonna die?" Jake pipes up, making me cringe and causing Tristan's face to pale at his bluntness, but Mom just smiles, a sweet loving smile.

"Eventually, we all do, honey. It's just life ... but I plan to stick around as long as possible, I promise ... Ok?"

"Ok, Mom," Jake says innocently and beyond comprehension of what was just told to us.

I want to scream, it's not ok. Tristan cries and my own eyes well up with tears. I'm confused and I want to believe that she will stay here, but the way they both are acting has me doubting their words.

Looking across the boat at Alyssa, I feel her pain as if it is fresh and happening to me all over again. I pop up without thinking it through and stumble forward closer to her until I reach the small padded bench in the center of the boat. Taking a seat, I quickly scoop her tiny hand up in mine and give it a gentle, heartfelt squeeze.

"I wish I could hold you right now, but I may flip the boat. I promise to as soon as we get to shore, though," I tell her, ready to pause our fishing excursion and dock the boat. *I have to hold her!* But deep down, I know more than anything she doesn't want to think about it. I assume that's why she came to the lake after all, to try and get her mind off of it. With that, I clear my throat and get busy harpooning worms onto both our hooks and lightening the conversation to fishing stories that will make her laugh, and she does.

After we have caught a few and thrown them back, we find a small clearing with some sand not far away so I steer in that direction. Once the boat is pulled to the shore and we unpack a couple necessities, she spreads a towel out, but I can't wait any longer. I grab her up in my arms and hold her as the minutes click by without a single word. Her fingertips run up my back in slow motions and I love it. Tilting my head to look at her, yet making sure to not turn this into anything less than affectionate and heartfelt, I move in for a slow, warm kiss that lets her know what's in my heart.

The sun beats down over us, warming the sand under our feet and sucking every bit of moisture from our skin, but we still stay put holding onto one another. Our lips find each other again and this time, it get more heated with her hands running up my ribcage then back down, settling on my abs. The positioning of her hands makes my head spin, my heart drums uncontrollably, and we pick up momentum as I slip my tongue into her mouth. I don't even take a breath; I taste her lips with my own, moving them in a seductive flow with hers as my hands work their way over her bikini strings to her back, past her small waist and stop, comfortably resting on her swimsuit bottom.

As we break away, both of us taking a breath, she speaks up, "You want to get in the water and swim for a bit?"

I'm relieved. With me pressed so closely against her body while we kiss, I don't even have to ask her if she knows just what that does to me; I'm sure she can feel it. She has a habit of letting out this tiny little whimper when my tongue touches hers and it always has me visualizing more aggressive actions.

I take off into the water, turning my back to her so she cannot see my state of arousal. The pitched tent is never a sexy look when you are trying to be smooth and woo a girl. Besides, she has already taken in that sight on numerous instances so I think she has pretty well gotten the point that I stay turned on around her.

Once I'm waist high in the water I turn back around to look at her as she wades in, stopping when the water laps at her thighs. Folding her arms over her chest, she crinkles her nose and looks around.

"What's wrong?" I snicker.

The water is pretty chilly today and with the thin fabric of her bikini top I can see just how cold she is.

"It's freezing." She shivers, running her hands along her arms.

Walking back towards her, I splash a little water up in her direction and laugh. "It's not that bad," I say, my situation already remedied from the cold water.

She puts her hands up as if she is defending herself. "Don't throw me in, Judd," she laughs.

I smile, "I won't. I promise. " I pull her into my arms and walk us back to the beach area.

After I lay her down on the towel, I reach into her bag and pull out the sunscreen. Her smile grows as I stare at her not even watching while I flip the cap and squirt a nice blob of lotion on my hand.

"Lay back," I instruct; she complies without hesitation.

I get busy rubbing it on, starting with her calves and working my way up her thighs. She lies back for only so long before propping herself up on her elbows to examine my technique. Slowly, I wander up her leg further to the tender flesh near her bikini line. I'm not even sure I have any lotion left on my hand, but just like back at the shower, no way am I interrupting this. Carefully watching her face as she puckers her lips, fighting a smile, I sneakily dip my pinky behind the fabric of her bottoms on each stroke.

She laughs, eyeing me the whole time. "You know, the sun is not going to penetrate that area, right?"

I kick my head back with a chuckle, not even bothering to answer her. She knows full well that I'm taking advantage of a perfect excuse to touch her. Moving up to her chest I use the same gentle motion and sneak a couple extra touches under her suit. *I have to be fair, giving all parts of her body equal attention.* We both laugh at my seduction methods while I finish slathering her with sunscreen. After I'm done, I slide on top of her with the slick sticky texture of lotion acting as a sort of glue that is sure to seal us together; *I'm hoping.*

"What are you doing? You're blocking my sun," she worms around, trying to sound stern and annoyed, even though a smile gives way.

My smile deepens and I squirm around playfully against her body, holding onto her shoulders with my knees sinking into the towel at each side of her legs.

"Don't be stingy … I'm getting some lotion for myself," I tease then plant a kiss on her beautiful moist lips.

Her face lights up as she pulls me in her for a deeper kiss. *No more playing; down to business.* I still myself and leisurely run one hand up the curve of her body.

"Mmmm," a whine vibrates on her tongue and I have to suck in a breath.

She has no idea, absolutely no idea what those little sounds do to me or what they make me want to do to her. Raising my face away from her, I look into her eyes and shift so she can get more comfortable. Her legs slide up along either side of my hips and I settle myself between her legs, both of us still dressed in our suits, but in my mind…there's absolutely nothing between us.

Running a hand up the outer part of her thigh, I move in to taste her lips again. My eyes flick down as her tongue grazes over her bottom lip, leaving a trail of moisture that is calling my name. She opens her mouth and I descend in on it, eager and already aroused.

"How many girls have you kissed?" she slams me with a question I didn't expect and I pull away quickly, completely forgetting my desires for a moment. *Where on earth did this question come from and why is she asking it now of all times?*

I laugh, lowering my eyebrows in confusion. "What? Umm … what brought that up?" I shake my head wondering how we went from making out to talking about other girls. *Never a good subject!*

"I'm curious," she says innocently as if it is completely usual to dead-end a moment of passion and bring up something that most men steer away from discussing.

I may not have ever been in a relationship before, but common sense tells me, never discuss ex's or particular situations from your past when you are in the position I'm currently in. Basically our easy-going-playfulness-in-the-sun day might have come to a crossroad.

Pausing before answering, I weigh my options of how to answer this, but then give in to just answer plain and simple. "Not as many as most guys my age, but like I told you before I stay pretty focused on football." I'm probably going to sound fairly inexperienced. I grit my teeth, mentally tallying them up.

Tiffany, of course.

I have no doubt that my lips probably landed on the girl I lost my virginity to a time or two.

After a huge football game my junior year, one of the cheerleaders tracked me down and asked if I was busy later. I told her I had plans; she congratulated me on the win and then slapped one on me. I didn't stop it ... it was unexpected and it was pretty nice.

Then there was a girl last summer that stayed in one of the cabins down from Evan's camper. I went for a walk late at night, alone and ran into her down by the dock. We talked for a good while and before she left to go back to her cabin, I figured what the hell and kissed her. There was absolutely no sparks or chemistry, nothing like what I feel with Alyssa.

"Four girls before you ... " *Yeah, that's it.* Then I add, "... that didn't kiss near as amazing as you do."

She bites her lip with a smile then pulls me down to kiss her. My whole body relaxes, knowing I may have escaped a major blow-up by throwing in that last comment which was totally honest. I love kissing her. But before my lips touch hers, I squeeze at the skin on her side and surprise myself.

"Wait just a minute. What about you?" I throw out with a grin. *Two can play at this.*

I look at her not really needing to know the answer, but noting by her reaction to my answer that we can pretty well talk to each other about anything.

"Oh, me? Well, I would be at a whopping three."

This surprises me and kind of makes me very happy.

"Including me?"

She nods her head and I smile. *So I am lucky number three; I think I'll keep her at that number.* Placing my lips back on hers, I run my hand back up her leg in an attempt to get us back where we were.

"So how many girls have you had sex with?" she drops this bomb, stopping me in my tracks.

Whoa! I close my eyes and laugh. "Do all girls do that?" I laugh harder, leaning my face into her neck.

"What? I just want to know," she says softly, drawing her fingers across my back and into my hair.

Suddenly, this conversation does not seem important. I take her face in my hands, nibbling at her lips before kissing her like I've never kissed anyone else in my life, as if she is my last drink of water. My tongue roams her mouth, tasting everything within her, every breath, and every word that she had left to ask. After slightly pulling away, I suck her bottom lip into my mouth then level her with a questioning look. She seems distracted now, a little dazed as she stares at me through heavy breaths. *I'm home free from discussing my past sex life. Not a subject I want to dive into with her or anyone.*

A wide smile spreads across her face and I've been caught trying to side track her. I mock her expression with an innocent grin that curls up my cheeks where my dimple is. Her eyes move to the right of my face like it always does as she leans forward and teases me with the thought that I'll get to devour her lips once again. Instead, she kisses the dimple in my cheek. I laugh; for some reason the dimple always gets to girls and I definitely like how she obsesses over it.

I retreat, holding one hand up beside our faces, "Ok, ok … but you have to tell me your number, too. Deal?"

She nods her head seeming awfully excited about this discussion. Most girls would be starting a war at the talk of other girls.

"Ok …" I blow out an uneasy breath and go on, "only two." I spit it out and wait. She doesn't laugh, doesn't change expressions, so I elaborate with a little hesitation. "There's a girl that I've had a thing with for a couple years … nothing serious, just kind of a mutual understanding," I pause, clamping my jaw in panic of how bad that may sound and that's not even the other one. *I'll keep some of that to myself; she didn't ask for details.* "Then there was the girl I lost my virginity to when I was fifteen … almost sixteen," I throw out the last part quickly, ashamed of how that all happened.

"So is the first one your girlfriend?" She speaks with caution and I immediately toss her doubts out the window.

"No!" I spit out then realize I probably sound like a dirt bag. "Her name is Tiffany and we're friends, that's it. She is a great girl, but we just sort of ended up getting carried away a couple times. We ended all that anyways." I make sure to toss that detail out there; after all, that is exactly what we did right before I came out here.

She doesn't huff up in an angry tizzy at my words, just smiles. *She must have forgotten that now it's her turn.* I clear my throat and wiggle my eyebrows to nudge her on.

"Oh, yeah. Umm well … I am standing strong at number …" she pauses, eyeing me. I groan and we both laugh. "One." She raises one finger up with her teeth gritted.

I am pleasantly surprised and extremely excited, but then she goes on.

"I've only slept with Kyle, my ex. I lost my virginity to him about three months ago, sooooo …"

I raise my eyebrows, nerves, anxiety and relief all bolting through me that she is just as inexperienced as me, yet feeling a bit like a sleaze in comparison. Considering I don't even remember the first time, I'd have to say her and I are fairly equivalent on our skill level. If we ever do go any further, I know I will more than likely fizzle out fast from the excitement so I am comforted in that fact.

We lie on the shore kissing until the sun goes down and I really do not want to leave. After a prolonged period of solitude and intimacy, she breaks our connection for a brief moment.

"Oh my gosh! I was so excited to see you earlier … I forgot what I came to find you for."

Hearing her say she was excited to see me makes my heartbeat drum in my chest and creates a monstrous smile across my face.

"We talked to my parents and we are staying til the fifth."

This is news I've been praying to hear. As if my smile could not get any bigger, she tells me this and my mouth breaks open into a half smile half laugh. I want to lift her into the air and spin in circles with her tightly in my arms, but the level of emotion that rises within me also has me somewhat scared. I knew she should have already left by now, but to hear that her trip was extended until the day I leave is music to my ears. *Damn, I love this girl!* My mind says the words so clearly for only a split second but there it is. I look into her eyes and everything inside of me is yelling for me to say it aloud.

"Alyssa, I …" I gulp down the anxiety that threatens to come up the back of my throat and spill out from how nerve-racking this is, but for the third time, I chicken out and veer in another direction. I don't want to lay all my cards on the table until I am absolutely positive that my words won't make her bolt for the door. "This has been the craziest, most wonderful, totally unexpected week of my life and I owe it all to you."

I smile at her; she in turn gives me the most beautiful, bright smile I have ever seen.

Later that night I decide to make things official and ask her to be my girlfriend. Her answering yes makes it more than clear; I'm in love with her. The craziest week of my life just turned into the best thing that has ever happened to me and I don't intend on ever letting her go.

Did that Really Just Happen?

I WAKE UP THE next morning by the sounds of my little brother tapping on the side window of my truck. My neck is stiff like a metal bar has been shoved up the back of it. I bend it from side to side, glancing over at the head rest that I had my head laid back on the entire night.

Holding my finger up, I signal to Jake to give me a minute at the same time that Alyssa's head moves in my lap. My fingers are wound up in her hair while my other hand rests on her stomach. I look down at her and am met with sleepy pale blue eyes and a smile. *My day is already complete.*

"Good morning, baby." *I can totally call her that now.*

In true Junior High fashion, I asked her out last night. I have no idea how those kinds of things are approached so I just went with what felt right, stumbling around my words like an idiot while she sat cuddled up in my lap.

"Hi," she says with a hoarse voice, rising up to cuddle up against me just like last night.

I wrap my arms around her then look over my shoulder to Jake, which is impatiently pacing back and forth outside of my truck. He has an hour before he has to leave, but I have something I need my truck for so I'm glad he woke me up early.

"Hey … my brother has to leave today to go back home, so I was hoping I could spend an hour or so with him to say goodbye." I hate even suggesting the second apart, but we have several more days at our disposal now, so I have something up my sleeve that I hope she'll love. "You want me to come find you after?"

She scrunches up her face, gritting her teeth as if she's hesitant to say what's on her mind.

"What? You want to spend the day with your sister?" I ask, sensing her uncertainty on answering.

"Want to?" She gives me another silly look as if I just asked the dumbest question of all time.

I laugh, "Ok, so neither one of us wants to but maybe …" I draw out my last word playfully, "… they'll leave us alone later if we spend time with our friends." I wiggle my brows, shooting her my best sly smile.

"You promise you'll come find me later?"

"I promise." *Without a doubt.*

She flashes me a full mouth of white teeth before agreeing. After giving her a quick kiss, I watch her walk off, grinning in a complete daze until my brother's hand swipes across my arm creating a bit of a sting.

"That's just weird," he says while shaking his head.

I look over and laugh. "What?" I'm sure I am smiling like kid on Christmas morning.

"You have the most ridiculous smile on your face and you stare at her like you're undressing her with your eyes," he cracks up, but I don't care.

I know exactly how I look at her. I look at her like my heart may explode like a volcano from all the love it holds for her; like she is the most amazing thing I've ever seen. I memorize the way she moves, the way she throws her hair over her shoulder and holds it up when the wind blows, how she bites her lip when she is nervous or excited. I tuck it all away in my heart, watching it all as if today is my last day.

"You mind running me somewhere real quick?"

He shakes his head and we automatically jump in my truck, jetting over to the other side of the lake so that I can rent a cabin.

Pulling my phone out of the console, I hesitantly dial Tristan's number. The hours he keeps whoring around, I'm sure he hasn't even woke up yet.

"You better plan on apologizing for waking my ass up."

Don't answer next time dumb-ass, is what I want to say, but I need a favor so I hold back my sarcasm and our differences. "Sorry. Hey … I was hoping you could do me a favor and maybe *not* give me shit for it."

"I'm listening." I hear the creaking of a mattress and wonder if he is even in our cabin at this time.

"Ok, well I know you've made some friends on the other side of the lake," I use the word 'friends' loosely, "I was hoping I could rent one of the cabins over there for the Fourth, but with it being a week out, I know that's going to be hard. You think you could sweet talk some of those girls into moving their party to one cabin for the night if I reimburse them double what they paid?" I wait then get anxious, adding "… triple if I need to, money isn't an option." *Now, I sound desperate.*

"Well … well, is someone planning a sleep over for that night?"

I roll my eyes, pressing my head into the phone impatiently and fully intent on sucking up any amount of pestering he has lined up for me as long as he can deliver.

"I'm headed over that way right now to check with the front desk if they have some cabins available, but if you can do anything to make it happen in the next fifteen minutes, I'd really owe you." *He actually owes me and he knows it.*

"Hold up … pull your panties out of your ass and give me a minute. Text me when you get here."

The phone clicks and my frustration spirals through the roof of the truck. *He's such a jerk-off.*

"Let me guess, either he flat out turned you down or he wants to know what's in it for him."

I breathe out a sarcastic chuckle and shrug. "I have no idea."

Jake lets out a deep sigh, his shoulders falling and chest receding on it. I'm sure he's more than sick of the animosity between me and Tristan.

"Well at least you won't have to worry about putting up with him for much longer."

His words hit me like a 300 pound linebacker, leaving me dazed and filled with guilt.

"Jake, listen…" I look down, hoping that maybe some of the guilt will be washed away before I leave if I talk to him about this. The decision to go away has never felt like something I needed to even think about. Packing my bags and getting on that plane was going to be as easy as breathing, until now. I never imagined a simple summer job would turn into a process of me discovering where my life is headed; to doubt whether I should stay on this road or possibly veer off onto the unmarked one. It's a sweeter ride, but it scares the shit out of me, to not know where it could end up.

"I've been meaning to talk to you." I stop and take a quick gulp of courage. "How do you feel about me leaving?" I finally move my eyes from staring at my hands and look his way when the truck jostles to the left. "Whoa!"

Jake's shocked expression swings from me back to the road as he corrects the steering which was leading us into a rut alongside the country road that winds along the lake.

"Well…" He draws his brows up thoughtfully before answering. "It's not up to me, Judd."

I start to stop him and correct his comment. In a way it is. If he asked me to stay, I would; I'd hate it because I'm dying to leave, but I would stay.

He goes on, before I can speak up, "Do what makes you happy. I want that for you and Tristan. I'm grown up now. I'll be fine and besides, this is my last year of school then I'll be out on my own, doing my own thing."

"And you'll be in college, busy with football and studying," I add, immediately noticing a funny expression cross his face.

"Yeah, that too. You'll also visit, right?"

My eyes light up with that, but then my thoughts take a nose dive wondering what will happen. If Alyssa is in Indiana and I'm in California, will I visit her there or will she come visit me or will we plan to meet back in Rosemore and Fairview?

"You do plan to come back, right?"

Jake pulls me out of all the questions that I have no way of answering until I work it out with her. I'm taking this too fast anyways. One thing at a time, right now I'll focus on getting the cabin.

"Of course, I'm coming back." The mention of coming back home doesn't ignite the same dread inside of me as it did before and I know that has so much to do with her.

"Well then, go…have fun and go play your ass off in football. Don't worry about me."

I sigh, smiling with a new found relief. I've worried that he would view me leaving as skipping out on us like Dad did, or maybe even as losing another person in his life; God knows we've faced enough of that.

As Jake and I wind down our conversation, we make it to the other side of the lake. Stepping out of the truck with my phone held in my hand, I slam the door shut, but don't even get my phone pulled up to text when I see Tristan stepping out of the cabin directly across from the office; the main cabin, which I thought belonged to the owner.

Holding his arms out on a stretch, he looks across the way right at me with a huge grin then reaches down to check his fly. *Of course he's there.* He jogs across to meet me as I shove my phone into my pocket, hoping for good news.

"Hey," I say blandly even though his smile couldn't get any bigger with those stupid ass dimples digging into each of his cheeks.

He stops just in front of me with a cocky expression and runs his hands through his tousled up bed-head.

"Done and you're welcome."

I cock my head back, annoyed and not at all positive of what is done. "Ok, so I have a cabin?"

Without a word, he turns and points right to the front cabin. My jaw drops and eyebrows rise in shock.

"No way! How?!" I spit out, nearly impressed, but I should know better; I know how.

He folds his arms over his chest, assertively and I know I'm about to be the recipient of details I really don't care to hear.

"Let's just say, the owner's daughter wanted something and …" he quirks his eyebrows igniting my gag reflex and goes on, "I wanted something. Of course, I gave her exactly what she wanted …" he bites his lip, thrusting his hips subtly. "Sweet ass in return for that there cabin." He twirls his hand in front of him and takes a bow.

Releasing an exaggerated breath, I look at him needing to say thank you, but it's always hard to be cordial with him. "Thanks. So what do I need to do? How much do I owe?"

"These front cabins go for $300 a night, but I dined in early this morning and got 100 bucks knocked off your tab," he smirks and my stomach turns. *I really didn't need to know that.* Changing to a serious tone, he stands up straight and flicks his hand through the air on a wave. "Just show up at the office that day … pay and the key is yours for the night."

I glance back, seeing Jake still in the cab of the truck lowering his hand from a wave. For some reason, Tristan seems to tone down the whole man-whore act around Jake. I guess he reserves it for me.

"Good deal. Thanks," I say, nodding my head.

With that we part ways, Jake and I head back to the other side while Tristan goes where ever the hell he usually goes. Jake drops me off a little ways behind my cabin so that I don't chance Alyssa seeing me and asking where I was. *I'm actually pretty pumped about surprising her.*

It takes no time at all for Evan to find me and hit me up to join him on a fishing excursion. I gladly tag along, because this is our norm when we come to the lake. Ever since we met, we would spend hours at a time out in his grandpa's boat catching anything from bass, blue-gill, trout, catfish, some gar and even an old torn up tennis shoe once.

However, today, anxiety sets in as soon as the engine cranks up and we push off from the dock. The clock is ticking and the realization that I will soon be leaving gets more and more real by the minute, especially when I'm with Alyssa. Every second we spend together is bitter sweet. Since Mom died, I pushed football to the forefront of my heart, turning it into my one true passion, my love in life; my dream. Now that dream is literally only a month and one flight away, but little-by-little I feel that passion being nudged a single millimeter at a time to the back of my thoughts as my love for her grows. So with each grain of sand that slowly seeps through that tiny hole in the hourglass of time, I get a pit in my stomach that I'll be leaving her; that this amazing thing that has been gradually healing each deadened fragment of my heart may come to an end. That scares the hell out of me and to choose football over that is starting to seem unfathomable. Do people really take leaps of faith this big? How can I know what the future holds? If I go, will I be making the biggest mistake of my life or if I stay will I be passing up the opportunity of a lifetime?

"Geez ... are you even listening to me? Earth to Judd?" Evan shouts from the bow of the boat as he holds one hand up waving.

I look at him and nod, slyly pretending as if I was paying attention the whole time.

His face goes slack with an expression that reads, "Really?! Seriously?"

I laugh. "Sorry ... I was sort of zoning out. What did you say?"

"No joke. Thinking about girlie, huh?" He shakes his head, steering the boat into a private cove where we have caught some pretty decent sized bass in the past. "So what warrants a day off from the ole' ball and chain? You guys break up or something?"

Chuckling at his choice of words that implies so much more than girlfriend and boyfriend, I correct him quickly, "No we didn't break up. I actually asked her out last night." I spit out a huff of air at the memory of how lame I felt asking her and how silly I probably looked stumbling around my words as if I was asking her to wear my class ring or something. "I have no clue how that shit is done."

Evan throws his head back on a howl and stomps his foot to the floorboard of the boat as if he's determined to knock a hole in it. "Ah oh, no more slumming ... it's official now! Did you drop down on one knee or what?" he pesters on, having a ball with my attempt at being romantic. *This is the reason guys don't sit around discussing their feelings.*

"No ... besides, I was in my truck, jackass," I laugh with a bit of a frown, curious and wondering. *Would I be sitting at the kitchen table with Mom telling her all about Alyssa right now, if she were alive? Would I possibly ask Dad for advice on my next move; about the night of the Fourth?*

Oblivious to my sudden silence, Evan clears his throat and brings his voice to a serious tone. "Seriously though, that's great. I can see that she makes you happy and you deserve that, you know?"

I look at him, a little stunned. His expression changes to his usual smirk and I expect the conversation to either barrel into the gutter or him to come up with some cynical remark.

"You know, I did the same thing."

Again he surprises me as I wait to hear the rest.

"The same summer you came out here for the first time …" he pauses almost in deep thought as he kills the engine a little ways from the shore.

I remember that summer, how he at first he was quiet down until the day I opened up, telling him how my mother had just died a few months prior. After that he became my best friend and someone I could always depend on to pull my head out of the sand and jolt me out of any feel-sorry-for-myself mode that I would indulge in.

Grabbing our poles, he stares out at the water a sense of genuineness masking every feature of his face. "I even went a step further." He laughs and looks at me, squinting from the sunlight that is blazing over my back. "I asked Piper out on the main boat dock under the moonlight after …" he holds his finger up to deliver a punch line I assume, "… carving our initials into it. Then I kissed her." I remain quiet; shocked that he is giving more details than he ever has about his summer with her. He speeds up his talking as if he's embarrassed or maybe even feeling something he wants to escape. *I know how that feels.* "Anyways, she said yes, of course. I mean who could refuse, right? Real romantical bullshit."

I nod slowly, getting my line ready to toss out, but still stay quiet in case he's not done. It's nice to see him open up for once. We cut up nonstop, but Evan is about as sealed off as me about his past.

"So she said yes, right?" He snaps his head around to me suddenly, his voice and expression laced in confusion. "I mean, you guys aren't together today for a change. Shit, she didn't say no, did she?"

"Oh no … she said yes."

He lets out a breath and I chuckle, casting my line far out into the dark rippling waters.

"Oh ok. I was about to feel like a horse's ass."

"You are a jackass, no use denying it, but while we are having this sappy little heart-to-heart," I roll my eyes, using one finger to air quote as he laughs. "I have a question for you."

"Yeah …" he draws out.

I wait, knowing this may get met with a thunder of laughter.

"So, I rented the main cabin across the lake for the night of the Fourth for Alyssa and me."

"Wait … are you asking me for sex advice?" he says in a flabbergasted tone, holding his fishing pole in mid air before casting out.

"No!" I snap and go on, "Well, not really. I know how to do that …"

"Oh good. I was going to say … dude, I'm not walking you through the birds and the bees. Go to Tristan for that shit. I'm sure he has a manual or a little black book or dictionary on moves to get your screw on."

Shaking my head, yet in absolute agreement with him that my brother probably does write that crap down, I finish with what's on my mind, "No, what I'm curious about is …" I pause. *How the hell do I put this?* "Well, I've got the cabin rented, but it's like this … I don't want her to think I expect anything … I just …"

"Yet, you rented a cabin for the night … clear across the lake from everyone you know …"

I ignore his interruption, but flinching from his comment, because it does look that way, like I am expecting sex. I'm not, but if it happens, I sure as hell don't want it to be in my truck or in a cabin with all my friends listening in and making crude comments immediately following.

"If it happens, it happens, but what do I do … I mean, do I just take her into the kitchen and sit at the table or to the living room and pull out a deck of cards? I mean, I want …" I ramble on not even knowing what the hell I'm saying anymore or sure of how to word anything floating through my mind at this point.

"Whoa … whoa … you're going to hurt yourself. Just chill out for a second," Evan finishes reeling his line in with a nice sized bass swooshing and flipping through the air as he secures the line and pulls it from the hook. "Just …" He stops what he's doing, holding the fish by the mouth for a second before he throws it in the cage. "Just go at her pace, ok. I mean, I don't know her history, but I'm sure you two have discussed that by now whether she's tested the waters or if she's still hanging onto her cherry for dear life, but …"

I chuckle at his always-colorful selection of words, a surge of reassurance swelling inside of me that we have already discussed the matter of past experiences, even though I was a little timid on the subject.

"… just let her lead. Seriously…" with no traces of a smile and a crease between his brows, he levels me with a completely humorless look, "You don't know what that is for her. She could have had an accidental pregnancy in her past, a bad experience … maybe she's not on birth control or you know …" his seriousness falters with his eyes desperately looking for something other than me to land on. I feel a tug at my line and we both look forward, but I quickly look back at him.

His signature smirk fills the edges of his face and he ends the male bonding in only a way Evan can, "… or she could have been with some dude that was really hung and then she may laugh when you drop your drawers." His shitty smile drops and he points to my line.

Twisting the reel at a steady pace and gripping the handle from the weight of the fish, I pull it in while setting him straight, "First off … I'm plenty confident that she won't laugh, but will more than likely be nervous as hell …" he snickers and I glance his way out of the corner of my eyes as he uses his finger as a gun, making a "pssshhhh" noise.

"Second …" I go on, tugging my line out of the water. "I'm not sure if she's on birth control. Our conversation hasn't got to the point yet, but I think you all have been very generous in that department with all the condoms I have found in random places each and every time I come back to the cabin." I roll my eyes and Evan spits out a snort. I have seriously got a gym bag full, finding them in my truck, my bag, under my pillow. Some were even lying under my towel when I got out of the shower the other day with a clever note from Tristan:

Judd, just so you don't worry after the deed is done. Remember, condoms were invented to prevent pregnancies.

Ha-ha, is all I can say. Nice stroll down memory lane, Tristan.

"Third ... I will most definitely not do anything she doesn't want to do. She's pretty good about acting on what she's feeling in the moment, I've found." I chuckle, with visions of our first kiss and how she actually licked my chest in the shower house. I still cannot get over that. *That was awesome.*

"Nice," Evan jokes while stumbling to help me with the catfish that I'm struggling with. "That's a big one."

Chuckling to myself, I nod. "And that's what she'll say."

Evan bursts out laughing as I smile at the hefty beast that I just reeled in.

The day stretches on with the blistering sun slowly torturing us and making us call it a day.

"What time is it anyways," Evan asks, packing the fish we caught into the Styrofoam cooler.

I pull my phone out of the bottom of the tackle box, thankful that I remembered to grab it out of the truck earlier. Luckily we've gotten good at not drowning the boat when we fish or my phone would be toast. Back when we were sixteen, we would usually drag back to the docks with about three inches of water lapping at our feet in the bottom of the boat. We'd end our fishing trips with a celebratory jump into the lake to cool off then carefully pull ourselves back over the edge, bringing in a bucket of water with us. It took us a few trips to figure out that it was best to wait until we pulled into the dock or to just pull into shore for a swim. That was only after out we managed to tip the boat and lose all our fish.

Pressing the main button, it lights up. "It's 3:11," I announce as my eyes land on my photos icon.

My mind wanders back to last night as Alyssa and I sat in the back of my truck, taking photo after photo. I hit the button and am immediately greeted with her beautiful blue eyes smiling at the camera as she pushes her pink cheek against mine. My heart bounces like the strings on a guitar, vibrating throughout my body with all that I feel for her.

"Oh shit … what's this?" Evan stands at the end of the boat, looking down at my phone with a perfect view of the picture I am marveling over. "Really?! You're acting like a girl," he spits out, pestering me as he takes a seat back on his side.

I shake my head with a laugh, "Don't think I haven't seen that picture that you keep peaking out of the lining of the camper *right above your bed* of Piper."

Evan's eyes light up and he stops for a brief second, gathering his wits or maybe shocked that I know about it. "Oooo … you're quick. Me so proud!" he chuckles, grabbing the boat cord to crank it up. "What were you doing lying in my bed, anyways?"

I cock my head back, amused that he never stops as we slowly wind our way along the now choppy waters back to the cabin grounds. Getting one past Evan is beyond me; *maybe someday.*

Once our feet hit land and we drag all our equipment back to the cabin, I rush down the path and across the lot to find Alyssa. Squealing and laughter reaches my ears as I near the beach and I see her. She's lounged comfortably across a towel on the sandy shoreline with a pair of big sunglasses positioned across her nose and her face pointed out towards the waters. Lucky for me, she's alone. I may very well have had a conniption if Tristan was sitting with her.

"Hey," I stride up behind her, a stupid grin pulling upward over my cheeks.

She flips her head around and instantly lights up. "Hi," she gasps, tossing her glasses from her face, and bouncing onto her feet right into my arms.

My hands fall around her and my chin lands on the top of her head with wisps of hair tickling at my neck. Evening comes and we swim, fry up some fish and try our best to stay within the group. Of course we sneak away a couple times, but with people like Tristan around that only lasts so long before dirty comments start going around.

As soon as darkness falls and the girls start to retreat to their cabin, we finally get some time to ourselves. Since I no longer have my truck, and seeing how my cabin is full of listening ears and hers is full of giggling girls, we have to be imaginative on finding a place to sleep. The jokes would run all night in my cabin, so without much of a discussion, we sneak off to the boat house with a bundle of sheets, a sleeping bag and pillow wedged in my arms. That's pretty much all I need to get comfortable with her by my side.

We reach the boat house and all that fills the night is the soft chirping of bugs and birds, the gentle whistling of the wind over the metal awning and a subtle slapping of gentle waves against the base of the dock.

With absolutely no light to guide our way, I hold tight to her hand as we both slide our feet over each board of the dock. Small bays open up every six to eight feet along the edge, offering us relief from the darkness and assuring us that we are not about to take a nose dive into the lake.

I stop at the end of the dock, my eyes pulled to the night sky where a full moon beams over the trees and illuminates the murky waters.

Assessing our plan to sleep here, I stare over the hard planks that stretches about five feet across into the bay with the boat Evan and I took out today. We won't need that much room, because I intend on keeping her very close to me through the night, so this is perfect...

Squatting down in front of Alyssa, I get busy making a small pallet by laying the sleeping bag down as a cushion over the hard surface, the pillow to the top then the sheet spread out last. The nights have dipped into the low 60's a couple times this week, but I'm confident I can keep us warm. I turn to face her and rub my hands together, ready to curl up at last.

"This good?"

She smiles and nods her head.

I pull the sheet back, motioning for her to get in and she quickly indulges, sliding her sandals off at the base of the pallet. I do the same and slide in beside her, already at ease.

We both squirm around to get comfortable then settle into a peaceful silence for a few minutes. Her head rests on my chest with one of her legs flung over one of mine and one of her arms wrapped around my side, her fingertips making a slow path back and forth over my ribcage.

My hands find contentment across her back, with her pulled so tightly against me that it pushes a deep sigh from her lungs that has the traces of a smile in it. *I feel exactly the same way.*

After about five minutes of quiet and right when my eyes start dipping back into darkness, she moves, folding her arms across my chest and laying her chin on them to look at me. Fully opening my eyes, I'm wide awake with the sight of her beauty. The moonlight that shines through the last bay illuminates her face making her eyes sparkle and skin look like porcelain. I take in a quick breath and reach my hand out, running my thumb up her jawline and over her cheek. She smiles but still says nothing, just looks at me with adoring eyes.

Ok, I can't help myself. I lift up forcing her to roll onto her back beside me, so I can slide over to lie against her. Our positions have reversed and I'm grateful that there is plenty of room on the dock. I think us falling in the water would really dampen the mood.

"Have I told you how beautiful you are today?" I whisper, the pace of my heart thudding rapidly.

"It's dark … you can't even see me," she laughs, writing off my compliment as empty words.

She doesn't know how wrong she is; I don't need to see her.

"It is dark, but I can see you. I have the contours of your face, every curve of your body and every strand of your hair memorized. I see you every time I close my eyes. So believe me when I say, you're beautiful," I enlighten her, not even sure where the hell those words came from, but feeling every ounce of them throughout my heart and soul.

At first she doesn't say anything, but as her face lifts, her lips cover mine. I lean into her, moving my mouth in a synchronized rhythm with hers. When she wiggles around beneath me, I pull back to end our kiss.

"Are you ok?" I laugh.

"Actually, my swimsuit is tied in the back and the knot is digging into me," she squirms some more, reaching her hand behind her back to reposition the tie.

"Did you bring anything else to wear?" I ask, knowing full well that she didn't have a bag or anything else with her; neither of us did. She shakes her head.

I sit up, sliding my t-shirt over my head. *I didn't plan to sleep with it on anyway.* "Here," I say, holding the neck of it open so she can slip it on.

She slides it on without hesitation and within a second pulls her swimsuit top out of the sleeve. *I really wish she would have done that before the shirt was on.*

Once the swimsuit top is flung to our feet to join our shoes, she lies back down. I take in the fact that she is in my shirt for a brief moment before sliding back down on top of her. Something about my shirt hanging over her bare body makes me feel territorial and animalistic in a way, damn near like a cave man that would like nothing more than to drag her off.

Our lips automatically pick up where they left off and we devour one another.

"I love the way you kiss," her muffled voice breathes out between my lips.

I stop and look at her, wanting to scream out how I feel about her; that I love her, because I know I do, but also really wanting to wait until we are in the cabin on the Fourth.

Instead I choose to say it without saying it exactly. "I love kissing you, too, Lyssa," I whisper then move in for a slower kiss. Keeping my lips close to her, I go on, "I love touching you." I run my hands under her shirt and up the side of her body. "I love feeling you against me." My hand continues a path over to the bare skin of her back as I pull her to me so that we are nearly one. "I love waking up next to you … I can't even sleep anymore unless I feel you near." I take a breath, noticing that she is staring at me as I go on with my declaration of how much I love her.

"I love listening to you talk. I love when you talk about your family." I smile, knowing there are not enough words that could fill the air with how full my heart has been since I found her. "I love everything about you, Alyssa," I whisper, then kiss her like there is no tomorrow.

My hand stays under her shirt, but before I know it I am flush against her and we are rubbing against each other in a mad frenzy for one another. Our hands are all over the place and I am getting extremely turned on. We still have our clothes on, but this is where we need to slam on the brakes. I pull my mouth away from hers and a small whimper escapes her lips.

"I think it might be best if I get over to my side of the dock," I laugh trying to make a joke.

Of course, I am not going to roll away from her, but if I don't want this to escalate, being on top of her probably isn't where I should be.

She wraps her arms around me and pulls me back to her. "I want you, Judd," she whispers into my ear and the small amount of will power I have hanging on starts to slip.

"I want you too, baby, but don't you want our first time to be special?" I pause, regrouping any amount of restraint that I can muster up. "You mean so much to me and I just want it to be perfect." I wish I could see her face right now. Last thing I want is for her to feel like I'm rejecting her, because that is not it at all.

"But what if I want to? I don't care where we are. It will be perfect because it's with you."

Her words send an arrow right through my heart. She's right, but what my heart holds for her is better than something quick on a boat dock one night; that just makes it sound cheap and she may regret it later. If it's going to happen, I'd prefer for it to be in a bed with light so I can see her; so we can see each other and explore one another all night long.

I kiss her lips and try to explain it better, "Don't think I don't want this ... right here, right now, but I would like to make it special, because you're special to me. I don't want this to be something that just happened one night when we got carried away and couldn't stop ..." I look into her eyes and gauge whether she looks hurt or possibly insulted. "I'm not saying no … I'm just saying let's save it and make it a night that we will look back on, a night we'll always remember."

She smiles a small convincing smile and I slide onto my back on the pallet, tucking her closely to my side.

"Judd, can I ask you something," she says as she nuzzles her body back against my chest.

"Anything, you know that."

"Are you worried about … ummm," she pauses.

"What?" It makes me uneasy for her to think I'm worried about anything, because I do want her more than she knows.

"I was just going to tell you that I am on the pill if that's what it is."

My brows bolt up with her announcement and the nervousness in me bursts from my mouth into laughter. "What?!" I spit out, trying to contain the surge of nerves and surprise that chose to come out of me in the most peculiar and appalling way.

She flips her head towards me, looking just as surprised.

Laughing probably isn't typical when a girl gives you the green light to take her … now.

"Sorry … no, I wasn't laughing about that. I just had this image that came to mind as soon as you said it. Seems the guys think it's funny to leave me condoms everywhere. I seriously have a stock pile of them, so all in all … I think we are covered."

She giggles, rolling towards me. "Well, the condom fairy has visited my cabin a time or two. So that's not it?"

"No, I'm not worried about anything. I just want it to be perfect and somewhere special. Not a dirty boat dock where Evan's grandpa brings all his friends to drink beer."

She laughs, but quickly gets serious.

"Ok, so … what if I'm curious?"

I'm half confused by her question. *Curious? What on earth is she curious about?* "About what?" As soon as the words leave my mouth her statement registers. "Oh…" I swallow hard, my entire body bouncing with excitement, nerves and so many other emotions that she wants to know what I look like or possibly what I feel like.

How do I respond to that? Most guys would probably unzip their pants and start directing traffic while silently shouting "Hell Yeah."

I'm right there with the "Hell Yeah" statement, but I don't want her to say this because she thinks that's what I want; I do, but only if she wants to.

"You know I don't expect you to do that, right?" my voice comes out a shaky puff of air and it almost pains me to not say, "Sure, yeah … go for it."

She smiles and wiggles her body against mine as if I am not turned on enough from this conversation. *She's killing me.* My body ignites a million tingles and electric pulses disburse through me. *Now I am verging towards painfully aroused.*

"I know…" She moves in closer to my face and whispers so quietly I can barely hear her, "but I want to touch you."

That statement alone is enough to make me climax. My heart speeds in my chest and if this had been my first physical experience with a girl I would swear I was having a heart attack. I don't know what to say; *yes please? It's right there for your curiosity? Hell yeah?*

I go with a subtle, mellow and as gentlemanly as possible approach, "Lyssa, that is up to you but I don't expect it." I gulp; mentally slapping myself for not shouting out, "Yes please!"

She doesn't answer me instead she slides her body to my side to get comfortable. The tickling sensation of her hand inching down to the waistband of my shorts instantly has my torso in flames, blazing a path right down to … *Whoa; this is really happening!* I suck in breath after breath trying desperately to catch it before I hyperventilate as her delicate hand falls beneath my waistband and she makes contact with every throbbing inch of me. *I swear I may lose it now.* My eyes roll back and my head falls against the dock with a clunk as soon as sensations buzz through my body.

She takes her time moving her hand back and forth in an open palm, slow, sensual caress. *Holy geez, her hand feels like satin.*

"Your hand's so soft," I breathe out in a strangled breath to myself.

I lower my eyebrows and look at her cautiously, not sure whether I will be met with her eyes or possibly even embarrass her from direct eye contact during this event. The moonlight is shining on her face, giving me a perfect view of her, only she is not looking at me. She keeps looking down at what she's doing and if it wasn't for the fact that I am about to fall over the edge, I may actually be a bit uneasy over how hard she is studying my anatomy.

I breathe in and out … in and out … in and out … trying desperately to catch one breath after another. My body feels like it has caught fire and shock waves pulse through my core. When the warmth of her fingertips shifts and moves in a more urgent motion, I can't hold back anymore. I toss my head side to side and squeeze my eyes closed tightly, my heart on the verge of rupturing as waves of pleasure wash over me … and over and over and over.

Once I regain my sense of thought and the lingering ripples to the lower half of my body subside, I look at her, expecting for her to possibly be grossed out because let's face it, the end game isn't always the cleanest. Instead, I see her looking at me with a proud, slightly shy smile.

Between deep breaths I chuckle, because honestly, I don't know what to say. *Wow? Thank you?* Speechless with excitement and disbelief was pretty much the dilemma I was faced with before this happened and once again I'm at a loss. The exhilaration meshed with my nerves and the sensations that still flicker in my body nearly make me want to laugh; it's almost sensory overload.

Staring at her, I realize, no words are necessary. Flashing a genuine smile that probably says everything, I gaze into her gorgeous eyes and keep to myself about all I want to say. *I love you. God I hope you love me, too. I cannot believe she just did that. Holy shit, did that really just happen?*

Good Friends

THE NEXT THREE DAYS rush by, bringing us near the end of our summer vacation. Every hour of every day we spend in each other's company exploring the lake, splashing in the water, going for Jet Ski or boat rides together or chilling with our friends. However, every night we slip into a peaceful, private bubble where only the two of us exist. After we leave here, it will be weird not lying beside her every night.

When I agreed to come here for the first month of summer with the work crew, I never imagined meeting her. She has managed to break through all the barriers that I have ever built up in my heart. Her sweetness, playfulness and beauty have penetrated every corner of my heart and filled it up with feelings I thought I was incapable of feeling. Although I have only known her a little under two weeks, there is utterly no doubt in my mind how much I adore her; how much I love her; she is everything.

Tonight we lie on the beach. Everyone else has already called it a night and we are completely alone. A sliver of moon shines above our head along with way too many stars to count. Silence surrounds us with the exception of the sounds of night critters and frequent splashes created from fish swimming to the surface. Beauty is all around us, yet my gaze is fixed on her.

Tangling one hand into her hair, my other hand holds steady

around her small waist. Her head rests on my chest, but her breathing tells me she is still awake. It's funny how in such a short period of time that I am able to recognize simple things like the difference in her breaths when she is asleep or awake and whether she is upset or happy by the expression on her face. With a flick of her eyes I can tell if she wants me to kiss her, and I can even read when she is holding back. I guess that is what it means to fall in love; knowing the other person inside and out.

"Did you want to stay out here again tonight?"

My ears perk up to the soft sound of her voice, as if it is my favorite song.

"I'm kind of getting eaten up by mosquitoes, actually," I tell her with a chuckle, not fond of getting the blood sucked out of me all night long and then itching like hell tomorrow. "It has to be well into the morning hours, so all the guys should be asleep by now. Do you want to sneak over to my cabin?" Her cabin is closer, but she hates sleeping on those cots; at least our cabin has twin sized beds.

She lifts her head and nods in agreement. I can barely make out her face, but I can tell she's tired. Every night we are together, I force my eyes to stay open as long as possible not wanting to miss a single moment with her; there is no hiding that she does the same.

We both stand and her arms instantly stretch high above her head. My whole body reacts to her movements and my arms automatically wrap around her so that I can pull her tightly against me. Resting my chin on the top of her head, she nuzzles against me and as always, *she feels so amazing.*

We break apart after a long embrace and trek back to my cabin. I keep one arm around her mainly because I always want to touch her in some way but also to help hold her up. Her repeated yawns and dragging feet tell me she is exhausted and ready to crash.

Once we get to the door, I release my grip on her so that I can push it open. Gritting my teeth, I hold my breath as it lets out a low creaking sound. I should suggest to Evan that we replace the hinges before leaving. I step through the doorway and grab her hand pulling her along behind me. My eyes sweep the room for anyone that may be awake as we tiptoe our way to my bed. Fortunately, everyone seems to have slept through our arrival. *Thank you!* The last thing I feel like dealing with is a bunch of cut ups and teasing.

As soon as I reach my bed, I pull the sheets back so Alyssa can slip under the covers. Once she is settled, I crawl in beside her and pull her snug against me so that the curves of our bodies fit together like a puzzle. I brush my lips across the exposed skin behind her ear and wait to hear her little whine she usually makes; nothing.

Letting out a quiet laugh, I lift my chin so that I can get my face closer to hers, immediately hearing her light steady breaths. She's out.

"Alyssa?" I quietly whisper her name, careful not to wake anyone else in the room. Our beds are spaced quite a ways away from each other, but Evan seems to have ears like a damn elephant; it's as if he's waiting for some emergency in the middle of the night.

When she doesn't answer I know she is asleep and that I should probably join her. Laying my head back on the pillow, I run my hand over her hip up to the dip in her waist and let it rest there, perfectly seamed against her skin as if that's where it has always belonged.

"Are you asleep?" I whisper even quieter than before; still no reply.

A small held in breath moves over my lips as I think over what I'm going to say next. It's silly, but my insides have been kicking me for not saying it yet. I lean in towards her ear, finally ready to say my secret out loud.

"Alyssa, I know you probably won't hear me or even remember this, but I can't keep it to myself anymore."

She squirms a bit in my arms and I instantly still. Shifting in her sleep, she then flips onto her back with her hands tightly clutching my shirt and her eyes still completely closed. After she settles and I'm re-assured that she didn't wake, I continue on, half hoping she will wake up during my confession and half fearing she will.

"All my life I've thought love was a sick joke; something that didn't really exist. I watched my dad walk away from my mom …" I tilt my head to look around slowly and quietly. I sure don't want Tristan to overhear me. Quieting to a nearly inaudible whisper, I go on, "… after that I swore I'd never put myself through that kind of pain. I sunk every ounce of passion I had inside me into playing foot-ball and figured that way, there would be nothing left for anyone. I kept my heart closed off … refused to open." I take a deep breath and stop talking long enough to hear if my ramblings have disturbed anyone. "Alyssa, no one has ever gotten to me like you. The day I saw you step out of that van, something hit me; it snuck up and sucked the breath right out of my lungs. I'm not sure what happened that day or the next or the one after that, but something happened that has never happened to me before and ..." I stop for a second, looking at her profile as she sleeps. My heart beats into my throat, vibrating through my ear drums. "I fell in love with you ... I *am* in love with you."

I swallow down the lump in my throat and focus on staying quiet. No doubt the guys would have a ball harassing me about this topic; I would never hear the end of it.

"I love you, Alyssa," I whisper so softly while looking at the outline of her face.

As soon as the words are out of my mouth, she lets out a quiet moan in her sleep and rolls back to her side to face me. I pull her in as close as possible and then rest my mouth against her ear.

"Do you love me, too?" I whisper, having a little fun to soften the intensity of what I just said.

I know I won't get a reply ... but then she surprises me. Her hands, which rest softly to her side against my chest, grab onto my shirt as she nestles closer to me with a faint sigh.

"Juuuuuud" barely reaches my ears, but I hear it. *I'll take that as a yes!*

I smile the widest grin I've ever felt then close my eyes in absolute happiness and completeness. *Sweet dreams.*

The next morning my eyes snap open and it's not to the sound of my alarm. *Damn it!* I had it set so I could wake up before Alyssa and set up the cabin across the lake for tonight. I look down at her face buried into my chest and breathe in relief.

As careful as I can, I slip out from her grasp and slide off the bed. I pull a fresh shirt out of my bag, throw on a pair of flip flops, and snatch up my phone then race out the door. Hopefully Evan remembered to leave his keys for me. I'll kill him if he forgot.

I make it to his jeep and snap open the glove box. Sure enough, the keys are there. I throw them in my pocket with my wallet and phone and run down to the beach where I can see most of the group hanging out. I'm not sure if she'll even be down there, but Abby might be able to help me with a few tasks.

My feet sink into the sand as I near the water and I raise my hand above my eyes to block the sun from my view. She's a little ways out from the dock and it almost looks like she is treading water trying to escape my brother. *Good girl.* It's about time someone didn't treat him like he was God's gift to women, because he most certainly is not; more like a nightmare.

"Abby!" I holler out, bringing all attention my way.

"Hey Judd, Get in!" Tyler yells out.

"Where's your girlfriend! Did you wear her ass out last night?!" Nick calls out from the dock.

"Last I saw he was all cozied up with her in bed this morning back at the cabin," Tristan replies. "Just make sure you wrap it, bro!" With that, all sorts of laughter and speculation start to fly.

Abby swims to shore and grabs a towel before running up to me.

"What's up?" she asks, running the towel through her hair as Tristan steps out of the water behind her.

I glance over her shoulder, watching my brother ogling her in the most obvious and obnoxious way possible, before speaking. *How does that work for him?*

"Hey, I was curious if you would lend me a hand today."

"Sure," she glances behind her. I can't see what happens, but Tristan cracks up and walks away without a word. Turning around, she rolls her eyes. "What do you need?"

"I sort of need …" I pause, looking around again. Tyler, Nick and Matt are bobbing in the water over by the dock while Evan and Skylar sit on the edge, deep in conversation. Tristan is settled in the sand over by Jesse and Piper while Mitch is nowhere to be found. I lower my voice anyways, not wanting to let everyone in on my plans. "I rented a cabin across the way for tonight and was hoping to …" a bit of uneasiness bolts through me, unsure of whether she will approve or jump into over-protective sister mode. If this was a girl approaching me about plans with Jake, I'd be rooting them on. "… surprise Alyssa. I'm not planning anything. I just thought the time alone would be nice and well …"

Pausing from towel drying her hair, she looks at me with an unreadable expression that's about to make my head explode from anticipation. Slowly a smile emerges on her face.

"Romantic?"

I smile with a flood of relief and nod, "Yeah."

"Come on," she waves her hand, already heading in the direction of the girl's cabin. I follow with no clue of what is up her sleeve.

Inside, she seems to already have something planned as she heads straight to Alyssa's cot and grabs a bag from underneath the bed then disappears into the bathroom. I sit down on Alyssa's cot, waiting patiently. On the floor, I spot a small bag that is unzipped and pulled open. Looking down, I assume it is her bathroom bag that I've seen her carry into the shower house on several occasions. A tall clear bottle with a pink-tinted liquid about halfway to the top peeks out like it's flagging me down for attention. Hoping this isn't an invasion of privacy, I reach down and grab it, noting the picture of a spilt bowl of strawberries on the front. I flip the cap open and pull it to my nose to take a deep whiff, already knowing the exact fragrance I'll be met with. *Geez, I could get lost in that.* It smells just like her; just like my pillow smelled this morning and the same scent that I've noticed on my shirt after she has spent the night pressed up against my chest. Snapping the lid shut quickly as a floorboard lets out a moan behind me, I slip the bottle back into her bag right as Abby comes out of the bathroom.

"Ok, so I figured I will just send her whole bag over. I doubt she will be back here today." She stops in front of me and leans down to gather all of Alyssa's things, pulling up the small bathroom bag with a smile on her face. Of course she probably caught me pilfering through her sister's private stuff.

"That sounds good. I'll drop it off at the cabin here in a bit. So, I wanted tonight to be sort of … umm …" embarrassment creeps in once again and I pause. I thought it would be simple to ask for her help, but I really hope she doesn't think I'm some asshole like Alyssa's ex, just in this for one thing. Like Evan said, it definitely looks like sex is what I have planned.

"Romantic?" Abby finishes again with a snicker as she stands up with Alyssa's bag in hand.

I quickly lift off the bed and pull the bag out of her hand. "Ahhh

… pretty much, but not so I can …" I look at her uneasy and just say it, "I'm not expecting anything, at all."

"Uh huh," she says skeptically, eye balling me like I'm some sexual predator that she desperately needs to analyze before she sets me loose back into the real world. Squinting her eyes for a minute, she slowly eases her unconvinced expression and shakes her head. "Ok, if you want it to be romantic, you need candles. Lots of candles."

"I have the keys to Evan's jeep this morning. You care to run to town with me and help me set things up?"

Abby doesn't even hesitate, turning to head to the door immediately. That wasn't so bad after all, but as we near the jeep she questions my intentions.

"So why did you rent a cabin if you're not going over there just to get in her pants?" Her bluntness jolts me to attention with my eyebrows raised, mouth drawn open and not a single word coming to mind as she goes on, "She said you're not like your brother, was she wrong?"

Her words challenge everything I have planned and turn this into anything other than comfortable. Of course, I'm not planning to throw her on the bed as soon as we get there and if I get the smallest inkling of doubt from her, I will hand the keys back to the front desk and gladly take her to the dock to watch the fireworks. Deep down, I do think that it will fall in that direction, but I would never force it or pressure her. When we are together, it is so hard to put the brakes on, but I really want our first time to be perfect. I've never had that. Nor have I ever had a relationship. I wasn't lying to her when I said this is all kinds of new to me and I love every cheesy, sappy moment.

"Ummm … I … Ahhh …" I'm at a loss, staring at her like a petrified animal backed into a corner.

Squeezing her eyes shut, she slaps her hand across the front of the jeep and bursts out, laughing. "Relax, Judd." She waves her hand before hopping into the passenger seat. "I know there is no way you could be as bad as Tristan."

Climbing into the driver's side with the keys already in hand, my shoulders drop as I spit out a nervous chuckle and release all efforts of finding the right words to convince her of my devotion to Alyssa. As soon as the engine roars, I catch Tristan running towards the jeep.

Shit! This is all I need while Abby and I are discussing my objective for the night. Let's have a damn Sex Ed class and school Judd!

"Whoa … hold up, you two!" He grabs a hold of the roll bar on the Jeep and in one swoop is lounged in the backseat as if we invited him. "Hey, sexy," he says, leaning into Abby's ear while tossing a strand of her hair aside.

"Oh great." She rolls her eyes and I laugh. "Seriously, are you invited?"

"Tristan, we were just running to town for a bit. Do you mind?" I sweep my eyes to the side of the vehicle hoping he catches my hint to take a hike.

"Great," he claps his hands. "I need to get some stuff, too … let's go," he declares in a more enthusiastic tone than I think I've ever heard from him.

"Perfect! What on earth do you need or is this just an excuse to pester the hell out of me?" Abby spits and I can't help but admire her feistiness. *Tristan needs that, although he probably views it as playing hard to get.*

"I saw a fireworks stand behind that old grocery store when we came in. We should stock up for tonight. What the hell is the Fourth with no ammunition?" Abby and I both stare back at him as he looks back and forth between us wildly with the resemblance of an excited little kid.

Coming to terms that there is no getting rid of him, I put it in reverse and we head off to the adjoining town that consists of only a gas station, super market and an old-time diner. We make it there in less than twenty minutes and the first place we go is a fireworks stand. Here we are, all at the lake for the Fourth of July and not one of us thought to get fireworks … well, except Tristan, it seems. Maybe the top half of his body still works after all; there may be hope for him yet.

"Would you stop blowing in my ear, Tristan," Abby huffs out as I put it in park.

I glance over, nearly wanting to crack up from her resistance to him. She jabs at him with her elbow as he leans towards her seat, dang near nibbling on her ear.

"Would you stop it!" she snaps but with the hint of a smile. *Oh no, not her too.*

She smacks him across the arm, but Tristan rifles back demolishing her efforts of refusal, "Oh yeah … hit me again baby. I like it rough."

I subtly toss my head back in exasperation of his usual perverse and demeaning comments.

"Geez, let's go." I kill the engine and jump out, noticing Abby's eagerness to exit the vehicle as well.

Beneath the canopy of the worn out red tent that nearly appears as a shade of pink, Abby wanders around table after table with my brother quick on her heels. From across the way, I manage to enjoy all his advances getting shot down with a swat of her hand, an equally quick witted comment or her just flipping around to give him the finger. I want so badly to rush over and give her a big hug. This is the first damn girl that I've ever witnessed not cave to his charm; it's about time.

I fill my basket up quickly, as does Tristan and Abby. Once he slips away to look at some huge ass skyrockets that look pretty enticing to me as well, Abby pulls me aside.

Grabbing me by the shirt sleeve, which is sticking to my skin from the strangling humidity, she leans closer to speak, "Ok so I'm assuming you don't want Tristan in on the whole sleep over going on tonight?"

I shrug, not even caring at this point. "It doesn't matter. He's the one that got the cabin so he can think what he wants."

"Oh," she sounds surprised as her voice raises an octave. "Tristan got it?" She looks over my shoulder then back at me. I nod. "Well, how about you stay here and keep him busy while I run to the store to see what they have."

Her offer fills me with reassurance that I've gained her trust and even though I should be ashamed for not going myself, I'm extremely thankful that she is willing to get the other things we came for. I'd surely screw it up and get some perfumed candles that Alyssa is allergic to or something that would make the cabin smell like a toilet; this is better left in her hands.

With a quick nod and a smile, I agree with her plan. Maybe this will keep my brothers relentless teasing at bay for today at least. I'm sure when we show back up on our side of the lake tomorrow morning the jokes will start to fly. The one lucky thing that all the teasing has done is stocked me with condoms for life.

She runs off, but not before casting a skeptical glance past me to Tristan. I waste no time joining him to pick out a couple more fireworks so we can get back quickly, but nostalgia has me remembering Fourth of July's when we were kids. I laugh and bring it up hesitantly, not sure of whether he may fly off the handle with me dredging up a memory.

"You remember the time we picked out a ton of parachute launchers and had Dad light them all at the same time? Then Jake, you and me all frantically threw firecrackers into the air in hopes to knock them out of the sky. It was a full on war in our backyard."

Tristan and I crack up.

"Shit, I remember that. We all yelled, 'arm yourselves for battle' and blam!" we laugh and he goes on with another story. "Hey, you remember when you were … oh gosh; I think you were six or so. Jake was a little thing and we went camping after the Fourth with a whole bunch of left over fireworks." He laughs while he talks and I get a glimpse of the brother I used to have; the one I miss; the one Jake and I always looked up to. "Dad thought it would be impressive if he lit up five or six fountains at once. You remember how Mom loved fountains …" He looks off and his voice cracks as my heart tightens.

I nod; *I remember everything.*

"So he goes up to those fountains with a lit punk and you and Jake are going all sorts of crazy, excited for the show to start. I was only nine or ten but I kept my eye on all the branches above the fireworks, thinking the whole time about how we learned about firework safety tips from the conservation department the week before that. I just kept thinking, is this safe, but then I thought, well … Dad is the adult. He should know whether it's ok or not." Tristan takes a breath and chuckles. "So I didn't say a word until he got them lit. Crack, crack, crack, they start going off and Dad runs over beside me and the first thing I do is lean over and say …" Tristan lowers his voice and mocks his motions from that night, leaning towards my shoulder with his hand held by his face as if he's telling a secret.

I burst out laughing at the memory, also leaning closer so I can hear what he told Dad that night.

"Dad, you think those branches are flammable?" his face breaks open into a huge grin as he continues his walk down memory lane. "I was so proud of myself for remembering that word because I saw it on several of the packages. Dad didn't say a word, his face goes white as a sheet and he snaps his head around right as the tree branch goes ablaze."

"Oh man, I remember that. Holy shit, the campers around us all ran over, tossing their crap out of their coolers, filling them up with water and throwing it in the air. It was crazy. Mom grabbed us and pulled us away from the whole thing," my mouth stretches and stretches, joining in with Tristan's rare laughter that I thought had died along with Mom.

"Yes!" he hollers and I look around to see how many eyes are watching us. "Oh my gosh … that was insane. The police showed up and gave Dad a citation for using fireworks after the holiday then the fire department ended up having to hose down the tree."

"What was left of it," I add.

"Yeah, it looked like a measly old, burnt French fry after it was all said and done."

"And that next year, Mom insisted on scoping out the perfect spot for fireworks. Even then, Dad set those fountains up with caution, looking around a hundred times and trying to scope out anything that could possibly blow into the line of fire … literally."

Tristan's smile deepens to the point where I think he may fall to the floor in laughter, his eyes animated with thrill and amusement as if we were right there again. July Fourth was always a big deal when we were kids. It was a favorite of mine and obviously his.

Placing his hand at his stomach, he finishes my thoughts, "He held his hands up, figuring the trajectory of each shot before he would light the damn thing. He was calculating that shit for about thirty minutes until Mom yelled, 'Come on Scott …'"

"I'll do it!" we both say at the same time, busting up in a fit of hysterics.

We make eye contact, the look of two brothers, two friends reunited after years apart, but then Tristan suddenly stands straight, clearing his throat. "Anyways …" he takes on a more serious tone with his smile long gone.

My smile falters and I look over at the table beside us, noticing a boat load of fireworks Mom would have gravitated to. "Hey ..." I smile, clasping a large fountain in my hand and holding it up to show Tristan. "You want to get some fountains ... kind of in memory of Mom ... in her honor?"

Before I can finish, Tristan is shaking his head with a frown on his face and his hand in a fist at his side. "No!" he snaps, his forehead crinkling as his frown deepens. "No fountains. Let's not talk about em!"

My heart and hopes fall with his bitterness and I don't say a word, I just watch as he walks to the check out. Sometimes, I just wish he would realize that holding onto the good times in the past isn't all together a bad thing. Yeah, the outcome sucked, but it wasn't always bad. Maybe keeping the better times close to our hearts would help bring us together instead of how we deal with it, which has most definitely pushed us apart.

After we have everything paid for we meet Abby back at the jeep and head back to the lake. Even though Tristan has tagged along, I move forward with my plans to stop by the cabin that I rented for the night. We go by the main office and pick up my key first then swing by so I can drop off Alyssa's bag and all that Abby bought.

"I'll wait out here," Tristan says as he eyes a couple girls splashing in the water in the distance, for once ignoring Abby. I guess she pissed him off with her constant refusal to play his games.

Inside, I go into the bathroom to place Alyssa's bag on the vanity while Abby goes in the back bedroom to set out all the candles. Exiting the bathroom, I see that she went all out in the candle department. There must be two dozen of them spread throughout the room. I laugh and look over at her as she places a few more candles on the nightstand.

"Ok, so assuming I'm going to have a crate full of matches and about an hour to sneak in here and light all these while she waits outside ..." I chuckle, giving her a sarcastic smile. "This is ... ummm ... great."

She claps her hands and squeals, possibly oblivious to my sarcasm or maybe just excited for her sister.

"You know, I'm only going to have a few minutes to light these, right?" I raise my eyebrows and gaze around the room to take in what Alyssa will see later.

"I know, but you'll get them all lit. If you want romantic then you need to go big," she holds her hands out and pivots back and forth so I can take in the entire view. "And … make sure you keep the bedroom light off…that way it's more magical," she lowers her voice to a whisper on the last word and I laugh, nodding my head at her cheesiness.

"I want romance, but I also don't want to start a forest fire." My comment is almost ironic, considering that's what Tristan and I just discussed.

Abby giggles then pulls a box out of the paper bag. *Good gosh, not more condoms! How long does she think we are going to be over here! A whole box!* All of sudden, with a sneaky grin on her face she tosses a bunch of red crap all over the bed. *What the hell is that?* Once they settle, I see she has covered the bed in rose petals. *Ok, this is going a tad bit overboard. I want romance but I'm not setting up a honeymoon suite or anything.*

I fold my arms across my chest and stare at her. "Don't you think that is a little too much?"

She quickly puts her finger up to stop me from talking and hands me the bag. "Shush … now go put the rest of this in the fridge so it is fresh tonight."

I, of course, oblige and head into the kitchen, without another word. *Wait, what the hell needs to be refrigerated?* Pulling the fridge door open, I reach into the bag, curious and a tad worried. My mouth drops open as I pull out one thing after another.

"Abby, what the hell?"

She laughs hysterically as she enters the room and takes in my expression. I stand with the door of the fridge open and with my mouth also wide open holding a can of spray whipped cream and chocolate syrup.

"I thought you might want those in case your night headed in a kinky direction."

I snap my mouth shut and shake my head, an ocean of ease and relief washing over me. I think me and Abby are going to be pretty good friends. *What the hell would I have done without her today?*

It's on

WE CONTINUE TO LAUGH our way out to the jeep and wrangle Tristan up from the group of girls he has latched onto down at the beach. I glance at the clock, my anxiety kicking up that it is already a little past noon. I've been gone an hour and a half. I really hope she isn't awake yet.

The discussion about Mom and Dad must have put Tristan on edge because the ride back is pretty quiet between the three of us.

Glancing into the rearview mirror, I think twice about his apparent foul mood as I catch him staring at Abby with a pouting expression like she just took away the last toy in the sandbox; only she's the toy. Fine by me; last thing I need is Tristan hooking up with Alyssa's sister and that going south. That could definitely pose a problem in my relationship.

As soon as I pull into the small gravel lot between Piper's family cabin and Evan's grandpa's, I hop out of the jeep.

"Thanks Abby," I holler out as I sprint back to the cabin.

"What no thanks to me?" Tristan calls out, but then his attention quickly turns to Abby. "Keep shooting me down, baby, but you know you want me … I just haven't worn you down yet …."

I shake my head at my brother's faith in his own never failing skills at picking up women and race off to get to Alyssa. My lungs burn from the run and I suck in a swarm of hot air like it's water. Shoving the door open, I look up and see her sitting on the edge of my bed. Her hair is all ruffled up from sleeping, she doesn't have an ounce of makeup on and the look she is giving me says more than either of us could express in words. She's gorgeous.

"Did I wake you?" I ask as I take wide strides across the room.

She nods her head and flashes a smile that could brighten anyone's day.

"I was hoping I made it back before you got up, so you could wake up in my arms," I tell her, silently praying that she doesn't ask where I was as I squat down in front of her and pull her forward so I can look into her eyes.

She instinctively places her hands on my shoulders, slowly moving them side-to-side in a slow caress that drives me crazy. Her hands run up my neck to my face and she plants a small kiss on my lips that leaves me wanting more.

"Good morning."

I snicker at her assumption of time, "Morning? Lyssa, it's a little before 1:00. We slept most of the morning."

My eyes focus on the way she puckers her lips into a pout and I want nothing more than to suck her lip into my mouth and taste her. Sighing, I force myself away from those thoughts and sweep a few hairs out of her face. Looking into her eyes, I find myself completely mesmerized by the crystal blue shade and her thick, dark black lashes that ark up towards her eyebrows and down to her high cheek bones, making them seem even brighter.

"Do you know how beautiful you are?"

Her nose crinkles and I have to laugh. Clasping both her hands in mine, I stand and easily pull her small frame into my arms and off the ground. The warm center of her body presses into my waist and her thighs quickly lock around me as if that is where they have always belonged. Her feet brush against the back of my legs and I squeeze my eyes shut for a second, filled with exhilaration from the movement. I can't help but wonder if every part of our body will fit together so perfectly.

She lays her forehead to mine and I instantly open my eyes, looking directly into hers. Biting down on her lips, she curves them into a smile as mine do the same.

"I have a surprise for us tonight," I say, turning in a slow circle with complete happiness and joy flowing through my veins.

I wish so badly that I could blink my eyes and make the day fade away. *I want to have her all to myself; across the lake; with no interruption; with no Evan; with a king sized bed and whipped cream ... Shit, I have to stop this or we won't be going anywhere anytime soon.*

"What are you up to?"

I place a soft tender kiss against her mouth and smile, excitement raging inside of me.

"You'll just have to wait and see." I lower her to the ground and pull her hand to my mouth for a small peck across her knuckles. "Come on. Let's go find Evan and see if we can get the keys to the jet skis," I suggest, hoping that the adrenaline rush from racing across the water may keep my mind off of activities that could possibly be awaiting me later in the night.

"Ok, that sounds fun." She bounces up and down on her toes.

We rush out of the cabin, hand-in-hand as usual. Not even ten paces out the door and we run into Evan.

"Hey guys." He sweeps his hand across his forehead and his eyes widen. "Thank God. I was really thinking I was going to walk in on something."

Alyssa laughs beside me, hiding her smile behind her hand.

"Is that why you came this way, ya ole' perv?"

"You betcha ... if that's the only way I'm going to see a naked chick this summer, then so be it," Evan winks.

"I don't think so!" I spit out, knowing he is kidding but still determined to put out into the universe that looking at my girlfriend is off limits to anyone.

"I gotta get my thrills some way." He quirks his brows and quickly adds, "So what are you two up to?"

"We were coming to find you. Do you have the keys to the jet skis down at the boat house?" I ask, hoping he has them with him to save on time.

"They're in the camper, but I can go grab them real quick." Evan points over his shoulder toward the camper that is parked between his grandpa's cabin and the second cabin on the property.

I look over at Alyssa, hoping she is ok with what I'm about to suggest; after all with Evan around I'll definitely be able to keep my excitement under wraps.

"You want to join us? I figured we would take the jet skis out for a few hours before we're supposed to meet up for the barbeque. Alyssa and I can hop on one and you can take the other."

Evan looks back and forth between us and laughs. "What, you think I'm desperate for something to do lately or something?"

I pause at his seriousness, wondering for a second if he is really taking me that way. "No! I didn't ..." I start as Alyssa chimes in with a sympathetic tone.

"I think Judd just meant ..."

"Hell yeah, I will ... I've been bored to tears since Jake busted out of here. Bout time you two decide to be a little social," he says shoving me. "I'll run and get the keys and meet you at the boat house." Evan takes off before we can say another word.

I look down and shake my head; I have been pretty preoccupied. Two weeks ago, it was usually Jake, me and Evan heading out to go fishing every night while the others headed to the other side of the lake. In a way it really sucks that in less than a month I will be heading hundreds of miles away from everything I've ever known and the people that I love. With that thought I look over at Alyssa. *Damn, leaving to go to college later this summer is going to be hard. That is something I did not feel weeks ago; I was desperate to leave.*

"You ok?"

"Yeah, come on." I nudge her along beside me and we both take off to the dock. *Right now all I care about is being with her. I'll worry about leaving when that time comes.*

I run a few feet behind Alyssa the whole way, not because I can't beat her but more for the sake of a great view. The way her body bounces underneath her thin shorts have me thinking X-rated thoughts. As soon as she gets to the edge of the dock, she bends over with her hands on her knees, breathing heavy from our hike. I step up beside her and run my hand along her back, still lost in my imagination.

"I really need to take up running like Abby," she laughs while standing up and turning to face me.

"Come here." I pull her against me in one swift motion and immediately the heat radiating off of her skin has my pulse racing. That and the sheer thought of what happened last time we were at this dock knocks my heart into overtime.

I run my hands down the bare skin of her back, an onslaught of goose bumps forming under my touch. My hands reach the soft fabric of her waist band and I slowly tuck my fingertips below it, continuing in my pursuit of roaming every inch of her skin. Rising up onto her toes suddenly, my hands thrust further beneath her shorts, cupping in every bit of her that I can. Her lips find mine and I dine on their sweetness, devouring each of her breaths along the way. My tongue grazes hers as she whimpers through a soft sigh. Instantly aroused, my fingertips tense up and I clamp down on a handful of the supple, smooth skin of her ass. Pulling her up. her legs worm around my waist and I have visions of our activities in the shower house. *Holy shit, I can't control myself around her.*

My hands tense and I squeeze and massage her skin, desperately wanting to have her bare. I gulp down a breath then move my lips along the contours of her jaw, swiping my tongue out to taste her. She whines again and my shorts instantly border on constricting.

I stumble around, holding my hand out and looking over her shoulder to make sure we don't take a dip right into the lake. My hand finds the small partition between two of the bays and I carefully press her body against the wall, using one hand to brace us. Her hips move against me and I drop my head back, not able to think or focus on anything except the incredible and intense pressure that she is pulling from my core.

"… wait! Do you …"

I'm breathing so hard and my mind is going a million miles an hour that I only hear clips of her voice, but then I notice the fire I felt from her just seconds ago is dwindling.

"Do I what?" I breathe out as if I just ran a marathon.

I struggle to zoom in on what she hears, but all I hear is the kicked up pace of my hammering heartbeat. But then … I hear it. *Shit, of course.* Before I can even get my left hand out of the back of her shorts, Evan rounds the corner whistling an out of tune song. He comes to a dead stop as I hastily rip my hand out of Alyssa's shorts and lower her to the ground simultaneously. I put my hands at her waist, while she reaches around and looks as though she is adjusting her shorts back

123

over her ass.

"Well hell! I wasn't even gone ten minutes. Seriously, is it going to be like this all day with you two?" Evan scoffs, shaking his head on an amused chuckle.

"I ..." I can't even think of anything to say, partially because all the blood in my body is currently rushing to one area, leaving me a little dumbfounded. *Well, maybe just dumb at this particular moment.*

I continue to stand braced against Alyssa, hoping to steer away any strange looks from Evan. Alyssa giggles and buries her head in my chest as I look at the wall behind her in embarrassment. *Why does this always happen. Someday ... someday, I will get him back for this.*

"Oh, aaaa ... do I need to go away and give you two a few more minutes? I totally can if there are things that need to be taken care of."

Even though I cannot look at him, I can hear the shitty ass grin in his voice. I shake my head, wanting to laugh; maybe cry. The pain flaring up between my legs right now definitely has me wanting to agree that he should leave, but I don't.

"It's fine, Evan. We were just ..."

Alyssa's laughter turns into snorts and I can feel her shaking against me from it. I chuckle and look over my shoulder.

"Seriously dude. You should put that away before you hurt some-one."

"I'm working on it, but it's not like I have a whole hell of a lot of control over it," I reply back, leaning toward Alyssa for more con-cealment, yet careful to not graze my body against hers anymore than need be.

Evan busts out laughing then wiggles the keys in front of him. "Once you get him in park, I have your keys. Don't come near me until you do though."

"Sorry," I whisper into Alyssa's ear as she tries desperately to control her giddiness. "Are you ok?" I laugh painfully.

"Mmmhhm ... I'm fine," she hums.

She looks up at me and her eyes are watering. I smile and decide to lean down for a small kiss.

"Ok, I am here. The party can officially begin," Skylar's voice calls out from the entrance of the boat house.

We all look over at her and she smiles.

"Oh yeah, some of the others are renting jet skis, too, so Skylar is going to hop on with me." Evan turns to where I can only see his face. His eyebrows quirk up and down as he bites down on his tongue in a deliberate effort, which tells me I'm not the only one with my mind in the gutter.

He tosses me a key and I step aside, my body finally relaxed enough that I can walk around without waving a red flag to my state of excitement. Unfortunately, a throbbing pain still serves as a reminder of what didn't happen.

Hanging onto the partition between the bays, I lean out and grab the handle of one of the jet skis and pull it closer to the dock so Alyssa can jump on. Once I have one foot placed on the ski, I take her hand and help her on then climb on in front of her.

Evan and Skylar settle onto the other jet ski and we both fire them up to head out for some fun.

Tristan and Jessie fly past us a couple times and it actually surprises me. I figured he would be rolling around in the sheets with one of those girls across the lake by now or aggravating the crap out of Abby. Evan and Skylar stick around for a few hours but then wave their goodbyes before heading back to the boat dock. I guess he gave in and decided to take a break from his pining over Piper.

Thankfully, the few hours we have before we need to meet up with the others flies by. I thought spending the day out on the lake would keep my mind occupied and off of the cabin that is screaming my name across the lake, but I was wrong.

The constant mayhem of boats, skis, wave runners and other jet skis zooming by did nothing to the adrenaline rush I get from being near Alyssa. Every wave we crash over, her thighs tighten on my hips like a vice grip and all I could think about is how I want them wrapped around me later tonight. However, as bad as I hope we take our relationship to the next level, I am going to leave that decision in her hands. There is not a doubt in my mind about how I feel for her so even though nothing about us has ever been slow, I am willing to wait. I just know if she decides we need to, I will be in utter agony.

We call it quits and make it back to the beach before sundown. The savory aroma of grilled meat reaches my nostrils and my stomach rumbles in response. One of the beachside picnic tables is filled with a spread of food and my mouth begins to water. With the craziness of the day it didn't even occur to me that neither I nor Alyssa has had a bite to eat. Doing our best to remain civilized, we all form a semi-single file line and start dishing up.

"Dig in guys," Piper announces as we all fill our plates. "There is more than enough for seconds and thirds and ..." her voice fades off, forcing me to look up.

"I'm freaking starving," Tyler belts out beside Piper.

She is stone still and looking past us. I glance over my shoulder and see Skylar and Evan walking hand in hand towards the beach. *What the hell? When did that happen?*

Evan smiles and immediately drops Skylar's hand, but she doesn't seem to mind in the least.

"Save some for me," she calls out, running up to the table to fix her plate.

"Hey, what did I miss?"

"What's up with you and Skylar?" I ask instead of answering his question as he strides up to my side.

"What do you mean? Nothing's up." He cocks his head back and furrows his brows into a pissed off glare. "I'm just messing around, man. Isn't everyone else?"

"Yeah, I guess ..." I pause, "but you know Piper saw you and Skylar, right?"

"Whatever. I'm over it and I'm hungry!" Evan glares across the table at Piper and the conversation is closed.

The last hours of daylight fade away as we all cram our faces with food and make casual conversation. Alyssa and I make ourselves comfortable around the fire, sitting side-by-side. She shoves a large bite of burger in her mouth and I have to smile. Usually I wouldn't watch a girl eat out of fear that I would get slapped or she may freak out and start eating lettuce, but something about watching her eat is sexy as hell. She doesn't just take little nibbles like a lot of girls I've met and she sure doesn't hold back, throwing a few twigs of broccoli on her plate. Rather, she goes for a greasy burger and takes some huge ass, monstrous bites. Her mouth opens wide as she shoves in more food and I notice a splash of ketchup drip onto her chest. The saliva glands in my mouth immediately go nuts and all I want to do is lick it off.

"You have ketchup right there." I lean forward, hungry for her, but instead of going in for it with my tongue, I use my finger to swipe it off.

As soon as I slip my finger into my mouth and lick the tangy tomatoey sauce off, she stops chewing. I stare into her wide eyes and snicker, aware that she was just as affected by that as I was. *Come on time, move faster.*

"What?" I laugh, my arm sliding around her to get closer. "I was actually going to …"

"Hey, come help me for a second." Tristan interrupts my thoughts, motioning for me as he steps towards the parking lot.

"I'll be back," I tell Alyssa then jump up and sprint after my brother.

We walk up to Evan's jeep and Tristan grabs a huge bag of fireworks. He tosses me the bag and reaches in to grab the other. I follow him silently back to the beach, not really having a whole lot to say. He glances over at me periodically as if he has something on his mind, but I keep my mouth shut.

Once our feet sink back into the sandy beach, he drops his bag to the ground, leveling me with a familiar kiddish smirk. I scrunch up my face, confused by why he is staring at me, but before I can ask, everyone is gathered around the bags, picking and choosing their favorite noise-makers.

Tristan darts off towards the bonfire then returns holding out several punks with fiery red tips. Handing them all out, he stares at me with the same mischievous look as before. He holds a handful of fireworks in one hand and a single punk in the other. Hastily shoving the unlit fireworks into his pocket he leaves one between his fingertips, slowly bringing the glowing end of it to the wick as he looks directly at me.

"Arm yourself for battle, boys and girls."

The look in his eyes tells me that he is remembering our conversation at the firework stand but his words take me back. For only a second, I see him as a kid again shouting a warning to me, Jake, Mom and Dad, before a full on war begins. The gleam in his eyes intensifies as he tosses the fire cracker right at my feet. Whoops and hollers sound around me as everyone scrambles to grab their own loot. Jumping back, my head snaps up to look at my brother and I return his smirk right before the firecracker explodes. *Oh, it is on!*

Go out with a bang

AFTER A VIGOROUS HOUR or so of running and tossing sizzling grenades until my arm is about to fall off, I am more than ready for the end of the night. Dripping with sweat from avoiding the possibility of getting my ass lit on fire has me opting for a dip in the lake. It doesn't take long for the cool waters to revive my tired limbs and calm the adrenaline rush brought on from our firework battle.

"I wonder where Evan is," I mutter quietly to Alyssa, noticing several people around the bonfire and a few out in the water, but no sign of him.

"Who knows," she whispers in my ear causing the hairs on my arm to stand on end.

The slick skin of her stomach rubs against my back as she hitches a ride on our way out of the water. As her arms tighten around my neck to hold on, so does my hold on the backs of her thighs.

"Last I saw … your brother and my sister were headed for the back of the cabin."

I sigh at the thought of Tristan screwing this whole thing up for me by pissing off her sister.

"That sounds all kinds of wrong," I say as Alyssa giggles.

She slides off of my back and plops down on a blanket that is spread out across the sand. I join her, quickly slithering into a clean t-shirt that I brought with me earlier. Alyssa does the same before subtly nuzzling against me.

"Did you see that one rocket bounce off my damn calf?" Matt carries on next to us.

"Oh my gosh, I was about to die when I saw you dive behind the truck," Tyler chimes in, "I just knew it was going to blow up when Tristan launched a rocket that way."

"No shit man, look at …"

"Hey, you ready to go? I have to start the firework display in thirty minutes and need to get there early to set up." Evan's voice directs my attention over my shoulder and I see Tristan walking back towards us with a pissed off look.

Not too far behind him is Piper and Abby. I laugh to myself, assuming that my brother must have been shot down again, before I jump to my feet more than ready to leave.

"Let's go … it's time for that surprise." I take Alyssa's hand in mine trying to tame the smirk that is emerging on my face. Her smile mocks my own as she walks beside me.

I mouth a quiet "Thanks" to Abby and she responds with a wink. Placing my hand on the small of Alyssa's back, I lead her up to Evan's jeep and hop in the passenger side.

"Come on." Patting my lap, I grin and raise my eyebrows to beckon her into the jeep with me.

Once her body slides onto mine, I place my hand along her thigh and make a slow, soft trail across the skin above her knee, focusing on looking out the front window instead of where my hand is. My insides are bouncing off the wall with anxiety and anticipation of tonight. The cyclone of thoughts spinning in my head is unreal. *What if I disappoint her? Was renting the cabin a stupid, impulsive idea? God, what if I go too fast or too slow or …*

"So the show starts in forty-five minutes so that should give you guys plenty of time …" Evan bumps his fist forward and backward above the steering wheel as he drives and I just about lose it.

I cannot believe he just said that. Wait, yeah I can … this is Evan.

"Shut up!" I rifle out instantly, watching Alyssa for any recognition of what he just said.

Unless Abby or Tristan spilled, she has no clue where we are going. For all she knows we could be going to this side to help Evan or to get a close up view of the 10:30 annual firework extravaganza that the lake puts on.

"Ok, what's going on you two?" she asks, craning her neck around to look at Evan then back at me.

"Hey, whoa … hold on. There is no *you two* involved in what is going on tonight, unless you are referring to you and Judd, but I will definitely not be attending …"

"Evan!" I say a little sterner, about to shove him out of the driver's seat and take the wheel.

"So are you not staying for the show?" She directs her question to him, clearly talking about the fireworks.

He chuckles, glancing over at me. I'm mentally choking him with a look that more than likely expresses that desire quite well.

"Oh come on. She walked right into that one," he laughs, "I told you once before, Alyssa, I'm not into that shit."

"Wait, what?" her confusion, Evan's sarcasm and the tight knot of nerves wound inside of me has me about to come unglued. One minute I want to laugh hysterically the next I want to panic.

"Don't listen to him," I growl.

She looks back at me for a second before sweeping her gaze to our surroundings as we pull into the large gravel lot. Evan steers us back to where I parked earlier today and slams the jeep into park. Looking over Alyssa's shoulder, I see him holding out a lighter.

"Bring it back out because it's the only one I have."

"Sure. I'll be right back." I pat her legs, motioning for her to scoot off my lap.

After grabbing the lighter and smiling a quick thanks to him, I dash for the door having absolutely no clue what is in Alyssa's head. Slipping the key out of my pocket, I quickly unlock the door and bolt into the back bedroom. *Damn it … Abby had to go and get a million candles. I need a freaking blow torch.*

Flicking the lighter with my thumb, an orange glowing flame instantaneously pops up. I act fast, aware that I just left Alyssa in a confused state out with Evan, the mother of all mouths. As my best friend he is armed with every detail of what I hope happens tonight and he has absolutely no filter. He is probably filling her head with all sorts of bullshit right now.

After the first two tall candles are lit, I start tipping them to the side so that several wicks are met in the center when I light it. It takes only a few minutes and I am darting back out the door, not even bothering to survey my candle-lighter skills before I leave.

"... of this. If you don't enjoy it, don't blame me." I hear Evan's amused tone as I walk up beside the jeep.

He sees me over her shoulder and his smirk deepens. *He is just eating this up.*

"Shut up, you ass! And here's your lighter."

Alyssa snaps her head around to face me.

Reaching past her, I shove the lighter towards Evan. "Come on." I help Alyssa out with the other hand. "Thanks for the ride, man."

"Go get her, stud," Evan mouths as he grabs the lighter.

I shake my head at him, trying not to grin and encourage him.

Once we step inside the cabin, I think it finally dawns on Alyssa what is going on. I flip on the light in the main living area and her eyes search the entire cabin. These cabins are so much different than the ones on our side, much more upscale and perfect for this night; for *the* night.

I stand silently behind her and watch her eyes dart to the rock fireplace in the corner, up to the chandelier hanging from the vaulted ceiling and then on to the flickering candle light barely filtering out of the back bedroom.

She spins around to face me, standing only inches away but yet too far for my taste.

"Did you rent this?" Her voice is laced in amazement and it brings a smile to my face.

I waste no time pulling her into my arms and flush up against my body. Bending my head down, my lips find hers and I slowly slide my tongue along her bottom lip coercing it open. She complies, and I taste and explore her mouth while carefully guiding her back past the doorway of the bedroom.

Brushing my elbow against the door, it lets out a quiet creak and Alyssa breaks contact to turn around. I stretch my neck, trying my best to look at her face while remaining behind her. *I wish I knew what she was thinking.*

Looking from her face to the room and back again, I focus on what she is seeing and what could be running through her head. The back of the cabin faces the lake and this bedroom has the best view of all, with a large picture window that stretches from the headboard on up. In the distance the lake sparkles with reflections of small fireworks going off here and there. Below the window, lies the massive bed which Abby had peppered with red rose petals.

Glancing back at her as she studies the room, I see flickers of candlelight sparkling in her absolutely content and happy eyes. She catches my look and twists around to face me again.

"This had to cost you a fortune."

I laugh at her assessment and the stunned tone of her voice.

She doesn't seem upset or fearful of any expectations I may have. She seems hopeful and that makes my heart thud like a canon.

"Don't worry about what it cost. You're worth more than this."

Doesn't she know that she is worth everything I own; every thread of clothes on my back? There is no jewel or gem that I would treasure more than her; I would give anything to have her near me.

"… how?"

I smile at her question feeling somewhat proud that I was able to hold out until today. There are so many things that I have been holding onto for tonight; just to make this moment as perfect as possible.

"I rented it the morning Jake left. I wanted our last night to be special with no interruptions."

She laughs at my confession and for a moment I think about the last part of what I said. *I really hope there are no interruptions!* Evan is supposed to come get us in the morning and take us back so I can leave with Tristan, but considering he is only about twenty yards away getting ready to set off fireworks for all the vacationers, that part of my plan could easily crash and burn.

Backing her up a little more into the room, she slides down onto the edge of the bed and continues to look up at me. *This is it!*

I scoot in beside her and run my hand along her back and to her waist so that I can pull her into my lap. She slides onto me with ease and looks into my eyes with a gentle smile.

"Alyssa, don't think I expect anything. I just thought…"

Her lips smash into mine and just like our first kiss, I made no movement to make this happen. *Definitely another one of those hell yeah moments!*

As soon as I feel her moving her legs to both sides of my waist in an effort to get as close as possible to me, my body blazes with need.

Sinking my hands into the soft flesh of her thighs, I greedily trace a fiery path up her back then flip her over. My actions are saying the exact opposite of my words, but there is no holding back now.

Desire and longing licks at my insides as my hand clutches her waist. I pull her to the head of the bed with me, sliding over rose petal after rose petal and never once breaking the rhythm of my tongue against hers. I drink her in, lapping my tongue inside her mouth as if I have to taste every ounce of her. Yearning, longing and craving burns through me, spilling into every limb of my body until I cannot touch her enough, taste her enough. My lips move from her lips to her chest down to her stomach and thighs then slowly back up.

Her shirt has wormed its way up her body with a little help and I have to feel all of her.

Trailing my tongue back up her slim waist to her rib cage, my hand drifts below the fabric of her suit. I softly graze my fingertips over her nipple and a moan escapes her lips followed by another soft whimper.

She quickly rips her shirt over her head and I immediately take that as a sign that the rest of her clothes have to come off; now. My mouth sucks and tastes a path up to her neck while I quickly untie the strings at her neck, sliding the fabric down to expose the plump and fleshy curves of her body.

I soon untie the rest of her suit and fling it to the side, ready to take off the few scraps of fabric that still remain on her body.

My lips join hers again in a slow melody of kisses as I slide back on top of her. Once the hard, pebbly skin of her nipples makes contact with my chest, my excitement intensifies to a nearly painful level and my mouth desperately seals to hers.

My head is in a frenzy and my body has a mind of its own. Sucking and licking my way down to her stomach and around her sexy ass belly button ring, I have one goal in mind as I slide my fingertips along the side of her shorts and swimsuit bottoms. *To hell with taking them off one by one, we'll knock out two tasks at once.*

My heart is hammering and my head is screaming at me to rip them off but I pause for a single second to gather my wits.

"Is this ok?" *Please say yes, please say yes.*

I can barely catch my breath as I suck air in by the gallons. Once she nods her head and lifts her hips off the bed, I let out a breath and pull both articles of clothing off in one swift motion. For a second I fear that I may have been too forceful and burned her thighs from the friction of the fabric, but as I toss the clothing aside my mind and body is stunned into silence.

I lean back, sitting up with my legs bent beneath me and barely grazing her inner thighs. My eyes roam and take in the most amazing sight I've ever seen; Alyssa completely and utterly bare and sprawled before me. Her legs are bent with both feet planted on the bed beside me. As I search my way up her creamy soft skin, a shiver rolls through her.

"You're so beautiful," I barely get out between breaths as my eyes land back on hers.

I lean down, anxious to run my tongue along every crook and curve of her body, but I halt in my movement when I feel a tug at the button on my shorts. Swinging my line of sight downward my heart jumps with excitement as I take in her delicate fingers nervously pulling at the clasp.

"What about you?"

Meeting her eyes, I struggle to maintain normal breathing. "Are you sure?" I'm ten seconds from busting out of them anyway, but I want to make sure that she wants this, too.

She barely answers with a slow nod before she has me unzipped and my shorts are pushed down to my knees. I help her out, shifting my weight from side-to-side until they are off and on the ground. Once I kick them to the side, I kneel back in front of her to scan her body a second maybe even a fourth or fifth time by now before sliding back onto her.

The moment my skin melts into hers, our lips connect in a wet, sultry kiss that has me nearly hyperventilating. Her legs graze my hips reminding me that there is nothing between us; no barriers to keep me from feeling everything that I want so badly.

I continue kissing her, moving my lips and tongue in a quick needy motion that has her tilting her hips and wrapping her legs around mine. Heat is barrels off of her and I can't wait any longer, but I have to tell her how I feel first.

Pulling away, I suck in quick breaths only centimeters from her face.

"Alyssa, I'm in love with you." I can barely speak, barely think. I take another nip at her lips and try desperately to catch my breath. Her eyes glisten with unshed tears, but I don't stop, "I've wanted to tell you so many times, but I was afraid I would scare you off but I can't hold back anymore." After scanning her face, I continue to let the words gush out of my heart like a river breaking free, "I'm so in love with you! I've never felt this way about someone before and I know we've only known each other two weeks but I can't imagine my life without you now."

My chest expands and contracts against hers as our hearts wage a drum war with one another. After tightening her arms around my back, she places a small gentle kiss on my lips. Pulling away to where I can still feel her breath move across my lips, I notice a small tear drop down her cheek.

"I love you, too."

I squeeze my eyes shut and smile, feeling relieved, excited, hopeful, happy and nervous of what's to come all at the same time.

Tenderly, my lips join with her as I slowly move my hips to connect us. I take it slow, making sure we fit comfortably together. Her head falls into the pillow and she instantly whimpers, making me want to move faster.

I want this to last; I want to take it slow, but her skin against mine sends sensations zapping through my body until I may come unhinged. Gripping her shoulders, I push and thrust while my tongue slides up her jaw to her ear lobe. I pull that tiny bit of flesh into my mouth, teasing it with my tongue. She whines and whimpers and wiggles beneath me, driving me insane. I kiss my way back to her mouth with a hunger I've never felt, then down to her chest while arching my back so I can deepen my movements.

Moving back up to her mouth, the pleasure within me builds,
Builds,
Builds,

Shoving my hips forward one last time, my mouth opens and an animalistic sound erupts from my mouth before I collapse onto her. My body quivers and shakes from the eruption of pleasure. I keep my head buried in her hair against her neck, trying to allow blood to flow back into other portions of my body so that I can think again.

Her hair tickles my cheek and I pick up on the sweet smell of strawberries mixed with a hint of sweat as I focus on calming my breaths.

Once I can think, I almost wish I couldn't.

I want nothing more than to flip her over and go for round two right now but I'm way too ashamed of my performance. *What was that a minute; two at the most? What the hell? I can't even look her in the eye. I'm so embarrassed!* As soon as I felt her, the zips of electricity from the friction sent me over the edge. No way did that even give her time to enjoy it.

I slide my hand into her hair and brace myself onto my elbow.

"I am so sorry that was so quick," I say, hiding my face in my hand from absolute humiliation.

Lowering my hand a bit, I lock over the top of them to gauge what she's thinking and go on, "Here I wanted this to be a magical experience and I built it up so much to make it just right and then I ended up …"

I take in her expression and am met with a beaming smile and bright eyes, so I stop reiterating my humiliation from getting overly excited. *Maybe it wasn't as bad for her as I assume.*

Her fingertips leisurely combing through my hair make me want to close my eyes and melt into her. Each pass of her hands has every nerve in my body unwinding and the embarrassment fading away.

"Well then you succeeded because it was perfect."

I narrow my eyes and stare at her, still skeptical and feeling I need to explain. I mean last thing I want her to think is that I have no stamina. *I have stamina, just apparently not the first time with the first girl I've ever been in love with. Damn, she felt so good.*

My lower extremities come to life once again right as loud popping ignites outside of the window. My attention has been so focused on everything that I didn't even hear thunderous sonic booms and see bright beams of light flashing just yards away. Still looking at her as she continues to ruffle her fingers through my hair, I realize she hasn't noticed either.

"I was really hoping it would be mind blowing for you. I even arranged for fireworks," I joke hoping to detour the conversation from my performance to the show outside.

She takes only a small glance out the window then looks back at me. Her hips tilt inward and my body heats up against her. As though someone just announced that half time is over, I begin planting small moist kisses along her jawline as she squirms.

"We could try again …"

I don't even need to think about her suggestion; I can't because my body is already kicking into action. I laugh and roll onto my back, firmly holding her against me.

"You read my mind …"

She looks at me nervously as she rises above me, placing one leg on either side of my hips with her knees bent.

"I want to look at you …" I say thinking, *bucket list time.*

Like a magnet, my hands find her hips, holding her steady in case she is uncomfortable with this.

"Ummm, I've never done it …" she breathes out with a quivering voice, "… like this."

I smile and loosen my grip on her hips feeling comforted that she never experienced this with that other guy.

"I guess we'll figure it out together then," I say, feeling goose bumps spread over her hips as I run my hand over them.

Her apprehension dissolves and she positions herself perfectly over me, slowly easing down until the warmth of her center settles onto me. I keep my hands glued to her hips and guide her as rolls of electricity shoot through me with our contact. Slowly allowing my gaze to sweep over her, I take in her voluptuous chest to her tiny waist then down to watch our joined bodies. Her head falls back and she lets out ragged breaths, whining and whimpering.

I continue to watch, to savor every tingle, spark, buzz and bolt of electricity as she moves. A couple times, I try to join in lifting my hips, but it throws off her pace and trips us up. *I guess I won't try that for now.* We both laugh at our inexperience but we quickly correct our position and waves of pleasure silence the joking. Within seconds we are back to gasping for breath.

Soon sensations begin to build within me and I need to have her closer. Lifting myself up to sit with one hand gripped on her waist, I begin pulling and pushing her at the perfect pace. My mouth roams any part of her body it can reach, wanting to taste it all, wanting to touch her everywhere, wanting to experience everything with her. I settle my lips on hers as she makes the most beautiful sounds that have me barely holding on.

"You're so beautiful," I gasp as my eyes devour her exquisite curves bouncing to the rhythm of our love.

Waves roll and crash within me as I feel the muscles in her body tense up. She arches her body towards me with her head flung back, and I can no longer hold on.

"Juuuuud ….." She calls to me on a scream as we both plummet, spiraling into a pool of ecstasy.

With my arms gripped around her, I pull her flush against me with my face buried in her chest. Her arms tighten around my back, holding onto me securely. Turning my face so that I can breathe, I marvel at small trickles of sweat sliding across her skin and how her heart beats wildly in my ear.

I turn my face back between her breasts, "Whoa …" I mouth against her skin causing her to bounce and giggle within my arms.

"That tickles."

My lips curve into a smile that I have never owned before in my life because I've never known this happiness and I've never felt so content. Dropping my head back so I can look at her while still holding her against me as tight as possible, I see that she is looking out the window at the fireworks. I break our hold and she slowly rolls off, both of us collapsing on our backs against the mattress. Silently watching boom after boom burst into a million sizzling lights, I turn and look at her, curious.

"Was that better? Did you…" *I know she did, but I just want to be sure.*

Her lips rise into a huge smile as she bites her bottom lip and I have no doubt that I have a stupid ass grin plastered on me as well.

"I did …" She giggles still looking above us at the blazing sky.

Crack,

Crack,

Boom.

Snapping my head back out the window to the sky, I see that Evan must have just announced the end of the fireworks show by blasting the biggest, brightest and noisiest rockets all at once. *Wow, perfect timing ... for all of us!*

"Just ... like ... that!" Alyssa announces, erupting with laughter.

I slide my hands behind my head feeling a tad bit cocky and whole lot pleased, "Yeah, I planned it like that." I laugh and look over at her, "I figured we could go out with a bang."

Blurred visions of her

THE NEXT MORNING, OF course, Evan busts in as usual putting an immediate halt in our morning passion. He has a way of choosing the precise moment that will destroy me the most. After he made himself scarce, the situation between Alyssa and I turned from playful to emotional as we both realized that this is the day that we have to say goodbye, so to speak. I know without a doubt that it is not goodbye, but it still scares the hell out of me that I won't have her near me every day. I trust her and I am confident that she loves me, but I do worry that her ex might realize what an idiot he was and try to get her back. Honestly, I'd say he doesn't have a shot in hell; his loss is my gain.

After closing the door of the cabin behind me, I grip her hand in mine wishing I could turn around and lock us both in it for the rest of the summer. Her fingers thread between mine and the grip she has on my hand may very well turn it blue.

Evan sits in his jeep with the engine running and a smirk on his face. I look at him and shake my head, praying that he reads my mind that this morning is no time for his dramatics. Once I get settled in the seat with her curled up in my lap, he throws it into drive and crosses the lot to the office so I can turn in the key.

Throwing it into park, he looks over at me as Alyssa nuzzles into my neck with her body turned away from him. I rub my hand along her back and let my lips settle against the top of her head.

"Hey, you want me to take the key in?"

I turn my cheek to the side, with Alyssa's soft hair brushing over my face. Evan looks at her with a sympathetic smile with his hand held out. Returning his smile, I gratefully hand him the key clasped in my hand.

"Hey, look at me," I say to her as soon as Evan jumps out.

She looks up and her tear streaked cheeks send a slicing pain straight through my heart. Running my hand to her face, I place it against her cheek and touch my lips to hers, expressing everything within my soul.

"I love you. This isn't going away ... .what I feel for you." I smile, trying to break through her wall of doubt. "I have a couple weeks before I leave for school and I plan to spend every second with you, ok?"

She nods her head and curls back against me as Evan climbs back in.

"Ready?" He grits his teeth after the word slips out and is met with absolute silence.

Neither of us says a word as the jeep bumps over the gravel lot until finally finding a smooth, quiet path on the main road.

Once we pull onto Mr. Jansen's property, I see a none-too happy Tristan pacing along the side of his red sports car. His work shirt is on and he immediately lowers his sunglasses to shoot me a pissed off glare.

Alyssa jumps off my lap and I hop out behind her, grabbing her hand as I walk towards my brother's car. Looking around, I notice Nick's red truck is gone and Matt seems to be missing too. I forgo my goodbyes to Evan and Mitch and wave to all the girls.

"See ya guys," I yell out in the direction of the girls as Abby skips over.

"Sooo ... would you like to say thank you for the chocolate syrup and whipped cream?" she laughs and I look around to see where Alyssa is.

She stands not too far away, saying goodbye to Evan and Tyler. She has a strained smile on her face and all I want to do is toss her in the car with me, take off and hide from the world and all the plans that

I have spent years waiting for.

"Hello …"

I look back at Abby, "Sorry," I smile then remember what she asked. "I didn't use them." I inform her bringing a shocked look to her face.

"Oh come on … that's no fun."

I shake my head and smile, knowing just how wrong she is. Some things don't need to be sweetened, and there is no doubt in my mind that my mouth enjoyed everything just as much as I would have had there been chocolate and whipped topping involved.

"Hey, but thanks a lot," I tell her as she sneaks back over to join her friends.

"Hey!" Tristan snaps as Alyssa walks back up to my side. "We have to go. I have to get to work." His wording bleeds together.

"Are you drunk, man?" I ask, lowering my voice as I move closer to him so everyone else doesn't hear. "What the hell went on over here last night?"

"No!" he shouts as he gets into the car. "I'm just hung over! Now get in!"

Furious that he is acting like this, I pull Alyssa to the side of the passenger door and wrap my arms around her, not wanting to let go. She looks up at me with blood shot eyes that hold the same concerns as me.

"Don't worry. I'll get him to switch seats with me when we gas up. I'll be fine." I kiss her lips gently then lean down so that my gaze is level with hers. "I'll give you time to get home then I'll call you a little later today … I love you."

Her arms fly around my neck and her shaky voice whispers "I love you, too," in my ear.

"There will be plenty of tail to chase at college. Let's go!" Tristan's choice of words has me spinning around, ready to rip the door off the hinges and throw him from the car.

"Shut the hell up and give me a minute," I snarl, leaning into the passenger side before returning my attention to her.

"Ignore him, Alyssa." I say beneath gritted teeth. "He doesn't know anything about us. I love you and I will talk to you later today. Ok?" I kiss her one last time then get into the car beside my brother.

"Aww … break my freaking heart," he mumbles.

I slam the door with enough force that I hope it leaves a damn dent in his precious baby. As I look up to see Alyssa's eyes brimming with tears, my mood softens and I reach out to grab her hand.

"Good grief," Tristan spits out as he slams the car into drive and spins out causing me to release my grip, letting go of her hand sooner than I had hoped. My heart and head are conflicted, filled with anger from Tristan's lack of respect and childish comment, yet overflowing with the sudden feeling of emptiness and loss. I stare out the passenger window until I can no longer see her beautiful face and golden locks of hair that spills around her shoulders. Images of Mom flickers through my mind for a second, as I headed out the door the morning before she had died. I could barely see her through the crack in the door as I held my hand up in a wave that I'm sure she could no longer register through the confusion of an oxygen mask, IV and feeding tube.

As I look away from the window, Tristan's foul mood reads loud and clear through a deep frown, low dipped eyebrows and an unyieldingly taut grip on the steering wheel. This is going to be a long trip but luckily, for now he remains silent. Slipping my phone out of my pocket, I type a message to Alyssa, not willing to wait to hear from her.

Me: I know I told you last night how I feel but I just wanted to elaborate for a moment while I have a good 4-5 hours on my hands. Alyssa, you have completely thrown me for a loop this summer. I never expected to come out to the lake and walk away in love with the most amazingly beautiful girl I've ever met. You completely own my heart. It's yours and I don't want it back, I just want you! Ever since I can remember, all I've focused on is football and making it to UCLA … that was my dream. That isn't my dream anymore. You are. You're everything to me and I love you more than I ever thought imaginable. This is fast and I know it is, but why fight it when it is right, when it is meant to be and I know we are. I feel it. I knew it from the moment I saw you. I will call you later. I can't wait to hear your voice. I love you!

After half a million back spaces to delete and correct my ramblings, I smile down at my phone feeling completely comfortable with everything I wrote then hit send. 'Message Failed to send' lights up on my phone and I glance up to the corner of my phone to see that I have no service.

"Damn reception," I say under my breath.

Slamming my phone down to my lap, I look up and see that Tristan is swerving. I twist in my seat and look behind us; another car is close on our tail, probably ready to report a drunk driver if there is any reception out this way.

Heaving out a sigh, I look over pissed off and aggravated over the way everything always has to end up when he is involved. His knuckles are white and his hands hold the steering wheel like he is imagining choking someone.

"Can I ask what your problem is?" I pause, but he never looks at me. "I mean from the second I walked onto the lot this morning, you were pissed off at me and ready to ruin my day. Is there ever going to be a day when we get along again?"

I stare over at him and back to my phone to see if I have reception yet. For a minute, I consider dropping it, but then he chuckles like what I said amused him; there wasn't a damn thing funny about what I said. Tristan has always had an acute talent of pushing my buttons and I always end up giving in, stooping to his level and playing right into his hands. Looking back, I see a small grin on his face. A blast of fury shoots through me and all I want to do is say something that will get to him as well, take a jab like he always does.

"What? No girls put out last night?" I ask sarcastically then stare forward at the road, like a scorned child. *At least he's driving straight.*

"No problems there. Why, you need pointers? Could you not get the deed done last night?" he laughs, unaffected by my words.

I need to keep my mouth shut and let this conversation end. A chime from my phone draws my attention away from the conflict at hand right in the nick of time. A message lights up across my phone notating that I only have twenty percent charge. I unfasten my seat belt and twist in my seat to reach the small back seat where my bag lies. Shoving my hand into the side pocket of my red duffel bag, I feel around until my hand falls on a long cord.

Once I have my charger pulled out, I flip back around and shove one end into the car as a loud thump sounds. Snapping my head up, I see Tristan's hand slamming down on the wheel.

"Damn she got under my skin!" He bites out in an angry tone.

This really came out of nowhere. "Who?" I ask totally confused.

He's been with so many different girls that I lose track of which one he's with at what point.

"Abby! Who the hell do you think?" He looks over at me for a brief moment then swings his eyes back to the road.

Abby … this makes me want to laugh. Sure the one girl that shot him down is going to drive him insane with questions. Affixing my phone into the other end of the charger, I grip the armrest along the side of the door. He's driving these roads pretty fast and I find myself holding on for dear life.

"Pull over and let me drive, Tristan. We can talk about it then," I say nervously.

"I'm fine! I'm just pissed off that's it!" He lets out a loud sigh and I immediately smell whiskey.

"Man, I thought you said you weren't drinking this morning! You reek of whiskey!" I yell out , ready to jump over and grab the wheel.

Thank God, Jake is not in the car with us. Damn his irresponsibility!

"I said I'm fine! I just…" He shakes his head. "I drank last night, not this morning." He sighs and I wonder when last night ended, because it sure as hell seems like he drank clear into the morning by the way he is acting and the way he smells.

"It's just a girl has never got to me like her. She's gotten under my skin ever since I met her three summers ago. Of course, that's when she was hung up on Mitch and wouldn't give me the time of day."

I'm more confused now. I thought him and Mitch were buddies. I also do not know what he is talking about with Abby. From what I could see, she was flat out refusing his ass these past two weeks and I was thankful to finally see a girl with some sense.

"Maybe someone needs to get under your skin. Maybe it would be good if you broke down that wall you built and let someone in," I mumble, knowing it won't go over well.

The last thing my brother ever wants to discuss is feelings or closeness with someone. He wrote love off the moment Mom left this earth.

"Shut up! Don't try to preach to me! Just because you have a new screw buddy doesn't mean you can lecture me."

I immediately get on the defense, my fist clinching with the urge to punch him. Now he is back to pushing my buttons. Serves me right, I should have just listened and kept my mouth closed, but he is definitely not going to talk about Alyssa like that. I turn and face him with my finger pointed in his direction.

"Don't freaking talk about Alyssa like that!"

"Come on bro, she's someone you can get your freak on with just like your little friend…what's her name…ahh… Tiffany. It's cool … If anyone gets it, I do," he taunts me with a smirk that pisses me off even more.

"No you don't get it," my veins bubble with anger and venom, "She is way more than that and you would see that if you could manage to look beyond yourself and your selfish needs for once! You would see that I am finally happy! That I have found something I never thought I would find! Neither of us should be giving lectures on relationships, but I'll tell you what, I've learned more in the past two weeks than I have ever known! And don't ever compare us! I'm nothing like you!" My body shakes from the rush of adrenaline.

Tristan doesn't say anything, just frowns with a hint of amusement. All of a sudden he busts out laughing. *He has to be drunk.*

"Damn man, since I can't get with her sister maybe I could just borrow your girl."

He's trying to bait me … don't fall for it like you always do.

"They both have those tight little asses and the most amazing racks. Oh man, I would love to bend…"

That's it! Turning in my seat, I poke my finger at his arm and yell loud enough that my own ear drums may rupture.

"Shut the hell up, man! Shut up! Does anyone like you? Seriously? Anyone?! Do you have any friends? Anyone that gives a damn whether you're alive! No, you don't and that's because you are a sad pathetic excuse for a man! You are a selfish asshole that just moves from one fix to the next! No wonder Dad left and I'm damn glad Mom died so she didn't have to see who you've become!"

147

With that my brother's eyes widen and he turns in his seat driving his fist right into my face. My head smashes into the side window and a sharp pain shoots across the bridge of my nose. Opening my mouth up wide in an effort to move the muscles in my face, a slick, salty substance drips across my lips and into my mouth; my nose is bleeding. Before I have time to register or react to my brother's extreme action, squealing and screeching booms in my ears. The smell of burning rubber rises into my nostrils as I try desperately to raise my head away from the glass.

"Shit!" Tristan yells out in a muffled tone beneath a storm of other chaotic sounds.

From my peripheral vision, he jerks and twists the wheel from side-to-side. All of a sudden, all the gravity has been released from the earth and somehow the car is weightless, flying through space; maybe it is me that is weightless. It all happens so fast that I have no time to think; to wonder what is happening or where I am.

Catapulting in one direction to the next, I am met with unyielding pain as the weight of my body turns into a lifeless doll being tossed around; flung into the door, the head rest, the roof. Something slams into my head and I yell but nothing comes out. It's as if my voice is trapped.

A crack like a baseball bat slamming into a ball rings out in my ears and I swear my arm has been ripped clean off of my shoulder. Knives slice through my chest, jabbing me across the rib cage until my heart may explode. I gasp and sputter, trying to get a breath in.

"Juuuud!" a voice barely penetrates all the other crumbling, jagged, crushing sounds.

I squeeze my eyes shut from the extreme pain that is coursing through every limb of my body and hear a loud grinding noise like metal scraping metal mixed with the piercing sharp shattering of glass. My neck snaps to the side and my back thumps forcefully into a hard surface. I gasp out, desperate for air. My name is being called out over and over; it is amplified in my ears, yet suddenly I am no longer moving; I'm still. My thoughts are fuzzy and my body is being drained of energy. Sleep … I'll just sleep.

"Judd," a weaker yell calls out in the distance, but it's muffled. I don't recognize the voice but it is laced with fear, pain and is fading.

I'm slipping; falling or drifting maybe even sinking. I'm not sure I'm on any stable surface.

"Judd…Judd, answer me," the voice calls out to me again and it sounds quieter.

My brain is telling my body to open my eyes, but any sort of control is lost and my eyes are being tugged back and forth, losing the battle; I can't focus. Sleep, I want to sleep despite the shooting, throbbing and thundering pains that bolt through every fragment of my body.

"Ju …." the voice in the distance fades away and all that remains is a faint strangled noise as my chest tightens. *What is that?* It's a steady gurgle raspy noise and each time it sounds out, my chest constricts and;

I can't breathe. I can't catch my breath.

"Over here," A different voice echoes in the direction of the earlier one.

"Oh my God, there's another one over here."

"This one isn't breathing," several voices sound around me.

"I can't get any serv …"

"Hold on," a female voice says from above me as the pressure of something soft lands in my hand or maybe another hand.

"You'll be ok … breathe," the voice is shaky and sad, but I cannot see who it is; where it is coming from.

I'm slipping again, floating and it's dark.

The pressure in my hand gets stronger and a bright beam fills my mind. It's like sunshine, but it is blurred. Then I see it; I see her.

She is sitting at the end of the fishing boat. Her mouth is moving and she's talking about her dad. I can't hear her voice; I want to hear her voice.

Her long blonde hair is draped over to one side and she is looking at me with so much love in her eyes. That was before we said we loved each other, but I can see it in her eyes now. I didn't see it before; she loves me.

I want to touch her, but I can't move. I look down and it all blurs. My feet are concreted to the boat. I look back up and see her fading, blurring.

Don't go! Please don't go! I love you!

Her face blurs and blurs as I hear a soft voice whisper, "Hold on."

Am I dying?

But I know I am and I know without a doubt that I will never see her again; that I will never feel her in my arms again; I'll never hear her say I love you and I'll never feel her soft lips against mine.

My chest tightens and pain rolls through me and although I struggle to reach for her; to touch her blurred face and hold onto it, the blurred visions of her soon fade to darkness and the pain slips away.

A dream

"JUDD ..."

Rolling my head, I get light headed as if I've been drinking all night. A splitting pain shoots across my skull and if I didn't know better, I'd say that I had been in a fight with someone ten times my size.

A throbbing sensation shoots up my right side causing me to scrunch my face in response. Slipping my tongue out of my mouth, I run it along my dry, cracked lips sparking a stinging sensation.

I make every effort to push the haze from my head, concentrating on summoning up just one thought, one memory of what happened. My mind reels with confusion and I cannot shake this heavy fatigue that pulls at my body.

"Judd ..." My brother's voice echoes, reminding me that I must be sleeping.

"Hey, buddy, you gonna join us here in the real world or sleep all week?" Evan's smartass voice joins the chorus and I re-evaluate my surroundings.

Drip ... drip ... drip ...

My ears zoom into the subtle sounds of liquid dropping into more liquid along with a faint humming and muffled chatter in the distance.

"Judd, hey, it's me ... Jake. The doctor said you should be waking up soon." My brother's voice is strained, almost hoarse.

"He's awake …" Evan draws out. "What? You think you worked so hard at the lake that you deserve a vacation now?" Evan chuckles, yet the sarcastic tone that is usually in his voice is replaced with a hint of worry and concern. "Well, I've got news for you buddy …" Evan's voice vibrates, "… carrying your whipped ass all over the place chasing after blondie *is not working*. Now, get your lazy ass up."

I snicker at Evan's words, but the laugh lodges in my throat.

Trying to clear it, I slowly wiggle a couple fingers on my left hand and pry my eyes open slowly and carefully.

Soft folds of fabric move beneath my hand and I can tell I'm in a bed. A sliver of light filters in through my half opened eyes and it is so bright my head immediately throbs. Sticking my tongue out to lick my lips again, a raspy vibration moves up my throat and out my mouth.

"Hhhh …"

"There he is!" Evan exclaims.

He's only a blur so I crease my eyebrows and concentrate on bringing the image into focus.

"Judd," Jake's voice fills the air once again, coming from my right, but when I flick my eyes to that side, my head is motionless as if it is welded down.

No matter what I try, I cannot twist it and with each muscle that tenses in my efforts, a shooting pain bolts down my back and something inflexible digs into my jaw.

"Hey."

My eyes waver, opening and closing in an attempt to adjust to the light. His face slowly comes into focus, automatically putting my heart on alert when I see tears welled up in his eyes.

Flicking my eyes down, I glance over, barely able to see the length of my body beyond the blur of my cheek bones. I take in rolls of soft, white pillowy clouds. *Wait. Why am I lying in clouds?* I seal my eyes closed then reopen them. Blurs of bright white come into view over my feet and like one of those hidden picture illusions, my eye sight pauses then focuses in on a white sheet draped across my legs down to my feet. I strain to look down despite something that is holding my neck still. Slightly nudging my index finger, I zero in on the movement and see that my arm is wrapped in chalky white bandages. No further movement reigns in my arm as I attempt to relocate the motion to my wrist. I center my vision in on the thing covering my arm, realizing it isn't a bandage at all.

"Your arm's in a cast."

I swing my eyes back to my brother at his words and the instinctive reaction ignites a series of sudden cluttered visions of me being flung around in Tristan's car.

"Wher …" I open my mouth to speak but it's hoarse and scratchy.

I gulp down nothing in particular, but work to assemble any amount of moisture so that I can form words. It's like someone shoved my mouth full of sand down my throat.

"Here, this will help," Jake says as something solid and pointy comes to rest at the corner of my lips.

Trusting my brother, I close my mouth around it, immediately familiar with the shape of a straw. I muster up enough strength to draw the contents up with a weak suck that nearly drains what little energy I have in my body. Greedily gulping down the bland yet thirst-quenching flavor of water, I cringe as a pair climbs across my chest and up my side. My throat screams out in relief and my stomach rebels with a roar.

"Take it easy. I don't think you should drink too much at first."

Bullshit. I'm thirsty as hell.

My brother obviously doesn't read into my desperation, because the straw quickly gets pulled from my mouth, leaving me impatient and frustrated.

"Where …" I stop, still feeling as though birds have taken up nesting in the back of my throat.

"Should I call the nurse?" Evan asks and I assume he is talking to Jake or someone else.

I have no clue what is going on but his words clear up a bit of the mystery that I continue to try and verbalize. Shifting my gaze straight forward, I stare up at the ceiling, hoping to steer off blasts of pain in my head. A loud buzz behind me has my heart airborn and my eyes stretched open further than I have pushed them. A slicing sensation splinters down my nose right as a female voice booms out from behind me, with a bit of static and crackling like an intercom or speaker.

"Can I help you?"

"The doctor said to let you know when he's awake," Evan's voice halts for a second then that sarcastic tone that I am so used to hearing rings out loud and clear. "Ahhh … so yeah, he's awake now."

"We'll send the nurse," the loud, crackling sounds of the same female voice replies.

Without full mobility of my head, I manage to flick my eyes back and forth over my surroundings and it becomes one hundred percent clear that I am in a hospital. With this revelation, all sorts of sounds, sights and feelings begin to stand out and my confusion is partially satisfied.

A tightening over my bicep clamps down and a hissing sound rises into the air. The vice on my arm gets tighter and tighter until I know every vein in my arm has to be bulging and ready to explode. After an extended hold on my arm, I clamp my jaw as the grip releases, allowing me to relax a bit. A slow and steady beeping bounces along and sounds as if it is behind my bed. More chattering rises from beyond my room with an amplified voice that sounds like it is calling out over a speaker phone. I stare ahead, looking up at the snow white ceiling that consists of large squares. Sweeping my gaze down without moving my head, a row of cabinets surrounding a sink that is cluttered with medical equipment finally comes into view.

Closing my eyes from the overwhelming knowledge of where I am, my mind fills with images. Pain and fear that I have never experienced in my life flicker in my head as I remember screeching tires and the panic on Tristan's face as he worked to regain control of the car.

We had a wreck. It's a single thought, but it is very clear as memories of my brother's screams and my own rise up to the forefront of my mind. Whirling through the sequence of events, I immediately slam on the brakes with one thought inside of me screaming, pleading and begging for an answer.

"Tristan," I whisper out as my body finally relinquishes moisture.

My eyes haze over with tears and my heart clamps with the thought that my brother could be dead. *Please, no.*

A sudden tornado of images and memories fly through my head, seizing my heart in its wake.

"Tristan, push me higher," I scream as he runs under my swing for possibly the twentieth time today.

"I am, I am," he laughs, two deep dimples adorning each cheek.

"This is how you build a snowman Right like this." He pierces the ribcage of the middle ball of snow then hastily shoves a smaller twig right in the center of Mr. Snowman's face. *"Then we can use these for the eyes and mouth."*

He adds several pebbles in a large, curved-up arc below the twig and two above it to finish it off. I stand back in awe. It looks just like the one on TV.

"I'm gonna make one just as cool," I shout in amazement, already on my knees, balling up a huge heap of snow.

"Me too," Jake yells, jumping to the ground with me.

Tristan cracks up, falling to the ground with us. *"We'll make a snowman family."*

Knock, knock ... I rack my fist on Mom's bedroom door. The door opens a crack and Tristan looks out at me.

"Hey, I was going to sit with Mom for a while." I try to glance behind him, but he has the door held nearly shut. *"Is everything ok?"*

Tristan's eyes seem dazed as he searches for words. *"The nurse just got here, so it's probably not a good day. Don't you have practice?"*

"Practice has been over for an hour."

"Well then wash up and warm up some of the leftovers in the fridge for you and Jake." He closes the door without another word, leaving me feeling shut out.

I know he takes care of Mom and I get that he tries to protect Jake and me from seeing everything this disease is taking from her, but sometimes it's too much. I'd rather see her sick than not see her at all. Maybe that's selfish, but she's still here and I miss her.

Bursting into the bedroom, the immediate sense of stillness and emptiness slams into me as I see Tristan sitting silently on the bed, his head hung over his knees as he rocks back and forth. He looks up and my heart explodes. This isn't real. I want to speak. I want to scream that it's not true, but the tears racing down his face tell me all that I need to know, everything that was explained to me before my guidance counselor drove me and Jake home.

Tristan shakes his head as he looks at me, pain and agony crum-

pled across every feature of his face. "She's gone ... she's gone," he barely gets the words out. He holds his hands out and stares down at them. "I was supposed to take care of her."

I want to fall on the bed with him. I want to tell him that he did take care of her, but everything inside of me is gone, vacated, gone with her. I didn't say goodbye.

A noise sounds behind me and I glance back. Jake is sliding to the base of the floor beside the doorframe, his body shaking and sputtering with every excruciating sob and that makes my heart clamp so tight that the crushing feeling may be visible.

"Jake, Judd, come here ..." Tristan breathes out in a quivering tone.

Jake jumps to his feet and runs to my brother, collapsing onto the bed with Tristan's arms immediately wrapping around his shoulders. I want to join them, I want to go, but all I can do is stare at the empty bed behind him, the hospital bed that took residency in our house the last year and a half as my mom deteriorated. I look to Tristan and his eyes land on me, but my feet are nailed to the floor.

"Judd ... come here," he sucks in a deep breath and reaches an arm out, while still holding tight to Jake.

I can't; I want to but I can't. I didn't even say goodbye. Turning in a furry of emotions and heartache, I race out of the room, flinging the door out of my way and run ... run ... run and run. I don't even care where I go.

Before the front screen door slams shut, I hear my brother call out, "Judd!"

Coming out of my thoughts, I look over at Jake and tears run down his face as well.

No, God, no, please, no! Not my brother, not like this!

Jake's breathing sounds labored as a loud beeping rings out over and over and over.

"Judd, calm down. Tristan is fine. He's alive," Jake's shaky words set my strangled heart at ease somewhat and I quickly realize it is my breathing that is in distress.

"What's going on?"

A movement in my peripheral vision and a thud has me looking past Evan's head to a female figure coming towards me.

156

"He's just scared I think," Jake says as the woman walks past my line of sight and the sound of papers crinkling sounds behind my head. A continual beeping makes me want to scream out in annoyance. Fingertips press down on my wrist and another soft hand slides over my temple.

"Your heart rate just shot up. You also look like you ripped open the cut on your eye. How are you feeling, sweetie?"

The beeping keeps going off, making me grit my teeth and forget about everything that is currently going on. *How do I feel? I feel like I just woke up from a damn car wreck; what does she think?*

"Call me crazy, and of course this isn't a medical assessment or anything, but I'm thinking he feels like shit," Evan says my exact thoughts out loud.

I drop my eyes to him. He has his signature smirk on his face and it automatically makes me want to laugh.

"Also, is there any way to shut off that annoying ass beeping noise?" he adds and I find myself chuckling despite the pain in my body and level of stress from what has happened. *Thank you, Evan.*

She belts out a deep laugh and counters Evan's sarcastic comment, "I tell you what, you're mouth is the only reason I keep coming back in this room. If I didn't know better, I would swear you were flirting with me."

Evan's stunned expression gives way to a huge smile and I glance up at the nurse who is leaning over me, making slow swipes at the skin near my eye. Evan mumbles something and she laughs.

"Your friend here sure has been keeping this floor entertained." Her body shakes as she laughs. "This may sting but hold still," she says as I study her face, finally able to see her.

The wrinkles around her blue eyes bunch up and her eyebrows lower as if she is sympathizing with the prickles of pain flaring up from my eyebrow to my cheek bone.

"Fortunately, this pretty little face of yours wasn't damaged too much, but it does look like you just got punched in the nose." Her thin lips curve into a kind smile and her eyes fill with compassion as I sputter out a laugh at her assessment of my injuries.

"I was."

Her brows rise as her face hovers a few feet above mine. She laughs, then a soft touch brushes over my hand and a pressure is eased off of my fingertip and then replaced.

"It sure must feel like that."

I huff out a small laugh, realizing she doesn't think I'm being serious.

"So, can you tell me how you feel?" She goes on.

Evan starts to pipe up, but quickly stops. "Oooww! You don't have to kick me. I thought you were supposed to be helping people."

The nurse grins and I get the idea that I may have been here longer than a day.

"How long …" My voice garbles as I glance over at Jake, hoping for another drink. The straw immediately finds my mouth and I guzzle down more, needing something wet.

"Careful. We don't want it coming back up. Throwing up is not good in your state."

Jake pulls it away from my mouth with her words and I snap my attention back up, quickly glancing at the name Stacey in bold print on her badge before my eyes land back on her face.

"How long have I been here?" I barely get out. *And where is here?*

Her face brightens with a sympathetic smile, "Three days, sweetie, but it has been very eventful. The doctor will be here to fill you in soon," Nurse Stacey pauses, looking at me for confirmation that I understand, I assume.

"Ok," I rasp out, shocked that I have been in a hospital for that long.

I wish I had a mirror above the bed so I knew what I looked like or the extent of my injuries. *Holy shit! Three days and I have no memory of it!*

"For now, let me check over a few things. I would prefer if you don't move around too much, but could you move the fingers on your left hand for me?" Her words surprise me, but it must be standard after an accident to make sure everything is functioning properly.

"He moved his fingers earlier," Jake announces as I twitch each of my fingers, mechanical with each movement.

"His feet moved around under the sheet when he woke up, too," Evan adds, my level of confusion growing by the second.

Do they think I am paralyzed? Am I paralyzed? I think as I instantly move my feet underneath the rough, coarse sheet.

"Oh, that's good. Doctor Raynes will be glad to hear that. Are you comfortable or are you feeling a lot of aches and pains?" She asks like I'm a child with their first booboo.

I think about the question for a moment and focus on my body. My mind still comes in and out of foggy thoughts, but my skull feels as though someone smashed a two-by-four over it, especially my neck. The skin at the base of my skull is wound so tight it may split and my head is throbbing.

Breathing in a large breath, slivers of pain vibrate through my ribcage and deep inside, making me very aware that something must have slammed into my side during the wreck. The pain is dull and muffled somewhat, but still hurts like hell. With each deep gulp of air I breathe pain slices through every inch of me as if shards of glass are coursing through my veins. I immediately shallow my breaths in an attempt to ward off that horrific pain.

My left arm seems to have plenty of feeling and moves like my joints have been put on ice, but they still move with minimal pain. In an effort to wiggle my other hand, a sharp piercing jolt shoots across my neck and down my arm.

"My …" I clear my throat, "right side, my neck and right shoulder," I tell her instantly. "My shoulder and side hurt pretty badly."

"Ok, I'll let the doctor know."

She messes with a few more things beside the bed and out of my line of sight before leaving the room. I take a couple more drinks of water, thanks to Jake, before feeling confident enough to dive into questions.

"What happened exactly?" I flash my eyes back and forth between Jake and Evan, pissed that I cannot bend at the neck. "What is on my neck?" I spit out, sounding extremely annoyed.

"It's a brace, dude. You'll get it off soon," Evan answers, but Jake quickly jumps in.

"Try not to move your neck for now. The brace is to stabilize your movement so no damage is done while your shoulder is healing. The doctor told me that any further trauma to your spinal cord could …" he trails off, but I keep my eyes on him.

What the hell is wrong with my shoulder and what the hell hap-

pened to my spinal cord or what could happen if I move my neck?

"Well, it wouldn't be good. Just try not to look around much." I raise my eyebrows, a tight and stiff tug festering up on the side of my face where the nurse was fiddling.

"Don't do that either." Jake jets around my bed and disappears to the other side of the bed.

"No, it was in the other drawer," Evan says as I hear a couple sliding and clicking sounds, which I assume would be the drawers Evan is referring to.

"Are you sure you should do that already? He looks pretty rough." Evan's statement lights a bulb in my head, making me want to bolt up and see what my brother is searching for.

"A mirror?" I ask, not all together sure if I want to see or not.

"Yeah, here it is," Jake says near my ear. "You look pretty beat up, but the doctor said you shouldn't have any scarring on your face. Most of it was just minor bruises and cuts. Do you want me to show you?"

Wishing I could nod my head because my words are stuck in my throat, I gurgle out a response, "Mmhuh."

"Geez, this is a bad idea," Evan says as Jake draws a mirror up in front of my face.

My eyes zoom to the image staring back at me, but I'm not sure if he is holding it right, because surely this isn't me.

Both of my eyes are swollen and black with streaks of yellow spread out beneath the sockets. My left eye has a cut that extends from my brow to my cheek bone and it looks as if it's been smeared with some sort of shiny substance, glue possibly. My nose is twice its original size and flaming red along the ridge with shades of blue and purple at the sides. It's a mess of colors and at any given moment I expect to hear a chorus of horns honking and bells ringing as the circus comes to claim me.

Moving my gaze over my cheeks, I see dozens of nicks and cuts, several with small bandage strips holding them shut. Sticking my tongue out to make sure this is my reflection, I run it over my cracked up, dry, flaking lips and breathe out a sigh. A couple more nice-sized cuts stand out on my forehead and another along my chin that also looks like it has been glued closed.

"Wow," I whisper, wishing this is nothing more than a dream.

Lost

I STARE AT MY bruised and banged up reflection for quite a while without anyone saying a word. I don't think Evan or Jake knows what to say; I wouldn't know what to say in their position. There is so much I want to know, yet I cannot find the words. The few memories that have surfaced have me jumping out of my skin. The aroma of burnt rubber mixed with the sounds of crunching metal, glass and bones make me wish I could tear the thoughts right out of my head.

"I know it looks awful," Jake starts with a shaky voice then stops.

"Yeah, you seriously look like a piece of crap, but I think what may be on your brother's mind is ..." Evan pauses as Jake drops the mirror and moves into my line of sight.

He doesn't let Evan finish, "I thought you were dead." My little brother's eyes fill with tears and it is at this moment that I finally think of something other than my pain.

"I thought you both were dead. I thought I ..." Jake looks at me through exhausted, bloodshot eyes and I just now see the toll this has taken on him.

My brows lower, reminding me of the cuts on my face. "Jake, I'm going to be fine. I'm so sorry." I can't imagine what he is feeling; what this did to him, knowing he may be alone. We've all felt that, I did only minutes ago, yet he felt it times two. "Have you seen Tristan?"

"I've seen him, but he hasn't woken up yet. You both have been in and out of surgery since you got here, so it's been hard going back and forth between you two. I'm keeping tabs on him and the doctors are keeping me up to speed."

Feeling as if a weight is suddenly pressing down on my body and pulling me under, exhaustion starts to set in and I slowly blink my eyes in an effort to stay awake.

A clicking sounds behind Jake and I hear an unfamiliar voice call out, "Good afternoon Mr. Michaels. I'm Doctor Raynes. I hear you have finally decided to join us."

Jake steps aside and a dark-complected, older gentleman with salt and pepper hair and deep brown eyes walks into my line of sight. His mouth tugs at the sides with a small smile as the same nurse from before comes up beside him. She flashes me a kind smile that somehow raises my spirits despite all that has happened along with my level of tiredness and confusion.

They both walk to the side of my bed and paper crinkles again. Jake and Evan take their seats on either side of me and the doctor's voice rises up as he walks to the edge of my bed by my feet.

"I hear you are able to wiggle your feet and hands. Do you feel any numbness in your arms and legs?" He asks as he flips the sheet off of my left leg and proceeds to slide one hand under my calf and places the other at the bottom of my foot.

"Can you lift your leg at the hip and bend your knee for me."

"Yeah." I do as he says with ease then repeat as he walks to the other side of the bed and grabs my right leg.

"It doesn't feel numb?" he asks, but doesn't wait for my answer. I am beginning to think he is speaking just to hear the sound of his own voice. "Good. Any tingling sensations?"

I chuckle to myself, just as Evan snickers loudly beside me. *Oh yeah, I have sensations all over my body; it's called pain.*

Even though all the silly questions are frustrating me, I refrain from being a smartass and answer the doctor with as much honesty as I can, "Not that I can feel, but I am pretty tired."

"You're going to wear out pretty fast. You've been through a lot not to mention the anesthesia from your surgery this morning is still in your system. I'm not sure if your friends have filled you in at all but you sustained several severe injuries during the car wreck. Do you remember anything?"

"Yeah, I think I remember most of it. It's sketchy but I've re-membered clips here and there, more than I want to remember," I say, widening my eyes to stay awake.

"Careful, honey. You keep busting this cut open."

Cool fingertips swipe along my brow and I glance up to see Nurse Stacey tending to my eye wound again.

"It's good that you are remembering. However traumatizing the event was, any source of memories with the blow you took to the head is a positive sign. When you were brought in, you had a large gash at the top of your scalp. The impact, either from being thrown from the car or possibly the landing, also put a significant amount of strain on your neck causing swelling around your spinal cord. With inflammation like yours it is typical to see temporary paralysis and sometimes even permanent. Although you have been unconscious or under anesthesia over the course of the last few days, when you were somewhat lucid you exhibited absolutely no movement in your limbs. I will order another scan in the morning to ensure that most of the swelling has gone down."

I struggle to hang on to everything that he says. "What's wrong with my side? I have a sharp pain when I take a deep breath."

"Ahhh, yes. First I want to say that you are a walking, talking miracle, son." He smiles again and moves to the side of my body that has been hurting. Positioning his hand above the right side of my chest he begins to explain, "One significant and nearly fatal injury that sent you immediately into surgery was a scrap of metal that was lodged in your right ribcage only centimeters from puncturing your lung. When the EMTs arrived on the scene, you had stopped breathing …"

A deep sigh comes from Evan's side of the bed and a blur of movement darts up in my peripheral vision. "I need to step out for a sec," Evan announces suddenly.

The door snaps shut behind him and Jake stands up.

"I'm going to go check on him, Judd. I'll be back," Jake says then races out the door, leaving me even more puzzled.

After Doctor Raynes explains all of my injuries to a point where I have no idea what exactly is wrong with me, he leaves and finally lets me rest. It takes no time for sleep to grab hold of me and pull me away.

The next morning goes by quickly with me being wheeled into room after room for scans and lab techs coming and going drawing blood and checking my vitals. Of course, I always have the company of Jake and Evan when I return back to the room.

The doctor checks in once, drawing a picture of positivity in terms of my condition and I try to stay focused but my attention wonders to Alyssa. With the chaos of everything, I haven't had time to call her yet or even ask Evan or Jake if they've called her. The fact that she is not here leads me to the conclusion that they definitely have not. She would be here, if she knew what happened. She has to think I forgot about her.

My ears tune back to the doctor, who stands by the bed giving a more in-depth assessment of my injuries.

"… extensive amount of damage to your shoulder. The break in your collar bone and damage to your rotator cuff alone will take six to eight weeks to heal, but you may very well always experience a little discomfort in your shoulder. Hopefully we can get you back to a 100% before you know it." His words immediately make me think of my scholarship.

"I'm supposed to leave for UCLA in a couple weeks for freshman football training. Will I be good to go by mid-semester?" I ask, worried that all my hard work has now been washed down the drain.

The doctor sighs and presses his lips together in a frown. "Honestly, I don't think football is going to be a good career to fall back on with the level of damage your body sustained. We see a lot of the same injuries in relation to sports, such as a torn rotator cuff and a broken collar bone, but you had it all and another blow could cause irreversible damage. I will put my recommendation out there by saying you definitely should not play, but the final decision is up to you. With that said, you will by no means be in stable enough condition to play this fall. You will also have to do physical therapy for a while to get your arm back to working order so I will not be able to release you. Give your body time to heal."

He gives me a sympathetic look and adds, "I would recommend you take a year off and then you have a tough decision ahead for next year." He smiles then exits the room, leaving an awkward silence behind.

I can't play football? That's all I've worked towards. I sacrificed my entire high school social life all for that scholarship and now I may have to kiss it all goodbye.

"So you transfer to the local college and get to hang around for another year. That's not so bad. By next year, you'll be good to go and can transfer." Evan tries his best to lighten the dark news that the doctor just delivered, but I still feel as though I've been told I'll never walk again.

"Judd, call them and let them know the circumstances," Jake says.

My world is spinning out of control and all I want to do is hear one voice; she's the only thing that can ground me right now; she's the only thing I'll choose over football.

"Jake, can I use your phone?" I ask, desperate to speak to her after what seems like an eternity.

"Oh, actually I needed to talk to you about that. I just didn't want to bring it up with everything going on."

"What?"

"Tristan has been getting behind on the bill the last couple months and I had called him the day before the Fourth because the phone company said they were disconnecting our lines if the bill was not paid by the fifth," Jake grits his teeth as he delivers this news.

I blow out a frustrated breath at Tristan's irresponsibility, but then quickly stifle it, remembering that he is laid up in a room just like me, hearing about life-changing injuries and possibly facing the same hellacious dreams that I have. *It's only a phone, but considering we are both racking up some serious medical bills at this point, the last thing we need is to add reconnection and late fees for our phones to the tally of bills.*

"Yeah, so not only is your phone gone … but if it had survived the wreck, we have no service," Jake adds.

"Actually, seeing how both of yours and Tristan's checks for your work this summer were also destroyed in the wreck, I was going to run out to my grandfather's office and re-cut you both a check today. If you want, I can swing it by here for you to sign, then Jake can go cash it and pay to get your phones turned on." I want to shrug my shoulders in question of how I'm supposed to afford a new phone at this point, but he goes on, "He could just pick you up a cheapy phone while he's at it to hold you over til your upgrade," Evan chimes in, bringing a whole new level of questions to my mind.

"I didn't even think about how we are going to pay for all this. Am I on the company insurance yet?" I look at Evan as he stands near the foot of the bed.

"Don't worry about that. I think it has all been taken care of, right?" Evan and Jake share a look and my brother nods.

"Ok, yeah … go ahead. Cash my check and get your phone turned back on. I'll worry about mine when I get out of here. While you're gone, can you get my laptop so I have something to do here?" Jake nods again as they both turn to the door.

"Wait!" They both stop. "Have either of you called Alyssa to tell her what happened?"

Evan's eyebrows shoot up and he looks surprised.

"Hell, it didn't even dawn on me to call her. I think we both have been so focused on seeing you and Tristan wake up that that was the last thing on our minds." Evan scratches his head while Jake shrugs his shoulders.

"Honestly, I wouldn't have known how to reach her anyways. I know you said she lived in Fairview but other than that I haven't a clue. You got her number?" Evan walks to my side with his phone already held out.

I laugh, wondering how I'm going to do this with an immobile head glued to a massive brace, a nonfunctioning arm and another arm that is too sore to raise more than three inches above the bed.

"Yeah, but I think I might …"

Evan laughs and quickly flips the phone around so he can punch in the numbers himself. "Oh. No problem … I gotcha. What's her number?"

Burnt into my brain since the night she sat beside me in the back of my truck and agreed to be mine, I say aloud each digit as Evan carefully dials. Even though every inch of me feels like it is tied down to this bed, my insides bounce with excitement at the thought of hearing her voice. What has only been a few days seems more like weeks from the time I last saw her face in the rearview mirror of Tristan's car til now.

Evan slides the phone against my ear with a clank as it taps the hard plastic of my brace. My heart drums with anticipation and the corners of my mouth tick into a small grin as soon as I hear the ringing. The ringing stops and I swear my heart does too, but then the wrong voice echoes in my eardrum.

"Hello."

"Hi…aaaa, is Alyssa there?" I ask hesitantly, hoping I dialed the wrong number. *Surely, I didn't remember her number wrong.*

"No she isn't. Who is this?"

Who's this? Who the hell is this?!

"Aaaaa … who is this?" I counter his question, unwilling to believe what could possibly be going on.

"This is Alyssa's boyfriend and this is…" he draws out his words, grating on my nerves and making me want to reach through the phone with my halfway good arm and choke his lying ass.

"What? You're her boyfriend? Is she there?" I demand, wanting to hear this from her.

What the hell! It has been four day; four days! What the hell kind of boyfriend could she have unless she went back to her cheating ex?

"No, she isn't. Did you need to leave a message?" he says in a smug tone.

"No…no, I don't!" I try my best to pull my face away from the phone, immediately sending a lightning bolt of pain straight down my neck and to my shoulder.

I look up at Evan and Jake who are both standing up against the bed looking at me with blank stares. No doubt they picked up on the whole conversation. *How freaking humiliating! How the hell is this possible?* Evan's hand slowly pulls the phone away, pulling it to his ear for a brief moment before tapping the end button.

"Ok, so that didn't sound like it went too well. Umm, do you want me to go kick…" Evan starts in with his humor, but I really can't handle it right now. *What is going on? Boyfriend?*

Shooting him a look that says not right now, Evan snaps his mouth shut.

"Judd, did you want us to hang around for a bit?" I know Jake is concerned, but I really don't want anyone around right now when I am helplessly hitting rock bottom over and over.

"No, I think you guys should go get the check and get your phone turned on. Don't bother with mine. I won't need it anyways."

To hell with taking the high ground; I plan on wallowing in my grief and feeling sorry for myself.

"You sure, because we can stick around?" Jake offers up once again.

"No it's fine." I give them a tightlipped smile as all the misery from today's news boils in my veins.

Jake and Evan hesitantly make their way out, leaving me with a cold, silent room and my screaming thoughts. *How could she?*

Laying in bed replaying every moment we spent together and every word we said to each other proves to be more torture than I can handle; I'm thankful when Evan and Jake return an hour and a half later.

"Here you go," Evan announces, striding up and placing my laptop on the side table.

"Thanks," I glance down at it, afraid to even look up anything I'm thinking. "Can you get the nurse and have her adjust my bed so I can sit up?"

"Here," Jake runs over and pulls a remote from my side; instantly the top portion of my body rises so I can finally see my surroundings. It feels good to actually be able see to where the hell I am. I look over to the door, saddened. *I just wish Alyssa would walk in and tell me that this is all a big mistake or cruel joke.*

"Thanks," I say again, this time to my brother.

"No problem. Are you going to be able to sign the check?"

I flick my eyes down to the paper he's holding. "Yeah, I can manage." Luckily with his guided hand, I sign it with minimal pain flaring up into my arm.

"Hey, you know what? I'll get your laptop hooked to wifi and ready for you to get on it, if you want."

He doesn't wait for my ok. He flips it open and gets it all set without another word, positioning the table in front of me so that it is low enough that I do not have to lift my hand much to tap the sensor pad.

"I think we're going to take off and get this cashed. Jake said there were some other bills that apparently Tristan *forgot* to pay before heading to the lake." Evan emphasizes the word forgot, knowing as well as I do how irresponsible Tristan is. "Last thing we want is for you to bust out of this joint and have no water, because you stink my friend."

I can only imagine.

"You want me to get you anything else before we head out?" I shake my head, but he quickly continues in on his waiting-on-me-hand-and-foot ritual that he's been on the last two days by refilling my cup with water and sitting it by the bed. "Ok … all set. I even opened a couple tabs for you with your newsfeed, UCLA's webpage and so forth." He stares down at me as Evan moves closer to the door, clearing his throat to signal that it's time to leave. "Ok," he says again before turning away.

"Thanks, Jake." I smile at him, a little worried about all he may be holding back. Tristan and I may be experiencing the physical re-percussions of this wreck, but Jake had to live through the emotional turmoil of hearing that his only two remaining family members were near death in some hospital.

They both wave their goodbyes and head off.

As I lift my hand to the laptop, I'm thankful for the stretching exercises that Stacey had me do this morning with my good arm. It is tender and sore, but in good working order. Every joint and muscle in my body feels eighty years old from the impact of being jostled around, so I consider being able to raise my good arm to my lap and tap on the touch pad a small feat in itself.

Slowly and carefully letting my fingertip glide along the smooth surface of my keyboard, my eyes follow the curser up to the search bar at the top of my newsfeed; n*ow for the challenging part.* Lifting my hand a couple inches to the left, I hit the 'A' key then shift it clear across the board and press down on the 'L.' Moving to the top, I hit the 'Y' followed by 'S' and another 'S' and then an 'A.' Letting my hand flow down to the space bar and up to the 'M', a shooting pain in my neck stops me in my tracks and I have no choice but to give it a rest. *This really sucks! Here I've worked my ass off to hit the weights 4-5 days a week through my entire high school existence and now a simple task like typing in a name presents a new level of strain on my body like I am trying to bench press a buffalo.*

As soon as my arm is softly cradled back into the mattress, the throbbing in my neck and shoulders lessen. I sure wish I knew when this brace would be off, but so far I have gotten no indication from the doctors or nurses of when that could be expected. Times like now, I am thankful that I am the patient, because if I were the doctor, I'd be out of this costume and more than likely doing all kinds of damage to my body.

My head sinks back into the lumpy, itchy hospital pillow and I close my eyes trying to will away all pain so I can continue typing. As soon as my eyes seal shut, the soft satiny feel of her skin surfaces in my mind at the same time that the sweet scent of strawberries rises into the air around me. Snapping my eyes open, I flick my gaze around the room, swearing she had to be right beside me. *Screw the pain!*

With strained movements, I raise my arm back to the laptop as if it is being levitated and rest my wrist against the bottom of the key-board for two more movements; left to the 'A' … tap and 'S' … tap then clear over to the right to finish off her name with an 'O' and 'N.'

With a deep, deliberate breath, I hit enter and instantly see a list of matching names pop up. The top picture catches my attention, but I quickly close my eyes when I see that it is of her and someone else.

After I've mustered up the courage to look, I peel my eyes open and stare at the picture. My gaze is unfailing as I am pulled in and staked through the heart again and again with the image. She looks into the camera with a closed mouth smile and a sparkle in her eye. I zoom in on her eyes and study the curves of her long eyelashes and swoop of her brows. Her nose is crinkled up like she has been laugh-ing and her high cheeks have the slightest hint of pink to them. She's beautiful.

My eyes wander over the picture, automatically straying down to her shoulders, then stop. An arm is casually draped around her neck and his hand is placed right above her chest. I snarl my lip, pissed as hell. Every fiber in my body is dying to rip his arm right off her shoulder. I finally swing my eyes over to this mystery guy; a guy I've only heard about, yet I despise everything he stands for; the guy who owns the same voice that I spoke to just earlier today; a voice I will not likely forget.

That's him? That's the guy she really loves?

His unruly blonde hair sticks out in all different directions and bleeds into hers as he leans his head against hers. He has dark eyes and a cocky grin plastered on his face, like he just got away with cheating on his girlfriend. *Oh wait, he did. Wow, what an asshole!*

"What the hell are you thinking, Alyssa?" I whisper to myself.

He doesn't look like anything special. Honestly, if I was a girl, I doubt I would even find him attractive. He's pretty goofy looking, if you ask me.

I glance back to her face and even though I know I was more than likely just some act of revenge to get him back for cheating on her, I can't help but feel crushed. I really thought I had found something. It felt so real, unlike anything I've ever experienced.

When I was with her I felt whole.

I felt peace.

Every minute of my life has been spent feeling as though I was drowning, sinking, being buried alive, but from the second I saw her, catching my breath no longer felt like a struggle.

It no longer felt painful.

It reminded me that I was alive and I was finally able to look at my life and realize that every turn, every crook in the road and every roadblock had led me to this moment ...

It had led me to her and I don't want to let her go; I can't let her go.

Now... ....

Now, I just feel empty

I feel lost!

Picking up the pieces

THE NEXT COUPLE DAYS are chaotic with nurses in and out of my room taking my vitals, blood work and wheeling me through the hospital for more scans. Luckily, the swelling in my neck has gone down quite a bit and I'm hoping to get this sheet of armor off my neck soon. I'm sure the doctor will veto that request as soon as I ask.

Sitting up in bed, I use my left arm which is more mobile with less pain today, to look up information on my shoulder injury. Not that I don't trust the good ole doc, but I'd rather look it up on the internet and read it for myself.

Going over several forums where athletes who had received similar injuries then proceeded to ignore their doctor's advice and ended up with permanent damage later, gives me a knot in my stomach. Comment after comment pushes all my hopes further away as I read about the potential repercussions and experiences.

One guy left a book long post stating that he experienced temporary paralysis due to a biking accident and despite the doctor's orders to give the dirt biking a rest he was back at it only months after his accident. That resulted in a harder hit the second go around, and now he is told he will never walk again. *Honestly, his post scares the hell out of me.*

I received a four year scholarship, however I need to call and let them know the situation. I'm hopeful that the coach can red shirt me for this year and start me as a first season sophomore. I have a lot of calls to make and things to figure out. Sitting out for a year will be more than enough recoup time, however, the fact that the injuries I've sustained are common for football players and just one hard hit could end it for me, has me on edge.

Shuffling sounds behind me, reminding me that Nurse Stacey is changing out the drip bag of my pain meds.

"Hey, look who we found," Evan announces with a dramatic eye roll as he, Jake and Tiffany enter the room.

Perfect! I shut my laptop and give them all as sincere a smile as possible. "Hey."

"Hi," Tiffany says quietly as she shoves past Evan and slides onto the bed beside me, immediately clasping my left hand in hers.

I stare ahead at Evan, wanting to choke him for bringing her here then gracefully slip my hand away from hers.

"I'm sorry. Are you in a lot of pain? Your brother told me you were in a wreck. Your poor face is so cut up" she says sweetly with a truck load of concern.

Leaning toward me as if she is going to kiss my nose, I shoot Jake and Evan a quick look that says "WTF" then my eyes shift back to her. This is the point when I really need this damn brace off my neck.

"Tiffany, I'm really not up for company."

Evan snorts out a fit of laughter at the same time that she draws back, puckering out her bottom lip. *That look doesn't even faze me today. Pout all you want. I'm lying in a freaking hospital bed, dealing with the fact that I may never play football, I just had my heart trampled on by the one person I would have given up anything for, I'm not getting any sleep with endless rounds of nurses checking on me all night, my body is stiff as if I've been sleeping on a steel beam for weeks on end, my chest hurts like hell and I am not in the best of moods.*

I glare at her and open my mouth to speak, but Stacey quickly cuts me off, "Ok, now I need to look at some of these cuts. I'm going to need your girlfriend to move for a minute."

"Ahhh ... she's not my girlfriend."

Tiffany looks at me as if she's hurt and a jolt of guilt shoots through me.

"Sorry … she's a good friend," I correct my statement and give her a strained smile.

"No problem," she whispers, stepping up and walking over to a recliner in the corner.

Jake smiles and looks back and forth between Tiffany and me. Everyone knows the story between me and her, so they all know just how awkward this is.

"She came by the house to see if you were back from the lake. I told her I was coming here and she asked if she could come," he explains quietly with a sorrowful expression. Lowering his voice more, he leans forward on the edge of his folding chair, "She is really worried about you … as a friend, you know?"

A cold draft brushes across my right side a little below where I had my surgery. Along with all the damage to my arm, the puncture in my side and a couple of cracked ribs all on my right, I also have several rather deep gashes that the doctor suspects are from me blasting through the windshield. I grit my teeth from the sting that burns at my skin along my hip bone as Stacey peels away the bandage.

Looking down to make sure she hasn't disrobed me completely in front of a room full of people, a wave of nausea courses through me when I see the nastiness of the wound.

"So what's the scoop? He's all healed up and ready to go home, right?" Evan snickers.

A bubble of laughter bursts from Stacey's mouth surprising us all. "Honey, that is not likely anytime soon."

I look at her alarmed. I never thought to ask her or the doctor how long I might be here, assuming they would be getting me on my feet as soon as the swelling in my neck went down.

"I think you are going to be hanging around for a couple weeks, sweetie," she says and my heart sinks.

"Great," I huff out, wanting to throw a temper tantrum like a little kid.

"Oh come on, it's not that bad here, now," she spits out a laugh. "I'm thinking the staff is enjoying your company anyways." She flashes me a mischievous grin and continues on her mission to change my bandages.

I crinkle my brows, still staring at her.

"Oh stop that before you rip open that cut again," she teases and for some reason I find myself wanting to smile at how tickled she gets. "You really don't think all those young nurses need to be checking your vitals as many times as they do, do you?"

I catch on to her comment, just as Evan does, "Who ... which one?"

My brother cracks up while Tiffany crosses her arms across her chest, clearly opposed to anyone trying to move in on what she has been trying years to claim.

"Oh don't worry, baby doll, they are talking about you, too. Three handsome young men all in one room is sending those nurses into a frenzy. You boys are the talk of the floor. We've never had so many requests for the nurses to work extra shifts." Her body shakes as she spits out a laugh.

Tiffany speaks up, more than likely in a deliberate effort to break up the conversation at hand, "So what happened anyways? I never heard the full story. Your brother just said that you wrecked."

"Good question? What did happen? Was Tristan ..." Evan asks, tipping his hand up to his mouth as if he is drinking.

I don't have the definite answer, but Jake pipes up, surprising me, "No, actually the doctor said they checked Tristan's blood alcohol level when he was admitted, assuming it was a drinking and driving accident, but he was below the legal limit."

"Seriously, because I swore I smelled alcohol when we were driving. Tristan kept arguing that he wasn't drunk, but I could smell something."

Evan jumps in to correct my assumption, "Dude, that pass to the lake is filled with distilleries. On windy days, you can nearly get a buzz just from breathing."

"So if he wasn't drunk, how did you wreck?" Tiffany asks, crossing the room then sliding onto the bottom of my bed.

She carefully places her hand on the exposed skin of my left shin, trailing her fingertips in a small circle over and over. I follow her gaze to my left thigh, where Stacey is checking another wicked slash in my body. Feeling uncomfortable with her affectionate gesture, I sneak a quick look at Jake and Evan. They seem oblivious to her actions as they vacantly stare at me, waiting for my answer her question.

I laugh, because I've already told them, but they all laughed it off thinking that I'm joking. "He punched me."

"You mean, he really punched you?" Jake asks with a look of awe.

"So your face looks like you just tangoed with a wrecking ball because your brother actually did hit you."

I laugh louder than I have since I have been in this bed. "Yes!"

"Holy crap! So you weren't just bullshitting us." Evan's eyes widen with this revelation. "Man, karma really bit him in the ass, didn't it?"

"Yeah, after he clocked me, I guess he lost control of the car. My face was buried in the passenger window so I didn't get to see too much before it happened," I tell them as a shiver rolls through me at the memory. "So how did you guys find out? I mean, do you know how we were found or how we got here? I vaguely remember someone kneeling beside me at some point, but it's pretty foggy."

Tiffany looks over to Jake while he looks dead ahead to Evan, sitting on the other side of my bed. The color drains from Evan's face and his throat wobbles as if he is gulping down a tennis ball lodged in his throat. *He looks nervous or scared.*

"Yeah, ummm … I left out only about fifteen minutes behind you." Evan takes a deep breath as Stacey's hand sweeps the sheet back over my leg.

Everyone is completely quiet, waiting to hear all the details that I'm now assuming only he has.

"As I rounded that massive curve that is right before you hit that little gas station, I saw a whole mess of traffic including an ambulance, which is totally unusual for that area. I've never seen more than one car along that road at a time, even during peak seasons," Evan rambles on nervously.

"Anyways, the ambulance pulled away just as I drove up and there was a group of girls that I recognized over to the side of the road watching as several police filed up and down that large embankment on the left side of the road." Evan's eyebrows crease together and he presses his lips together for a moment before speaking again. "When I walked up to the girls, one of them ran up to me crying saying how sorry she was. She had blood on her shirt and I had no idea why she was telling me she was sorry."

He chuckles an insecure, strained laugh, then looks up to meet my eyes. "After I asked why she was sorry, she told me that my friend that rented one of her father's cabins the night before had just died in a car wreck with his brother." Evan's eyes look glassy and he quickly looks down at his hands, which are folded in his lap.

Leaning forward in his chair, he keeps his eyes directed to the floor as he goes on. "I ran to the edge of the embankment and watched as the police men took pictures of Tristan's smashed up little ass sports car. I was hoping to God I would see a different car, but no … it was his … all mangled and smashed up. I stood there frozen." He chuckles again and glances up to me for only a second before looking back down at his fidgeting hands.

"I couldn't move. She said you were dead, that you both were dead," his voice cracks on the last word he says, and my body is exactly as he explains his own; I am frozen.

My heart crumbles with the thought of what that did to him. Since the summer after my mom died, Evan and I have always had each other's backs. We met through our brothers and after a while that is exactly how I thought of him; as a brother. He may have a brother and a father, but Jake and I have been his family for the last few years and he has been ours.

"After the wrecker got there, she filled me in a little more while I kept trying to get a hold of Jake. I found out that she stayed by your side until you stopped breathing and one of the other girls stayed by the car where Tristan was trapped. I left soon after and went to your house to find Jake. My phone rang as I pulled up and it was him calling from the hospital. He said you both were alive and in surgery. I don't think …" Evan takes a deep breath and looks at me with watery eyes. "I don't think I took a breath until I got to the hospital and knew you were alive."

The room is dead silent as we all imagine the scene that he came upon. I am a crucial part of this story, but listening to him relive it is like watching a tragic movie. A loud click sounds as the door opens, snapping us all out of our trance and I see a good looking blonde peak her head inside.

"Are you done with him? I was going to see if he wanted to get cleaned up." She smiles, stepping into the room with a large blue sponge in one hand and a small square plastic tub in the other.

I shoot my eyebrows up and look over at Stacey. *Just what does she plan to do?*

She laughs while nodding her head. "I bet they all fought over who was going to get to sponge you down," she says under her breath, yet loud enough that I can hear.

I look back at the slender blonde walking toward the sink across from my bed. I really have no idea what to say. *What on earth does she intend on cleaning? I have one good arm and am fully capable of washing myself. Geez, I wish I could get out of this bed.*

"What'd I tell you?" Stacey laughs with a wink, "Ok kids, let's go and give them some privacy."

Evan smirks at me, glancing back to the new nurse then back my way. He nods his head dramatically with wide eyes and mouths, "Oh yeah." On his way to the door, he flips around to face Stacey.

"So you're telling me all I have to do is go out there, have some dumb ass car wreck and I get to spend weeks on end having her give me a sponge bath?" he says, nudging his head toward the blonde.

The girl giggles and a shade of red spouts up across her cheeks immediately reminding me of another blonde. Jake busts out laughing and I look over at Evan, who is silently trying to get my attention by pointing out on his own body the exact areas I should have the nurse pay particularly close attention to. I hold in my laughter, too nervous to give in to his amusement. Evan spins around as soon as the nurse turns her attention to them.

"Oh come on, Lover boy! This isn't that kind of hospital." Stacey rolls her eyes, motioning for him to get his butt out the room.

The door snaps shut behind them all and I can barely hear Evan and Nurse Stacey joking back and forth. He gets a kick out of teasing her.

Nervously, I look at the new nurse and lay there feeling completely defenseless and somewhat exposed. She smiles and I desperately try to return her friendly smile, but instead I must look like I'm about to jump off a cliff.

"Relax. I'm not going to strip you down or anything. We do this for any patients that are stuck in bed. All I'm going to do is help you wash off," she says plunking a sponge into the now full plastic tub then quickly pulling it out, dripping with water.

Clinching her fists around the sponge with a squeeze, water runs over her hands and back down into the tub as she looks back at me. I gulp, a strange mix of anxiety, curiosity and thrill as I watch the water roll down her arm to her elbow.

"Here," she says placing the sponge in my right hand. "You have to be feeling pretty uncomfortable. Sometimes something as little as getting freshened up can enhance your mood."

Her face lights up with a bright smile and I slowly feel all the nerves in my body unravel, now knowing that she is not planning on fondling me while I lay here, staring into space.

The following week goes much the same, except by midweek, I get the pleasure of trading in my knight gear around my neck for a snazzy looking foam neck guard. Apparently the swelling is gone, but they still want to limit the movement in my neck. At least I can turn my head side-to-side now. The nurses continue to come and go at all hours of the night. By the end of the second week, they wean me from my drip bag of pain meds and switch me over to oral medicine.

Throwing the door open, the two faces I wait all day to see stroll in and automatically brightening my mood. Jake has finally been going home to sleep and Evan has been working days, but they are both completely predictable and undeniably loyal when it comes to showing up a little before six every single day. Once in a while I even get their company when my lunch tray is delivered.

Jake holds up a brown bag with what looks like a hint of grease soaked through one corner. "I figured hospital food has to be getting old by now."

He walks up to the adjustable table that holds my laptop and food tray that was just delivered a bit ago. Shoving the tray to the side, he slaps the bag down and rolls the table so that the oblong portion is hovering above my lap.

Digging into the bag with an extreme amount of excitement, my hand finds a wrapped up burger and a carton of fries. I pull them both out eagerly and sit them in front of me. The chargrilled aroma of bacon, cheddar cheese and hamburger meat filter through the air, making the caged beast inside my stomach pound its fists and roar out its demand for real food. Quickly tearing the wrapper off the burger, my mouth begins to water when I see the avalanche of cheese sliding out from under the bun and the ketchup oozing over two thick hamburger patties.

"That's what I'm talking about," I say with a smile right before I shove a massive bite into my mouth. "Mmmm," I murmur over and over as my tongue flings an array of flavors from one side to another.

"Oh wait; I come bearing gifts, too." Evan plasters on his cocky grin as he pulls a phone out from his back pocket. "A new phone, just for you," he sings out very proudly and places it down by my fries.

I swallow the heaping bite of food in my mouth and quickly gulp down a large swig of water from my enormous hospital cup. Grabbing up the phone, I look at Jake and then Evan.

"I'm not up for an upgrade yet. How much did this cost, because I don't think we can …"

Evan holds his finger up to stop me. "It didn't cost you anything. It's not even on your plan but good news…I worked with the cell company and was able to request your old number plus … drum roll please." Evan throws his hands through the air as if he is playing the drums. "All the info on your old phone was backed up so they were able to upload all your contacts, pictures, everything. Boom!"

I laugh at his delivery of this news and push the button to power the phone up. Immediately clicking on the photo's icon, the last picture I took pops up on the screen. My fingers push down on the main button instantly to get out of the picture and back to the main screen before my heart realizes that I was just staring at a picture of me and Alyssa; *too late.* A stabbing sensation vibrates through my chest and it has nothing to do with my injuries. *Damn, I miss her!*

Looking back up at Evan, who is still standing with an ear-to-ear grin, proud of his gift, I quickly speak so that I can refocus my attention to something other than thoughts of her. "Ok, so who's plan am I on and how is it not costing me anything?"

Evan slides down into one of the folding chairs that have come to rest on either side of my bed and kicks his feet up on the edge of my bed.

"Well, since you are now an employee of my grandfather's, he needs all his job foreman's to have company phones so that he has direct contact with them at all times."

"What are you talking about? An employee … a job foreman? Man, I cannot even get out of this bed at this point. How am I supposed to oversee construction sites?" I ask, clearly not following where this is going.

I worked a summer job and filled out the proper paperwork and W-4 for two months of work, but nothing past that, that I know of.

Sliding his feet off the bed, he slips a folded up stack of papers out of his back pocket and places them on my table.

"Well, I talked to my grandfather and told him you would be hanging around for a while and he said he would set you up. You're already hired … he just needs a few more employment forms filled out. Then as soon you are sprung from this place, you'll be helping me oversee that building site downtown where they're putting in that new mall."

"Wait, who said I'm sticking around? I already called the coach at UCLA the other day and he said he would redshirt me as long as he could get a release from my doctor here and the doctor they use for the players. Actually, I asked Doctor Raynes to send my medical records to the coach just the other day."

Jake and Evan share a look then stare back at me, completely dumbfounded.

"Judd, Doctor Raynes called me this morning. He wanted to tell me that Tristan finally woke up."

I immediately cut Jake off and smile, "Really? How is he? Have you seen him?" I ask impatiently, a million thoughts flooding my mind.

"No, I haven't. He doesn't want to see or speak to anyone. I'm just going to give him time. You know Tristan. I think he is probably beating himself up pretty good over this."

Jake's never failing optimism and forgiving heart shines through even in this situation. *He doesn't want to see anyone? Not even me after he nearly got us both killed? Will he ever think of anyone other than himself?*

"Yeah, I know Tristan," I mumble, looking at my unfinished burger like it is the enemy. *I'm not even hungry now.*

"Anyways, Doctor Raynes said he heard back from UCLA already. I assumed he had talked to you." I pull my chin up to level my gaze with his, not liking the hesitation in his voice as if he is delivering bad news.

"And?" I spit out, drawing my brows down in fear of what he is going to say.

"Judd …" he pauses and looks at me with compassionate eyes and a sympathetic heart.

My left hand flies to the call button and I press it so hard that I am sure my thumb print is embedded in the remote.

"Yes …" A female voice calls out.

"When will Doctor Raynes be making his rounds?" I demand.

"Ummm … it looks like he is on the floor so he should be in to see you in just a bit," she says before the line goes silent.

I don't even have it in me to say thank you; I just sit there numb and at a loss.

"The doctors in California don't think I should play, do they?" I pause but don't need to hear the answer.

Jake and Evan both look at me blankly, neither even able to respond. I look down at my tray, my heart once again torn from my chest as the bad news keeps rolling in.

"I'm never going to play football again, am I?" I don't wait for or expect an answer.

I let the silence surround me and I drown in the revelation that everything I've ever worked towards is gone. All the hours I spent playing, practicing and working out even when my mother was alive; was all for nothing. Endless hours of studying to keep my grades up, for what, so I could come close enough to touch my dream then watch it slip right through my fingertips? For an instant I want to hate Tristan for this, but I don't even have the energy to do that. All I can focus on is how am I going to move on? How do I pick up the pieces and go forward when there is no longer anything to move towards?

Breathe

AFTER A LONG, HEATED discussion with my doctor, he confirms everything Jake said and I am left with one thing on my mind; getting the hell out of this hospital.

The next week, I struggle and fight to keep my head above the dark cloud of depression that is threatening to pull me under. *I refuse to give in to it.*

Week three comes at me with the pace of a slug, but manages to bring brighter days.

"Ok, today's the day. We are going to see what those tough little legs of yours can do," Stacey says, throwing the door open with a few other nurses behind her.

"Great! Do I get wheeled to physical therapy or do I just stand and race out of here?" I ask, hopeful that they will hand me my clothes and turn their head so I can dart away.

Two younger nurses behind her, including the sponge bath nurse giggle and smile at me. *This must be part of my fan club that Stacey told me about. I really think she just likes to try and embarrass me.*

"Not so fast, sweetie. It's going to be tough, but no, we are going to stand you up right here and get you moving. The physical therapist has already been coming in daily and having you do leg exercises to keep your muscles strengthened so you should be able to stand fairly easy, but running is something you won't be doing right off the bat.

First thing is first though … we need to take your catheter out."

Oh Thank Goodness. Uncomfortable does not even cover that feat.

Twenty minutes later I open my eyes and let out a breath I was holding, trying to summon up any visual other than the nurse that is now standing at the side of my bed finishing up on removing it.

"There, all done," a brunette nurse says while patting my knee. "Now we just have to get you up and going."

"I'm ready to walk now?" I question.

She smiles, pulling her gloves off and tossing a tube into a small trash can lined with a red garbage bag in the corner. "Yeah but we need to see if you can go to the bathroom. Sometimes it's hard to urinate after your cath is taken out, but eventually you'll go. Do you feel like you can?"

"I could try …"

I smile at her and let Stacey and the blonde help me sit up without the support of the bed against my back. *Holy crap!* My chest feels as though it's been split in two with splinters of pain and soreness from lying in one position for so long. Bending slowly to one side to scoot to the edge of the bed, my stiff back screams to be stretched out.

"How are we doing so far?" Stacey asks once I settle on the edge of the bed with her arm draped around my back, gripping at my waist.

"I'm feeling like shit, how are you?" I mumble through gritted teeth.

She laughs as sponge bath nurse runs to my other side.

"Ok, do you need to rest or are you ready to stand?"

No time like the present. "Let's do this," I say, nodding my head slowly and not wanting to bring on new pain in other areas.

Slowly standing up, I bear most of my weight towards Stacey, who is someone I've come to trust completely.

The way these other two giggle and stare at me, makes me worry that they may just let me fall right on them just so they can have something to talk about. Not to mention, sponge bath nurse looks to be all of a hundred pounds and seems to be more interested in glancing behind me instead of to where my feet are supposed to be moving.

"Hang on." The blonde darts past me to a closet by the sink while the other nurse with short dark hair, quickly rushes over to brace me up on my right side.

Running back over, the blonde hands Stacey another gown and it is at this moment that I notice a cool draft blowing right up the back of my ass. *Great!*

"Oh yes, we don't want to be flashing everyone." Stacey laughs "Let's slip this on. You're liable to give some of these gals a heart attack walking around with your robe flapping open."

The other two giggle while Stacey helps me slip the garment on the opposite way from the first one. After it is secured around the arm brace on my right arm, they have me take small steps at first. My legs wobble and bend in a mechanical effort.

A few minutes later, Stacey helps me into the bathroom. *This has got to be the most humiliating experience of my life.* Luckily my feet are steady enough that I can stand alone and have some privacy, but after weeks of going without knowing I was my body doesn't wanting to work quite right.

"Ok, well … it's not working," my voice echoes in the small bathroom after a two to three minute stand-off with the toilet.

She belts out a loud laugh, "That's normal, honey. I assure you, all the plumbing will be back to working condition soon," she hollers from right outside the bathroom door.

Giving up for the moment, she helps me back out of the tiny room as I level her with a quizzical look. She says nothing, just laughs and as usual places her hand on my right elbow to gently guide me back to the bed. Not even ten minutes on my feet and fatigue soaks through me down to my bones. Once I sink into the bed, exhaustion from such a small task renders me defenseless, but after a little rest I am determined to try again.

A couple more days stretch by with my life falling into a semi normal routine of playing on my laptop, eating, pacing up and down the hall and visits from Evan, Jake and even a few from Tiffany. I finally cancel my flight to California and also go online to apply for a grant to the local university. Even though I can't play football, I would still like to go to college. Who knows, I may find something that I want to do with my life some day. This is the light at the end of the tunnel that I've waited for.

This morning, I'm taken down for another chest x-ray to make sure that my internal injuries are healing well. After the doctor evaluates the scans and gives the all clear Nurse Stacey returned to my room with discharge papers. I've never been so happy in my life to sign my signature to a piece paper.

"I am going to miss you, kid."

Sitting on the edge of my bed, I smile at her then stand to give her a hug. She is almost six inches shorter than me, but when I'm around her I feel like a kid. She has a motherly air about her that has put me at ease and managed to keep a smile on my face for the past three weeks. This road would have been far bumpier if she had not been assigned to my room.

"I'm going to miss you, too, but hey, I think I owe one hell of a hospital bill so they may have to come repo my ass in a few months. I might have to get a job washing dishes in the cafeteria to pay off my debt," I huff out a laugh, being partially serious. Our *bill has got to be ridiculous.*

"Ohhh … you'll be fine. Besides, I don't think there will be any complaints from the nurses if you have to come back," she chuckles then steps back to look me over. "You better get changed up and swing by the front desk before you leave. You need a hand?"

"Hey, hey, guess who is here to finally break you out of this hell hole." Evan's voice is a surprise.

"Oh hey," I crinkle my eyebrows over to Evan then quickly look back to Stacey. "No, I think I can manage. Evan might have to help me with my shirt and shoes."

"No way … I am not dressing your ass."

"Watch your mouth," Stacey walks over, patting him on the cheek in a teasing manner. He smiles, eyeing her mischievously as she walks out of the room.

"I thought Jake was taking me home."

"Something came up and he asked if I could come get you. Besides, I was hoping to get one last look at a couple of the nurses on this floor before you were sprung. So what's up? We gonna get going?"

He looks me up and down, scoffing at my awkward method of slipping one leg at a time into my jeans with slow, pained movements and only the use of one arm and a jacked up side.

"Instead of laughing, you could help you know," I point out, breathing through a sharp jab down my rib cage as I wiggle my jeans over my hips, carefully.

He snickers, "What?! No way!"

I cock my head and look up for a second, standing there, clumsily pressing my thumb and index finger together against the hard metal snap of my shorts. Gritting my teeth in frustration, the clasp makes a popping sound and I tilt my head forward, back to Evan.

"Got it," I huff out, pissed off that the smallest of tasks presents the biggest challenge at this point. "You wanna get the zipper for me," I smirk, fully screwing with him as I tug it up slowly with one hand.

"Hell no! I am not going near that." He looks down and I crack up. Walking past me, he grabs my shirt off the bed. "I'll help with this, but if you can't zip up your fly … you're just shit out of luck, man. I say just let the nurses window shop."

I choke out a burst of laughter as he helps maneuver my arm into the sleeve carefully, and then back into the sling. After I'm back in normal clothes, he helps me slip on my shoes, tying the laces like I'm a little kid.

"Count your lucky stars that I'm helping you with this. I knew I should have said no when Jake asked me to come. I wouldn't even do this crap for my brother or Dad if their right side was busted up."

I crook a smile and look at him as he gets the second shoe tied. "Yeah, but you don't like either one of them."

He huffs out an amused chuckle and stands up. "That's true."

I nod my head and stand with him, thankful that I've had a friend like him through the toughest times of my life.

Walking out the door of my room and down the hall for, I am hoping, the last time, I quickly make eye contact with another person that I owe so much to. Stacey sits idly behind a computer screen at the nurse's station in the hallway. She swiftly spots me, her cheeks lifting into a motherly smile.

"Well, I guess I'm out of here," I say, tapping my knuckles on the counter with a grin on my face. "Ok, sweetie," she says with a sigh, "Here …" Sliding some paperwork and an appointment card towards me, she starts going over the details of my release, "I already scheduled an appointment with your doctor for Monday, August 18th. He will decide whether you get your brace off your arm then and set you up with weekly physical therapy. So now for the motherly advice …"

Her cheeks puff up again, as she points her finger and raises her eyebrows in a semi-serious expression. Her words make me smile wider than I have in weeks.

With her index finger held up between us, she starts a count down, "No more wrecks." Raising a second finger, she adds, "No more getting punched." A third finger is held up and she grins. "… and you better quit flashing that dimple of yours around here, because it's driving these girls mad," she lowers her voice for the last part and laughs.

I ignore her request and grin anyways, looking around at several women, all of which have seemed to notice my presence as they giggle, whisper or return a friendly smile.

"Take care of yourself sweetie." She pats the palm of her hand against the top of mine and leaves it there for a minute, looking at me with nothing but concern and compassion in her kind eyes.

"I will. You, too, Stacey … bye … and ummm … thanks, for everything."

Evan trudges back down the hall after carrying my things down to the truck. "Alright, we're out of here. It's about time."

I turn and walk towards him as he walks closer, looking past me at Stacey with a smirk.

"Oh boy, what are we going to do around here without you?" Stacey and several of the other girls start laughing, bringing all attention our way as we head towards the door.

Holding his hands in the air like he is about to make a huge announcement, he flashes the nurses a cocky grin. "Ladies, I know your lives will no doubt feel vacant and worthless without seeing my face everywhere, but if anyone is looking for something to do on a Saturday night, I live only ten minutes from here and I'm always up for a sponge bath." He chuckles and spins around by my side, headed for the door.

Several goodbyes are called out, along with more giggling and smiling faces as we pass by.

"Judd, wait."

I crinkle up my eyebrows in confusion. All the time I was here, everyone referred to me as either Anthony or Mr. Michaels. They had listed me in the system by my legal name and no matter how many times I corrected them; they still called me by the wrong name. Turning around, the good looking blonde that introduced me to sponge baths runs towards me. "Here." She presses a piece of paper into my hand with a twinkle in her eye. "Call me."

No sooner than I grip the paper, she takes off down the hall before I can say a thing. Running my fingertips over the torn edge of the paper, I open my hand and look down.

"Candy," I whisper to myself with Evan peering over my shoulder.

"Man, that's a stripper name. Nice." He nods his head and smiles. Staring down at the seven digits that she scribbled down on the torn scrap of computer paper, Evan adds in a shocking tone, "And you said she let you sponge yourself off … yeah, right. Apparently she saw something she liked during your supposed rub-a-dub-dub time."

I laugh at Evan's attempt to rile me up as we head to the elevator and out the sliding double doors at the entrance of the hospital. *I'll let him think what he wants.*

Once we are headed down the highway, the last place I feel like going is back to the house. Jake is apparently busy, Tristan is still laid up in the hospital and the last thing I want to do is go home to an empty house when I'll end up dwelling on the fact that my football career is over and that Alyssa tossed me aside.

"Hey, can you swing by my mom's?" Evan nods his head and takes the next exit. *He knows where I'm talking about.*

Ten minutes later we pull up to the small playground that I played at as a kid.

"You mind if I go alone?" I ask, feeling bad for bumming a ride then asking him to stay put.

"Yeah, sure thing … I have some calls to make anyways." He gives me a thumbs up.

Pushing limb after limb and piles of brush out of my way with the crunch of dry, brittle ground under each of my footfalls, the tranquil sounds of water spilling into more water welcomes me to Mom's fountain. After shoving one more branch out of my way, I step into her sanctuary and look around, breathing it all in. *This is where I feel at peace; where I feel close to Mom.* The sunlight filters through the trees, blanketing the fountain in a soft glowing light that sparkles across the water like shimmering crystals that have been cast along the surface.

I slowly stroll over to the bench, careful to walk along the side of the walkway and avoid stepping on our carefully constructed pictures. Bending down to sit on the concrete bench, I gaze at the angel that looks up at me from the path. It's just like my mom; beautiful and one of a kind. She would have been proud of us for finishing this place. This was our haven, our place to come to relinquish all our worries and fears. It became part of Mom when she was alive and when she died, she became part of it, surrounding us when we are here and wrapping us in her presence and love as if she is sitting right beside us.

"Mom …" I whisper with a quivering voice, instantly losing all sense of control over my emotions as my eyes fog up. "I'm ok. I thought … I thought I was dying at first."

I clear my throat; I should tell her the whole story. So I start from the beginning, from the day I laid eyes on Alyssa. I ramble on and on as the daylight slowly flees from the sky. I've no doubt been here for hours, and although I keep expecting for Evan to call and tell me to get my butt back to the truck, I go on.

"Mom, I wish you could have met her. She … I can't even describe how beautiful she is. She made me happy." My throat wobbles with that confession. *God, she made me happy.* "She made me happy like I've never felt; like everything in my life was finally going in the right direction," I pause, looking down at my hands and fighting back a river of emotion. "I miss her." I look up to the sky and the emptiness that was inside me before I met Alyssa is stronger than ever. "Mom, I wish you were here."

I talk for a bit longer then walk around the path, carefully brushing off crumbles of dirt, dried up leaves and stray pebbles that have littered the walkway. After a bit, I head back to the truck to find Evan passed out, with his head resting against the open driver's side window and his feet kicked up across the seat. A loud creak sounds when I open the door to his grandfather's old company truck, sending Evan nearly through the roof.

"Geez!" he yells out, pulling his feet to the ground and bolting up.

We both laugh, not even bringing up how long I've been gone. He understands what this place means to me. Aside from my brothers, he's the only other one that has ever accompanied me here.

The next several weeks run relatively smooth after I get used to the use of one arm. With my right arm in a sling and a massive brace that runs up to my neck, I have to learn to do a lot of things differently and slower. Television, which used to be something I had very little time for has become my best friend.

Jake ended up running me to the college administration office a few days ago, and I am all lined up to start fall semester at the local college in Rosemore. Once I left the office with my line up of classes, I had a pit in my stomach knowing this is all real. I will not be going to UCLA and I will not be playing football. That mixed with the knowledge that Alyssa is miles away at Perdue happily in love with someone other than me, twists the knife a little further into my gut. *I wonder if she has left for Indiana, yet.*

August 18th rolls around and I finally get my brace off. After the secretary sets up weekly appointments with a physical therapist and they give me a couple pages of at-home exercises, Evan and I head out. We go by his grandpa's office so I can set up a schedule that will work around my classes and physical therapy. So far it is looking like I am going to be going 24/7, but I'm ok with keeping my mind busy.

Hopping back in the white work truck that Evan drives most days, I have an idea that has been bouncing along the surface of my mind.

"Hey man, you remember that gas station in Fairview that we used to drive a half hour out of our way after school just to get that insanely delicious buffalo chicken pizza?" I ask, reminiscing about good times from high school.

"Oh, I forgot all about that. Yeah, I remember that. Why, you hungry? I can totally go for a slice right now." It suddenly feels as if we've picked up speed and I laugh.

"No ... well, I mean sure we can get something to eat while we are there. Do you know that subdivision that is down the road from it? Twin Lakes or Spring Lakes ... something like that?" I look over at him and notice a deep frown.

"Yeah ...." He draws out the word and I get the feeling he may talk me out of my idea if he knows I want to go see where Alyssa lives. "I think I know where you're talking about. It has that small dance studio right on the corner by the entrance, right?"

Now he has lost me. "Since when have you taken dance?" I cock my head back in confusion.

"Noooo … I didn't take dance, dipshit … Piper did. That's how she and Abby met. They started taking dance when they were kids. I went to this silly dance recital of hers back when I first met her. Actually she didn't know I was there so I sat all the way in the …" Evan looks over at my scrunched up, baffled face and stops his ramblings. "Oh yeah, ok, so back to what you were saying. Why are we going there?"

"Just go to the gas station and we'll get a slice of pizza and go from there." I throw that out, hoping he won't ask any questions.

"O … K …" he says staring ahead at the road.

I need to hear from her what happened; I won't be satisfied until she can look me in the eyes and say what we had meant nothing.

Forty five minutes later, we are walking out of Ed's Quick Stop with our bellies full and our mouths on fire from the flaming buffalo chicken goodness that we just crammed down our throat like we hadn't eaten in weeks. *I forgot how good that pizza was.*

Evan and I stand side-by-side on the curb in front of his truck.

Stretching his arms up in the air, he lets out a loud yawn then speaks up, "So which way to Alyssa's house?"

I snap my head over to him, instantly sparking a spurt of pain in my neck from the sudden movement. "You know where I want to go and you're not going to talk me out of it?"

Walking to the driver's side, he pulls the door open with a creak and looks back at me. I haven't moved. I'm still in shock that he knew and never once thought to change my mind.

"Yeah, well, her older sister took dance right there," he points a block away to a small ancient looking brick building, "and the girl lives in Fairview. It's not hard to figure it out. And no, I'm not going to talk you out of it, because she owes you an explanation. Hearing it from her would be one thing, but being told by her boyfriend is just shitty."

With that, I jump in and we drive into the subdivision, making slow turns so I can eye the house and look for the one she explained. I'm not sure of her house number and I came up blank when I searched online, but I do know that she has a row of flower boxes in the front yard that her and Abby planted flowers in the year her father had cancer. I also know that there is a large birdhouse, painted to match their home along the side corner, another project she enlisted Abby to help her with when they were depressed over the news of their dad's sickness.

Finally spotting the house that looks like hers, I raise my hand to signal Evan to stop.

"That's it, I think." I stare ahead and don't see any cars in the driveway.

"Do you want me to park in front of the house?" Evan asks as he rolls slowly by the house.

"No … park across from the next house so I can sit here and gather my wits before I face her." I gulp down a truck load of anxiety and nervously rub my hands together, feeling a tugging sensation in my right shoulder.

"This ok?" Evan pulls to a stop where I told him to. I nod my head, unable to muster up any words at the moment. I'm about to jump out of my skin with the thought of seeing her after six weeks. This may very well kill me, hearing her say we meant nothing.

Just as I'm about ready to get out and face her, I watch as a silver truck pulls up to her house. A blonde guy jumps out of the driver's side and rushes to the passenger door. For a minute I think of telling Evan to just forget it then she's there. Right there … only steps away from me again.

The guy helps an older gentleman out, holding his arm around his waist to support him. She hops out of the truck behind him and all three of them slowly walk to the door and inside. I crinkle my brows up in confusion. The older man I am guessing is her father. He looked sick. My heart plummets, thinking over how scared she was to find out her father's results. I can't even think it.

All of a sudden the blonde guy comes back out with Alyssa on his heels. She walks behind him to the truck. My heart drops further, knowing full well that this is the guy on the opposite end of the phone only weeks ago. She isn't holding his hand, she isn't walking beside him, there's not anything that would lead me to the conclusion that this is her boyfriend as they stop and face each other talking.

She flips her hair behind her shoulder, looking down at the side walk and even from here I can read the sadness in her body language.

"I have to go talk to her," I tell Evan, my heart ready to leap out of my body and blaze a path to her on its own.

"Whoa, wait. Look." Evan grabs my arm to stop me from getting out.

I look up and over at Evan before looking back to where he is pointing.

Alyssa still looks down at the concrete drive, but the guy has moved closer to her and is holding her hand between them. My pounding heart drops into my stomach, causing it to churn and my blood pressure to rise.

Sucking in a quick breath that I'm unable to let out, I stare at him as he pulls her into an embrace. She doesn't fight it; she doesn't pull away, in fact she clings to him just like she used to hold onto me. I strain my eyes, trying to see where their faces are. *Are they kissing?*

"Man, I think we should take off," Evan's voice breaks through my thoughts, but cannot pull me away from the spiraling freefall that I feel in my body.

My hands tremble and my lungs become deprived of air until they pull away from each other, waving their goodbyes. She runs up to her porch and he jumps in the truck; I finally take a breath. It's on the tip of my tongue to tell Evan to follow the truck, but then I look back to the porch. Alyssa stands there looking out at the nearly vacant road in front of her house. She doesn't look happy, she looks deep in thought. Then my mind ventures to the frail man they helped inside; her dad. I clamp my eyes closed, a familiar heartache intensifying within me; the same heaviness she may be holding right now.

Sniffling in a trembling cry, Mom spots me peaking in through the crack in the door.

"Honey, come in."

Sucking in my stomach, I stiffen straight as a board, hoping I can conceal myself from my nosing around. I didn't mean to listen in, but when I passed by her sobs caught my attention. I couldn't help but inch the door open just a tad so I could see what was happening. For a moment, I thought maybe Jake or Tristan had gotten in trouble, possibly even gotten a whooping, but then I saw Mom. My eyes followed each and every marbley-ball of water rolling down her face and collecting on her shirt.

"Honey ..." The door swings open and her face smiles down at me, completely free of anger or aggravation. "Come in here so we can talk."

She returns to the bed and I follow, taking a seat beside her, but hesitant to say a word. She already explained to us that she was sick, we've discussed it separately and I've even asked Tristan questions I was curious about, but still day after day I've caught her crying all to herself. It's crushing watching her hurt and there's nothing we can do.

Her entire body rises a little with a deep sigh and her arms lie slack in her lap, empty and quivering. I glance up at her face, watching another escaped tear. Without a single thought, my hand reaches out, grasping one of hers.

"Mom ..." I stare at her, not sure whether to ask why she's sad. I know why and I know why she cries; she cries because she's sad, so I just stare. She glances over to me, both of us looking at each other eye-to-eye with no words; silence, yet so many things that need to be said or asked. Suddenly her arms fly around me, pulling me into a hug as she quietly weeps on my shoulder. I hug her back, automatically, wishing the pressure of my hands on her back and my chin buried in her shoulders could stop her tears.

Once I realize she may be at a loss for words like me, I speak up, "Mom, are you sad about being sick?" I still don't quite understand the gravity of the whole disease, but from Tristan's reactions, I've came to the conclusion that this is serious. "Are you in a lot of pain?"

She leans back, dipping her chin and holding me at arm's length so she can look into my eyes. I give her a small smile, leaning my head to the side, confused and scared for her.

"Oh honey, I don't even know where to start ..." she pauses, searching my face. "I'm not sad for myself, but I am worried about you boys. I can handle the pain and I will handle anything that comes my way, but you boys ..." she looks at me and her eyes glaze over again making the vice on my heart tighten. "I don't want you to have to go through this ... .seeing me sick and maybe even ... "

I look at her face and although she never answered Jake's question directly, I can see it in her eyes.

"Will it kill you ... this sickness?" I'm not sure where the question came from or why I worded it like a sickness is some sort of a murderer, but the thought of it stealing my mom away makes me feel like it is and suddenly, a slow burning hate for this disease starts to bubble in my veins. "You didn't really answer Jake the other day. Will it?"

Her eyes flick over to the side of my head and cool fingertips are instantly swiping my hair back behind my ear in a steady rhythm back and forth and again. Ordinarily if Tristan or Jake was a around, I'd shy away from this sort of affection that makes me feel like I am five rather than ten years old, but I don't mind it right now. Her tears have slowed and she has a slight smile on her face as she watches her own hands ruffle up my hair, so I'll welcome her treating me like her little boy, because I am.

She sighs with a bit of a laugh and stops moving, bringing her hands into her lap along with mine. "Sometimes you're too smart for your own good." I don't laugh, I'm too afraid of her answer. "Yes, it will."

Now my eyes fog over before I can even think to stop it. Spilling over, I take a breath and ask what I need to know. "When?"

"Oh honey," she looks shocked by my bluntness. Usually Jake and Tristan are the inquisitive ones that throw what is on their minds out while I sit back and take it all in, quietly. "Maybe three to five years. I have plenty of time, but I still worry. It's not leaving that I'm most worried about."

"Then what is it?"

"It's that this disease will rob me of my life gradually ... everyday. I fear the day when I won't be able to take you to the park or give you hugs or just say goodbye."

With that I understand; I see it. I throw my arms around Mom fiercely, knowing now that each day has to count.

"Hey," Evan gets my attention as I stare out the window deep in thought. "She's going to see us if we stay here. You saw her. Now I think we should go. After all that, I don't think this is a good idea anymore," Evan says in a tone I'm not used to, all joking and pestering set aside as if he can read just what all of this is doing to me.

"Yeah, let's go."

Ten minutes later we are headed to my house.

"Just keep driving for a bit. I need to think."

Pressing my forehead to the glass, my mind flashes with images of the car wreck and the last time I felt the cold panel of glass against my skin. I squeeze my eyes shut, forcing all thoughts to the back of my mind, especially the thoughts of her. *She did move on. She went back to him. Why would she go back to him after what we had, not to mention after what he did to her?* Despite the cool glass my face heats up, from what I'm not sure; maybe anger at him for taking her away from me or maybe humiliation for thinking what we had was something. Pulling my head back for a second, I tap it back to the glass with a thud.

"Hey, ok! No, slamming your head through my windshield. This is my grandpa's truck and I'm not covered on his insurance."

Slumping down in my seat, I glare at him.

"Ok listen. It's hard for me to be serious, you know that, but…" pausing, he glances over to me as if he's thinking.

There are no words he could possibly offer to help pull this knife out of my heart.

"Ok…" His tone is serious, so I sit up straight and give him my full attention. Looking forward at the road as he drives, he goes on, "I used to know this gir…person and something had happened to them that was…" He takes a heavy breath before continuing.

"Well it was pretty traumatic and sometimes certain things would trigger bad memories for them," pausing again, I frown in confusion of where this discussion is going, yet curious to hear the rest. Letting out another deep breath, he pushes through the topic, "When those memories would surface, this person had a tendency to hold their breath so that's where I came in. I figured it out pretty fast what was happening and I would always remind them…" Evan glances back at me, an unhealed wound flickering in his eyes. "I would always remind her to breathe."

He looks forward again, clearing his throat. *Piper.* A part of me thinks to question what happened or ask if it's her that he's talking about, but I know it is. Staring down at my hands, guilt and foolishness engulfs me. Here I am feeling sorry for losing a girl I barely knew and he has been hung up on the same girl for years. *Life just sucks sometimes.*

As if reading my mind, Evans voice fills the small cab of the truck, "My point is that sometimes life is shitty! You don't always get what you want, you know that, but you have to just keep breathing. When you think about the crappy points of your life, just remind yourself to breathe."

I stare at him taking in every word, knowing he is right. I watched my mom get sicker and sicker until she died, I watched my dad walk right out of my life and never look back and I nearly lost my brother and my own life; I can survive this … I can move past it; I can.

Looking up at the road, her face flickers through my head, her soft smile and bright blue eyes so clear I could nearly reach out and run my hand over the softness of her skin. *Breathe,* I tell myself silently.

"Turn around."

"What? Where we going?" Evan asks as he takes the first exit we come to.

"You feel like doing something ridiculously stupid and permanent with me?" I laugh.

"I'm always up for doing something stupid, but the permanent part sounds a little like marriage so I might need you to elaborate." Evan's smartass tone returns as he turns back onto the interstate, headed towards downtown.

An hour and an half later I am sitting back in Evan's truck, parked in an alley behind a store called Tatt-it. Evan has his arms crossed in the driver's seat, staring at me like I just willingly let someone saw off my arm. Looking down at yet another bandage on my body, a stinging sensation pricks at my skin feeling as if I just dipped it in scalding hot water.

"Ok, so that was more stupid than I can do right now. I hope that solved your problems, because that is going to look ridiculous when you're eighty years old and sporting bat wings instead of biceps. All you're going to see is some blob of ink and all your grandkids are going to be like …" He raises his voice an octave to sound like a child and I laugh at his sarcasm. "Papa, why'd you scribble all over your arm? That's a funny looking birthmark? What's that black thing?"

I crack up, pulling my seat belt over my shoulder before Evan fires up the engine. Looking back down at the bandage, I take a deep breath and let it out.

For years I've felt like I was jumping from one life altering event after another. It's been ongoing since I could remember. When my life would find some sense of normality, disaster would strike and I'd be back to dealing with some bullshit that left me wondering why, just like now.

Even though I used to stay busy with football, kept my grades up and worked my ass off every available second, I still continued to try to catch my breath from a sequence of events the led to me being one of three brothers trying to raise ourselves.

I'd catch my breath between being a positive role model and supportive friend to my younger brother.

I'd catch my breath from struggling with nonstop training and studying to ensure a scholarship along with working every available second to help make ends meet, that I hardly had time to enjoy being a teenager.

I'd catch my breath between remembering every moment that I had watched Mom's ALS get crueler and harsher until eventually her worn out body had to give up the fight.

Now, catching my breath has become second nature.

So this, this will be my reminder to stop and breathe when I'm drowning; to breathe when my life is spinning out of control; to breathe when I think I can't go on and to breathe even if it means I won't have her in my life.

Going through the motions

S UNDAY NIGHT COMES IN a hurry and suddenly it is the night before fall semester starts, the day I will begin to move forward in a whole new life … without football … without her. Grabbing my phone off the nightstand, I hit the button to light it up and see that it is only 9:21. Sighing, I run my hand over the picture icon then tap it before I change my mind. I have forced myself to not do this since I saw her in front of her house on Monday, but I have to. I have to see her like she was when we were together and she was not with him.

Bringing up the first picture, I smile at the looks on our faces. Alyssa has her eyes crossed and her tongue hanging out of her mouth while I am cracking up. I tried to play along for most of the pictures but her insane, goofy expressions had me laughing so hard I couldn't match her dramatics.

Swiping my hand across the screen, I flip to the next picture and chuckle. Her attempt at a duck face looks more like a kissy face while mine looks like I'm trying to roll my tongue. Shaking my head, I flip to the next and grin wider as my heart slowly slides into the pit of my stomach. In this one, I'm looking at the camera, smiling while she is pulling me to her side planting a huge kiss right where my dimple is.

Pressing my lips together, the familiar presence of that feature dips into my skin and I wish so badly I could feel her lips brush across it. Sinking back into my pillow, the softness surrounds my face and I close my eyes, wanting to get lost in memories of her for just a moment.

My hand vibrates and a loud chime sounds from my phone, startling me and interrupting my sulking. Looking down, my mouth drops open in shock; it's Tristan. For weeks he has refused mine and Jake's calls, even after Evan kindly dropped off a new company phone for him as well. Now out of the blue, he is calling. I don't even let it get to the third ring.

"Hello." I lay still in bed. *What on earth prompted this call and do I really want to hear what he has to say?*

"Judd …" His voice shakes. "I just wanted to hear your voice and know that you're alright."

I should be touched, but instead it lights a fire inside me that I have been holding at bay since the day we were in that car.

"Had you picked up the phone the last twenty times I've called you over the course of three weeks, you would have probably come to that conclusion a little faster, Tristan." I spit out, fury racing through my veins."Did it ever occur to you that for weeks I was sitting in the same hospital as you and I may have needed someone to talk to?" I raise my voice and grip the phone until my hand is numb.

"To hell with you, Judd, I'm still laying in a hospital bed," his venomous tone now matches my own.

Honestly, I don't even know the extent of his injuries. The doctors had relayed to Jake and I as to when Tristan had woke up and that he was doing better, but never the details of his condition.

"And I know this, but you ordered the hospital to keep all visitors out. I'm your brother and you almost killed me because you had a bad day, yet you won't even see me. Really? What the hell, Tristan!"

I'm so sick of him being so selfish. I know he is still in the hospital and I know what it feels like to want to be out of that bed so bad that you can practically taste it, but I don't think I would have made it if it hadn't been for Jake and Evan being there nearly every day. They kept me from sinking into despair. I've lost a lot just like him, but I'm not shutting the people that care about me out. All he does is run from everything.

"I shouldn't have called."

The phone goes dead before I can say a word and I stare forward at the wall of my bedroom in utter shock that he called then hung up, just like that. *Does he really care or is he trying to ease his conscious over the fact that his temper nearly cost both of us our lives?*

Still gripping the phone in my hand with it pressed to my ear, a tap, tap, tap sounds to my right and I glance up to the window. It slides open with a sharp scraping noise and Tiffany's face comes into view.

"Why don't you just use the front door?" I roll my eyes, rising out of bed in nothing but my boxer briefs.

After setting my phone back on the nightstand, I grab her hand to keep her from falling face first again as she climbs inside.

"It's not like I have parents that are going to ground me."

She gives me a bleak look then jumps down off of the ledge. "I know, but this makes both our lives seem more normal. You know, typical teenager sneaking in her boyfriend's window after his parents tell him to go to bed."

The word boyfriend in that whole scenario is highlighted like a neon sign with sirens going off in every direction; s*o much for our agreement to keep this at a friend level.*

"I thought we agreed to be friends." I sigh, slouching back down into my bed.

She falls onto the mattress beside me and blows out an exaggerated breath. "It was just a joke of what normal non-parentless teenagers may be doing, not an assumption of what was going on between us." She lies back on my bed, throwing her arms out to her sides. "Are you going to kick me to the curb?" she asks in a bland tone, looking up at my ceiling.

I scoot sideways to position myself better so I am not straining to look at her face.

"No. It's been a bad week and honestly I could use some company right now."

Sitting up quickly, she looks me in the eyes. "Can I borrow one of your t-shirts?"

"Yeah, they're still in the second drawer." I point at my dresser not wanting her to grab any of my shirts in the third drawer; that's where I put the one that Alyssa wore on the dock.

Tiffany quickly shuffles out of her clothes and slips on my shirt.

I browse on my phone while she changes with my back turned to her. As soon as the bed dips with her weight, I flip over gladly, unable to support my body on my right side for very long. The lights from the streets cast shadows all across my room and I can barely make out her clothes in a pile on the floor with her bra and panties at the top of the heap. *Just friends, huh?*

"Do your foster parents ever wonder where you are at all hours of the night? I mean they have to worry about you."

Her head tilts back with our faces only a short distance apart.

"They don't care. They already told me that I need to start looking for my own place since I'm eighteen now."

Her mention of her birthday reminds me that I have one coming up the beginning of next month. That in turn makes me think of Alyssa. Both our birthdays are in September, mine at the beginning of the month and hers at the end.

Tiffany scoots closer, her arms sliding over my waist and instantly making me tense up.

"Hey, this isn't really a good idea. I am kind of hung up on ..." No sooner than I start to tell her about Alyssa, I'm hit with a sweet breeze of strawberries in the air as Tiffany nuzzles into my chest. "Are you using a different shampoo?" I whisper with my pulse racing.

"Hmmm…oh no, it's this new strawberry-honeysuckle lotion. Do you like it?"

I barely register Tiffany's voice as I bend my head down and breathe in the aroma. Closing my eyes tight, I caress my lips over the skin on her forehead just to feel its softness. Instantly seeing an array of shiny blonde hair, I allow myself to slide my hand across Tiffany's waist, gently tugging the shirt up over her hip so I can feel her skin more. *God, I miss her.*

With my eyes still closed, I imagine Alyssa lying in front of me, turning her head so that her lips can meet mine. Warmth floods my mouth and my tongue goes into overdrive, needing and wanting to taste all of her. *Where is the whimper, that sweet moan that always escapes her mouth when I kiss her deeply?*

Opening my eyes, Tiffany is against me with her right leg drawn up over my hip. Her pelvis rubs against me and her hands run up my chest and into my hair pulling me closer. It feels good, but it doesn't feel right. I should stop; I need to stop now, but my heart hammers from the memory of Alyssa and the ache in my heart lessens with each wave of nostalgia.

I close my eyes again, wishing desperately for Alyssa to be right here again, even if it isn't real. She wiggles and worms against me as my hands glide up over the curves of her body. Grazing my fingertips beneath the loose-fitted shirt, I caress her skin inching up further and further until I hear her moan. *That's not the sound I wanted to hear at all.* I close my eyes tighter, fighting the inner voice that is yelling, "Stop … this isn't right."

"Get these off."

Tiffany slides her hands under the covers, tugging and pulling my briefs until they are down past my ankles and I let her with a knot in my gut, but the drum of my heart overpowering any sense of reason that I can pull up. I open my eyes for a second, but have to immediately close them back before flipping onto my back. Alyssa fills my mind, her hair flowing around her shoulders as her legs graze my hips. My eyes trail up her body as I suck in a savory breath of strawberries.

"Alyssa," I whisper, ready to feel her.

My fingertips run across her hips and I grab ahold of her gently, yet firmly with a sudden eagerness. Pressing my head back, another whimper fills the silent room and my eyes fly open.

"Wait! I can't do this!"

I look down at our bodies, a storm of relief blazing through my conscience when I see that we didn't get that far. My fingertips sink into the soft flesh of her hips in an effort to hold her firmly in place so she doesn't move around and make this any harder on me, literally.

"A part of me wants to, but I shouldn't because it isn't right. I have been so adamant about us just being friends and here we are falling into the same routine as before," I say squeezing my eyes shut. *I'm such an asshole.* "The truth is I love someone else." I look at her and instantly see the hurt welling up in her eyes.

I take a deep breath as she shifts her body back to sit on the top of my thighs.

"This is going to make me sound like such a jerk and I'm sorry, but when I kiss you, when I touch you and when you touch me, all I see is her face." My heart pounds rapidly with each word, because I know Alyssa has moved on, yet I'm not ready to. I go on, not that she wants to know this but more because I need to say it, "… when my hands run down your body, I feel her skin not yours. I smell her skin. All that is on my mind is her and the whole time I'm wanting her … not you and that is not fair to you." I gulp down a massive ball of hurt, anxiety and guilt and continue more for my own benefit, "No matter how crappy she did me, she owns my heart. I'm still in love with her and that is not fair to you."

No tears are shed as Tiffany looks at me with a deep, profound look like she understands. Gently leaning forward, her lips barely graze mine in a sweet and completely honest sense of care and compassion before sliding onto the mattress beside me.

"Are you mad?" I ask, afraid that she may unleash Niagara Falls with this question.

"No," she says weakly and unconvincingly then turns to look at me.

I slide onto my side, completely unable to read her. Using my good arm, I wedge my head up above the pillow, waiting.

"Really?" I'm stunned and not sure whether I can believe her.

"Is that so hard to believe?" She laughs and flips onto her side only a foot away from me, both of us still damn near bare.

Running her finger down my chest and stopping just below my sternum, she gives me a content, peaceful look.

"I'm glad you found that. I want you, Judd, but most of all I want you to be happy. I want both of us to be happy. I think we both deserve to find that, don't you?" For a second it seems like my comment to her from the night of my graduation party; maybe it did sink in. "I just hope this girl appreciates what she has."

I pull her into my arms for a hug, hoping her words are real and that my naked hug doesn't send mixed signals.

"Thank you for saying that. You mean so much to me, Tiffany. I care about you; I really do."

She leans away and smiles. "So you wanna talk about it?"

Letting my fingertips glide across her cheek, I realize just how much I miss Alyssa, just how much I wish this was her. A sharp, piercing pain echoes through my heart with that thought and so I decide to talk. I keep most of our time together to myself, but I talk to her in a way I can't talk to my brothers or Evan. I can actually tell her how Alyssa made me feel; I can explain my heart without fear of future harassment about me being whipped. Tiffany listens all night, just like a friend.

The next morning, I sneak out of bed quietly, letting her sleep in. It's weird waking up with a warm body beside me that is not Alyssa; that's probably why I faced the wall with my back to her most of the night. Last thing I want is to fall into a deep sleep with hot and heavy dreams of Alyssa then mistake Tiffany for her. The vivid dreams that I've experienced lately tend to wake me to a full on pup-tent.

Once I'm dressed, teeth brushed and ready, I race off to class. My first class goes relatively smooth and I make it around campus with no trouble. After my second and third class, my shoulder becomes a lead weight and it's painfully clear that parts of my body may not be completely 100% yet. As soon as the professor excuses us in my last class of the day, I dart out and head for my truck, shooting Evan a text in the process.

Me: You out of class yet?

I continue on my route to the parking lot, still clutching the phone in my hand at my side. Usually Evan texts right back like he spends his days staring at his phone waiting for messages, but not this time.

"Hey, wait up," a girl yells not far behind me.

I look around at all the bodies rushing to and from class.

"Hey hot pants," the same voice yells out a little louder. My eyes widen and I snicker at her choice of words. *They are definitely not calling for me.* Glancing over my shoulder to see this supposed 'hot pants,' a short, blonde-haired girl showing a whole lot of skin is practically on my heels.

"Wait up," the same voice calls out, looking right at me.

Is she talking to me? Hot pants ... what the hell?

Mid step, I halt all movements when a hand tugs at the back of my shirt. Lowering my eyebrows in a frown, I spin around and face her.

"It's about time. I've been chasing you clear across campus," she giggles, squeezing a book to her chest and spilling right out of her low cut shirt in the process. "I'm Bethany. I was sitting a couple seats over from you in English 101."

I offer her a half-hearted smile, pondering over what she yelled to get me to stop.

"Hot pants?" My eyebrows shoot up as she stares at me not the least bit intimidated by my question.

"Well, it was the only view I had." She bites down on her lip and casts her eyes down my body and back up to my face. "It was either that or 'hey, green shirt', and that just didn't sound very original. Besides, from where I was standing hot pants seemed to fit the bill."

I don't think this girl has ever read up on playing hard to get.

"Is that right?" I laugh, opening my mouth to introduce myself when Evan's voice stops me.

"Holy shit, you are not going to believe who was in my first class," he says, looking down at his phone as he rushes up. Tilting his head back up, he stops and drops his hand to his side. "Oh, hey," his normal cocky smile emerges as he turns to face me. "… and who's this?" Wiggling his eyebrows, he shoots me a smirk that shows his approval of the blonde.

"Oh, this is Bethany." I point over at the girl just as a chime sounds on her phone.

Glancing at her phone quickly, she shoves it into the bag at her shoulder along with the book she is carrying.

"I'm sorry. I have to go. I forgot I'm meeting my roommate for a late lunch. I'll see you in class though." She turns to leave, but suddenly turns and races over, pulling my hand into hers. "I work at Aftershock Bar and Grill downtown. You should come down sometime and see me, or…" she draws out her last word as her ink pen digs into the palm of my hand, making me grit my teeth.

The sensation reminds me of the wreck, making my pulse race with the thoughts of shards of glass tearing through my skin. If only this girl knew what I went through less than two months ago, maybe she would have chosen the soft edge of a marker to doodle on my hand.

"… you could just give me a call."

Slapping the lid on her pen, she steps backwards swaying her hips in an exaggerated effort and keeping her eyes locked on me. I really want to laugh at her bluntness, but in a way her confidence is attractive. As she spins around and races away, Evan lets out a low whistle, still keeping his eyes in the direction that she ran. His hand slams into my back, knocking me forward a bit.

"Look at you … Judd the Stud!" he belts out on a laugh, reminding me that the first number ever pressed into my hand is what landed me that nickname.

I glare at him through the corner of my eye, a bit amused as my feet stomp down grass on the way to my truck.

"Come on … what's with all the blondes coming out of the woodwork and giving you their numbers. That shit never happens to me. It's like you have some sort of wounded puppy syndrome that their sensitivity satellite is tuning into."

"Good choice of words," I snap. "It's like the universe is hell bent on reminding me of her."

I squint and finally spot my truck a few yards away buried in a mass of cars burning cement to get off campus.

"Whatever …" Evan challenges me, clearly annoyed by my ongoing hang-up with Alyssa. "You need to move on and speaking of blondes …"

I look over at him again with an expression that urges him to back off, but this is Evan; he says what is on his mind.

"Yes, I said blonde."

It's as if he's childishly shouting, "Nana-nana-boo-boo."

"So what I was saying earlier, guess who was in my first class." I open my mouth to throw out a guess but he won't shut up. "Guess, just guess." I cock my head to the side and laugh at his excitement. "Ok, you're never going to guess … little-miss-stripper-sponge-bath nurse and one of her hot nurse buddies."

"Candy?" I say, pulling my truck door open and sliding into the seat.

Evan scoots into the passenger side, immediately reaching for the stereo as I fire up the engine.

"Oh yeah, you know who I'm talking about," I don't even bother to look over at him as I steer out of the parking lot and onto Main Boulevard. Without a doubt, he is sporting that lame ass crooked grin he has when he has already roped me into something I'm not going to be too happy about.

"So apparently the brunette is in to me, and well … Candy must not have gotten enough out of those sponge baths, because she is begging for more." Snickering, he slaps his hands together and rubs them like he is trying to start a fire. "So this Friday, we are going out. You, Candy, me and … Lauren. There is nothing you can say; you're not getting out of this. I need this and you need this."

I glance over and take a deep breath, reminding myself … *Breathe.*

He goes on before I can get a word in, "Man, you need to move on. It was two weeks." Immediately shooting him a look with my eyebrows dipped down into a frown, he holds his hands up. "I know she meant a lot to you and made you feel all kinds of sappy and lovey-dovey and all that other sentimental bullshit, but she screwed you over … it is time to *move on.*"

My mind tumbles every syllable of his pep talk around until all I can do is agree to go Friday night. I'll just hold on for the ride and hope for a miracle. *It is time to move on.*

Fury

THE FIRST WEEK OF college flies by and although it isn't what I've dreamed of or imaged, I am fully determined and motivated to make this a good year. My past has always seemed to rule my future and hold me back, but not anymore, starting with to-night's date.

Evan arranged the whole night with the girls, so I am at their mercy. With a knot in my stomach and a ball of nerves, we walk into the theater ready to meet them; at least Evan is. The whole way over he was bouncing off the walls about "what could happen" this evening.

"Hey," I say, gulping down all my nervousness as we walk up to the girls.

"Hey you," Candy says sweetly, smiling with a soft, delicate expression in her features. "How is your shoulder?" Her hands run over my bicep up to the sleeve of my shirt.

I stare at her hand, watching the gentle way she touches me.

"It's good," I breathe out, my insides shaking like a damn leaf as if I've never been alone with a girl. *I was never like this with Alyssa, was I? I miss the easiness of being with her.*

"Good. Well as much as I enjoyed waiting on you hand-and-foot, I'm glad you're on the mend," she quietly laughs, hiding her mouth behind her hand.

Watching how her dark blue, almost steel gray eyes sparkle and how the sides of her face crease with her smile, I can't help but grin from how sweet and equally nervous she seems.

"Ok, so you guys ready?" Evan's voice breaks through my thoughts and motions for us all to head inside the theater. "Let's go."

After the girls take a quick trip to the bathroom and after Evan ropes me into joining him to get snacks, we settle in our seats, sitting boy, girl, girl, boy. The lights go down and the boom of the speaker rises around us, drowning out the chaos and excitement of all the movie watchers. I sigh, ready to get it going and sink myself into something other than worry about what comes next.

Fifteen minutes into the movie, her arm grazes mine as she positions her hand face up on the armrest next to mine. I stare down at it, analyzing it more than I should. *She's cute, she seems sweet and she's obviously attracted to me.* I go over Evan's words once more, *you need to move on. She has.*

Moving my hand just a fraction of an inch, I let my fingers slide between hers while nervously sitting up straight in my seat, unable to move anything else on my body. The texture of her skin is soft yet it's rougher than Alyssa's was, a different texture; just different. She immediately responds to my gesture of affection by gripping my hand in hers, but her movements are tense and unsure. With Alyssa it was always simple; she moved, I moved.

With her hand still held in mine, my ears pick up on a soft sigh from her mouth and I barely turn my head to see her expression. Her lips curve into a soft smile and she slowly crosses her opposite arm over her body, finding a resting spot on my bicep as she pulls closer to me. Laying her head against my arm, the flowery scent of her perfume assaults my nostrils and quickly makes my head start to pound.

I draw my attention back to the screen, now tensed by our closeness. Every once in a while, my gaze wanders to her small frame nuzzled against me like my arm is a rope that she is desperately clinging to. The top of her head sits right below my chin and something about the way the soft lights from the movie screen hit her blonde hair puts me at ease. Laying my head back against the stiff theater chair, I close my eyes and sigh, letting each nerve and muscle in my body unwind and relax. My heart pounds and I think about Alyssa, before gritting my teeth. *Geez, am I ever going to get her out of my mind, out of my heart?*

The end of the date comes and Evan takes Lauren home while Candy and I take off in my truck. Putting it in park in front of a ritzy, two story home that her parents own, my head pounds and heart thuds, but definitely not in the way it should at the end of a date. All night, I've tried to make myself feel something. I've searched for a spark, some sort of electricity that zips from her body to mine when I held her hand; anything. She's attractive and she's sweet, but that is where it ends and now I'm alone in a dark truck with her.

Sitting here worried about how I do this, my mind ventures to the day I saw Alyssa for the first time. It was like a power surge inside of me, igniting more love in my heart than I thought a person could hold. It actually felt as if Cupid himself had pierced me with his arrow, linking me to Alyssa and raising my expectations so high that anyone else in the world would be incapable of reaching them.

A low squeaky sound breaks my focus and I turn to see Candy sliding across the seat. *I guess I was hoping she would sneak out while I was lost in thought. No such luck.*

I turn my head as the heat from her arm lands on mine.

"Listen, Candy …" I start but the sweet somewhat reserved sponge bath chick instantly sticks her tongue down my throat. *Whoa!*

I gently place my hand on her arm, which is now eagerly drawn around my neck with her hand swimming through my hair; I break our connection. Running my hand to her shoulder in an effort to brace her from lunging at me again, I nearly want to laugh. Maybe it's nerves, but I guess she's been reading a lot more into tonight than I've been. The beat of my heart remains steady, my body is free of any sort of reaction and I'm about as uncomfortable as when a doctor asks me to cough.

"Sorry, it's just I've been wanting you to kiss me all night."

Her hand roams from my hair to my neck and I'm not sure me holding her back is getting my point across.

"Candy, I'm sorry if I have in any way led you on tonight, but I'm kind of in a weird place right now and starting something new may not be a good idea," I say as she remains quiet. *How do you nicely put the whole "it's not you, it's me" speech?* It's dark so I cannot see her expression, but I continue, "A lot happened this summer and I'm sort of still picking up the pieces."

As soon as the words are out of my mouth my abs tighten as her hand snakes up my shirt. "Your injuries?" she whispers, lightly running her hand over my rib cage

"Ahh … listen," I grab her hand out from under my shirt and place it on her lap between us, making every attempt to be a gentleman. "I am trying to go about this respectfully. I think you're nice, extremely pretty and I really did have fun tonight, but I'm just not … interested."

"Why the hell did we even go out then?" She raises her voice as she shoves her body across the seat, swings the passenger door open and steps out.

Last thing I really want to do it piss her off or hurt her feelings. "Candy, I just need to get past some things before I jump into anything."

Her expression softens and I watch as her lips pucker to the side as if she is biting the side of her mouth in heavy concentration. Pressing my lips together and glancing around uncomfortably, a deep breath brings my gaze back to her as she finally breaks the silence.

"You're lucky you're cute. You're also lucky I saw just what you had to go through while you were in the hospital." A gentle smile touches her lips. "I really like you, but I understand."

She places both her hands on the seat and raises back up on her knees into the truck. *Great, now what?* Sliding her knee forward, she leans in to plant a small kiss on my cheek. Of all the things tonight, this tiny act is the one thing that got my pulse kicked up. I smile at her as she hops back out of the truck.

"When you get it all figured out, give me a call." She swings the door shut.

On the drive home, I suddenly feel a weight easing off my heart; maybe eventually I can move on.

The next week goes much the same, without any dates of course, and then my birthday rolls around on the eighth. Surprisingly enough, I receive a text message from Tristan.

Tristan: Happy Birthday, Judd

It's short and to the point, but completely shocks me. In four years, he has never so much as shown his face on mine or Jake's birthdays, much less acknowledged them. Sometimes he makes me feel as though he is in agreement with what my father said the night he left; that we were a mistake. I don't reply, not because I don't appreciate it, but really because I'm not sure what to say. This is when I wish I had Jake's never-failing, forgiving heart, because I just haven't been able to set aside my bitterness, and then the wreck on top of that. It happens every time; he pushes my buttons when he is in a pissy mood, but this time it nearly killed us and took a lot away from us in the process. I think we've lost enough in this life; the last thing we need is his irresponsibility adding to the tally.

Two weeks into college, Tiffany's midnight-hopeful booty calls become a bit much and I start staying at Evan's apartment more and more. I can't make myself go there if my heart is somewhere else and I guess the friendship zone isn't good enough for her.

Plus with Jake so busy in his senior year and Tristan still laid up in the hospital, living at home is lonely. By mid-month, I settle into Evan's two bedroom apartment, which is only fifteen minutes from campus. Between physical therapy, work and college, I have little time to myself, but Evan never gives up. He tries to rope me into a few more dates with girls that he has seen around campus, including that Bethany girl, who is relentless, but I remain constant in saying no.

Tonight is no exception.

Evan: Get your ass to the apartment, shower, shave, spruce up or whatever the hell you do to get ready then we are going to a party. Bethany invited us to some Frat bullshit on campus. Yes, I'm not too keen on Frat parties, but I heard a lot of people buzzing around campus about this one, so we are going! Time to move on and hot chicks that are incredibly drunk with one thing on their mind, is just what you need!

Jumping in my truck from the downtown worksite that I help oversee, I throw my hardhat into my backseat and chuckle at Evan's persistence.

Me: On my way.

I hit send and peel out of the gravel lot to get home.

As soon as I stroll into the apartment, Evan is bouncing off the walls like he is a five year old on Halloween night.

"Come on, get your ass in gear. Get ready!" he hollers, waltzing into my room and pouncing down on my bed.

"What is your rush? Are we putting on this party or something?" I swing my eyes over to the clock on my nightstand, while throwing a long sleeve shirt over my head.

A thought enters my mind and I turn to him in a panic as he lazily slouches on my bed, rifling through the top drawer of my nightstand.

"You did not set me up with anyone, did you?"

Evan's snaps his head up to look at me with an offended look, "What? I wouldn't do that!"

I drop my mouth open. *What the hell did he do?*

He pinches a package between his fingers and holds it up. "Dude, these have expiration dates on them, you know!"

I rip the condom package out of his hand, tossing it back in my dresser drawer and hoping to steer this conversation back to what is going on tonight. "Leave my shit alone! Go rifle through your own drawers. What is going on tonight?"

Stepping back to the closet, I grab a pair of sneakers and walk over to the bed, noticing that Evan once again has my drawer open.

"Man, you have a ton of these! You might as well sell them; you're never going to use them. Let's go online and post these." Placing his hands in the air in front of him as if he is laying out a banner or sign, he says in absolute seriousness, " Truckload of condoms … never used … ten bucks or best offer."

I roll my eyes. "Are you done? Besides, those are all the ones you guys left as a gag in Alyssa's cot and my bed this summer. Trust me, even if I started using them today and had a week long marathon of sex, I still wouldn't get through them all."

I slip on my other shoe and rise up to head for the door.

"Ok, so you going to tell me what's going on tonight?"

My phone buzzes in my back pocket, so I slip it out and tighten my grip, staring down at an unknown number that has texted me so many times over the course of the last several weeks.

"Evan! Really?! Her?" I look up from my phone, annoyed and

aggravated.

Evan slams the drawer shut while sliding a couple packages into his wallet then glances at me with a smirk. *I swear he is going to kill me!*

"What? She wanted to meet up with you, so I sort of told her we would be there by 7:00." Evan laughs and exits my bedroom behind me. "It's time to move forward and if that takes getting you highly drunk and in the sack with her annoying ass, then so be it."

"Anyone but her!" I say dropping my head in exasperation. "She's more annoying than you and borderline stalkerish. I'd rather meet up with Candy than her. Her aggressiveness is kind of scary; I keep waiting for her to tackle me on campus."

Striding over to the kitchen island, I grab my wallet and keys, cramming them both in my pocket.

"So would that be so bad? You always loved getting tackled on the field...same difference just with more bouncy, perky body parts that brings the game to a whole new level of fun when they crash into you," he jokes, cupping his hands in front of his chest.

"Maybe fun for you, but this girl will not leave me alone. Do you know she sent me eleven text messages by 11:00am yesterday? Eleven, and she doesn't even know me. The extent of our conversations leaving English class is ..." I do my best valley-girl accent, batting my head side-to-side, "Did you understand what the professor was talking about or OMG, I need a manicure." I squeal my voice trying to mock her bubbly tone. "Oh and the pictures." I flip my phone around and show him the one she sent me recently.

Evan grabs my phone and squints his eyes, bursting with laughter. "Wow! And you're not into her? At least she's hot!" He laughs and hands me back the phone. "Come on! Give it a shot! You might just have fun tonight and wake up a changed man tomorrow." Unable to keep a straight face, he shakes his head with a huge grin and heads to the door.

Glancing down at the picture in my text messages, I stare at a selfie of Bethany, displaying what I believe she takes as her more admirable features. She has on a low cut shirt that appears to have less fabric than the black lace bra that sticks out and hoists her chest nearly up to her chin. *Come on, leave something to the imagination.* With bright red lipstick that makes me think there may be a circus in town, she puckers her lips out prepared to kiss the camera. Under it she wrote "XOXO."

"So annoying," I mumble. *This is going to be a long night.*

Three shots, a couple of hours and two very strong concoctions of alcohol later, I find myself sunk into the plush cushions of a sofa with a pair of plump lips attached to mine. A body sits across my lap with a vice grip around my hips. Numb and feeling as if I'm backed into a corner, I push my body into the back of the sofa, watching as the room spins so fast that I reach out for something to grab onto. My hands make contact with something soft and smooth that is definitely not the couch.

Sealing my eyes closed as a soft pillow wraps around my head, a voice calls out my name and forces the weight on my eyelids to retract and spring open.

"… to my apartment." Bethany's syrupy tone echoes through my head and every nerve in my body vibrates with unease.

My lap suddenly is freed of her weight as a blurred image rises in front of me. I'm jostled to the side as the cushion sinks down and Evan leans into my view.

"Hey buddy. You're trashed," his voice is solemn.

I try hard to focus on only one of the forms that I see as a hand slaps down onto my knee.

"Let's go," Evan laughs.

Go where? My mouth opens, but my tongue trips over itself, unable to work properly. *How the hell much did I drink? Why did I drink so much?*

"Come on, buddy. Let's get you somewhere so you can sleep this off," Evan says into my ear as an arm wraps around my back, under my arm then lifts me onto my motionless feet.

Laughter erupts from my chest and I put one rubbery leg in front of the other. "Whoa," I mumble, "I shouldn't drink, Evan."

Taking a deep breath, coolness surrounds me and a slight breeze sweeps across my face, forcing my head to snap backwards in an attempt to look around. All I see is blackness, though; pitch black. *Did I fall asleep?* Peppers of blurred dots come into view as I stare into the darkness and I think of Alyssa and all the nights I spent under the stars with her.

"No, you shouldn't. I should have stopped you, but you were having fun and loosening up. You're definitely going to feel this in the morning, though," Evan's voice sounds crystal clear as the numbness in my body lifts just enough to register another pair of arms wrapped around my waist.

"Hold him for a second so I can get the door."

The steadiness I felt before as I was pulled forward leaves my side and I sway back and forth like a teeter-totter. My head slumps forward and my exhausted eyelids give up the fight of staying open.

"I don't know if I can hold him."

There's that shrill voice that grates on every last nerve in my body.

"Holy shit, you whine toooooo ... damn ... much!" I mumble as Evan snorts out an eruption of laughter.

"Ohhh ... sorry," I barely hear him grumble following his outburst.

With my eyes welded shut, my rubbery legs finally give out and I am plummeted against something hard and solid with a loud thud.

"Whoa, buddy. That might leave a mark." All humor seems to be drained from Evan's voice, but then again it can't be easy lugging your drunken friend back home when you're stone sober. "Work with me, Judd. Move your legs."

I snicker at the train of thought it takes for my mind to carry that message down to my immobile limbs.

"There ya go," he strains to say.

My butt plops down onto a lumpy surface and I drop my head back with a clunk. Two doors slam behind me and a hand lands on my leg.

"What are you doing?" I ask, a bit creeped that his hand is fondling my leg.

"Not me, dude."

Evan's laughter fills the truck as I struggle to center my bobbling head on my shoulders, despite the fact that gravity keeps tugging it forward and back. Turning to the left, I widen my eyes to focus on the body next to me. Bethany's bright red lips come into view and it's all I can do to not open the door and jump out.

"Freaking perfect," I slur, looking at her. *Why is she coming to our apartment?*

Dread floods my mind as the truck comes to a stop and the door beside me quickly springs open.

"Come on, jump out," Evan says with a smirk in his tone.

"Evan, no! Take her home," I whisper, leaning my head out the doorway while my feet work to find solid ground.

Erupting with amusement, he corrects my assumptions, "I am taking her home. Now, watch where you're going."

His arm slips around me as my hazy mind tries to compute what he said.

Did I imagine her in the seat or ...

"Please tell me you live on the first floor," Evan's voice calls out directly in my ear.

"Yep, first apartment on the first floor," Bethany's overly cheerful voice chimes in as my wobbly legs carry me inside a building that I'm sure I wouldn't even recognize if my vision was fully functional.

Where has he brought me? The answer that immediately pops into my head sends tingles of sobriety through my body, urging my thoughts to clear and my wits to get back on track.

"This is me."

Another door opens in front of me and I stiffen my legs like a dog being guided into a vet's office.

"Evan, I know what you are doing, but just take me home," I say quietly, making a point to try and enunciate every syllable and appear unaffected by the amount of alcohol I guzzled down earlier.

My body falls back on a soft pillowy cushion as Evan releases his grip on me. "He's all yours. Take care of him now."

Using my arm to brace myself up into a sitting position, I squint my eyes from the bright light streaming down from the ceiling and level Evan with a glare. My body still feels numb from the alcohol; my eyelids seem to have been coated with lead and the two legs that made it through a horrific car wreck with very little damage now feel like strings of stretched-out rubber.

Evan laughs at my attempt at a scowl and sits down beside me, slapping me across the back.

"My dad's in town so I'm not headed back to the apartment, but I have it on good authority that you will be well taken care of." He quickly glances to the far wall where I can make out Bethany's voluptuous figure standing up against a tall dresser. "Oh and you can thank me tomorrow," he whispers, turning his attention back to her as he stands. "Seriously take care of him. He's still kinda got a thing for his ex."

I do my best to roll my eyes then drop my arms out from beneath me so that I can bounce back into the mattress and hopefully pass out.

"Don't worry, he's in good hands," she giggles and I quickly grab the pillow out from beneath my head and flip it across my face to drown out her voice.

I keep both hands pressed into the feathery soft pillow, hearing the sounds of a door snapping shut, then fabric rustling, another snap like something clasping shut and then …

What the …

Pulling my head out from under the pillow a few inches, the brightness of the light is gone and Bethany's shadowy form sits at the end of the bed taking off my shoes. Her hands snake up to my snap and zipper before I can so much as muster up a single word. *This girl is relentless.* I quickly slam the pillow back over my face, unable to watch her wrestle with my jeans in an attempt to get them off. *I am not helping her out, but I give up on stopping whatever is doomed to happen.*

"Bethanyifi'mgoingtostayherejustletmesleeeep!" I mumble out through my pillow shield, making my entire sentence run together in an aggravated moan.

Each time she yanks at the leg of my pants, my body slowly slides down the bed and I want to laugh at how difficult this is for her. *I am not helping her out.* Her fight seems to let up as a burning sensation crawls down the outsides of my legs like I just slid across the carpet. *I thought Evan said I'd be taken care of, not rug burned to death as she tears my clothes off.*

"Here, take this off."

Stealing away my hiding spot, the pillow is pulled from my face and the fabric of my shirt is tugged over my head, sending a dull pain through my shoulder. *I get the feeling she has done this before, but she sucks at it.*

Once again the weight of her body is draped over mine as she gets completely comfortable straddling my lap. Using one hand, I run it along the wads of sheets until my hand connects with my fluffy retreat from this situation. *I liked it better with the pillow over my head so I didn't have to be reminded that my best friend threw me to the lions.*

Pulling it to my chest as a barrier from her, I decide to talk my way out of this one just like I did with Candy. However, something tells me that Bethany may not be the kiss-on-the-cheek-after-she-has-been-rejected type. A hard smack across my face or swift kick to the groin may be more her style.

"Hey, Bethany, I don't know what my friend told you ..." I use the word friend very loosely at this point. *I'm going to kick Evan's ass when I am sober enough to do it.* "... but I am not looking for a one night stand or a hookup or anything like that."

She giggles, making my head thud and spin. My stomach churns as her hands slide over the skin of my stomach and her body wobbles around like she is swaying her hips to music.

"I know he told me you weren't over your ex, but I bet I can help you get over her." More giggling and bouncing create a wave of nausea through my stomach up into my throat.

I clear my throat, hoping to regain my composure and steer off vomiting. "Ahh, I don't think so," I say, aggravated as I glance back at her. I want to laugh at how sure she is of herself.

"Oh, I bet I can." Her bubbly voice grates on my nerves as her hand runs up my rib cage and over my scar, igniting another pulse of nausea through me.

Maybe that's what I need to do. Maybe that will send the message that this is not happening.

Gulping deeply, I let out an uneasy sigh, "I think I'm going to be sick."

She shifts a bit and for a second I think, *really ... not even that is going to get you off of me*, but then finally lifts her body away from mine, allowing me to roll onto my side and deliver my very best performance of a near vomit induced drunk.

I can barely make out anything in the room, except for what looks like a bed across the aisle and piles of clothes or towels littering the alleyway between the beds. Bethany's feet brush across the carpet as she runs out of the room then quickly returns, tossing a small trashcan down beside the bed.

"Here …"

I lean over, pulling the pillow up over the side of my face. Her hand rubs over my back in a tender way, but instead of soothing my supposed sickness it aids in the realism of the situation. *Maybe I'll puke after all.*

I have no idea why I loathe her so much. There is just something I don't trust about her and I most definitely do not want her to get the idea that there is anything going on between us, regardless of what Evan thinks is best for me.

"Do you mind getting me a glass of water?"

She bolts off of the bed and darts back with a glass of water in hand. After taking a couple sips, she slips back in bed and nuzzles up to my back. I grip the trashcan, leaning over the edge of the bed, knowing very well that I'm not going to vomit but also being completely uncomfortable with her lying so intimately close to me.

My mind whirls around with thoughts of Alyssa. *What the hell am I doing? How did I get here? How am I such a mess over two weeks?*

"I miss her," I grumble into the trashcan, sounding as if I just shouted into a large vacant room.

Bethany makes a couple more trips for a washcloth and aspirin before I shove the pillow back over my head, wishing I would wake up back in my own bed; better yet, that large cabin across the lake.

"Judd … Judd …" Bethany says my name a couple times as my mouth curves into a smile and I slowly start to drift off. "Well, shit …" I hear right before I am plummeted into a quiet, relaxing darkness without her relentless efforts of trying to wake me and get me interested; only me and memories of Alyssa.

Cracking, pounding jolts of lightning shoot from my temple around my head and straight down into the base of my neck.

"Mmmmhhh …" I let out a moan with my eyes sealed shut and a soft warmth against my back.

I squeeze my lids shut, trying my very best to function, to move any limb of my body. *Why did I drink that much?*

Bethany's curvy body presses into my back, making me desperately want to flee before she wakes, but at this point I'm not even sure if I am 100% sober. Gripping my hand hard into the soft folds of the pillow still clutched over my face, my ears pick up on a subtle sound in the room. It's not coming from behind me so it can't be Bethany. I lie motionless and focus on the sound. A scraping or grating noise that sounds similar to two surfaces scratching across one another rings in my ears. The room goes silent and all I pick up on is Bethany's breath against the base of my neck. *Please let her stay asleep so I can make a quiet exit.*

I keep the pillow firmly held over my face as the scraping sounds again, followed by a loud thump. More aggravated than anything that this noise could potentially snuff out my chances of a non-drama filled morning, I push the pillow away from my face so I can see what is disturbing the quiet of the room.

All of a sudden my heart stops; it stops. I swear it stops beating and I am no longer breathing. *I'm not breathing!* I crinkle my brows together and tighten my hold on the pillow to help ground me because I know I am dreaming. Alyssa stands frozen in front of me.

Waves of blonde hair hang over her shoulders and are tipped with moisture, dripping onto her shirt. My eyes roam down her body past her small waist and tight denim jeans that hug her curves. She has a pair of black knee high boots on and she looks sexier than I've ever seen her. Quickly pulling my line of sight back to her face, I take in her beautiful crystal blue eyes; the eyes I could look into forever; the ones I have dreamed about nearly every night for the past three months. The eyes I have prayed I would get the chance to look into again, only today is probably not the day for gazing because right now she looks pissed.

I toss the pillow over to the side, not caring where it lands or who it wakes. My eyebrows shoot up, shocked and confused at how this could be. *How is she here? How is she in the exact apartment that I am?*

Her eyes fill with a mixture of hurt and anger as she clutches her arm across her stomach much in the same way as I did last night. Continuing to glance back and forth between me and the other side of the bed, a slight brush of fabric moves across my arm that is bracing me up into the sitting position, and it is then when I realize just how this looks. I look down at the sheet slung over my midsection, covering up the fact that I am still wearing my boxers then swing my gaze to the side to see Bethany's barely covered up naked body. *Shit, this looks bad! I didn't do anything with her, but that is definitely not how it looks.*

"Lyssa." My raspy, dry voice calls out but it doesn't even sound like mine. "What are you doing here? I thought …" I gulp down the knot in my throat and let out a shaky breath as she holds up her hand for me to stop talking. *This is bad!*

My chest heaves up and down with equal amounts of relief and dread that she is here. *How is this possible? I thought she would be at Purdue. Did she stay because of her boyfriend? Maybe they broke up.*

My headache has temporarily taken a backseat and my mind spins with questions, hopes and scenarios that I can't possibly find out at this moment, given the unfortunate way we have been reunited. I look her up and down once more, wanting nothing more than to wrap her in my arms and kiss the beautiful lips that I have been dreaming of, but then an icy tone I've never heard emerges from her lips, leaving me dumbfounded.

"Did you tell her you love her, too?"

I cock my head back in confusion and stare at her. *What the hell does that mean, when she is the one …?*

I'm left with no time for thought as she races for the door, tripping over her feet in the process. Jumping to my own feet, I immediately realize I am completely sober and now pissed as hell. *Where does she get off questioning my intentions?!*

"Wait a minute! Where do you get off being mad at me?"

I tear my pants off the floor where Bethany must have thrown them and dart after Alyssa who is nearly out the door. Coordinating my efforts of jumping a leg at a time into my pants as I run after her, I yell out with anger coursing through me at her accusation.

"What! You can dish it out but you can't take it!" *She shacks up with me for two weeks then races back to reunite with her boyfriend without a second thought and now she feels like she has a leg to stand on. Sucks to be on the receiving end!*

I stumble, nearly going headfirst onto the carpet as I try desperately to get to her before she can get away. *Three months of wondering why; I just want an explanation.*

"Go back in and enjoy your slumber party!" she yells from outside the apartment building.

"Lyssa, wait! Just let me talk to you!" I plead right as I round the doorway and my eyes collide with her cheating ex.

I would know that face anywhere. It's the same guy I saw in her profile picture, the one that haunted me, knowing that she was touching and kissing him and not me. He is also the same guy that stood right outside her house, grabbing her hand and holding onto her like I used to.

He steps forward with a defensive stance between me and Alyssa as if I mean her harm. Honestly, just that action makes me want to punch him in the nose, because it should be my place to protect her, not his. After all, he is the one who ultimately hurt her by sleeping around on her, yet she still chose him. That thought shoves the piercing knife in a bit further, but then I hear a sound that splits my heart in two; his voice; the same voice from my call to her.

"Is there a problem here?"

I narrow my eyes and grit my teeth, fully prepared to lunge at him and fight for her. Opening my mouth, I'm fully intent on questioning this douchebag that can go out one night and shack up with another girl then run back to her with an apology and make everything right. *Come on, Alyssa! What are you thinking?* But no sooner than my lips part, her once alluring voice calls out with such animosity that it leaves me frozen.

"It's ok! He is one of Bethany's overnighters and I accidentally walked in on them. They were more than likely so busy last night that she failed to mention she has a roommate," she says as if seeing me like that meant nothing; as if it had no effect on her, but I know I saw hurt in her eyes.

I know I did!

Anger and pain course through my veins as I look into her eyes, and I freeze from the lack of love I see. Every section of my pounding heart has been mauled and left for dead.

Her mouth moves again as she turns, pulling him along with her as if they are a package that goes everywhere together. I watch as they walk off and the blond asshole slowly slips his arm around her waist. I even watch as she turns and looks back at me one last time like she did at the lake as I drove off.

My legs have become one with the sidewalk; completely cemented to the ground, I watch …

I watch and let fury flood my mind and heart.

Answers

STORMING BACK INTO THE apartment for my shirt and shoes, I come face to face with a very confused Bethany. My bare feet slam against the plush carpet while I glare at her sitting lazily on the couch in the living room. *At least she has clothes on now. I'm thankful that I got to skip that awkward moment.*

"What was that all about?" she asks as she kicks her feet up on the coffee table, focusing on sliding a file across her thumb.

I have no desire to talk to her or play nice. *Was this a damn trick to get me in bed? How could she not know that Alyssa and I know each other?*

Gritting my teeth so that I don't blurt out what I think of her, I take large strides into the bedroom, hastily knocking the door out of my way as I enter. As soon as my eyes take in the room with sunlight filtering in through the window, I immediately notice a second bed on the other side of the room. My lungs temporarily stop filtering air as I glance at the pillow wondering if it smells like her skin.

I suck in a deep breath as shuffling sounds from the next room. Glancing around quickly for my shirt, my eyes skim over her neatly made bed, a perfectly lined row of shoes peeking out from beneath it and a large dresser along the far wall that separates the two sleeping spaces. My eyes zone in on a small frame that lies tipped over on top of the dresser. Mustering up all the willpower in my body, I refrain from running over and examining the picture. My heart stills in my chest at the thought that the picture could be one of ours from the lake.

"What was that all about with my roomie?" Bethany says in a giggle as she slinks against the doorway.

Looking towards her through the corner of my eyes, I bend down and grasp my shirt and shoes then slowly lay them on the opposite bed; Alyssa's bed.

"Yeah, good piece of information to share when you bring a guy home."

I slide my shirt over my head then take a seat on her roomies bed; Geez this is Alyssa's bed. Lowering my brows in a serious glare, I take in her cool facade and lazy stance. *Is it even possible that she is clueless about Alyssa and me; that Alyssa possibly never said anything?*

Caving in somewhat, I play along just to feel her out, "So that was your roommate, huh?" I raise my eyebrows in question as Bethany nods.

Slipping a foot into my sneaker, I go on, "I had no idea. All I know is, I woke up and there was some strange person at the end of the bed. I must have startled her as well because she took off running," I say, using basically the same excuse Alyssa did earlier.

Bethany huffs out a laugh, moving into the room. Positioning herself onto her mattress in a seductive manner, she opens her mouth as I lace up my other shoe then walk over to the dresser.

"It sure sounded like a heated discussion. I woke up and saw you bolting after her and yelling about dishing out something. Do you two know each other?"

I swing my head around and am met with a vacant look that tells me any answer will suffice. It is clear that Alyssa never shared the details of our summer together.

Pausing for a brief moment to answer, I swing my gaze back to the dresser and hold my breath as I carefully lift up the flipped over frame. Once I scan the picture of an older man surrounded by four women including Alyssa and Abby, I carefully place it upward on the dresser with each of their faces staring directly at me.

"Nope, she doesn't look familiar. She scared me, honestly. I wasn't expecting someone else in the room. It was a huge misunderstanding." I stare straight ahead at Alyssa's baby blue eyes in the photograph.

Casually pointing at the frame, I play stupid, hoping to get some sort of information from Bethany. "This must have been what fell over and woke me up earlier. How long have you two roomed together?"

Swinging my gaze back to her, I see her face light up as if I'm trying to get to know her.

"Just since the beginning of the month. She and I have been friends for a while, though. We're from Fairview, but couldn't handle the commute back and forth ... sooo ... we decided to move closer." She smiles and stares at me as I glance back once more to the frame and nod. "Her father is sick so things could change soon and she may want to move back home."

Finally Bethany takes a u-turn and guides the discussion in the direction I want; however, this isn't the information I was hoping for.

"Sick?" I ask calmly, keeping all traces of concern out of my tone.

"Yeah, she found out her dad has cancer this summer and ... or well, actually he had it a couple years ago, but it returned. It has really hit her hard and I'm not sure he is going to beat it this time."

My heart is hammering from the thoughts of how much this has got to be tearing Alyssa up. *I wish I could have been there for her; if only she had wanted me there.*

"That's awful," I throw out in a bland tone, but my mind is focused on the single vision of Alyssa's face when she told me about her dad the day we went fishing.

"Speaking of my roommate, I'm having a birthday party for her Wednesday. Care to be my date?"

Moving away from the dresser over to the door, I stop mid-step, snapping my head around to look at her. She still lies sprawled on her side, across her bed like she is trying to lure someone. Unfortunately, I believe I'm the victim in this scenario.

Date ... not a chance. I open my mouth to answer then stop to think about what she actually said. *Alyssa's birthday is Friday*; a detail that I have continually forced to the back of my mind this week, wondering what she would be doing, where she would be or who she would be with. Maybe tagging along wouldn't be such a bad idea, but first I need to make some things clear.

"Listen, Bethany ..." I say, taking a seat back on Alyssa's bed so that I can look at her as I talk and hopefully get through to her that I am not interested in her in any way other than friends. "I'll be more than happy to join you, but would you mind if I come as a friend? I had a pretty bad breakup this summer and honestly, I haven't gotten back on my feet from that yet."

It isn't entirely the truth. Even if I were over Alyssa, Bethany is definitely not the type of girl I would get mixed up with. There is something about her that I don't trust and there is definitely no chemistry between us. With Alyssa, fireworks were ignited way before the Fourth ever hit.

"Well, if you gave me a shot I just might be able to end that summer with a bang, although I can't promise you'd be on your feet after that either." She sticks her tongue out from between her teeth and crinkles her nose. *Not.a.chance!*

After staring at her for longer than I should and all my words forming into a pool of nausea, I blink quickly and remind myself: *Bethany may be my key to seeing Alyssa now; be civil whether you like it or not.*

With my eyes dead on her, no emotion over what she laid on the table and a small insincere laugh, I elaborate, "Thanks, but I never resolved things with her and I'm not completely sure where we stand. Until I find out, I'm keeping any relationships at a friendship level." I squint my eyes, curious whether her deer-in-the-headlights expression is usual or if it means she's not computing a dang thing I said.

Laughing as if this is joyful banter between us, she relents in a way, "Ok so if I agree to go as friends, you'll come on Wednesday?"

I nod, keeping my face free of any hint of excitement or dread.

"Ok then … friends it is," she pauses, giving me what she must think is a sexy look with her eyes narrowed. "Until I wear you down at least." She winks and I'm about ready to leave.

"Yeah … ok, so I'll just meet you there. Where is it at?"

"It's here."

"Here?" I look around at the small apartment that looks like it may hold twenty to thirty bodies max.

"Or, well … at the community hall out back." She points over her shoulder.

Nodding, I grab my phone and wallet off of the floor where they must have landed when she tore my clothes off before shooting Evan a quick text.

Me: You sure the hell owe me! Now come get my ass!

Evan: Ahhh … try you owe me and you're welcome. What's your rush? Have a little more fun. I'm not due back til Monday.

Me: Are you kidding me? Fun?

Evan: Ah oh … so you didn't enjoy it? Is she all talk? Does she use her teeth? Does she have rough hands, hairy legs, saggy boobs …?

I glance up at Bethany still standing in the doorway.
"Is everything alright?"
I hesitate, not wanting to ask, but also … I look over at Alyssa's bed, a dull pain thudding inside my heart.
"Hey, do you mind giving me a lift to my apartment?"
"Sure."
I agree with a nod, grateful, even though I'm not looking forward to the drive. I'm hoping for an uncomfortable silence, anything but her talking, but I doubt I'll be so lucky. Running my fingers back over the buttons on my phone, I quickly dismiss Evan's ridiculous line of questions.

Me: I wouldn't know! Good try! I got a ride. See ya on Monday …

Twenty minutes later, I'm shifting around nervously in the passenger side of her car, wishing I had not drunk a drop of alcohol last night. It was bad enough sleeping in her bed all night, and although we agree to a normal friendship, it is exhausting listening to her carry on about her upcoming hair appointment and party décor for Wednesday.
"It's the building on the left." I point at the large brick building that houses my apartment. *I really am going to kill Evan when I see him on Monday, not only for abandoning me last night, but also for*

not at least making sure I had a way home. Last thing I want is for Bethany to know where I live. It's bad enough that he gave her my number, because now I never get peace from endless text messages and selfies.

"Hey, thanks for the ride."

Pulling hard on the handle, I fling the door open relieved to be back home. My feet hit pavement and I quickly rise up, spinning around to slam the door before anything else can be said between us, but then I pause.

"About Wednesday … what time is it?" I ask, dipping my head back into the car.

Bethany's face illuminates with delight highlighted with an ear-to-ear smile and wide eyes like my question just made her year.

"It's at 7:00. Just come by a little before and you can head to the party with me and Alyssa."

It's my turn to glow with excitement, because the prospect of going anywhere with Alyssa has 'hell yes' written all over it.

"Sounds good. See ya then," I say with a sincere smile and a thudding heart on the verge of leaping out of my chest and scorching a path to find her, now.

I'm pissed off about seeing her with him, but honestly all I want is a moment to talk to her. That is something that always seemed so simple between us; we could talk. I mean really talk! I've never been able to talk to anyone like her; I miss it.

Saturday and Sunday rush by like leaves in a storm and by Monday afternoon all I can do is stare at my nemesis; the clock. It seems like any significant moment in my life brings me to a standoff with it as I implore the minutes to click by faster than time will allow.

"He's just scared to face you or call you. He thinks you blame him." Pressing my cellphone to my ear, I hop into my truck to head home from class and listen as Jake explains Tristan's avoidance of my calls and visits. It seems he is always mysteriously gone when I make plans to head that way. "He's changed a lot and I'm not sure it's all for the good. That cool, confident persona that he always put off is gone. He just seems …" Jake hesitates, taking a quick breath, "… empty. It's like when Mom died all over again."

Holding tight to my keys as I crank up the engine, I close my eyes and think back to the day he finally cracked. Jake and I had just come home from working at a big dairy farm right outside of town. It was how we pitched in with the bills while Mom was sick and after she died it helped to keep our minds busy. As soon as our feet hit the floor, Tristan started yelling at us, claiming he had never signed up for being a makeshift dad at eighteen years old. It had been nearly a solid month since Mom's death and a week after his graduation. That day he snapped and stormed out of the house. We didn't see him for a week and a half. When he came back, he was different. He was the good old Tristan I've come to know; quick to drink away his worries and with an endless rotation of girls at his side. That was the summer he introduced me to Evan, the younger brother to his new best bud.

"Hey, I gotta go. I'm in the parking lot of the hospital and he should be done with therapy anytime," Jake explains in a regretful tone.

"Yeah, ok. Just keep me posted on how he's doing. Despite what he thinks, I do care," I say, hearing a whistle in my ear indicating that I have an incoming text from someone. Maybe it's Evan. He hasn't answered my text messages the last few days. He knows I'm ticked; however, I haven't had the chance to fill him in on what happened the other morning.

"I will and I'll keep trying to talk to him. He'll come around, Judd."

"Thanks." I whisper and tap my fingertip on the screen to end the call.

I sit in my truck, thinking about my brother for a while before remembering that I had a text. Clicking on the messages icon, I see Bethany's name highlighted with a new message. *Great!*

Bethany: Hey, I was just packing to go stay at my parent's house for the night and I noticed your hat on the floor by the door. I think your friend brought it in the other night and left it there. Anyways, I am getting ready to head out the door so let me know if you want me to swing it by.

Slamming my head back onto the headrest, I push my phone against the fabric of my jeans and blow out an exasperated breath.

Maybe this is a good thing. Lifting the phone back up, I frantically type out an answer and hit send.

Me: I am in my truck now leaving campus. Give me ten minutes or so and I can be there.

Bethany: I'm in a hurry, plus I'm going in the opposite direction. Ok if I leave a spare key under the mat? My dad has this big company banquet that I have to go to tonight and I am already running late. :P Your hat is on the coffee table and I'll get the key when I see you Wednesday. Sound good?

Just as I am getting ready to throw my truck into reverse and speed over to her house, hopeful that I may bump into Alyssa, her words hit me. Why would she need to leave a key if Alyssa is there?

Me: Yeah, sure. Will your roommate be there? I don't want to have another surprise run-in like before.

I bite the inside of my lip while staring at my phone, willing her to answer back that Alyssa will be there.

Bethany: Actually, Alyssa is in Fairview until tomorrow morning and I won't be back until tomorrow afternoon. I have already left, but the key is there. Just keep the key until Wednesday … don't put it back under the mat. Freaks me out to leave it there while we are both out of town. TTYL

Me: I am already on my way!

I quickly hit send and throw my truck into gear.

Pulling up to her apartment in a matter of minutes, my feet barely register a physical surface beneath them as I dart to her door. Glancing around to make sure no one is watching, I scoop the key up from under the mat with a quiet chuckle. *For a girl that is wigged out about someone breaking into her apartment, she sure hides her key in the most obvious place. I'm sure the last place a crazed sick lunatic would look for a key is under a mat.*

Gripping the key in my hand, I knock just to make sure no one is inside. The tap-tap-tap vibrates through my wrist and down my arm as my knuckles make contact with the solid wood door; no answer. I slip the key into the lock without a second thought and slowly creep inside as if I am the intruder. *What am I doing?* As if I am being watched, I straighten up my stance and walk as normally as possible over to the table. My eyes find it quickly, exactly where Bethany said it would be.

Pivoting to walk back to the door and exit their apartment, my legs stop working as if I'm an old bike with stiff, rusty gears. I flick my eyes over to her bedroom door, glancing only through the corner of my eyes, hoping that this will signal my body not to do what my heart and mind is telling me to do. I look back down to the carpet, still stationed in the same spot by the coffee table and only a few feet from her bedroom door, but I can't fight the pull.

I walk slowly, careful as if I may wake someone. The door is open, still sporting a fuzzy purple scarf that makes my stomach turn. *It doesn't take a genius to know what that is code for. To think Alyssa saw that coming into the room and finding me in bed with her roommate. A good idea to let Tristan in on though.* Once I'm standing between their beds, I glance to her side and slowly feel splinters of my heart chipping away with the thought of her body laying here. I slide down onto the bed, my legs sinking in the mattress and thick comforter.

Without thinking, I clutch my fist around her pillow and pull it out from under her blankets. My arms engulf it as I bury my face in the fabric, breathing in the scent of her hair and skin as if she were right here in my arms. Inhaling a deep breath, I think over what Bethany said about her father. She was so frightened waiting on her dad's tests, and here it ended up being what she dreaded the most. The strong hold my arms have on the pillow goes limp and I drop it into my lap, staring at it like it may have some answers for me.

"I wonder how many times you've cried into this over your dad," I whisper to myself.

An aching pain pierces my heart as I look so hard at the white pillowcase that I can see hundreds of tiny balls of lint that cling on for dear life. Letting out a soft, somber laugh, I interrupt the silence of the room again, "I wonder if you shed any tears for me?"

Shaking off any selfish thoughts, an idea immediately crops to mind at the exact time that my phone chimes. *A text from Evan.*

Evan: Ok so I assume you're probably pissed so meet me at Joe's Cafe for lunch and I'll let you slap me around for a bit! Go easy on my face and I'll even buy you lunch.

I chuckle at his approach to last Friday night after two days of not texting me. He knows if he waits it out the storm will pass; it's a rare instance when I stay mad at someone other than Tristan.

Me: Sure, I'm right around the corner. Be there in a bit.

After, gently placing Alyssa's pillow back under her comforter as it was and after another quick glance at the picture on her dresser, I head to meet Evan.

As soon as I walk through the door of the cafe, I see him slumped down in a booth towards the back of the building. He hangs his head low staring at a basket of French fries with so much ketchup doused over the top of them that you would think a mass murderer was set lose on the poor crinkled pieces of potatoes.

Continuing to study the frown on his face and the way his eyebrows are drawn down in concentration, I stride across the room and slide in opposite him. With one fist wedged under his chin, he looks up at me briefly then back down to the murder scene of fries as a waitress slides two plates in front of us.

"Two cheeseburgers with everything. Can I get you anything else," she says with a cheerful smile.

I nod quickly knowing Evan will probably have some smartass remark that will more than likely make the waitress want to stick around or wipe the grin right off her face, and right now I need to talk to him.

"No thanks," I say politely then look back at Evan. "Don't ever do that again. You have no idea what happened after you deserted me." I shake my head, widening my eyes over this weekend's events.

"I think I can imagine what happened but I'd rather not," he jokes with an unconvincing chuckle.

"No, that definitely did not happen!"

236

"Ahhh…" Evan says with a nod of his head and his eyes intensely focused on the basket of fries between us.

What, no sarcastic remark? He's got to be sick. Pausing in my eagerness to tell him about my Saturday morning discovery, I study his drab demeanor and how normally he would be shoving his face like a homeless person, where now he idly slides a French fry back and forth through a river of ketchup.

"Ok, what's wrong? You're in a pissy mood, I can tell," I point out, a bit concerned considering he just had a visit with his dad and brother. Those visits usually always end up disastrous. "Did something happen this weekend?"

Evan's body bounces up as he huffs out a large breath of air from his nose. Keeping the same fry busy swimming, he glances up to me clearly bothered by something more than letting his family getting to him.

"Surprisingly enough that went good for a change, but then again my grandpa was there as a mediator."

"What's up then?" I ask, fully prepared to listen, especially after nearly an entire summer of venting over Alyssa.

"It's her … she's in my econ class and all she does is give me the cold shoulder. She won't even acknowledge me. It's driving me nuts." Evan shakes his head as if he is trying to push a memory out of his mind. "Technically just seeing her everyday through the week is driving me insane, but her not talking to me is the cherry on top of this shit cake I've created!"

I snarl my nose at his choice of words as I steal a fry and dunk it in some ketchup. "That's disgusting."

Evan glares at me, rolling his eyes.

Whatever there is between him and Piper has been boiling inside of him for years; no way can I lighten the mood by cracking a joke like he usually can, but I can offer advice.

"Listen, I know you said you couldn't tell me everything about what happened, but from what you have told me, it sounds like you just need a chance to talk to her."

Evan looks up at me with a look of complete and utter frustration. "Ahhh…did you not hear me. She will not give me the time of day! I say so much as hello and she bolts! Trust me, I would tell her if I could at least have that opportunity, but she hates me." He sighs, angrily throwing his fry back into the basket.

I stare at him, unsure of what to say or how I can help him through this.

"You know, I don't even want to talk about this. What happened between you and what's her name?" he switches the subject quickly, pushing his foul mood to the side. "It had to be good if you're not lunging across the table to strangle me right now for leaving you there."

Looking at him to be sure he isn't just shoving this whole issue with Piper down so deep that it will eventually explode, I wait for a moment before diving into the details of my weekend. I know better than anyone how to bottle things up; I've been doing it for years.

"You sure?" I raise my eyebrows in question.

Evan sinks his teeth into his burger and lets out a muffled, "Yeah …"

"Ok," not knowing where to start, "Well, nothing happened between Bethany and me, that's for sure. I had to play sick after she got nearly all my clothes off, but finally she fell asleep."

I take a quick bite of my burger; the savory flavors of beef, melted cheese and tangy sauce slide over my taste buds.

"Well that sounds boring … and you don't think I would believe that? After you turning down sponge bath chick, I definitely believe it."

With extreme effort I swallow the half-chewed-up bite, unable to contain my eagerness in telling someone about my run-in.

"No, I knew you would believe that. The next morning was the shocker." I stare intently at him as if he can guess what is on my mind.

Irritated, he tosses his hands out on either side of his plate, urging me to get on with it.

"I woke up face to face with her roommate the next morning …"

Evan's eyes immediately light up. "Whoa … *Nice,"* his mind immediately crashes into the gutter.

"No! It wasn't anything like that. Guess who her roommate is?"

Evan tears off another large bite with his teeth, but answers me anyway, "Canny …"

I barely make out his attempt at a guess through the half chewed up cow tumbling around in his mouth, but I shake my head. *I wasn't really intending on this becoming a guessing game.*

"It was Alyssa!" I belt out, barely believing it myself.

His eyes bulge out and his throat bobs as he forces his food down.

"No freaking way! I thought she was in Iowa or somewhere."

I correct him, "Indiana," still wondering the same thing.

Dropping my burger which I had gripped in my hands so tight that all the toppings slide out onto my plate, I ramble on with all the details of our argument and finish with speculation.

"I guess she stayed because her dad got sick." I take a breath and Evan jumps right in.

"That's crazy! What are the odds? So what happened? Did you ask her what the hell?" he asks, pounding his fist on the table.

I shake my head, retracing my words and steps from that morning in my mind. "No ... well, I tried to talk to her, but then she yelled at me asking if I told Bethany I loved her, too." Cocking my head back, I crinkle my eyebrows as anger and bitterness rise into my chest as if I am right back in that moment. *What the hell did she mean by that?*

"What?!" Evan bites out.

"I know. It's strange. Where does she get off questioning my loyalty to her, when she is the one that ran right back to her ex the second she was away from me."

Frustration and anger slowly starts to flare up inside of me, pushing away all enthusiasm and longing I felt for seeing her after three long months.

"I ended up running after her trying to talk to her, but she seemed ticked off," I swallow and take another deep breath so I can finish my story and add in the clincher of it all. "As if that wasn't traumatizing enough, she ran outside while I was chasing her, trying to put my clothes on in the process and there stood her cheating deadbeat boyfriend himself; face ... to ... face with me, asking if there was a problem." I go quiet and stare directly across the table, yet seeing the scene from the other morning so clear in my head. I am back in that moment, in a standoff with the one guy that I have every right to give a piece of mind, yet I said nothing.

"Well did you finally tell them both what bullshit this is or did you at least deck him?" Evan anxiously bounces up in his seat waiting for the rest of the story; a story that I have no more to tell, because I said nothing. *Three agonizing months without her and I said nothing. I couldn't. I felt like a bird that had just gotten their wings clipped. Seeing her with him took everything from me; she was all I wanted and she acted as if she hated me. Why?*

Pressing my lips together, I look down and shake my head.

"What! You had to say something! What happened then?"

I look back up, shame creeping over me that I was such a coward.

"I didn't say anything. She was pissed off then she left ... *with him.*"

"So wait, you've moped around all summer wondering what happened, you get the chance to ask and you don't. And of course she was mad ... she just found her ex in bed with her roommate," he states in a tone that says this should all be common knowledge.

"But I didn't break up with her, so why would it matter whether I slept with Bethany or not." I slap my hand across my forehead, bringing my index finger and thumb to my temples in a circling pattern to fend off the impending headache this conversation is going to bring on.

"Yeah ... but what are you doing telling me to fess up everything when it comes to my problems, yet you're not taking your own advise. Why wouldn't you have unloaded it all on her? "

I slouch back in the booth, crossing my arms already on the defense. *Wonderful, now we are both in lousy moods.*

"Totally different scenario! She didn't even give me a damn week before she moved on! I was just a cushion for her to get her mind off her boyfriend cheating, either that, or I was a way for her to get revenge. She probably went back home and told her boyfriend all about us just to get back at him then they made up!"

The more I talk about it the angrier I get. I can't believe I allowed myself to fall in love with a girl who had just gotten out of a one-year relationship the day before. I was worried the whole time that I may have been the rebound guy, but convinced myself that it was real. *Damn, it felt real.*

Evan's voice slams me back to reality, "It still doesn't make sense." He draws his brows down in confusion.

"I know it doesn't! None of it does! I mean I really thought there was something there, otherwise, I would have never told her…"

Evan interrupts me mid sentence. "No, I mean why wouldn't you first clear up that you did not sleep with her roommate."

I stare at him, totally annoyed that he pointed that out. "What?! You're the one that has been trying to get me to shack up with random girls all summer just for the sake of moving on, and now you think I should explain myself to her when she is all cozied up to a guy that cheated on her, right in front of me?" Leaning down in my seat, I look at the table knowing my next words are going to make me sound like a complete jerk. "In a way, I want her to think I slept with Bethany, because I want her to feel a little of what she has put me through; to think I am with someone else."

I love her...God, I love her so i should not want to hurt her like that, but if I never meant anything to her, then she probably could care less. My mind flicks to the look on her face after she looked from Bethany to me. I know what I saw; there was definitely pain in her eyes. She looked stunned, more so than the fact that she was seeing me for the first time. Not to mention her words, "Did you tell her you love her, too?" I'm still confused about that. *Does she think I wasn't honest when I said that?*

Evan shakes his head disagreeing with my reasoning.

"I guess in a way this is me listening to your advice about my dilemma, but I'm going to throw it back at you first ... if you love her, you probably need to fight for her, because you really suck when you're not with her."

I look at him and laugh. *I do suck without her.*

My thoughts toss and tumble around that entire morning once again: the look on her face, the pain in her voice, the tears that welled up in her eyes that I seemed to miss until this moment, her running away, something I do so well when I am hurting. Plus, everything that Bethany told me about Alyssa finding out about her dad. Obviously there is a bigger issue on her plate than me or this other guy.

I do love her, even after seeing her with him for a second time; I still love her, so it's time to act like it ... to fight for her.

"I'll do it if you do it?"

Evan raises his eyebrows and sighs out a small laugh. "You got it."

It's time I get some answers and remind her of what we had.

Follow her anywhere

"HEY, I'LL CATCH YOU later. I need to do something before I head to work." I wave over my shoulder as we both exit the café and swing around to the left to the pastry shop that is three doors down.

"Hey, I forgot to tell you," Evan calls out as he opens the passenger side of his work truck. Pulling out a large paper bag, he adds, "I was cleaning out my camper while I was at the lake this weekend and I found this." He holds the bag out towards me. "It's all the fireworks that we didn't use this summer. I wasn't sure if you wanted them or not, but I just loaded a bunch of junk I didn't need laying around out there and figured I'd give these back to you or Tristan to hang on to."

"Yeah, sure. Just take them to the apartment," I say, turning to dart away. Another idea springs to mind and I pause, mid step. "Wait."

Turning on only the balls of my feet, I turn back to Evan as he halts on depositing the bag back into the passenger floor board of the truck. He stares at me blankly, holding the bag between us. My hands clutch onto the crinkled grocery bag that now feels like coarse leather from being crumpled closed for the last several months.

Pulling it open with one hand while I brace the other palm up, at the bottom of the bag, I reach my hand in and peer down at the maze of fireworks, fountains and rockets that were abandoned after the Fourth. My eyes swiftly land on a small red, white and blue diagonally striped fire cracker. *Perfect.*

"What, you planning on setting off some rockets on that dude's front lawn? Maybe we could set them up on the lawn to spell out 'get lost scumbag'," he says excitedly with an over eager grin painted on his face.

I shake my head, "Not a bad idea," I chuckle. "But no … I'll see you in a bit at the job site."

Thirty minutes later, I'm standing back in her apartment, staring at the little white container that I just got from one of the best bakery shops in Rosemore. Mom used to go there and buy us fudge every week when we were younger. They made it right there in front of you on a huge marble slab. I remember how it would melt in your mouth and slide down your tongue, making your taste buds scream for more.

Flipping the lid up on the container, I stare down at the warm, gooey brownie that I hand-picked just minutes ago. Still holding onto the small firecracker, I squeeze it tighter in hopes of relaying just a bit of what she is to me with this. Last thing I want is for this to come off as some pathetic and lame attempt at winning her back.

I love her, so of course I want her back, but more over, I want to remind her just how much.

I want her to know that I heard every word she said when we would talk for hours.

I also want her to think back to the night I finally found the guts to say I love you, because I have never meant those words more than I did when I said them to her.

With a deep breath, I push the firecracker into the center of the soft creamy square of chocolate, spongy chunks crumble up around it instantly. The warmth of it reaches my fingertips, as I stare down at it perfectly cradled into the center and think back on the day when she told me about the significance of brownies. I smile, proud that I decided to do this, even if it doesn't mean the same thing to her. It reminds me of all the notes, cards and flowers that my brothers and I would leave on Mom's nightstand as she grew sicker, after her legs refused to work anymore. Up until she could no longer work her mouth to even eat, it managed to put a smile on her face, despite the pain of the disease that was ripping her apart.

Leaving Alyssa's apartment and heading to work, my shoulders are lighter and my heart is hopeful for the first time in months.

The day swims by in a current of thoughts, confusion, and frustration, leaving me waking up the next day from a dream that was so vivid that I can still taste her lips on mine. *I refuse to only dream about her for the rest of my life. I need to talk to her. No matter how badly the answers may hurt and tear me apart, I have to know what happened. There is no way I imagined what she felt for me; I saw it. The night we finally gave into our desires, I saw it in her eyes and I felt it in every touch. I could see that same look in her eyes Saturday morning; love. Some things are not adding up and I won't give up until I find out why.*

After my first mid morning class, I stride across campus, anxious to get through the day and figure out a game plan for contacting her. *Surely she has the same number and I know where she lives, but the last thing I want to do is ....*

My train of thought comes to a screeching halt as I round the corner of the Music and Arts building. *There she is.* The air seems to get thicker as my breath catches in my throat. Fumbling for my phone, I stare in disbelief as she sways her hips side-to-side with a black and white wavy patterned backpack slung over her shoulder. My eyes drop down and sweep over her small frame from her tight jeans to her dark purple v-neck sweater that falls just below her waist and clings to her hips. The small scrap of lace that hangs from under her sweater has my mind doing flips and turns with thoughts of what lies beneath.

Nodding my head, I shove all those thoughts to the back of my mind and quickly type out a vague message to her and hit send.

She instantly stops, ransacking through her bag until she holds her phone in her hands. I'm still several yards away, but I can see her clearly and the look that crosses her face confuses me; almost angry or hurt. *Why would she be hurt over me wanting to talk about this?* Hastily shoving the phone back in her bag, she continues in the same direction that she was headed before. I drop my mouth open and let out an exasperated breath, not sure how to take this. *What the hell? Really?* Raising my phone up to eye level, I scan the text I sent to make sure that there is no way for it to be interpreted wrong.

Me: Hey, I doubt you still have my number in your phone, but I figured I would give it a shot anyways. I think we should

talk, plus I wanted to see if you got my gift?

How can that be taken wrong? Confused and a little pissed myself, my fingers speed over the keys of my phone, impatient and desperate to get her attention now.

Me: Ignoring me! Really!? The least you could do is talk to me!

I hit send, pushing off from the corner of the building where I have been standing. My chest rises as I suck in a deep breath of courage and I stroll towards her, desperately wanting to be able to just walk up to her and throw my arms around her waist like I used to. *Why does everything good in my life always have to change?*

As I near her, I see the features of her face shift into a vicious lioness determined to defend her cubs; if I had to go off of how I feel myself, I would say it is her heart she is protecting.

Out of all the noise and chaos going on around us, my ears zoom in on the thud her phone makes as she recklessly throws it back into her bag, again without responding. With that, my footsteps slow and I'm second guessing confronting her at this moment. She's a little thing, but by the scornful look on her face, I'm half thinking it's me she'd like to body slam rather than the phone. Unfortunately my mouth must not have gotten that memo, because without any further thought, words vibrate up my throat and out my mouth before I can stop them.

"So, I take it you don't want to talk to me?" My voice comes out in a resentful and defeated tone, so unlike how I used to speak to her.

Lowering my brows, I shove my hands into my pockets to keep them at my side, because all I want to do right now is to pull her into my arms and erase all the pain and hurt in her eyes. It takes every ounce of will power I have in my body to keep my face drawn into an angry glare, but like her, I have to protect my heart.

For a brief moment, when her lips part and her sky blue eyes lock with mine, the love that used to shine for me in them flickers by and the entire barrier I'm holding up nearly falters. The frown on my face melts and I draw my eyebrows up in hope that I can get her back; maybe not today, but eventually. It's only a second, then her arms defensively slide across her chest and the hope that rose within me takes a nose dive into a pit of dread. We're right back where we were.

"You really aren't going to talk to me, after everything that happened between us this summer?" My voice cracks as I attempt to sound stern and unaffected by her, all while my heart is being ripped right out of my chest and crushed into a million pieces.

Words erupt out of her mouth as if she has been waiting months to throw them at me, "What we shared?! Are you kidding me! As if that meant anything to you! I mean really … how many notches have you put in your belt since I last saw you?!"

What … the … hell! Did she really just accuse me of being a player? Seriously? My first attempt at whooing her into a night of pleasure lasted all of ten seconds and she thinks I'm a player? I have literally spent three months enduring cold showers and batting off good looking girls that were throwing themselves at me, but I am now finding out I am putting notches on my belt. *Does she even know what that phrase means?*

"What is that supposed to mean? And why on earth would you think it didn't mean …"

Pieces of the puzzle slowly start to slide together and an understanding for what has happened between us starts to sink in just as 'sugar and spice' herself walks up, wedging herself into our conversation. Her bubbly voice takes a back seat as I listen to my own screaming thoughts. *She still loves me; she never stopped.*

My eyes flick back to Alyssa who looks at Bethany in utter confusion, but all I can think about is this summer.

A marathon of thoughts run through my mind, looking back at our time together at the lake to the morning I woke up to see her face again. Making record time in my thoughts, I go over the conversation Bethany and I had after Alyssa left with pretty-boy. *Her dad's cancer returned and she went back to a guy that treated her like complete crap. Is that a coincidence? Maybe since I had been unable to be there in that moment, it left her needing someone's comfort; anyone's comfort when her world was falling apart.* This revelation leaves me hopeful and a bit delusional, yet still does not douse the anger and hurt I feel over her letting me go.

My eyes swing to Bethany as I work to catch up on what they

have been talking about.

"Were you guys discussing your initial meeting or something else?" Bethany asks, looking from Alyssa to me and positioning herself as close to me as possible.

I decide to stay quiet for now. It's very clear that Alyssa never told her about me, which I find extremely odd. Honestly, I thought girls told each other everything.

"I was just apologizing for busting in on you two the other morning."

Pushing my eyebrows down into a frown in an effort to resist smiling, I watch as Alyssa uncomfortably shifts and comes up with a bland excuse for our argument. My amusement is quickly snuffed as Bethany's arm brushes up against mine. I move, trying my best to put a little space between me and her. *I'd much rather prefer Alyssa to be the one standing so close.* I cast my gaze back to Alyssa, my heart beating harder and louder once her eyes meet mine.

"Well it sure looked like a heated discussion."

I keep my eyes glued on Alyssa, watching for any sign of emotion from the memory of that morning, but I see none, just anger and frustration as she dismisses the conversation and walks away.

"Sooooo …"

Bethany's voice shreds over my nerves like a sharp pair of scissors as I stare longingly at Alyssa, heading towards the parking lot. Bethany's arm swipes across mine once again, but I cannot even focus on her presence.

"You and me … Wednesday?"

Her face suddenly blocks my view of Alyssa as her lips brush the corner of my mouth.

"Whoa …" I jolt backwards and away from her, firmly yet carefully placing my hands on her shoulders to form a barrier between us.

I sure the hell hope Alyssa didn't see that. What the hell does it take to get across to Bethany that I'm not interested? My first instinct is to lash out and ask her what her deal is, but then her words sink in; *Wednesday, Alyssa's party.*

"Hey, I thought we agreed to be friends; just friends?" I grit my teeth as her arms cross over her chest, as if this is news to her.

Something tells me that Bethany does not get turned down a lot, so maybe letting her down easy is not the best way to go here. Quickly flipping through any tid-bit of knowledge and experience I have with women, which isn't much, my mind starts flashing and blaring alarms to deter the conversation. *Distraction! No way am I going to burn a perfectly laid bridge to get closer to the girl that I love.* I have no intention of using Bethany to gain ground, but I can keep things cordial between us.

Right as she grudgingly turns to walk away from me, I open my mouth to steer the discussion to something that hopefully will peak her interest and lighten the mood.

"Hey about Wednesday, sure I am still coming!" I spit out eagerly, not wanting to miss the opportunity to be there.

Without hesitation, her posture perks up and she spins back around to face me, this time with a comfortable amount of distance between us. Her eyes glimmer with excitement like a cat eyeballing a dangling string; now I have her attention.

Think, think! If I have learned anything from this girl's over reactive personality in the past few weeks, it is that me agreeing to go to a party only as her friend is not going to be good enough. What else can I possibly throw out there to soften the blow of "let's just be friends?" All of a sudden, my mind slams to a stop as I see Alyssa's little red car drive out of the parking lot.

Bethany's eyes widen and a huge smile forms on her face at my announcement to go to the party with her, so I decide now is the time to snuff that out just enough to still be invited and not have to deal with too much added drama.

"It sounds like it will be a blast to hang with you and your friends." Her expression falls quickly, so I add, "By the way, does your roommate like fireworks by any chance?"

Bethany's face glosses over with confusion which seems to be a normal expression for her. She wears it well. "The reason I ask is because I have a whole slew of fireworks left over from this past Fourth." I smile at my proposal, knowing if anything will get to Alyssa and spark emotion from our time together, this has to be it. "It'd make one hell of a grand finale, plus I'm sure we could grease the wheels with the cops so that we don't get in trouble for a mid-fall firework display."

Bethany squeals and although I would like nothing more than to rip my ears clean off my head, it actually sends a bolt of delight through me knowing that a few leftover fireworks may be my key to holding Alyssa again.

"Oh my gosh, that is perfect! You know I didn't plan anything for the end of the night other than a last call, but that would be epic! Plus you know what, Kyle has a friend whose older brother is on the police force, I bet we could get him to ok it, we'll just have to be careful because …"

The name Kyle flares in my mind and I shut everything else she has to say out as she gushes about her plans for the party. After a ten minutes walk back to my truck, my mind is doing flips over why Alyssa would subject herself to comfort from her cheating ex. Not to mention, I literally feel like my ears are bleeding with Bethany's endless chatter. No way could I tolerate putting up with her obsessive need to go on and on about every detail of her day unless it meant it would end with me possibly having Alyssa back in my life.

After my escape, the day crawls by laughing in my face and leaving me impatient and anxious.

The following day I rush around work as if it is my last day on earth, then speed home to get ready to see her again. Right now I may be the last person she wants to see, especially if Bethany has made it out that this is a date, but with any luck at all by the end of the evening I'll be the only thing on her mind.

Racing up to their apartment after practically burning the tread off my tires, I think back to some of the sappy movies that Jake and I would watch in secret on the living room floor. Mom and Dad would be snuggled up on the couch as a couple on TV clung to each other in a passion-filled kiss or hug after a quarrel. At the time, that stuff made me want to puke, but what I always remembered from those movies is when I would glance over to Mom and Dad, her eyes were always glazed over while Dad would quickly brush away the escaped tears with a smile.

If this were one of those movies, a few sparkles in the sky tonight would have Alyssa running straight into my arms. My shoulders raise and my chest expands as I take a deep breath, savoring that thought.

"Hey," Bethany calls out behind me, making my nerves bounce.

"I thought I saw you drive up. Go in and I will be back in a sec to get the birthday girl," she giggles and darts away, leaving fate screaming my name and pushing me forward.

Twisting the knob slowly, I nudge the door open not knowing what to expect. She said she was coming back for the birthday girl, so Alyssa has to be here, only I'm not sure if that jerk-off could be here as well. *I refuse to call him her boyfriend.*

Sticking my head in first, I am met with complete silence. The door swings open with a shove and I walk in, my heart dropping once I see an empty room. Looking around, there are very little traces of her other than a ring of a dozen keys bound together with a bright pink keychain that reads 'Cancer sucks.' Drawing my eyebrows together, a jolt of pain slices through my heart as I think of the agonizing grief losing a parent creates in your life. Everything in my soul is pulling for her to not have to endure that.

Striding forward, I make my way to the couch as a rattle in the next room bounces me out of my thoughts and instantly has my nerves wound up tight in my stomach. I press my hands into the soft cushions to keep from springing forward when another sound interrupts the silence. Lowering myself to sit, my eyes dart to the door beside her bedroom, which I'm positive is the bathroom. Closing them tightly, I let my mind imagine what she may be doing in there in preparation for her party. My hands ball up, clutching the plush fabric of the couch as I remember beads of water flowing through her hair and over her delicate skin.

"Stop thinking about crap like that," I mutter quietly to myself.

Opening my eyes back up and releasing the death grip my fist has on the couch, my already pounding heart is thrown into overdrive as the bathroom door swings open and out steps a sexy as hell Alyssa in a tight blue dress and boots clear up to her knees. *Wow.* Snapping my mouth shut to keep from releasing slobber that is pooling in my mouth, I jump off of the couch and step forward towards her.

My eyes automatically take on a mind of their own, slowly sweeping down her body and back up. Wildly pounding in my chest, my heart does a flip when I look into her eyes and see complete vulnerability. It's the same look she gave me the night we were together. She laid beneath me as I finally reveled in every inch of her beauty.

"Wow … you look beautiful," I choke out as I relive a time when she was much less clothed, yet she is just as breathtaking in this very moment.

We stare into each other's eyes and although I should be talking, asking questions and getting to the bottom of what happened between us, I cannot speak. Words have escaped us both and all I want to do is touch her, kiss her, wrap my arms around her and never let go. Every muscle in my legs twitch, needing to move, imploring me to get her, to grab her.

As I lift my foot to step forward and close the few feet between us that seems like miles, Bethany's all too cheerful voice calls out, "It's all set."

Clinching my jaw to keep from blaring out the multitude of curse words whirling through my head, I clear my throat and walk to the door as Alyssa joins Bethany to go downstairs. The moment is lost, and all I want to do is slap myself for not blurting everything out. Once I get to the door, I pause gripping the knob to help stabilize my quaking body and my accelerated heart beat. Keeping my gaze down to the floor so that I don't give away all that I am feeling, Bethany and Alyssa make their way past me.

After closing the door behind me, I keep my eyes trained on her boots, listening to the clicking sound they make each time it snaps against the concrete hall floor.

Click

Click

Click

My heart thuds out in response to each step as we continue out the apartment complex and around to the back. I don't need to be told where we're going, I don't even care, because the truth is as long as she will let me, I will follow her anywhere.

I'm Done

STAYING ONLY A FEW feet behind them with every fiber of my body zinging with anticipation of the end of the night, we walk across the back parking lot to a one level building. Bethany grabs hold of one of the big glass doors at the front of the building, but I quickly press my hand flush against the cold glass to hold it open for them both.

As soon as Alyssa steps inside, the room erupts in cheers and shouts, wishing her a happy birthday. I can only make out a hint of her smile as she throws her hand over her mouth, but through the deafening noise of the party, I don't miss the beautiful sound of her giggles.

It doesn't take long for Alyssa to get lost in the crowd, without a single glance in my direction. I, however, position myself towards the front wall of the building separate from her and Bethany. Last thing I want is for Bethany to be hanging on me, plus a part of me enjoys being able to see Alyssa smiling and laughing with her friends at a distance.

Until I can figure out a way to break through this wall that has been built up between us since the day I left the lake, it's probably best that I don't try to mingle and party with her like there is nothing there. Standing with my foot braced against the wall near the keg, I watch as everyone around me gets a bit more unstable on their feet with each passing minute.

Abby and Piper walk by quickly, giving me a snarled glare that tells me Alyssa must have some seriously pent up feelings about me that she has been sharing with them. I wave in reply, but slowly let my hand fall to my side as they swing their heads around and storm off. Other than the morning she walked in and found me with Bethany, I'm not quite sure what any of them could be mad about and by now she should know from Bethany that absolutely nothing happened; if she told her.

A couple classmates swing by carrying on idle chatter, but I can't stop my eyes from swinging back to her.

Little by little, I watch as her legs wobble beneath her, how she throws her head back belting out laughter until her face turns red and even the way she begins to talk with her hands, swinging them about wildly. *I've never seen her drunk like this; tipsy yeah, but never like this.*

My lips curve up into a smile and I can't help but remember all the things that made me fall in love with her. It happened so fast, yet I've never been surer of anything else in my life.

She looks in my direction and finally we make eye contact when a familiar face comes into my line of view.

"Hey Judd. Wow, crazy seeing you here." Skylar walks towards me with a booze induced grin across her face and a beer bottle clutched in one hand. Slinking up against the wall beside me, she turns her head and looks me up and down. "Aren't you drinking?"

I dip my chin down and laugh, thinking over the few times I have indulged.

"Nahh … I don't drink much." Looking over at her I smile, "I don't have much of a tolerance and it is *never* a pretty sight."

She cracks up at my answer and peers around the room. "I really don't think drunk is pretty on anyone, including me."

I look through the crowd to Alyssa, which looks to be on a losing streak in a game of quarters. She tosses back another shot then slams the glass down, bursting out in laughter. I definitely have to disagree with Skylar; drunk is pretty on some of us.

"So are you two still hooking up?"

I snap my head around and see that she too is looking out at Alyssa. *Hooking up?* I've never cared too much for that phrase, but to associate it with what Alyssa and I share, at least what I thought we shared, hits a sour note in my mind and I immediately crinkle my brows in irritation.

Opening my mouth to correct her, I am met with even more aggravation.

"Hey handsome!" Bethany's slurred voice rings out like a shrill siren that's meant to make people take off running.

I turn from Skylar to Bethany, barely able to see Alyssa in the distance over her shoulder.

All I can muster up is a weak smile as she adds, "Why don't you come over and join us in a game of quarters?"

She leans in closer to me, running her hand over my bicep then swings her gaze over to Skylar as if she is marking her territory. I flinch at her touch, swiftly looking back over her shoulder. Alyssa giddily sways back and forth on a make shift dance floor with a group of girls. I breathe out a sigh of relief as Skylar pushes off from the wall.

"I think it is time for another." Skylar wiggles her empty beer bottle in front of her face and gives me one last smile. "I'll see you around. Tell Evan I said hi."

"See ya," I say as I wrap my hand around Bethany's small wrist and gently pull her wandering paws off of my body.

"I was actually getting ready to run out to my truck and get that bag of fireworks." I discretely sidestep out from between her and the wall.

She pivots her body back in alignment with mine as I back away. "Oh, I'll go with you," she states confidently.

My eyes widen as I resist the urge of bolting. *She is halfway blitzed, clingy as hell and no way am I walking alone in the dark with her out to my truck. I have no doubt that this chick will flat out attack my ass.*

"No really, I'll be right back," I say holding my finger up then quickly pointing over her shoulder to Alyssa and the rest of the group she has been drinking with. "Actually, you know I think they were motioning for you to come join them."

As soon as she turns to look in their direction, I dart off through the double doors at the front of the hall, blazing a path to my truck. *Damn, is it normal for a girl to intimidate the hell out of a guy like that?*

A few minutes later, I have the bunched up edge of the brown paper bag of fireworks firmly grasped in my hand and head back to the worn down brick building. My phone vibrates against my leg and I immediately shove my free hand in my pocket to retrieve it. Like a magnet, my finger goes right to the home button with a push and my phone lights up a new text. Swiping my hand across the screen, I open up the message, shocked.

Tristan: Hey, I just wanted to say hi and see how you were doing …

It's brief and vague, but a surprise after Jake explaining that he doesn't want to talk or see anyone the last several weeks.

I stop my trek back to the building, wedging the crinkled bag under my arm as I stare at the screen not quite sure what to say back. The days' light is faded away stretching into a sky full of shimmering stars and a sliver of moon with the muffled thumps of bass and music filtering out from the hall. I stare down, the light from my phone going black until another message pops up.

Tristan: Listen, I know I've been an ass …

Raising my eyebrows in disbelief of his confession, I nod to myself in agreement and wait.

Tristan: Ok, maybe an ass is putting it lightly, but I would like to talk. I'm pretty tied up the next few days, but I'll be home this weekend if you want to stop by. Maybe you, me and Jake can watch some football.

My hand shakes, but I still cannot make myself type anything. This is him trying; I know he is trying, but why is it so hard for me to do the same. For so many years there has been this barrier between us. We rarely get along and when we do, it ends in a fight or worse. The emptiness that fills my heart echoes with an intense need for so many people that have disappeared from my life. It burns inside of me every day.

Taking a deep breath I type …

Me: Sounds Good!

I hit send and let out the breath I was holding when I hear no immediate reply. Speechless and a little taken aback, I wander back into the hall and come face-to-face with Bethany standing near the doors.

"Hey, is this them?" She reaches for the bag and I gladly hand them off, ready to get to the end of the night.

"Yeah …" I say with a lump in my throat and my mind now set on Tristan.

A part of me wants to go back outside and call my brother. There are so many things that I'd like to be able to talk to him about, but in the back of my mind I always fear it turning into a fight, so I hold back.

"This is great," Bethany squeals, knocking me out of my thoughts. "Go get a drink and I'll find you in a bit. I'm going to go get this all set up."

I watch her race away, not at all paying attention to the path in front of me until I run smack dab into someone. The subtle scent of strawberries mixed with a conglomeration of whiskey and beer penetrates my senses and I instinctively reach my hands out to pull the small body against me. I don't even need to see her face to know it's her; every cell in my body is tuned into the way she moves, feels, smells and sounds.

"Whoa, are you ok? I whisper, turning my head to look at her.

Alyssa's glossy eyes meet mine and my heart speeds out of control. The heat from her hand against my chest breaches the fabric of my shirt, scorching my skin and leaving me hungry for her. The desire to kiss her overwhelms me, tugging and pulling with a storm of emotions that I can barely keep at bay. Swiping my tongue over my lips to fight the urge, her eyes flick down to my mouth and then back up. *There used to be no question in my mind as to when she wanted to be kissed; I knew her needs just like I know my own.*

My reaction must be obvious, because like clockwork Alyssa mutters, "I'm fine," swiftly pulling away and leaving my arms bare.

Still grasping my phone in my hand, I shove both hands in my pocket to avoid pulling her back to me and making a fool of myself.

I want you … I love you … I need you … all fly through my head and work their way to the tip of my tongue, begging to be said, but I don't.

"Alyssa, can we go outside and talk?" The ache in my heart breaks through and my voice quivers out in pain with my words.

I look down as her hand flinches a fraction towards me. Instantly looking back to her eyes for a trace of what is going through her head, her defiant expression that has masked her face the last several times we've had a run in, has softened. For a moment I think I have her won …

"Just the two I was looking for," Bethany's voice breaks through our seclusion and nearly sends me through the roof with frustration.

I swear this girl plans her interruptions; just like Evan; only Evan knows when to back off! My head pounds in irritation to the point of bursting.

"Ok so I keep catching you two talking like you've known each other forever. So spill … what are ya'll chatting about all the time?"

My eyes widen and I glance at Alyssa with a smirk that I definitely cannot hide. I'd like to grab a bull horn and holler out at the top of my lungs … *finally, Bethany … you're getting a clue.* It would be so much easier if this was all out in the open. I'm still a little confused as to why Bethany wouldn't know about Alyssa's summer with me, but I'll play along. Eyeing Alyssa, I eagerly wait for how she will talk her way out of this.

"We were just discussing school and fall season football. You know, since him and Kyle both play."

Her answer both amuses me and serves as a reminder as to why I should be pissed off. *Frankly, I cannot believe she used his name and mine in the same sentence, let alone right in front of me. What a slap in the face.*

A mist of beer shoots out of Bethany's mouth as she drunkenly rants on about school and partying, but I keep my eyes on Alyssa, tuning out every word that drops from her mouth.

"You play football?"

Bethany's question catches me off guard until I realize this is the perfect gateway for cluing Alyssa in on a part of my life; she's got to wonder why I'm not at UCLA, yet she's never asked. That alone crushes me that she cares that little for me. My head whirls with confusion on what the hell is going on with her. There are so many crucial pieces of this puzzle that seem to be missing. I only want a chance to understand; I need to, or this hole in my heart may swallow me up.

"No ... I don't play. I used to play," I say calmly, not caring in the least if Bethany notices how I cannot take my eyes off Alyssa.

She stares at me with a wounded expression, a crease forming between her eyebrows and her glassy eyes taking on a tint of remorse.

"We have a little surprise for the Birthday Girl! So if everyone could make their way out to the parking lot, we can fire it up!" The MC announces, bringing a small smile to my face.

Looking completely mystified by either my reply or by the knowledge there is a surprise waiting for her outside, Alyssa looks at me wide eyed with her lips parted as if she is on the verge of saying something. Bethany, true to her interfering-self, swiftly grabs her by the arm and Alyssa clamps her mouth shut, giving me a long look before Bethany drags her out the door for her grand finale.

As the mass of people flood out the door; I get held up behind a couple lollygaggers taking their sweet time, but manage to get outside and within a couple bodies of Alyssa. As soon as the first boom goes off, *Ooo's* and *Ahh's* sound all around, however I don't bother to look up. My eyes automatically drift to Alyssa, my heart hammering in anticipation of her reaction. At this point I'm not sure if this subtle attempt at getting her attention will make her angry, sad or happy, but I'm hoping it stirs up a storm of nostalgia in her heart.

Blood races through my veins as my heart rate picks up at the expression on her face. Bethany and Abby both stand by her side saying something, but the look of utter shock and surprise on her face is unmistakable. Sparks of light above us illuminate everyone in the dark parking lot, but all I see is her. Her eyes swing over to mine and I see it; she's remembering the night we spent under the spray of fireworks. Her face is etched in pain, yearning and tenderness all wrapped together to create one of the most beautiful expressions I've ever seen.

Pulling my brows together in sorrow of these many missed months together, I open my mouth ready to spill out all the feelings my heart holds for her. She stares at me with an equal amount of love and regret and at this very moment, if I told her I love her, I have no doubt that she would say it back.

Just as the words are about to slide over my tongue and spill out of my mouth, I remember how much she had to drink earlier.

I pause, wanting her full awareness when I say those words again, so I take a quick detour and say the words that make the most sense at this time, "Happy birthday." My voice comes out in a low whisper and although no one else could possibly hear above all the cracks and booms overhead, I know she did.

She offers me a small, loving smile then quickly slides away in the direction of her apartment, only a second after the last firework explodes in the sky. Barreling through the sea of people cascading back inside the building, I try to catch up with her. Not even thinking about it, I round the corner of her apartment complex not far behind her and watch as she slips inside. Quietly, I guide myself to the door, but as soon as I see her, Alyssa's phone chimes and she lifts it to her ear. My heart is still soaring with hope and optimism for us, but with one word all of that is swept away.

"Hi Kyle," she says in a quivery tone, walking into her apartment and turning just enough for me to catch a glimpse of her tear-streaked face.

The last thing I notice as her body disappears through the door is the small smile that emerges on her face as she grips the phone to her ear, hanging on to whatever he is saying to her. Turning away from the door, I meld my back against the cold brick surface of her building, feeling the uneven, sharp edges of brick jab into my skin. There for a minute, I was so lost in her that I overlooked how she threw me aside, all to go back to a guy that did the same to her only for a moment of pleasure. *I made her cry, he made her smile.*

Shaking my head, I bolt away from the building toward my truck with the fabric of my shirt clutched in my hand so hard that it feels as though the blood supply to my knuckles has been cut off. A razor sharp pain slices through my heart and it is all I can do to hold it together from shattering. All I care to do at this point is drag myself back home and fall into bed, hoping that sleep will wash away all the emotions from this night. *I'm done.*

Back in my arms

T HE NEXT DAY I wake up with a renewed sense of faith and urgency blazing through every ounce of my body. Last night I felt hopeless, but a new day brings determination; I have to see her; I have to get to the bottom of this once and for all. There is no way I will be able to move on until I hear her say she doesn't love me, that she never did. I need to hear that she wanted him all along and not me, that I was just a side-line until she got back home to take him back. Until those words flow from her mouth, I will forever sway back and forth between anger and hope, hurt and happiness; I will always, always wonder why.

With no morning classes, I head out the door an hour before Evan wakes and fly to the work site that I am helping to oversee. After sliding my key into the padlock on the chain link fence that surrounds the site of the soon to be new downtown mall, I push the gate fully open then jump back into my truck.

Once I'm parked in front of the tiny white trailer that I spend most of my time in during work hours, I jump out and run inside to get my day started. I just need to stay busy until this evening, then I have every intention of marching over to Alyssa's apartment and demanding we talk. She avoids any amount of confrontation with me, so it's obvious that I will have to catch her at a susceptible point when she cannot run away from all that needs to be discussed.

Hours stretch on and glancing at the clock becomes almost torturous. Some early morning drama and stupidity at least manages to keep me busy until it is mid-morning and time for me to clock out. Luckily, today is jam packed with an early physical therapy appointment so when 10:30 comes, I head to my truck ready to get it over with.

Throwing my hand up in the air to wave at Evan as he drives onto the lot, I hop into my truck, slam the door and fire up the engine to head out. He stops his truck beside mine and rolls down his window as I'm pulling out.

"Hey, anything interesting going on or can I just go back home?" Evan says with a grin.

"Not much. I had to send one of the guys to get his back checked out. I don't know if he is planning a career in weight lifting or if he suddenly thinks he is a super hero, but he was trying to move one of those steel beams by hand. Dumbass could barely stand straight when I got over there, so I had Jerry run him to get it looked at. I called your grandfather and let him know. There are also a couple loads of cement that should be on their way, but it was held up so I told those guys to finish what they could and head for an early lunch."

Evan shakes his head, taking everything in. "You got class?"

"No, therapy."

"Aren't you almost done with those?"

I laugh, raising my shoulder up to test it out.

"It feels pretty good, but my muscles get fatigued easily."

Evan laughs, a shitty ass grin forming over his face. "Use your hand a little more, that'll help get the muscles back in shape."

Rolling my eyes with a sigh, I shake my head at Evan. "Bye, Evan." Throwing my hand up in the air, I speed off as I hear him laughing over his own joke.

My therapy session goes smoothly, as always, and after a brief lecture on how I am putting too much stress on my shoulder too quickly and following several silly band exercises, I head through a drive-thru then over to the college for three afternoon classes. By the time my last class lets out and I make it back to my truck my dashboard clock reads 4:55.

The whole way to Alyssa's apartment, my speedometer reads ten miles over the speed limit, but my pulse races faster. Pulling into the front of her apartment building, I see car after car pulling into the back lot by the hall and spilling out into their parking lot. Knowing I will never find a spot, I choose to park along the road adjacent to the building.

Gripping my keys in my hand tightly, I hop out, dodge oncoming cars to get across the street and sprint to her door.

My knuckles drum against the solid wood door creating an echo in the vacant hall as I stand there silently, staring at the faded red paint and square patterns on the door. Impatience ricochets off every nerve in my body pulling up an overpowering excitement and anxiety within me. A minute passes by and all my nervousness starts to unravel, creating a knot in my belly. Raising my arm, I tap my fist to the door once again, this time with more force and vigor. Once my arm drops back down to my side, a throbbing flares all the way up into my shoulder.

Eagerly waiting and hoping that the door will fly open, I turn and lean against the wall beside the door. *What now?* I didn't even think that she may not be home. Turning my head sideways, I look at the quiet lonely door with all my excitement, hope, and determination slowly dripping into the pit of my stomach.

Not moving an inch but ready to jump out of my skin with impatience, I rap my knuckles on the door one final time before I give up. I keep my arm raised, my hand only millimeters from the door. Everything in my body seems to have paused as I hold my breath and silently wait, straining to hear inside the apartment for any movement or sound. Slowly all the sounds in my body pierce my ear drums as I hear the steady beat of my heart, the wisp of my eyelashes as I blink and even the moist sounds of me gulping down the last bit of hope I have left.

I give up and head back to my truck, with my head hung low and both hands shoved in my pockets. Feeling a little like a child who just lost a game of kickball, I take my frustrations out on a stone in my pathway by kicking it across the road.

After hopping into my truck, I insert the key in the ignition and jump from the sudden chime of my phone breaking through the silence. I temporarily abandon my keys, leaving them dangling in my truck as I fetch my phone from my pocket.

Once I see Bethany's name, my disappointment in my evening

plans quickly turn to irritation, until I read the beginning of her message. **Hey handsome! How about you come have a bite to eat on me? :P Alyssa just ...**

My eyes widen and I swipe the screen to read the full text, curiosity racing through my veins when I see Alyssa's name.

Bethany: Hey handsome! How about you come have a bite to eat on me? ;)
Alyssa just left to head back home and now I am all by my lonesome and it is super slow! Any chance you would be up for a free meal and a visit? Maybe after we can go back to my place to hang out? :0)

My first instinct is aggravation, since the winky-face following the "a bite on me" comment says she clearly cannot take a hint, but then I see that she says Alyssa is headed home. Immediately, I look up at the parking lot, my eyes fly past the traffic flowing into the conference center behind the complex. The same car that Alyssa was driving the day she raced away from me on campus still perfectly parked to the left side of the building.

Me: Thanks for the offer, but I have something going on.

I type out a simple response, hit send then throw my phone onto the seat beside me, not caring whether or not she'll text back.

Looking back up at her car and listening to the chaotic ramblings of my mind wondering if she is out to dinner with another guy, I sigh and slam my hands to the wheel. *I should just leave.* With the smooth metal of my key pinched between my fingers, I stop all efforts of leaving and freeze, staring straight ahead down the sidewalk. A small, slender figure walks into view and even though the face is not clear, there is no mistaking the curves of her body.

I jerk the keys out of the ignition and rise up off the seat to slide them back in my pocket right as she walks up to her building. The front light of the complex cascades over her silhouette as she walks to the door, bouncing off her long, blonde hair and making my pulse quicken with eagerness to see her.

As she steps inside, I fling the door of my truck open, jet out into the night air and sprint across the street, ready to get all that has been between us for the last several months out of the way once and for all.

It takes all of a few seconds for me to make it back to her door. Wasting not a single minute longer, I tap my fist to the door lightly, suddenly nervous, then wait … and wait … and wait. My patience has worn thin and my jittery insides are flipping, spinning and whirling about. *Come on, Alyssa, answer the door.*

My hand falls to the knob and I stare ahead, my face so close to the door that I can nearly feel the vibrations of the earth through it. Gritting my teeth, I test the knob to see if it is locked. When it lets out a clicking sound and refuses to move any further, my heart plummets. *Locked … dammit.*

Without a second to think about it, I reach into my pocket and pull out my keys with a smile on my face. *That's right.* Staring down at the extra key that has found a resting place on my keychain this week, I silently say my thanks to Bethany.

As soon as I slide it into the knob and hear the familiar clicking of the lock, a sigh trembles out of my mouth. Aware that breaking in will more than likely startle her, I push the door open slowly, ready for my ears to be greeted with a scream from my intrusion.

Holding it at arm's length, my eyes widen as I see the orange sweater that I swore I saw on Alyssa just a few minutes ago, sitting on the floor not far from me. Picking up on the sounds of running water directly in front of me, my eyes dart over a path of garments ending in a pair of black lace panties right in front of the closed bathroom door. My eyebrows draw upward in amusement. What do you know … a *shower.*

The corners of my mouth twitch until I am smiling from ear-to-ear with memories of Alyssa and I caught up in the moment in the lake shower house. I shake my head and chuckle; this is precisely the exact opportunity I've been waiting for. *Now she can't run or refuse to talk to me and I really don't give a damn how creepy this may seem; this is me and Alyssa.*

Crossing the room, I have one thing on my mind and it is not sex or seeing her naked. I want answers; I want to know what the hell happened, finally.

As my hand wraps around the bathroom door knob, I silently pray for courage and strength to accept whatever her answers may be, with grace and maturity. After my quiet plea, I turn the knob and step into a steam-filled bathroom, my heart pounding up into my throat.

Stopping right past the doorway, I see a small wooden vanity only a couple feet from the shower. Although the shower curtain is a thick, white vinyl material, I can still see her silhouette as she stops what she's doing and frantically looks around.

"Hello!" Her trembling voice calls out, "Bethany, is that you?"

Guilt burns in my chest, knowing that I have scared her.

"No, it's me." I speak up, seeing that she has picked up an oblong bottle, more than likely hell bent on launching it at her mystery intruder's head.

The sudden movement of the shower curtain being torn to the side and Alyssa's barely covered dripping wet body, instantly have my attention.

"What the hell are you doing in here?" she snaps out.

The way her brows crease and her forehead crinkles has me second thinking my plan of confronting her, yet something about the way she stands there with a shampoo bottle clutched in her hand as a form of defense is pretty comical. A part of me really just wants to forget the drama and ask her, "Really, Alyssa … a shampoo bottle?"

Holding back all my desires to look further down than her chin, and trying my best not to snicker from how riled up she is, I slouch back against the counter, crossing my arms over my chest and my feet over one another.

"Well, I've been trying to talk to you all week so I figured my best bet was to catch you in a compromised position …" I chuckle, looking dead ahead at her face. *Don't look down, don't look down!* "… like this. That way you can't run away," I finish, clearing my throat to keep from laughing.

"Like hell I can't! I can leave if I want to!" Her voice is amplified in the small room, but her words only seem to spark more laughter inside of me; laughter that is threatening to spill over and more than likely will make her all sorts of angry, but I might as well have some fun. Besides, I'm seeing that she is actually sexy as hell when she is mad.

Bending to the side with my eyes locked on her, my hand smoothly finds the knob. I pull the door open, letting in a blast of cold air from the living room.

"Really? Leave then," I tease, knowing full well that she won't but desperately hoping she walks her naked tail right out of the shower and into the next room. *I would pay to see that.*

Waving my hand in front of my body towards the door, I politely point her towards the exit, no longer able to hold back the fact that I am amused. I flash her a huge smile, feeling my cheeks stretched to the max and my chest vibrating from the impending laughter that is sure to follow.

Her wide eyes drop as she looks around and reevaluates the situation. Still gripping the bottle in her hand as if it is the last lifeboat on board a sinking ship, she pulls the curtain tighter against her and gives me a look I'm sure could kill.

"Just how the hell did you get in here, anyways?"

My smile does not waiver with her spiteful tone as I fling the door shut, my head still half hoping she darts out of the room in the buff.

"I used a key Bethany loaned me." I actually should have given it back by now, but keeping it with me everyday has felt a little like having a piece of her with me. Now, I'm thanking my lucky stars that Bethany forgot to bring it up on Wednesday.

Feeling pretty clever, I fiddle with my key chain until I have only the key to her apartment in my hand. Slipping the ring onto my index finger, I hold it up between us and jiggle it like a bell. She lunges for the key, nearly falling forward in the process and igniting a burst of laughter from me. In a way, I'd love it if she slipped so I could have the chance to catch her; to have my arms around her for just a second. Maybe that is what she needs to remind her of us.

Straightening her stance and looking even more annoyed, she spits out, "Why do you have a key and why are you in my bathroom?! Do you mind?"

Her aggravation tickles me, but the actual question reminds me of my reasons behind getting the key in the first place, which is definitely no joking matter.

Keeping my body relaxed against the vanity, I twist at the waist and carefully lay the key on the counter. *I might as well give it up now.* I stare down at it for a second, lying alone on the vanity before looking back at her. *It may not be the only thing that I am giving up today and walking away from.*

Clearing my throat, I try my best to propel the conversation past the point of my breaking and entering, "I left my hat here and when I came to get it, I decided to leave you the brownie," I pause as her breath hitches in her throat at the mention of my gift. *Maybe it did mean something to her.* "I wanted you to know I still cared and that I still thought about you, even if it was too late," I say with an ache piercing my heart.

As soon as the words flow from my mouth, her expression changes; softens. "Why?"

I can barely hear her whisper, but her face soon twists and transforms to an expression of pain and hurt.

Raising her voice, she goes on gaining more venom with each word, "Why, when all you did was play me?" I move away from the counter and open my mouth, ready to stop her but she goes on, "What, was Bethany not enough? Did you want …"

Wait just a minute! What the hell! My heart goes from a blissfully-in-love beat to an irate pummel in my chest filled with fury and disbelief in a matter of milliseconds. I have no desire to let her finish that sentence.

"What the hell are you talking about? Played you? I never played you!"

Anger courses through me, making me ball my fists and step closer to her. *How could she accuse me of being a player?! No way am I going to stand here and let her make me out to be the one that did something wrong.*

"Lyssa, I told you I was in love with you. How do you figure I played you?" Narrowing my eyes, I swallow a lump in my throat and raise my voice, "It felt more like I was the one that was played! How do you think it felt to know I was just some summer rebound for you until you got back home to your boyfriend?"

Her temper ignites as well, as she tosses the curtain aside and screams, with her finger raised in front of my face, "Wait just a minute! Rebound?! Kyle and I were over when I met you! Why would you think you were a rebound?!"

Her yelling fuels my anger, but pointing her finger in my face for some reason has my adrenaline surging out of control and rage boiling in my veins.

Grinding my jaw, I nudge her hand away from my face and roar out, "I don't think that. I know I was! How long did you wait to go back to him, Alyssa? Was it the day you got back home or the next?"

My chest heaves in and out as her movement catches my attention and has me sweeping my eyes down to her arms. Folding her arms across her bare chest, she cocks her head back looking baffled. Any other time, her standing there with nothing but drips of water covering her body would have me going crazy, but at this point, it just makes me look quickly back to her face.

"What? I never went back to him! Where did you get that idea?" she hollers, her voice piercing my ear drums, "Just because he came to my apartment the day I saw you with Bethany? News flash, we ended almost three months ago when my life was falling apart and you were nowhere around! Did you expect me to sit around and wait for you to call this whole time?" she huffs out.

Her words offer my heart no relief from the pain, but aids in my confusion and ferocity. *Why is she lying to me? There's no point in it!*

Flinging my finger up into the air much like she did, I look her square in the eye and call her out, "Don't give me that shit! When I called you, the guy that answered said he was your boyfriend. That was only four days after we left the lake. Four days!"

I want to stomp my feet, slam my fist into the wall, anything to bring me down from the rage that is blazing inside of me. My heart hammers in my chest and my entire body shakes, until I take in the shock on her face.

"You called," she whispers.

The shock and remorse that trembles through her voice instantly has my arm falling slack at my side as my anger begins to diminish.

"Yeah, I called. Four days after we left and a guy answered the phone saying he was your boyfriend and asking me who I was." I keep my voice steady, toning down my irritation.

She looks away, swaying back and forth as she stares at the floor, but then she stops. Her head snaps up and a shadow of understanding flickers in her eyes.

"Four days after I got home, my dad told me his cancer was back."

This one sentence completely and utterly melts the last bit of anger left in my body. A sharp pain slices through my heart and suddenly all I want to do is hold her, to take her pain away and to go back to that one single day when she found out so I could be there.

"I'm sorry, Lyssa. Bethany told me about your dad. That's why I left the brownie the next day. I remembered you telling me that your mom made them when you were upset. I just figured it might make you smile and maybe ..." The throbbing sensation in my heart intensifies and my voice catches. Clearing my throat to regain some composure, I go on and finally ask what has tormented me for the last few months, "I am sorry to hear about that and I wish I had gotten the chance to be there for you, but why ..."

She doesn't let me get that far and every fiber of my being wants to beg her to let me finish talking.

"You said you called?" Her voice is laced with sorrow, confusion and so many other emotions that I am also feeling at this moment. "But I never saw your number on my phone. And what guy?! There wasn't anyone that could of ..." I don't need her to finish; I know who answered the phone.

Her voice fades and everything inside of me unravels as I slowly start to go over a few thoughts that have always lingered in the back of my mind. *She never knew I called. She waited for me; she waited and I never called when she needed me most.*

"I called from Evan's phone ... mine was crushed so I had to borrow his to call you." Looking down and taking one step closer to her before looking her in the eyes and letting her in on my secret; the reason I couldn't be there when I would have given everything to be. "I called as soon as I got out of surgery and was awake enough to think."

The look on her face as I say the word surgery is indescribable, and it says everything I need to know. *She didn't know. She thought I had stood her up this entire time. She thought I had just written her off.*

"Lyssa," I speak softly and calmly, my heart thumping the extreme opposite beat from a few minutes before. "Tristan and I had a wreck an hour out from the lake. I was in the hospital for three weeks. I couldn't call you right away because I wasn't even conscious. Then I was in and out of surgery. When I finally was able to, I called. I wanted you there so bad. You're all I've thought about."

I get it all out and watch as her eyes fill with tears. A loud thump fills the room as the shampoo bottle that she had been clutching in her hand falls to the tub floor, but the vacant stare on her face doesn't waiver.

"I didn't know. I wish I would have known. Oh God … you were hurt?" she says through heavy breaths.

With cautious steps, I slowly step forward and inch my hand up to touch her face. The second my fingertips make contact with her skin, everything inside my heart, soul and body comes alive and it takes all my strength to hold back from taking her in my arms. Closing her beautiful tear streaked eyes; time stands still as she leans her face into my touch and lets out a sigh at the same time as I do.

Alyssa's eyes open and she straightens up away from my touch.

"I didn't know. And that day … it must have been Kyle. He came over to try and get me back, but I told him I had met someone and then my dad came home."

She pauses her rambling and I move my hand over, smoothing my fingers down her jawline toward her lips. I don't need her to say anything else. All I want is to feel her in my arms; to taste her lips.

"My dad needed to speak with us and I couldn't get rid of him. He waited for me and he must have answered my phone and felt threatened when he heard your voice. I promise you, I never …" Her breath tickles my fingertips as they trace over her lips to end all conversation.

"I get it … I believe you," I barely get the words out over the raw emotion that has built up in my chest.

Her eyes glisten with tears and love, so I take one final step forward, feeling the heat from her body as we stand only inches away. My boot hits the wall of the tub almost as if it is reminding me that there are still some words that have to be said.

Slowly letting my hand feel its way across her tear slickened skin into the thick threads of her water soaked hair, I swallow down my fear of rejection and ask the only thing I still need to hear. "Do you still love me?"

My heart stops, the waves of air that naturally flow to and from my lungs halts, my body goes limp as I drop my hand to my side and all I can do is stare, hoping and praying for the reaction I long for.

"Yes. I love you!"

She throws the words out at me so instantaneously and with such conviction that my body immediately resumes function, seeming weightless as I hop over the edge of the tub and lunge against her. Pressing her bare body to the shower wall and mine flush to hers, I finally allow my hands to explore everything the water has so effortlessly been enjoying the whole time we have been talking. *This is where I belong. This is where she belongs; back in my arms.*

Heaven

WHEN MY MOUTH MEETS her soft, supple lips, a tidal wave of emotion washes over me and spills into every limb of my body; I cannot touch or taste her enough. My heart hammers in my chest so hard it leaves me gasping for air, but all I can do is share her breaths; sucking and tasting them with each kiss. The familiar whimper that I love so much moves over her tongue and vibrates against mine, sending my body into hyper drive. Every inch of my body hungers and thirsts for her as if she is my last meal.

Water sprays over my back, drenching me in wet warmth and molding our bodies together like glue. *I need more of her!* Chills race over my skin as her leg lifts and grazes the back of my calf, beckoning for it to also be touched. I answer her call, grasping the flesh of her thighs and pulling her up and around me so that we can be as close as possible.

While nipping and biting at her neck, my hand feels its way over her slick, wet body from the back of her knee, up her thigh then pauses cupping the soft flesh of her ass and pulling her to me.

My head is whirling and spinning with so many thoughts; so many words that I want to say to her, yet I can barely take in enough air to breath. My chest heaves in and out against her plump breasts as her hand claws its way under my shirt and up my torso in a fiery path. The feeling of her velvety skin on mine is so intense a moan escapes me and has me in a frenzy to get her in the next room.

Holding tight to her and ready to carry her away, I realize I have to tell her how I feel as well. With one hand supporting her weight and holding her as tightly against me as possible, I run the other up the side of her body, igniting a blast of goose bumps over her skin. As my hand finds a resting place in her wet hair, her entire body shudders against mine and I break away from her lips.

Looking deep into her eyes, I see everything I feel reflected back to me.

"I love you, Alyssa. I couldn't stop thinking about you these past months," I swallow, trying to take a breath, "I missed you so much."

Her lips part and another whimper calls to me, drawing me back to her. Sealing my lips to hers, I kiss her deeply and push both our bodies against the wall for support.

After blindly reaching for the faucet and turning the water off, I step over the side of the tub and make my way into the other room, with Alyssa wrapped around me.

The trip to her bedroom is a sweet mixture of confusion, thrill, pain, and pleasure as I stumble through barely-known territory with my lips locked with hers, a burning sensation in my shoulder and bursts of electricity shooting through me.

Once my shins hit the edge of the bed, I collapse with her onto the bed and throw a hand over my shoulder to peel off my shirt. Pulling and tugging with extreme irritation that it has formed to my body like a second skin, I finally pull it over my head and throw it aside.

My lips automatically land back on her skin trailing a path to her neck while I put a truck-load of effort into shoving my boots off. Drawing my head back in irritation, I manage to get one off, but realize I need to focus on getting out of my wet clothes.

"Hold on one second," I breathe out, completely ticked off that I have to pull back from the momentum of this moment.

Jumping to my feet, I push my other boot off with my other foot at the same time that I unfasten my pants. Shoving and pushing my jeans down with a strenuous effort, I manage to get them down to my hips then lose my footing, nearly falling to the floor. *Perfect!*

A laugh erupts from Alyssa's mouth as she lays motionless on the bed, eyeing my every move. One look at her perfect body waiting for me and I am beyond determined to get these glued on jeans off. Wiggling from side to side, I grit my teeth with a half grin and push until they are off.

After all wet articles of clothing have been removed I slide back over her, blanketing her with my body. She looks at me with a gleam in her eyes and I can already tell she witnessed my klutziness. *Oh wow, what better way to fizzle out the passion than for her to see my comical act of playing tug-a-war with my jeans.* I laugh and hang my head low against her neck, heat spreading across my face. *Smooth, Judd, real smooth.* Lifting my head only a fraction, I look into her eyes and smile down at her.

"And here you thought I was a player this whole time," I breathe out a laugh at the irony of her assumptions, "I can't manage to be smooth with you … ever."

"Well, you're smooth enough for me."

Her lips brush against mine for a quick encouraging kiss that makes my heart drum into my throat.

We both chuckle, as her soft hand winds a path over my jaw and up to my cheek where her fingertips trace a circle. I nod my head at her little obsession over the dimple in my cheek, but the whole time I cannot take my eyes off her. As I stare into her beautiful eyes and watch her cheeks rise into a gorgeous smile, relief spreads through my whole body and fills my heart with an overwhelming desire I've never felt.

Pressing my lips back to hers, urgency courses through me telling me to take her now; yet I wait. I take my time, drinking in every ounce of her love and desperation to have me closer. Her hands roam my body driving me nearly mad, but I pace myself, not wanting this moment to end too soon.

My body yearns for her and my lips crave the smooth, delicate curves of her body. Taking my time, I greedily taste her skin as my hands explore every single inch of her body, until there is no more holding back.

As soon as my body is aligned with hers and I join us as one, my world spins out of control. Electric currents pulse through my core, fueling my need to be closer,

And deeper,

So close not even air could penetrate this perfect bubble we have wrapped ourselves in.

Pulling her tighter against me, our skin melts together and it's all I can do to hold on. I suck in a deep breath and start to fall.

Through the most astounding feeling I've ever known, I manage three single words that my heart has been screaming, "I love you," I barely get out.

I hear my name muffled out through her lips as she squirms and bucks beneath me, but my mind cannot focus on any one thing except the sensations rocketing through my body. My chest heaves in and out as a deep moan vibrates up my throat and out of my mouth. With one last desperate push, my body quakes and trembles until I cannot hold myself up any longer.

Completely depleted of any energy, I collapse onto her body, burying my face in the creamy skin of her neck.

I lay there silently, huffing and puffing, trying to climb back down from the clouds. My mind is hazy and fogged over still, but little-by-little I register the soft caresses of her fingertips in my hair. That touch grounds me and brings me back to earth, although each wisp of her fingers ignites tiny sparks through my core telling me that we most definitely are not done. Planting a few gentle kisses against her neck, I bring my breathing back to a normal state then slowly slip lower down her body so that I can look at her.

As soon as I rest my chin against her chest, I look at her with happiness flooding my heart, but a single teardrop sliding down her cheek immediately has me panicked. For only a second, I worry that I may have rushed this; that I could have hurt her, or even assumed she wanted this as much as me when she actually didn't, but then I look into her eyes. Those eyes tell me everything. She is feeling exactly what I am feeling. *I cannot believe she is back in my arms.*

Normally tears would have me freaking out, but this time it doesn't. A small grateful smile itches at the corner of my lips as I reach my fingers up to swipe a few more escaped tears away from her cheek.

"Hey, don't cry. I'm here now," I assure her, because I know with absolute certainty that I am not going anywhere. *I will not lose her again. This is the girl I am meant to love.*

"I thought I had lost you forever," she croaks out, making my heart shatter in two.

Digging my elbow into the mattress, I pull myself up level with her so I can look her in the eyes and assure her that I am not going anywhere.

"You never lost me. Didn't I tell you that it wasn't goodbye forever?" I repeat the same thing I told her before we left the lake. Little did I know that day, that it would take months before I would hold her again.

An immediate smile touches her face and I know my words have offered her some sense of comfort.

Softly smoothing my fingertips along the contours of her face, I lean in closer until her breaths feel as if they are my own.

"I love you so much, Alyssa," I say right before capturing her moist lips with mine. Pulling away only enough to speak, I whisper more of my heart against her lips, "Do you know how much I missed you?"

Her hands instantly frame my face and pull me in for a more fulfilling kiss and I know she missed me just as much.

After my thirst for Alyssa's lips is somewhat quenched, and after I have told her at least a dozen times how much I love her, she slips off the bed insisting on putting my clothes in the dryer. Even though the fight with my pants earlier doesn't sound like something I want to repeat, I would rather wrestle with them than miss a moment of being with her, but she goes anyway.

"I'll be back in a second," she says with a sweet smile as she quickly balls up all my wet clothes and races out the bedroom door.

I crane my neck to get the full view of her hips swaying side-to-side as she disappears out of the room, already feeling the loss of her by my side.

When she returns only seconds later, I laugh to myself. Her eyes light up and she freezes at the door, her eyes sparkling with love and happiness.

"Get your butt back in bed," I playfully say, wiggling my eyebrows with a smirk.

She wastes no time doing as I say and as soon as her body grazes against mine, all I can think is how I wish she hadn't gotten dressed. Cuddling up as close as possible to me, we fall right back into our old ways as if we are back at the lake.

We spend hours talking about the time we were apart and the more we talk the more that dull ache in my heart from missing her begins to fade, although when she asks about the wreck, I can't help but get tripped up going over all the painful memories. Our conversation unexpectedly takes a detour when she surprises me by asking if I will come to meet her parents. *That was the last thing I expected tonight. Honestly, even though I had hoped I would get her back, the way this night has gone has completely blown my mind and left me stunned.*

After a few teasing comments and a sense that she is now nervous about her invitation, I get serious and speak to her straight from my heart.

"You know, it wasn't the physical part of our relationship that I missed as much as the way we talk." I smile at her thinking over the many conversations we shared in such a short span of time. "We could talk all day and never run out of things to say. It's so easy being with you; so right; like I've never been without you." I trail my fingertips across the satiny skin of her cheek and go on, "I love when you talk about your parents and sisters. So meeting your family definitely doesn't feel sudden to me. It actually feels like I already know them."

I pause to let everything I said to her sink in. She has no idea what that tiny gesture of asking me to meet her parent's means to me. To most people this would be a huge step; a sign of moving the relationship forward, possibly even a deeper sign of commitment, and where I feel those same emotions, it is still something much more sacred to me. Getting to see her with her family and letting me be a part of something so special, something I barely remember myself is a treasure worth millions to me.

I haven't had a sense of a family in years, but I've longed for it and most definitely needed it. I cannot even count the times that I came home from school with a problem that only Mom could solve, to find that the only way I could cope with it was to bury it in my thoughts. There were days when I'd come home from practice wanting to give up, and all I could think about was, I wish Dad was here to give me some words of encouragement. That day in the hospital when I found out I would never play again, that was exactly the first thought that came to mind.

"So my answer is yes. I will definitely come with you to your parents'," I say with a smile while squirming around from the thrill of this entire night and what is yet to come.

The words are barely out of my mouth before Alyssa crushes me in a huge hug, letting me know how much my saying yes means to her in return. I wrap her tightly in my arms, and cover her lips with mine, wishing one single kiss could express all the love I hold for her in my heart. *I'm fine with spreading the kisses out over time, though.*

After a long while of basking in each other's presence, we finally take a breather from the kissing and touching to get up to date on our lives. Aside from the ache that still rises in my heart from missing her so much, it seriously feels as though we have never been apart.

Lying on my side adjacent to her, I run my hands along the soft tender skin of her forearm that her head rests on. This is one thing for sure that hasn't changed between us; we cannot touch each other enough. I just want to be physically linked to her in any way. Being near her makes me feel alive; makes me feel whole; like I can finally breathe. It makes me look at all my past heartaches and be grateful, because without each of those stepping stones, I wouldn't be here with her.

"Ok, so now that I am going to meet your family, do you mind if I ask how your dad is doing?" I ask the question hesitantly, knowing this is sure to stir up a lot of emotions for her.

I know he is sick and her fears from this summer were in fact brought to life, but I can't help but mentally beat myself up for not having the opportunity to be there for her when that news was delivered. It makes me sick to imagine what she felt in that moment; I've been there, and I will never forget the day I found out my mom had a disease that would end her life. For a fraction of a moment, a twinge of anger sparks in me at Tristan. A stupid fight between him and I took so much away.

"Well …" she pauses, tilting her head to meet my gaze. "His tests showed the cancer had returned a few days after I got home from the lake." A pained expression crosses her face and I know it is partly from knowing I wasn't there.

Lifting my hand away from the same wavy pattern I've been tracing back and forth over her arm, I run it softly through all the tangled waves of hair that hang carelessly over her shoulder. My fingertips quickly find a resting place behind her ear and I pull myself forward to place a kiss on her forehead.

Pulling away, a small smile touches her face as she goes on, "After that he started chemo. It all seemed so familiar and I hated that he had to go through it all over again, you know?" I nod my head, but don't say a word. I know right now she just needs me to listen, to be here for her.

Nervously, she reaches up and pulls my hand between us, clasping it in hers so tightly that I can feel all the pain that is surging through her as if that energy is being transferred from her to me. She shifts her body and moves in closer to me, leaning her forehead against my chin while she busily squeezes my hand in both of hers now.

"I found out this week that he has stopped all treatments and the doctor said he only has …" She trails off and I completely understand how hard what she's truly trying to say is. Moving the topic away from such a finalized comment, her voice grows hoarse as she speaks again, "Have you ever wondered why me?"

I breathe out an exaggerated sigh at the irony of her question. *Only a million times a day, up until I met you.*

"I mean it's almost like a tease. We celebrate that he is cancer free and then wham … not anymore," her voice cracks as she grasps my hand as if it is a stress-ball.

Leaning away from her body, I move so that I am eye level with her and place my hand under her chin. "It's normal not to understand and you should be mad. Seeing someone you love get sick is one of the hardest things in this world, but I also think those extra years that you got with him were a gift. After his first battle with cancer, I'd be willing to bet it changed how you looked at life and family. You learned how to truly be grateful for each moment. That was a gift, Alyssa."

I know my words probably offer her no sense of comfort, and honestly even though they make sense to me now, they may not even register with her. A part of me wants so badly to throw out how sick my mom got, how me and my brothers watched her wither away, day-by-day, until one day I came home from school to find out that she was gone, but I don't want to make this about me. I don't even want to make it as if I know what she is going through, because my mom didn't have cancer. Our stories are completely different and this is Alyssa's story; this is her time and I pray with every ounce of my soul that her story will end differently than mine.

A tear drops down her cheek and my hand instinctively brushes it away in an instant, wishing I could stop them all along with the pain. My heart is crumbling at the sight of seeing her hurt and I'm at a complete loss for words. If only words could mend an aching heart, but I know it can't.

I can't tell her everything will be ok, because I don't know if it will.

I can't even assure her that it won't hurt, because I know without a doubt that this entire journey is killing her, so I say the only thing that I know with complete certainty to be true.

"I can't wait to meet your dad tomorrow."

With a sniffle and tear streaked eyes, she looks at me and smiles. "Me too."

Quickly kissing her lips, I decide I'd love to see that smile grow just a bit more. I run my hand from her chin down to the neckline of her shirt and give it a gentle tug.

"So about all these clothes …" I raise my eyebrows and grin, knowing she is probably thinking I'm trying to get her to take them off, so I quickly add, "I really cannot get used to them. Here I thought you just wore bikinis every day."

Half the time at the lake, I swore I was going to have a heart attack from watching her traipse around in her swimsuits. The truth is, she could go around wearing a garbage bag and she would still be the sexiest, most beautiful girl I've ever seen.

Wiggling my eyebrows, she manages out a giggle and I take that brief interruption to steal probably the hundredth kiss tonight. From there, our conversation shifts to a more playful topic about the day we met and memories from the lake; I think those two weeks will always be our heaven.

Alone at Last

I NTENTLY LISTENING TO HER tease me about the morning she saw me for the first time, I glance over at the clock and see that it is after midnight. It's Friday; Alyssa's birthday. I knew the night of her party was not her actual birthday, so I was really hoping to get the chance to see her today. *Wish granted, thank you Lord!*

"… I proceeded to strip you down one layer at a time." I laugh at what she was actually thinking when she saw me that first day and she joins in, her eyes dancing with happiness.

Slowly letting my laughter die down, I look at her and my heart hammers in my chest. "Hey, happy birthday," I say, but I actually mean, *I love you and I want to be with you today and every birthday to follow.*

Her face lights up with my words and she giggles, "Thank you but it's not my birthday until tomorrow," she says as she tilts her head back to look at the clock on her nightstand. "Holy crap," she shouts out and I am automatically confused at the panic in her voice.

"What's wrong?"

"Well … it's just that … Bethany really likes you."

Whoa, so what is what I want to say, really sick of her friend and not sure I can tolerate her any longer. "Yeah and so? I love you, not her. I've never been with her … .*ever.*"

"I know you do and I love you, too, but she is really into you and since I never told her I knew you, it will seem like I made a move on her boyfriend."

This sends a bolt of frustration through me. *How is it that this girl can dictate my life even after I've got back what I so desperately wanted and waited for?*

"Ahhh ... I was never going out with her. I told her I just wanted to be friends and that is all she's ever been; a friend. Besides, technically you're still my girlfriend, because we never officially broke up." I add that part, jokingly, but Alyssa is in full-throttle-freak-out mode.

I say let her walk in and find us, but just as that thought enters my mind, her pleading, worried eyes shoot right to my core, fracturing my sensibility and urge to argue what I feel is the right move her.

Opening my mouth, I hesitantly suggest it anyway, "Maybe we should just tell her about us and this summer." Like a band-aid, rip it off and it'll be fine the next day. There is no use in letting it simmer and risk added drama later.

"I agree and I will, but for now, I don't think she should come home and find us together. Either way, it will hurt her, plus I think seeing us in bed together would be a bad way to break this to anyone."

Her words catch me off guard. "Do you want me to leave?"

"No!" she snaps and I'm thankful for her sudden dismissal of that suggestion, because on my way out, I'd be awfully tempted to make sure Bethany knew how I felt about Alyssa. "I just meant maybe we could go somewhere else together."

This slaps a smile right across my face. It takes no time for Alyssa to grab my clothes from the dryer and for us to be out to my truck. A part of me is bothered that she doesn't want to confront Bethany and let her know that we are together right this second. *If it were up to me, everyone would know!* Guilt still tiptoes over my conscience for being in the same bed as Bethany when Alyssa and I found each other again. The last thing I want is for her to think there was ever anything between her roommate and I.

In the end, I agree with the no drama tonight part. Tonight is for us. We found each other and I'd rather just have her all to myself all night long without a clingy roommate listening in on every word we speak. With that, we take off to my apartment for the night.

Jumping into my truck, my body zings with excitement; she is right here, right now, with me. Feeling as though the console creates a barrier between us as soon as we are in our seats, I fling it up and smack my hand on the seat to coax her nearer to me. She immediately complies by sliding flush against my side and it instantly has me wanting her back in my arms.

I pull her to me and capture her lips with soft wisps of my lips and tongue. All of a sudden her sitting beside me is way too far away. Wrapping my arms around her small waist, I pull her onto my lap, keeping my mouth on hers the whole time. Her hands frantically run through my hair and down to my shoulders with the same desire burning inside of her that has me going ninety miles an hour. All too soon our fire is extinguished by a passing car, pulling out of the community center.

"Maybe we should go?" I suggest, not at all wanting to stop. "We can be at my apartment in ten minutes tops."

She laughs, nodding her head and moves to the side, but I hold tight to her hand.

"Where do you live?"

I throw the truck in gear and take off with one hand clasping hers and the other gripping the steering wheel.

"About ten minutes north of campus," I glance over at her quickly as I take a left off her road.

"Judd, that's about fifteen to twenty minutes away."

I grin, pressing my foot down on the gas as I answer, "Yeah, but like I said … I'll have us there in ten."

And that is pretty much all we wait, because no sooner than my doorway is in sight, I have her in my arms, hastily ripping the door open and making a mad dash to my room. *Three months … it's been three months.*

Unlike only hours earlier, my clothes come off like wrapping paper and I eagerly await a silent show that Alyssa is offering, standing tall on my bed. My heart thuds at the thought of her stripping right here on my bed as her hips sashay side-to-side and she slowly inches her shirt up, up, up and up. This is at the top of every guys bucket list. The need inside me grows and my whole body feels as though it has been set on fire, burning out of control. Once her bra hits the ground, I truly lose all my willpower.

I pull both of us the rest of the way out of our clothes and blanket her body with mine, ready to feel her, taste her and kiss her again. My mouth quickly forms to her skin, gliding from the corner of her lips to her neck, across her jawline and pulling the tender flesh of her earlobe into my mouth while my hands feel their way down her body.

Barely skimming my teeth across her earlobe, I pull away and whisper, "I love you."

My heart slams in my chest in anticipation, but a familiar snapping sound of my doorknob is the only warning I have before, "Hey man, are you asleep? I need to talk toooooo ...." Evan's voice calls out and I immediately tear the sheet up over me and Alyssa's bodies.

Luckily I manage to get us both mostly covered before roaring at my friend for his interruption. "Damn it, Evan! Could you knock?!" I spit out, completely annoyed with him. *Any other day, any other time, but not tonight!*

I glare over my shoulder at him and see a smirk cross his face as he looks to the bottom of my bed. *Oh perfect! Keep your mouth shut, Evan, Please!*

I'm silently pleading for him to keep quiet, because I know the last person he will think I'm with is Alyssa, but of course Evan stays true to himself.

"Hey, it's about time! Hell, I thought you were going to join a monastery and take a vow of celibacy. Good to see you're finally moving on!"

Great ... no, no, no! I just know he is thinking I brought Tiffany back here, or Candy, or geez ... maybe even Bethany. I have to defuse this before he says any more.

Just as my mouth opens to cut the conversation off and get him out of my room, Alyssa pushes the covers out of her face so she is in plain view. Evan's face immediately lights up with disbelief as he looks from her to me. "Well cool! You got her! Way to go!" My fear of him saying the wrong thing diminishes and my chest swells with pride as he carries on. "I was just kidding about the whole moving on comment," he says, getting comfortable like he plans to hang out in my room all night. *Not gonna happen.*

"Get out, Evan!" I holler out, desperately wishing for one time, just once, that he would choose not to drive me nuts.

Another ornery ass grin spreads across his face. "Oh yeah, I guess you guys are busy, huh?"

No, I just wanted to spend my morning laying here naked with a beautiful girl that I just happen to be completely in love with ... Not busy at all!

I open my mouth, fully intent on unleashing all my venom until he leaves but then I think I may have the perfect way to drive him insane tonight; all night in fact. A small smile rises onto my face, but I try my best to sound irritated as hell.

"Yes! We are! Would you leave?!"

"No problem." The door shuts and for a minute I think he's gone, but that would be way too easy. "So are you guys going to be making lots of noise?" he says, peeking his head back in.

I'm going to choke him, I really am! "Yes! Now leave!" I plead with him

"Ok, I'll go take a drive for an hour or so. You guys have fun; go nuts; get crazy," Evan says, pumping his fist in the air to root me on like I just threw the winning pass in a game.

The door finally snaps shut and I hear the front door click as well. Turning my attention back to Alyssa, I pull the sheets further down away from her face and flash her a smile. *Oh revenge is going to be so sweet!*

"I guess I forgot to tell you that Evan is my roommate."

Giggling over him walking in, she shifts beneath me and I know getting Evan back is going to be exhausting but well worth the effort.

"Well it just wouldn't be normal if he wasn't included in this re-union," she jokes having no idea what I'm thinking, yet she is so on track with my thought. *Invited ... no, but I'll make sure he's aware of our reunion.*

Deciding to let her in on my evil scheme, I ask a question I already know the answer to, "Are you staying all night?"

"I don't have my car with me so I guess I'm your hostage for the night." I widen my eyes in excitement at her use of words then laugh.

Slowly trailing my lips down her neck, a shiver rolls through her and I have no doubt that I can keep this up all night.

I pull my mouth away for only a second, "Then he is going to be real disappointed when he gets back in an hour because I don't plan to let you get any sleep tonight," I say then sneak another kiss in along her jaw.

Shifting my body, I'm hit with a wave of sensations. I gulp down a deep breath and look into her eyes. "I say we don't hold back. Let's be noisy, *all ... night ... long.*"

She giggles through heavy breaths and I try to smile, yet it's as though my brain has already shut down in anticipation of the sheer bliss that will be engulfing me in no time. We move together with a flawless harmony, our hands and lips exploring each other and leaving not a single trace of skin untouched.

Alyssa's whimpers grow louder with each movement and before long the ripples of pleasure start to build inside of me, making my hips move in a frantic pace. With one hand firmly wedged beneath Alyssa, I clamp down on her shoulder and run the other hand up into the palm of her hand, intertwining my fingers with hers. My grip on her hand tightens and I push them into the pillow beside our heads as I slowly begin slipping, diving, plunging and falling over the edge.

Just as an animalistic sound claws its way up my throat and out of my mouth, I hear Alyssa's strangled breaths turn into a loud moan mixed with what sounds like my name. I drop my head into the curve of her shoulder and take in a deep, exaggerated breath to calm my racing pulse.

The smallest of movements from her has me nearly coming un-glued from the sensitivity and spasms that keep rolling through me.

She lets out a content, satisfied sigh against my shoulder as her velvety, soft fingertips make soft steady strokes from my waist to my shoulders, creating another spasm within me. Tilting my chin, I look at my clock and see its only 2:37 am. *We still have the entire morning ahead of us. Who needs sleep?!*

On that thought, my lips take over and Alyssa falls right into step; both of us staying true to our plan to make this reunion last all night.

Hours pass and we are utterly exhausted and drained of energy, but somehow our vigor and excitement for one another never dies. With the exception of a few loud thuds on the wall coming from Ev-an's room, we both stay lost in our own perfect little bubble, reveling in our desire for each other.

"What time is it?" Alyssa says against my chest through heavy, sleepy breaths.

Rolling my head, which takes more energy than I have on supply, I look at the nightstand clock and lazily cradle my head back into the comfort of my pillow.

"A little past six," I mumble out to the ceiling, my eyes growing heavier as the seconds pass.

Alyssa blows out a laugh, her breath heating up my already sweat soaked skin.

"Have we really been up all morning?"

Closing my eyes, I murmur a quiet "Mmmhum," before letting sleep carry me away.

A loud clanking startles me and has me snapping my head in the direction of my bedroom door. Rapidly blinking my eyes to work out the hazy, sleep deprived feeling from my head, I see that my door is still closed, but I can make out the sounds of movement in the other room. I quickly glance down at the door knob, annoyed that my bedroom door doesn't have a lock on it, then over to the clock that reads 8:41. *What the hell is Evan still doing home? He was supposed to be at the site over an hour ago.*

A part of me wants to crack up, knowing I may be partly to blame for his tardiness, but then I look down at my chest and see Alyssa. *He can get over it ... It was totally worth it.*

Her small frame still lies completely draped over my body with one leg wedged between mine and the palms of her hands hugging my sides as if she is staking her claim. One look at her and I instantly start to get aroused. *I didn't even know I had anything left in the tank, but I'll take it.*

Carefully sliding out from beneath her, she curls up on her side and nuzzles into my chest, making me feel guilty for wanting to wake her up. *I guess I should let her sleep,* but then my ears pick up on a tiny content whimper moving over her lips as they curve into a hint of a smile. Something about seeing how worn out she is makes me feel satisfied and accomplished. Squeezing my eyes shut, I try to focus on controlling my arousal so that she can get a few hours of sleep before we leave. I'm driving, so actually I should be sleeping too, but I can't.

Opening my eyes, I gaze at her beautiful, angelic perfection and repeat that thought again. *No way can I sleep. I'd be happy with just staying awake all day and watching her sleep*, I think as I breathe a sigh of relief that I am not waking up from a dream. Another sound comes from the other room and this time it sounds like a crash or something falling. I sneak a quick kiss on Alyssa's lips and decide it's time to investigate.

"I'll be back," I whisper so quietly against her lips, immediately getting another soft moan as a reply.

Sliding off the bed and into my jeans, I head for the door and nudge it open, careful to not make a sound until I am out of the room. Spinning around to face the kitchen, I am met with a grumpy, run-down Evan slumped over a bowl at the kitchen island.

"Why aren't you at work?" I ask, trying to control the smirk that is threatening to take over my face.

With heavy eyelids and an etched on frown, Evan looks up at me and it's very clear that my method of payback worked.

I cover my mouth to stifle a laugh.

"What the hell, man! You look awfully chipper for not getting one minute of sleep ... *all night!*" Evan rolls his eyes and I can't hold back my laughter. "But then again, I guess I'd have a smile plastered on my face too if I had an all-night-sexathon with the girl of my dreams." Evan whirls his fingers in the air to emphasize his sarcasm.

I burst out laughing, throwing my arms around my waist as I stare at the bland, ticked off expression on his face.

"Oh and yeah to answer your question ... I'm not at work because *I ... didn't ... sleep ... all ... night!*" Evan raises his voice in annoyance and I quickly stop laughing, glancing back at my bedroom door, hoping that he is not waking Alyssa.

With no sound heard from beyond my bedroom door, I make my way over to the bar and take a seat at one of the barstools. Snickering, I fold my arms across the island and look at him.

"Payback's a bitch, huh?"

Evan's head snaps up and there is a mischievous gleam in his eyes that tells me I may regret challenging him.

"Oh! Oh!" He points over to my bedroom, a huge grin painted on his face. "So that was revenge for me busting in on your play day?" He throws his head back and laughs, holding his belly for emphasis. "Oh it is *sooo* on! I can play this game!" Evan points at my face clearly amused.

"Great," I grumble, knowing full well that Evan does not back down from a challenge. "Let's not make this too disgusting, ok? I really don't want to know about your sex life and every time you bring a girl home," I chuckle, "Last night we did get a little crazy and … loud …"

Evan's eyes widen, "Ya think? I thought the walls were caving in on me and Ho-lee shit, your bed frame slamming into the wall … you seriously need to move your bed to the other wall or something. I seriously stuffed cotton in my ears, held the pillow over my head until I was damn near suffocated and still all I could hear …" He looks at me amused and ready to deliver. I grin, enjoying the replay of what was heard from the other side of the wall. "… Oh Judd, Oh … Oh, Judd … Oh, ah, ahh, oh, mmmm … Judd until I really just wanted to gouge my ears out. Oh and your grunting … Oh my …"

I quickly cut him off knowing he isn't going to shut up otherwise. "… but that was just sort of a onetime thing."

He looks crazed for a minute, "Bullshit … that is not a onetime thing." He points to my door, "You have her back now, so this is going to be a nightly occurrence."

I hold my hand up to stop him, "We will keep it down from now on, plus we are going to be at her parents this weekend, so you will have plenty of time to catch up on sleep." I shoot him a goofy grin then stand up, stretching my arms over my head.

"Her parent's house, huh? Judd, I really don't think her parents are going to stand for all that racket."

I squint my eyes and cast him a shut-the-hell-up glare.

"Ok, so we are going to hop in the shower and then we're headed to Fairview for the night. I'll catch you later!"

I jump up and take quick strides to my bedroom so that I can wake Alyssa and hopefully relish in another shower. *This time clothes will not be involved. I'm really beginning to love showers.*

Evan's eyes widen and he nods his head.

"Holy shit, man! Do you guys ever come up for air when you are together?! I mean seriously, what was that four times last night … five … six?"

I raise my eyebrows, feeling a sly grin sneak onto my face.

"Not if we can help it and I'm really not sure, I wasn't counting," I chuckle as I grab the door knob to my room and open it slowly, careful not to wake her. I have plans on how I want to wake her up.

Before I sneak inside, I hear the rattling of Evan's keys as he grabs them off the counter.

"Well, I'm off to work, only two hours late. Have fun shaking the banana tree and whatever else you plan to do."

I squint my eyes at him and laugh. He thrives on getting under my skin. The front door closes and we are alone at last.

Family

"**Y**OU'RE RIGHT, WE ARE never going to leave if you keep attacking me," I laugh as I place warm kisses down her neck and back to her mouth.

"Me!" She giggles, trying her best to act like she is trying to worm away. "You jumped on me no sooner than I took my towel off."

As soon as we were out of the shower and back in my room to get ready, I slipped into my jeans and sweatshirt, then patiently proceeded to watch her dry her hair in nothing but her towel. That's just torture. Once the towel hit the floor, I pounced.

Speaking between kisses against her neck, I say in an amused tone, "Is that how that happened? I'm pretty sure I remember you jumping me."

She laughs some more but once I swipe my tongue just below her earlobe, her breaths pick up and all giggling stops. Her legs slide up the sides of my thighs and wrap around me, igniting a trail of goose bumps over my skin. I have to laugh at how fast the tables can turn.

"You're right, we're going to be late, huh?" I say pulling my face up so I can look at her.

Her eyes widen and I seriously do not think I have ever seen this expression on her face. She looks like someone just stole her ice cream cone. I crack up, quickly planting a hard kiss on her lips. Pulling away, I look at her again and lick my lips. Her eyes flick down to watch and I immediately have to give her another kiss, this time slower. We eventually come up for air and get on our way.

Thirty minutes later, we are headed down the interstate and my nerves are wound up.

"Ok, so they know you're coming," Alyssa says, scooting a little closer to me.

The movement of her hands in my peripheral vision catches my attention and I glance down. She places her phone in her lap then reaches over, wrapping her arm around my bicep.

"What did they say?" I ask anxiously.

I snap my eyes over to her and chuckle as she covers her mouth with a shocked expression. *What is she doing?*

"Are you super nervous?" she asks, sounding somewhat amused while the contents of my stomach feel as though it may come up and make an appearance at any given moment.

Looking back and forth between her and the road, I shrug my shoulders as she slowly settles back against the seat, nestled tightly to my side.

"Judd, you have absolutely nothing to be worried about. Like I said, they are going to love you." Her grip on my arm tightens and she presses her head to my shoulder, instantly putting my nerves at ease.

"It's not that I'm afraid they won't like me. I guess I just haven't had a whole lot of experience being around a family," I tell her not really wanting to admit all the emotions that stir within me with the thought of being around a Mom and Dad. "I just have a bunch of mixed emotions. I'll be fine," I say, waving my hand above the steering wheel.

"You don't regret coming do you?" Her voice comes out in a worried tone and immediately has me looking over to her.

Her head lifts off my shoulder and I catch a trace of sadness in her eyes. *Holy crap! That did not come out right.*

"No, not at all!" I spit out quickly, guilty that I made her think that for even a second. "I am excited to meet your parents, like I said. Seriously, I am fine, Alyssa. I meant mixed as in excitement, nerves and is your dad going to pull a gun on me, all blended together, that's all."

I laugh and manage to get a laugh out of her as well. She lets out a sigh and nuzzles against me so close that all I want to do is turn the truck around to head back to my apartment. *How did I make it three months without her? I should have raced up her driveway and stole her back that day I watched her from the street. I think if I would have introduced her douchebag ex to my fist that day, it would have corrected his assumption that he was her boyfriend.*

Right then, it dawns on me that Alyssa and I have some things we need to talk about, plus there are things that I need to get off my chest. This isn't the best timing, but honestly there are things I should have said before we ever even fell back into step with where we were before.

"Alyssa, hey … I need to tell you something …"

She instantly leans away, looking at me.

"You don't want to go, do you?"

I swing my eyes over to her for a brief second.

"No, I seriously want to meet your parents," I assure her while glancing back and forth between her and the road, afraid this whole topic is going to blow up in my face. "But I'm not sure if you're going to want me to after …" I lower one hand to my lap, nervously fidgeting with the seam of my jeans. Her hand covers mine and melts every hesitation in my body. "So this summer when we were apart, I went on a date with someone …" I get it out and wait.

"Did you sleep with her?" she asks me slowly, her voice laced with concern.

My eyes widen with her question and I steer the truck to the side of the road, right outside of Fairview. Once the truck is in park on the shoulder, I turn, grab her hand in mine and pull her close.

"No way!" I gulp, knowing I need to tell her everything. "Ok, I went on a date with a girl named Candy, but nothing happened. I took her home and she tried to kiss me, but I couldn't stop thinking about you." I cannot stop my rambling at this point. "Then Tiffany, my kind of ex, started coming over. We kissed and that was it. I kept thinking about you. I wanted you and I couldn't …"

She cuts me off and my entire body heats up with anxiety and embarrassment as I scrunch up my face in fear of her response to my confession.

"Judd, it's ok," she says, squeezing my hand tightly to her chest. "You know, I let Kyle kiss me the night of the frat party and it could have gone further, but as soon as it happened you're all I could think about."

My jaw tightens and visions of him touching her surface in my mind, making me ball my hands into fists.

Obviously feeling the tension in my body as well as my hand clutched beneath hers, she goes on in a soothing tone, "My point is … we both thought the other had moved on. I'm not going to be angry or hurt from anything that happened during that time. I have no right to."

I loosen the grip of my hand with her words and she immediately threads her hand through mine, causing a wave of relief to break open inside of me. The truck vibrates with the passing of a semi on the interstate, concealing my shaking body and pounding heart.

"Besides … the fact that neither of us could go any further is sort of a testament to how much we love each other, right?" She gives me a beautiful smile and my heartbeat kicks up. "None of it matters. It's like you said, we're together now so let's focus on that and not the past."

I suck in a deep breath and draw her into my arms, not completely sure I'll ever be able to pull away. *She has no idea how true that is.* It is only with her that I can truly let go of the past. Once I met her, my past stopped holding me back. The loss of Mom and Dad no longer felt as if it decided my future for me.

After a few more minutes of basking in the security of knowing that we can survive anything as long as we have each other, I throw the truck into drive and merge back onto the road. Exit 121 to Fairview comes up quickly and although there are three more exits past this one, I know exactly where I am going.

Right as my hand gets ready to hit the turn signal, Alyssa speaks up, "Take this exit then make a left."

I turn my head as I slide onto the exit ramp and give her an all knowing smile.

"I know where I'm going." I laugh. *Now for my next confession.*

"After I got out of the hospital, I ummm … sort of made a pit stop."

From the corner of my eyes, I catch her snapping around to look at me.

"You came to my house," she gasps in disbelief

With my jaw clamped down in apprehension, I grit my teeth wondering how much of a stalker this may make me look like.

"Aaaah, yeah," I spit out and glance over.

She smiles, causing me to crinkle up my face with a grin and restoring my confidence in admitting my need to see her.

"I came by because I wanted to talk to you." She stares at me with a question in her expression, so I go on, "You and umm … your ex and I think your dad pulled up. I watched from across the street as you both helped him inside."

I leave out all that I felt about her being with her ex, because we've already established that none of that matters. Honestly, I will always harbor hard feelings toward him for his deceit when I called Alyssa that day. After all, I would have been with her this whole time had it not been for his stupid ass lying to me, but I will let that go. I got her back in the end so in my head I am already sticking out my tongue at him, chanting "in your face" and doing a celebratory fist-pump in the air.

Recognition lights up her face, as she opens her mouth, "Oh," she sounds sad and it hurts me to hear it. "That was probably one of his chemo appointments. Kyle helped me take him to a couple. They made him real sick and pretty weak."

She kneads her hands together in her lap and I quickly scoop one up, bringing her knuckles to my lips to let her know I am here, that I understand, that I'm hurting with her and that I am not going anywhere.

Five minutes later we pull into her driveway and I jump out with Alyssa quickly on my heels. She grabs my hand in hers, dragging me up the stairway to the door like I'm some cartoon character digging my feet into the dirt in resistance.

As soon as I stumble through the doorway, sweat tickles my skin, my heart thuds up into my ears and my nerves erupt like a volcano.

Being nearly a whole head taller than Alyssa, I quickly find no matter how anxious I am there's no way to hide. My eyes immediately collide with a blonde that is just as gorgeous as Alyssa and definitely doesn't look old enough to be her mom.

"Hey sweetie," she says, crossing the room with Abby and a man that I assume is Alyssa's dad.

"Hi Mom," the woman pulls Alyssa into a huge hug, giving me a small smile over her shoulder.

Drawing my eyebrows up, I smile back, but cannot open my mouth to even say hi. *That's her mom?* The extreme amount of nervousness that is racing through my blood stream has apparently woven my mouth shut and has me holding my breath, until I hear my name.

"Hey Judd. How have you been?" Abby says, folding her arms across her chest and squinting her eyes as if she's trying to zone into my brain waves.

"Hey …" I start.

"Abby, can I talk to you?" Alyssa quickly pulls away from an embrace with her mother and father, hauling her sister along with her and leaving me in the completely awkward situation of facing her parents alone.

"You must be Judd?" her mom speaks up, allowing me to relax a little.

Clearing my throat, I smile and stick my hand out to shake hers. "Yes ma'am, you must be Alyssa's mom?"

"Angela," she says, putting her hand to her chest then letting out a laugh. The sparkle in her blue eyes and the way her cheeks rise into perfect circles, reminds me of Alyssa. "I've heard a lot about you." With that she engulfs me in a warm, welcoming hug that has my heart tripping all over itself with nostalgia.

There is something unmistakable about a mother's hug. It's warm and nurturing and usually comes at the exact moment when you need it most, but never realized how bad. I swear as soon as babies are born they pull the mom's aside and teach them how to hug; how to kiss your wounds and how to love so effortlessly that simply the sound of their voice makes the world better.

I wrap my arms around her in return and close my eyes, remembering how my mom used to hug. *God, she gave good hugs; they were life altering and until this moment, I forgot how much I missed them.*

Angela says something, but I cannot even focus on her words. For a brief second, I'm feeling my mom's arms around me, the way she would rub my back and whisper words of wisdom or encouragement in my ear. At first when she got sick, it was barely noticeable, but as time moved on it was unmistakable. A year before she died she experienced paralyses in her limbs and her arms lied vacant at her side no longer able to wrap around us. When I would sit with her, I would hold her hand and wonder if she needed to be hugged as bad as I needed her to hug me.

Pulling away before Angela thinks I'm a weirdo from clinging to her, she squeezes my shoulders and looks at me.

"It is so good to finally meet you. Alyssa has said very good things," she goes on then crushes me in another small hug. Her words have me somewhat confused considering this whole time Alyssa thought I was a player and moved on to her roommate. *Maybe her mom is just being nice.*

"Judd," her dad says with a nod of his head as Angela steps aside. He quickly grips my hand in a firm handshake, looking at me suspiciously.

This is where my adrenaline level should shoot through the roof, fearing what her dad thinks of me. I hope he doesn't know I slept with his daughter, but the mere fact that I broke her heart is enough for a dad to want to break me.

"Good to meet you, son," he adds then slips a little closer to me. For a moment I think he is going to hug me as well so I raise my arms to the side. Instead he places one hand on my shoulder, looks me square in the eyes and says, "Do I need to keep my gun handy with you around?"

My mouth and eyes both widen in alarm. I joked with Alyssa about this, but I truly did not expect it. *Do fathers really say this? I guess so! Holy shit, I want to vomit!*

Or run!

I open my mouth in an attempt to croak out a response that can excuse me for months of trauma he might feel I caused his daughter and possibly an apology for what he may view as me stealing her innocence. Before I can muster so much as a word, he bursts into laughter that has me letting out a stunned breath as he squeezes me in a slap-on-the-back hug.

Leaning towards my ear to speak, I realize he is a bit shorter than me and so frail-like that I'm afraid he may collapse if I reciprocate his friendly gesture.

"I'm only kidding. It's nice to meet you, Judd."

I break out in a huge smile of relief and breathe. I didn't even realize I had held my breath. Restoring the air in my lungs and probably the color to my face, I give him a gentle pat on the back before we break away, him with a kind smile that makes me feel perfectly at ease.

"I'm Alex and we are very glad to have you. Abby told us we were going to have an extra member of the family this weekend."

His statement has me feeling all sorts of uncomfortable like I just planned a sleep over at a girls dormitory.

"Yeah, Alyssa ..." I start to explain right as Alyssa's velvety, soft fingers thread through mine and have my heart drumming to an entirely different beat. A single touch from her replaces all my anxiety with absolute affection and love as I look over to her.

"I hope you don't mind. I asked him to spend the weekend." Her other hand entwines with our already joined hands and she looks up at me, with a breathtakingly beautiful smile. "We have a lot to catch up on so I just didn't want to miss a minute," she easily explains our intentions.

I stare over at her and for a minute I forget we are surrounded by her family, because I am completely lost in the depths of her ice blue eyes.

"Oh geez, get a room!" Abby's voice calls out, breaking the enchantment that Alyssa and I have became so used to when we're together.

My eyes instantly flick from Alex to Angela then down to the floor. *Get a room ... perfect wording, Abby. No doubt her dad is planning on keeping that gun by his bed this weekend.*

"Oh Abby, leave them alone." Her mom waves her hands in the air while her dad gives me a grin that I'm not sure how to read. "Are you two hungry?" Angela asks, her voice filled with excitement.

"Starving," Alyssa says as my stomach grumbles in agreement.

In no time at all, I feel at ease, completely welcome and with a full belly thanks to her mom.

After lunch, Alyssa shows me around the house making sure to give me an at-length tour of her dad's workshop. I don't miss how her hand smoothes over each tool as she talks like they are priceless jewels that should be displayed in a museum. It's no secret how much she loves her dad and that makes me fall even deeper in love with her.

Nearly an hour passes by with just the two of us rummaging through her dad's somewhat abandoned looking work bench and all the left behind projects that never got to reach their full potential.

Coming back into the house from the garage, we all gather in the kitchen, and although I've been away from the whole family scene for years, it's oddly familiar. Looking around, I catch glimpses of my mom and dad's playful banter as my brothers and I would set the table.

Glancing away from Alyssa and the flirty game of footsy we have going on under the kitchen table while everyone else works to prepare dinner, I notice how much of a struggle it seems to be for her dad to get from one side of the room to the next. He slept most of the afternoon, but it doesn't take a genius to see how ghostly white, thin and weak he is. Honestly, it would take a load off my mind if he would plant himself in a comfortable seat and leave the rest to all of us.

Letting go of Alyssa's hand, I dart over to the counter and grab the plate of pork chops that he is working so hard to get to.

"I'll get those," I announce, scooping up the plate along with a large bag of corn. "Do these get grilled, too?"

Angela flashes me a confused look.

"I was just going to boil them. Are they good grilled? I've never made them that way."

I immediately smile, feeling useful. "Oh yeah ... Tristan ..." *Wait they don't know my brother.* "umm ... my brother, makes them like that all the time. You just grill them up husk and all," I proudly tell her, excitement buzzing through me with the memory.

We used to help Dad grill when we were little. It was the one normal pastime that we kept up after he left; everything else seemed to change with no more late night movies, no more big holidays. We eventually even stopped going to church when Mom got too weak. Grilling and backyard dinners were the one thing that stayed the same. I guess we had to eat, but I never missed how Tristan made sure to do everything exactly how Dad had showed him and that included the way he grilled corn right in the coals.

"I'll come out and help you with the meat and we can grill these up, too," I politely say to Alex, making sure that I do not step on any toes and give him the sense that he is unable to fill the role of taking care of his family.

No doubt this disease is taking enough away from him already, last thing I want is for my gesture to give him the idea that I think he is feeble and obsolete, because I most definitely do not.

Before stepping out to the patio, I flash Alyssa a huge smile feeling like a little boy going on his first fishing trip with his dad. Thankfully, when I go up to the grill to throw the meat and veggies on Alex excuses himself to one of the cushioned patio chairs around a large circular table with an umbrella. A few minutes later, I sit in a chair across from him and lean forward with my hands clasped together on the table.

"I hope you don't mind me joining you."

I've been here all day and this is the first conversation I get to have with him with the exception of our introduction.

Alex looks at me with a smile, slouched back in his seat as if it pains him to sit up straight.

"Actually, I'm glad. You saved me," He chuckles and shifts in his chair restlessly, crinkling his eyebrows and frowning in the process. "Honestly I'm not feeling too well tonight and I really hate for them to see that."

I look over at the patio window as he goes on, and see Alyssa sitting at the kitchen table next to the sliding glass door talking to Abby. Looking back over at Alex, I see that he had followed my gaze. Turning back to me, he asks a question I'm not quite prepared for but 100% certain how to answer.

"You love her, huh?" He looks away and breathes out a small laugh as he pulls his coat tighter around him. "I'd know that look anywhere," he says then makes eye contact with me again.

I can't help but grin, "Look?" I suddenly get uneasy as if I've been walking around with an ear-to-ear smile or drooling into a puddle when I'm looking at her. *Is it really that obvious? I guess I definitely don't have a poker face.*

Alex kicks his head back with a laugh. "That far off look … like you're not just looking at her, but maybe past to a future with her." I shift in my chair, glancing over to Alyssa in the window as he goes on with a chuckle. "Don't worry. I get it. I used to get teased by my friends about that look when I was your age."

I laugh and think about what he said for a minute. My mom used to carry this soft, thoughtful look in her eyes. When she would run her hands through my hair, no matter what we were talking about, she would stare at me with a slight smile on her face; a look of pride, of absolute love. I know that look, too, only my mom probably wasn't looking to a future with us but maybe imagining what the future held for us. I wish she could see that look on my face like Alex does now.

Clearing my throat to hold back a fog of memories and emotions, I answer his initial question, "Yes sir, I do … very much." Feeling the need to elaborate, I go on, because nobody could possibly understand how Alyssa and I could fall so completely in love with each other in only a two weeks time. "I know we've only actually known each other for two …"

He chuckles and holds his index finger up in front of his face to stop me from talking. I do, grateful that I do not have to dive into any details of my relationship with her. My nervousness has the lead over my common sense right now and I'd more than like stumble over my words trying to avoid particular topics.

"You don't have to explain. I absolutely believe in love at first sight." He points over to the back kitchen window only a couple yards from the patio doors where Angela is standing in mid laugh.

I turn back to him and there is no missing that same look in his eyes that I feel each time I watch Alyssa.

"I saw Angela one night when I was out with my friends. We were both seniors and lived fairly close to each other, but until that night I had never noticed her." A soft smile touches his lips as he goes on, still staring at her in the window. "We went to school in two tiny little towns about three and a half hours from here. That night she was with a group of friends outside this old fashion soda shop. You know I think it's still there, too."

He looks out in the distance with a thoughtful expression, perhaps reliving a memory or wishing he could revisit it. Looking back my way, I smile urging him to go on.

"Anyways, as soon as I saw her it was kind of like nothing else existed. My buddy kept trying to get me to jump in the car so we could get to a party, but I couldn't leave. That night, I asked her to go to prom with me and I don't think we took a breath without each

301

other for weeks." Holding his hand back up, he pulses his finger in the air. "It took one second, one single second and I knew." He swings his hand over to the patio window and points at Alyssa, which is also laughing. "Just like I'm sure you knew. I've seen how you both look at each other, so I believe you when you say you love her."

He stops talking and for a moment I think he may go on, but he doesn't. He stares into the window and watches his family laugh and smile. My heart breaks for him at what must be running through his mind.

"How much later was it before you asked her to marry you?" I have no idea why I ask this. It literally spills out of my mouth as if I have no control over my body, but it gets his attention fast.

He spins his head around and a burst of laugher erupts from him, wearing away some of the shock from what I just asked.

"Well now that is fast." Laughing hard, he crosses his hands across his waist and leans forward. "Are you asking my permission, Judd?" My eyes widen and I start to speak up to explain that Alyssa and I aren't quite ready for that yet but then he adds, "It's ok … I'm only teasing you."

I sigh, relaxing back in the chair.

"It was a couple months later … the summer after we graduated actually. It was fast, but we didn't want to wait."

I snicker at his excitement and the glimmer in his eyes as he speaks.

He goes on, "Ohhhh, but our parents and friends most definitely did not approve. Her parents went ballistic, forbidding us from seeing each other and we broke up; took time away from each other. We actually let others decide that we didn't know what we felt. It went on like that for years."

Looking at him in an utter state of confusion, I now realize I am on the edge of my seat, wanting desperately to know what happened; even though I know where the story goes.

"We eventually got married despite our parents disliking each of us then we had Andrea. It was a struggle, but we stuck it out. After Abby and Alyssa, we finally decided to live our own lives and we moved here; left everything else behind. We figured out that our love started out fast and effortlessly, so why let everyone around us tell us that it was wrong? We were in love, bottom line. Once we stopped letting others dictate our lives for us, things became easy again; that's when that same love we felt in the beginning came back." He looks at me with a wide smile and I automatically glance over to Alyssa in the window as I make my way to the grill so I can check on dinner.

Alex speaks up again, breaking me out of my thoughts, "So Judd, I've managed to talk your ear off and wear myself out. Tell me about yourself. Are your parents from around these parts?"

I've never went down this road with anyone; discussing my parents, so the question completely throws me for a loop. "Ahhh, no. I mean well, they went to school in Rosemore like me."

"What do they do now?" Alex asks, seeming generally interested in me and my family.

After flipping the meat and seeing that it is nearly done, I head back to the table and think over his questions.

Memories of my family sit on a thin line in my mind. I love thinking about my mom, yet I try not to because it hurts so much. Then there is Dad; I stay far away from those thoughts. They always lead me to the night he left and that only confuses me. To this day I still don't understand what happened. Looking over at Alyssa's father and the desperation in his eyes, thinking about this relentless disease that is trying to pull him away from this earth, I decide to open up.

"Actually my mom died four years ago and I haven't seen my dad since I was nine."

I put it out there and say it out loud, for one of the first times in my life and it doesn't kill me. It stings, but I'm still standing. I've always thought it would strike me dead if I had to relive the entire experience. I stay away from the subject like the plague, steering it in any direction other than my past out of fear of the pain overwhelming me.

Nodding his head and pressing his lips into a tight line, I see the sympathy in his eyes and it doesn't bother me like it once did. "Well that's a shame. Do mind if I ask what happened?" he pushes on and for some reason I just keep opening up, reliving the night my dad left and made it clear to us that we were simply a mistake. The whole scene flickers through my mind before I can even open my mouth and the ache in my heart thunders just as loudly as it did back then.

"Come on Jake," I say in a loud whisper, bouncing up and down

on the balls of my feet. "I hear them turning on the movie."

"Ok, I'm ready. I got fruit snacks and some chips." He holds them up with a glimmer in his wide eyes and a devilish smile.

Jerking the chips out of his hand and tossing them under the bed, I lean closer and whisper, "Chips are too noisy ... we'll go with the fruit snacks. Now, shhhh." I crack the door open, slowly and easily, barely pulling on it so it doesn't make the never-failing squeak noise that it does when Mom comes in to check on us. That is usually our cue that they are getting ready to sit down and watch a movie deemed unworthy for child eyes.

The door comes open soundlessly, a skill I learned after the first time when that squeal sent us tumbling back to bed, our hearts thudding in our ears with fear that we had been caught. Once I have the door fully open, I glance down the hall. Music filters out of Tristan's room with his door sealed shut. Looking the other way, I find a dark living room with the soft glow of the TV flickering off the ceiling and walls. I wave my hand over my shoulder, motioning for Jake to follow. Dropping to our knees, we crawl down the hall in complete stealth mode, slithering along the floor with nothing but the quiet sound of our stomachs scraping the carpet.

When I see the back of the huge recliner that sits against the wall at the entrance of the living room, I know we've reached our rendezvous point. Settling down on our bellies, I kick my feet up behind me and peer around the edge of the chair where we can barely make out the screen of the TV. I immediately relax when I see a movie we've watched before and know this isn't one that will have me dragging my brother back to bed before we see more than either of our eyes can handle.

Half way into the movie, our gummy candies are eaten with the wrappers shoved under the chair and my eyes slowly slumped down, threatening to close. Widening my eyes, I focus on the movie then glance over to Jake. His face is down in the carpet with a drop of slobber dripping from the corner of his mouth. Gross. Well, I'm not going to miss the movie.

Turning back to catch up on the show, I quickly clasp my hands over my eyes as a girl in the movie creeps into her basement, alone and with nothing but a flashlight. Stupid. Her flashlight drops to the *ground in the dark room and scraping sounds in the distance. No way. I slam my face to the ground, fearful to watch the TV and see what happens. I'll scream.*

Keeping my head down, my eyes get heavier and heavier until ....

"I can't do this! I can't! I won't!" Dad's voice booms like a crack of thunder.

I bolt up from the carpet to the sound of glass shattering and a piercing scream. Pushing up to my hands and knees in a hurry, I look around the recliner to get a view of what is happening.

I'm not sure how long I was wisked away in dreamland or what transpired between movie time and now, but looking around I see a completely different scene from before.

Mom pulls herself up off the floor by latching onto the arm of the couch and Dad has a crazed look in his eyes, impatiently pacing back and forth a few feet away in front of her. Why doesn't he help her? They both look scared; frightened.

I glance down at Jake still flat-on-his-face-passed-out-sawing-logs asleep. Great! The one rule we set for ourselves during operation 'Crawl in Movie': never fall asleep. It figures, not only did he fall asleep, we both did.

"Scott, I'm sorry. I don't know what to say," she pleads, tears streaming down her face.

"Hailey, do you know what this is doing to me? Do you even care?!" he shouts out.

Looking around, I survey the situation and see a turned over lamp with shards of thick, amber glass littered across the floor. Mom is finally standing, but seems unstable, leaning some of her weight onto the end table which used to house the lamp.

"I just don't think I can do this. I've questioned this for years." He places his hands to his side and looks down with Mom staring at him in confusion.

"What do you mean?" she barely gets out between the tears as she lowers herself onto the edge of the couch.

He snaps his head back up and squints his eyes in an angry glare.

"I mean I cannot do this anymore." He motions between her and him. "You know what? I never wanted this in the first place. We got stuck together when you got pregnant ... you know that." He sighs and

Mom dumps her head into her lap, sobbing uncontrollably.

"Wait, I don't understand. I thought ..." Mom manages to get out in a quivering voice.

I have no clue what Dad is talking about either, but I want so badly to go hug Mom. I hate seeing her hurt. He knows she's been getting clumsier lately, she's even been to the doctor several times, but I just don't understand why Dad doesn't go over to tell her it's alright.

They assume I don't notice little things like her losing her balance and the way her legs don't seem to cooperate as they once did. Another thing I haven't missed sight of is how Dad prefers to keep us all at a distance lately. He watches her when she cries, he even looks sad for her, but he doesn't hug her like me and my brothers do. I don't understand it, and it bothers me more than they see.

The other day, out of the blue, Mom ran to her room after one of her spells. Tristan was loading the dishwasher and Jake was taking out the trash, but she ran right past me in the hall as I went to help my brothers with our chores. Once her quiet sobs filtered through the air, I snuck back and peeked through the crack in her door. She sat on the bed, her face buried in the pillow crying. Dad sat on the floor in front of her with a sad expression on his face, just watching as she shouldered the pain alone. A little while later she came out with a painted on smile pretending like nothing was wrong.

"God, I have been trying to make this work. That's why we had Judd, but then you got pregnant again, and it just seems like too much. You know, I never even wanted kids, Hailey. Did you know that? Do you even think we would have stayed together if you wouldn't have gotten pregnant with Tristan?"

Watching the entire scene unfold, what he is saying finally starts to sink in. Is he saying we are a mistake?

Looking up through tear streaked eyes her voice comes out shaky and confused, "Where is this coming from? I don't understand where all this is coming from. You could have left years ago, if that were true. You're just scared and I am, too," she huffs out. "It doesn't have to be like this, Scott."

I look back over to Mom and see that she has stood up and is inching closer to Dad, her hands out as if she is trying to tame a wild stallion.

"Hailey, no, please! I just realized I never wanted this and now with you being sick...I'm just...I'm out!"

Mom runs to Dad, tripping over her feet in the process and grabs onto his arms before she tumbles to the floor again.

"You don't mean that ... you don't! I know you're just scared, but I know you can do this. I know you can," Mom's voice softens and I crane my neck to watch. *"We'll face this together."*

She has her arms against his chest and for a moment I think everything is better; that the fight is over, but it isn't.

Grabbing her by the arms, he shoves her away, yelling with more anger than I've ever heard; the sound of a stranger's voice, not my dad's.

"It's over! This is over!" He points his fingers towards the hall where all our rooms are located and then lowers his voice; almost too quiet for me to make out. *"This was a mistake...they were a mistake and this is not the future I want."*

Confusion and disbelief fill my mind and I begin to rise up to make my presence known. I need to defend my mother, but suddenly hands grip the back of my shirt and pull me back into the hall. Tilting my head, I see Tristan's face above me, crumpled into a scowl.

"Get back to bed now," he says in an angry tone.

My first instinct is to protest, but one look into his eyes and I know I better let this go. Something about the way he continues to look over the edge of the recliner with a storm of rage in his eyes that tells me I better listen.

Not even a second after I am within the safety of my bedroom, he rushes back out and down the hall without another word. What had been only the raised voice of my father with a background melody of my mother's hurtful sobs is soon joined by Tristan's amplified hollers. His furious tone rises over Dad's and immediately muffles out Mom's cries.

"Don't you ever ... ever touch her or shove her! Get the hell out of here! We don't want you anymore than you want us! We don't need you!" The anger in his voice sends chills down my spine. *"Leave, just leave!"* he blares out.

"Tristan ..." Mom's voice calls out as I lean in the doorway of my room, trying to strain to see what all is going on. *"Honey, you don't*

under ..."

"Get out I said," Tristan's shrill tone vibrates through me, bring-ing tears to my eyes.

What's going on? Why is everyone yelling at each other?

Something crashes in the other room and I flinch against the door frame, fear gripping every corner of my soul.

"Get the hell out of here," he yells out again, his voice laced in rage.

Turning my body, I slowly slide down the wall beside my door much like the tears that now drip down my face. With my body planted into a ball on the floor, I think over everything that I heard, feeling lifeless and drained of emotion. Pushing my palms over my ears as more noise ignites from the living room, I look up at the ceiling not understanding, yet not sure that I want to.

A few minutes later, a muffled slamming noise penetrates the pro-tection of my hands over my ears and all goes quiet. Assuming it was the front door, I race to my window; watching just as Dad climbs into his car and speeds out of the driveway.

My heart hammers in my throat and I wonder when he will be back? Maybe he is leaving to cool off. With that single thought, his words come back to me, "I'm done ... I'm out", "I never wanted this", "It's over", "They are a mistake". He didn't want us...he doesn't want us? He's not coming back? Rejection, grief and sorrow engulf my heart as my mind spins out of control in a tornado of questions and doubt.

The door eases open behind me and I watch as Tristan carries Jake in. Folded in his arms like a big baby, I see that somehow he managed to stay asleep.

I remain quiet, holding back a river of tears as Tristan lays Jake into the bottom mattress of the bunk bed. His jaw is tense and his eyes are red as if he had rubbed them raw before coming into the room.

"Tristan, is Dad coming back?" I ask quietly, not wanting to wake Jake and involve him in this daunting catastrophe.

Tristan pulls his arms out from beneath Jake's back, stands straight and levels me with a firm glare that I've never seen on his face before. Suddenly my brother looks older; bitter and angry.

"Judd, go to bed. You're up way too late and you should not have been out of bed anyways," he says calmly and then slowly walks to the

door, shutting it without another look my way.

I turn back to the window and touch my hand to the cold glass, my crushed heart pleading that this whole night is only a dream. It's at that moment ... that solitary second that I recognize the significance of what just happened. This is the last time I will ever see my dad. We're on our own.

Blinking my eyes, I look at Alex still waiting for me to go on, so I do, starting with Mom.

"My mom had ALS for years. My brothers and I watched her get weaker and sicker every day until she just couldn't do the smallest things for herself," I fade off, thinking over the last morning I saw her, before going on. "And my dad ... you know I'm not sure what happened. He took off one night and the next day my mom broke the news to us that she was sick. The doctors hadn't yet diagnosed her with ALS. She went through test after test before they figured out what it was, but my dad high-tailed it before we got the news. My brothers and I took care of her. My older brother was with her day and night."

I go silent and sit there on the memory of Tristan missing day after day of his Junior and Senior year of high school. He had sacrificed so much back then; I forgot about that until now.

"Judd," Alex says my name and I realize I must appear lost in thought. I look up, met with a grateful smile. "Thank you for telling me all that. I'm sure it wasn't easy."

I nod my head and smile with a lump forming in my throat.

"I'm glad my daughter has you. You're good for her and she will need you. There is a plan for everything in life and I can see a magnificent one taking shape right now." He lets out a sigh and looks out to the yard behind us.

I stare at him wondering how he can be so strong in such a hopeless time, but movement from my peripheral vision gives me the answer. Through the window I view all the girls laughing hysterically like they are having a party and I completely get why he would hold on so tight; why my mom held on despite the pain: *love.*

Love can bleed light through the darkest clouds. It can give hope when there is absolutely none and it can give you the strength to break free when you are chained down and being pulled into a pit of despair. It breathes life into vacant lungs and helps you catch your breath when you have no air to breathe; I know this.

I get up and walk back to the grill as Alex sits in silence. After taking the meat and corn off the grill, we head back inside and discover three giggling girls.

"So what's so funny," I whisper next to Alyssa's ear as we all take a seat at the kitchen table.

We both get settled across from Abby, with her parents sat at each end of the table. Leaning towards me, she places her hand on my thigh to support herself from falling over.

"Mom was checking if we were being safe," she says at a barely audible level directly into my ear.

I instantly shift around in my seat, now uneasy about her hand being where it is and scared to death that someone heard her. Looking around, I fight the urge to grab her hand and move it back to her own body. Everyone digs in, dishing up and passing bowls from one person to the next, oblivious to us. Abby is the only one that looks directly at me as I finish dishing up my plate and grab my steak knife. *Oh God, what is she thinking?*

"Careful," she spits out quickly, steering all attention my way. "You always … want to be safe."

Alyssa and her mom both break into a fit of laughter as my face heats up and I snap my head around to look at her dad.

"What did I miss?" he asks mid-bite, finally igniting laughter from me.

Luckily no one answers and we all quickly move on to a less invasive topic.

As dinner moves on, all five of us laugh and talk as if I have known them my whole life. My heart warms with feelings I have not felt in years; something deep inside that I thought was lost, unreachable and I smile remembering what it is like to be part of a family.

My Home

THE NIGHT FLIES BY and after being shown to the spare bedroom with another extremely embarrassing moment of her mom directly telling us no sex under their roof we are then left completely alone at last. We talk for a bit, but with each passing minute and countless yawns from us both, we eventually fall into a peaceful sleep beside each other.

After what feels like a full day of sleep, I wake up clutching a pillow with Alyssa nowhere to be found. It takes me only minutes to change, make my way downstairs, and find her sitting alongside her father while he sleeps.

Standing in the doorway I watch in silence, filled with gratitude that I could be here at such a personal, meaningful, and intimate time in all of their lives. These may very well be some of their last moments together and I am allowed to be here for it.

My brothers and I didn't let anyone in at times like this and I think that is part of the reason why we were alone afterwards. The whole time Mom was sick we pushed everyone out of our circle; neighbors, co-workers of my mom's and anyone else who just tried to be there for three scared boys who would be left with nothing once she was gone. That is how it was too. After an endless stampede of casseroles and baked goods brought to our door, Tristan, Jake and I, who had always been close growing up, went in three different directions while everyone left us alone. It was just us, but by that time, not even the three of us pulled together as a family. We each grieved alone and in our own way. Thankfully, after a while I came to my senses and Jake and I became closer.

Alyssa kisses her dad's forehead before joining me, but all I can do is smile at the love she holds for him. Two strides backwards and I'm out of the room, not taking my eyes off of her as she quietly closes the door then melts into my arms. I immediately cover her mouth with mine, feeling as though a few hours without her has been way too long.

"I love watching you with your dad."

She nuzzles closer to me like I'm the only place she has ever known.

"Good grief, get a room," Abby's voice comes out of nowhere, making me jump.

Alyssa's face falls into my chest with a snort and I spit out a chuckle at Abby's sarcasm. *I should set her and Evan up, although that could be a disaster waiting to happen.*

"Going to Piper's for a bit. You two going to be here when I get back?" she asks on her way out the door.

"Yep … all day … all night! You are stuck with us til tomorrow." Alyssa sticks her tongue out.

I look back at Abby and catch her matching Alyssa's goofy gesture with her eyes crossed and her tongue also hanging out of her head just as the door closes behind her. I nod my head and turn my attention back to Alyssa, ready to crush her beautiful, plump lips with my own.

Just as my mouth is close enough to feel the tickle of her breath across my lips, the sound of someone clearing their throat breaks the moment and has my hands rethinking their descent into the back of her sweatshirt. *Close one.*

"Sorry to interrupt," her mom announces from the dining area of the kitchen while gritting her teeth as if she was doing something wrong.

Here I was considering fondling her daughter right in their living room, completely forgetting where I am.

Alyssa presses her lips together and gives me a bashful smile as if she feels just as caught as I do. *What was she thinking?*

"Would you two mind a quick trip to the store for me this afternoon sometime? I just need a few things for dinner."

Alyssa nods and her mom quickly gives us a list.

Five minutes later, we are alone in my truck and Alyssa is perfectly tucked against my side.

"Take a right up here," she says pointing in the opposite direction that we came.

"This isn't the way to the grocery store." I crinkle my eyebrows and look her way, curious again. *What's she thinking?* My cheek dips in and I can't fight the monstrous grin that is creeping across my face.

She has an all-knowing smile painted on her face as she stares dead ahead, completely unwilling to give me any clues.

"I know. Take a right."

I, of course, follow her new route plan. Winding along a street I've never been on, she instructs me to take another turn and we end up in a tiny parking lot right off the road, directly in front of a small ball field. I pull the truck into a spot and throw it into park, leaving it running for the sake of music and heat. A little confused on whether she has a sudden urge to play catch, I look over ready to ask what's going on, but it becomes clear in no time.

Alyssa snaps her seatbelt off, scoots around in the seat and slides between the steering wheel and me, settling into my lap. *Much better than playing baseball.* Thinking on their own, my arms fall around her, drawing her close enough that we share the same breaths.

"I thought some alone time was way overdue."

I chuckle at her statement because I have been dying to be completely alone with her.

"Besides, I don't think Mom will even notice."

My mind flashes back to all that Alex said about how he and Angela met, about how fast they fell in love then to how her mom just up and left us alone in the bedroom last night. A smile emerges deep inside of me. *No, I don't think she will even mind, in fact, I think she will understand an extra fifteen minutes away.*

Her soft hand brushes the back of my neck as she slides closer and places tiny kisses along my cheek. Once her path leads to my ear, I pick up the suckling sounds of her kisses and my body reacts. The hairs on my arms stand on end and I drown in the blissful sensations she stirs within me as her breath dances over my earlobe. Advancing my state of arousal, she starts to shift and moves into my lap creating a fiery friction between us that is not a good idea given we are at a public, children's ball field. I doubt her parents would approve of us getting arrested for indecent exposure.

"Whoa," I whisper, half out of breath. Pressing my hands tightly against her hips, I halt her efforts and concentrate on forming words. "Ahhh … we better stop before I hit a point of no return." *I'm damn near already there.*

Her face falls into a cute, irresistible frown that takes all my self control to not just throw the truck in drive and race to the nearest hotel. Running my hand from her waist up to her face, I lightly trace the soft texture of her skin while letting out a calming breath to cool me down. She looks back with the sliver of a smile surfacing.

"I missed you so much."

The words barely come out over the extreme amount of emotion that wells up inside of me when I look at her. *I can't believe she is here; that I am here with her. It doesn't matter how many hours pass by, I still can't fathom that after three long months that she is finally in my arms.* You would think loss would be something you get used to, but it never is; it never gets easier. It just hits you differently every single time. Losing Alyssa, or thinking that I had lost her, knocked the wind right out of my lungs.

Looking at me with nothing but love in her eyes, her soft hands slide under the front of my sweatshirt, triggering a tidal wave of chills throughout my body from her warm caress over my abs and up my chest. *She's not going to make this easy. Maybe I should just call Evan now and tell him to plan on bailing us out of jail later.*

"What all did you miss?" The alluring tone she uses is totally working to her advantage.

She could play me like a banjo right now if she wanted to.

"Everything," I whisper, moving my hand to the back of her neck and pulling her to my lips.

Her mouth touches mine and I am instantly starved for her, hungry for her touch and craving her body against mine as an unquenchable need burns within me. The heat from her hand has every muscle in my body tensed, anxiously awaiting more. Just as my resolve starts to chip away, she pulls back.

"Tell me something specific."

She is killing me here. I meant it when I said everything. I longed for her lips every night; dreamt of touching her everywhere. I heard the sound of her voice in everything; music, movies, in the dark, in class, it was always in my head. Then something very memorable surfaces and I smile.

I slide my hand into her hair and look her in the eyes.

"The way you smell."

"I smell?" She crinkles up her nose and I drop my head back laughing. "Great." She subtly turns her head to the side and sniffs as if she's doing a pit-check that you see a lot of jocks do before leaving the locker room. I want to roll on the floor laughing. *Probably not something girls want to hear.*

So I clarify the meaning behind my words, "You smell good ... all the time. I know you use some kind of strawberry shampoo, because I saw it in your bag back at the cabin and you also were using it as a weapon in the shower the other right."

She giggles at my teasing, but continues to look at me intently, urging me to go on with her eyes.

"I can't explain it. It's overpowering, as if the fragrance of your skin was formulated for me alone. Anytime I'm around you, it hits me like a truck. It was nearly unbearable when we were apart."

After resituating both of my hands at her waist I smoothly run them into the back of her shirt so that I can feel her silky skin.

"I use a strawberries and crème shampoo," she giggles.

I smile, still reminiscing over how the smell of her skin haunted me all summer long.

"There was this day this summer when Jake and I went to the grocery store. We were shopping around like any other time, but as we walked through the bakery aisle this sweet fragrance that smelled just like you slammed right into me." Her mouth opens slightly in surprise as I go on. "Jake asked me what was wrong, but all I could do was look around. It was so embarrassing. Finally, I looked over the counter where they were making the cakes and stuff. There was this woman making a strawberry shortcake dessert thing. Here she was placing little slivers of strawberries all over the top of this cake." I drop my chin down, nodding my head from the memory.

Alyssa laughs, cupping my face in her hands so that I will look at her. "So what was so embarrassing?"

I squeeze my eyes shut and grit my teeth at the last part of the story. *I am such a freak of nature!* "I ran off because I thought it was you …" Cocking her head to the side, it's obvious she's still confused by my half ass answer. "I ran off to the bathroom because that smell is like an aphrodisiac for me," I chuckle and hang my head, looking down to the wrinkles of my shirt.

She frowns at first, her expression blank, then her eyes widen, "Ohhh …" she mumbles tipping my head upward with her hand under my chin. "That's sweet."

I burst out laughing at her interpretation of that word.

"Sweet?" I stare at her, amusement rising in my chest. "I was turned on in the bakery department at the grocery store …" She drops her arms around her mid-section as if the laughter may tear her in two. " …In front of my little brother." I finish, my stomach now hurting from how hard I'm laughing. "Ok, ok … what about you?"

She stops laughing abruptly and her eyes flick down to my lips.

"You know," she says with a devilish smile that has my lips rising up slowly.

"What?"

Her eyes quickly gravitate to my cheek and I cannot stop from the full on smile that spreads across my face.

"There it is." Her lips go directly to my dimple for a gentle, loving kiss.

Swinging my head to the side, I capture her lips and drink her in, bringing a soft whimper out of her; that little noise I've always loved so much.

Nibbling at her bottom lip, I whisper against her lips, "I missed that, too."

Inhaling a mouthful of air between luscious, wet kisses, she whispers, "I missed how you kiss.

Her breaths kick up as my hand glides up her back to unclasp her bra. *So much for will power.* Just as my fingers find the hook, her phone buzzes, distracting us both from our current goal. Alyssa leans up and grabs her phone out of her back pocket, but my hands continue fumbling with the hooks at her back.

"Oh shoot, it's my mom calling." Still breathing heavy, she accepts the call and slaps it to her ear, annoyance ringing out in her voice. "Yeah?"

I drop my hands, suddenly feeling as though her mom has x-ray vision to see what's going on as my ears barely pick up on the quiet murmuring from the other side of the phone.

"Ok, yeah … shredded cheese and eggs. Got it … anything else?" she huffs out gasps of air.

That's not noticeable at all. Alyssa's voice is laced with irritation and there isn't a doubt in my mind that her mom can tell something is going on; definitely not shopping.

"No … not yet," she stutters and I can hear her mom laughing on the line. "Ummm … well we are parked and getting ready to go in." She glances at me, her eyes wide and her teeth gritted.

Great … we're busted!

"Ok … yeah …" she twirls her hand around in a circle, "… Ok … sure. Love you, Mom. Bye."

As soon her finger punches the end button, she flings the phone to the seat and grabs my face back into her hands. I laugh as her lips crash into mine. Soft tingles rocket up my torso and down my legs as her hands quickly climb back under my shirt and graze over my chest. I instantly find that her mom's call did nothing to put a damper on our fire; it's still raging, in fact. She tugs my shirt greedily and pulls back a couple inches, barely able to catch her breath.

"Do you think we could real fast?"

My pulse races and I may actually go into cardiac arrest at any moment. Gripping her shirt in my hands as well, I look her in the eyes.

"Oh, I think I can real fast," I spit out, leaning forward so she can pull my shirt up as I work hers off as well. *I have no doubt. Replay of our first time, here I come.*

Right as my shirt is around my neck and I have hers pulled halfway up her back, her phone chirps. *What the hell!*

"Just ignore it."

Alyssa proceeds to rip my shirt off, tossing it to the floorboard. The backs of my fingertips run over the lacy fabric of her bra as I raise her shirt further and further up her body. *This is totally going to hap-*

pen! In my truck! A blaring horn screeches out behind my truck at the same time as Alyssa's phone starts ringing, sending all my excitement plummeting to the ground.

"Oh crap!" she yells, ripping her phone off the seat.

I snap my head to look over my shoulder, bracing my elbow on the back edge of the seat and dropping her sweatshirt back in place.

"Are you kidding me? What the hell are you doing spying on us?"

My eyes make contact with Abby sitting in her car on the road behind as if she was passing by. Her eyes land on mine and a huge smile stretches across her face.

"Very funny! Fine! Bye, Abby!" I watch as she slams the phone down into the seat then I turn to catch Abby's fingers fluttering in a small proud-of-herself goodbye before speeding off. I flip around and rest my hands against Alyssa's waist.

"What did she say?"

She throws me a half annoyed look mixed with a half smirk. "She said she told us to get a room, not to go park."

My lips twitch up and my chest tickles with the urge to laugh. Once Alyssa falls forward onto my shoulder, shaking with laughter, I can't hold back any longer. We laugh and laugh until our lungs burn and voices are hoarse then decide we better head to the store.

When we get back, her sister, Andrea, and her family show up and I get to experience the full effects of being a part of her family, complete with wrestling around with her two nephews in the backyard. I remember seeing a football in the garage, so after going to fetch it, I stay busy in the yard teaching them how to tackle and run a passing play. We have an absolute ball and I truly do not want the night to end. Although it pulls up nostalgia of doing the same thing with my dad, it's an amazing feeling playing again, even if it's just goofing off.

Alex ends up drained and goes to bed early, leaving a storm of worry in his daughters and wife's eyes. After Andrea, her husband Greg, and the kids leave, Angela and Abby head to bed leaving Alyssa and I alone on the landing outside her bedroom and the spare bedroom I'm designated to. Wrapping her in a tight embrace as if we won't see each other for a couple days, I let my lips linger against hers, not wanting to let go for even one night. She lets out a loud sigh.

"You know, you could just sleep in my room if you want," she says with her cheek pressed to my heart.

"I don't know. With everything that went on earlier, I'm not sure we would be very disciplined," I snicker, "and the last thing I want to do is disrespect your parents by breaking their rules."

She lifts her head from its resting place and looks at me quizzically.

"Their rule wasn't that we couldn't sleep in the same room. It was that we don't have sex under their roof."

I laugh. "Yeah, and that is exactly what may happen. We seriously have no self control when we are together," I crack up. *She knows this; we cannot keep our hands off each other. She could sneeze and I'd find a way to find it sexy as hell like watching her chest bounce or the way she opens her mouth when she does it. We suck at holding back.*

"Sorry, I forgot to wash my face." Abby's voice comes out of nowhere once again, and I have to chuckle at her timing. *If it isn't Evan, it's Abby.*

Abby slips into the hall bathroom and Alyssa looks up to me with a sweet smile.

"We better get to bed," I pause, reading her small smile as a way to try to make me bend. "In separate rooms," I add, watching as her bottom lip bubbles out into a pout.

I quickly capture her plump lip and mold mine to hers for a second; not nearly long enough but if I kiss her too long, no way will I go in a different room. She kisses me fiercely, gripping at the side of my waist in an attempt to keep me near. Pulling away, I run my hand over her face as I move backwards.

"Good night." My heart pounds up into my ear drums as I look over her standing there in a tight black tank top and small, white shorts with a lace trim. *Oh geez! I need a cold shower.* "I love you." I stay true to my determination to be respectful under someone else's roof.

Her hand latches onto mine just as it is falling from her face and she flies back into my arms, her lips landing on mine. My hands run into her hair and I kiss her like there is no tomorrow, like this is our last day on earth. I let my tongue guide its way into her mouth, feeling the soft caress of hers in sync with mine. My mind shuts off and every nerve in my body is at attention.

A creak sounds behind me and I flinch away.

"Oh come on. Really?" Abby mumbles sarcastically as she walks to her room.

I turn back to Alyssa and smile. Her chest rises with a deep, irritated sigh that says exactly all that I am feeling. I seriously just want to be beside her tonight; all night, but I concede.

"Night ... I love you." I tell her one more time before walking to the spare room doorway.

Her feet don't move and I find myself silently pleading for her to walk away before I pick her up and drag her into the bedroom with me; breaking all of the rules in one wham.

"I love you, too." She slowly moves backward towards her room and I let out a breath. "Night."

She disappears into her room, peering around the door one last time as she pushes it halfway closed. Once her face is out of sight, I finally make my legs move and crash land onto the bed, clothes and all. Kicking off my shoes, I push and shove at the heels with my opposite foot until they both fall to the floor with a thump.

I stare up at the ceiling, watching the shadows of one of the backyard trees creep across it like a ghost. Twisting onto my side, my head settles into the pillow and I glance over to a prehistoric looking wind up clock on the dresser that reads only 10:23 and blow out a puff of air. *It's going to be a long night.*

After closing my eyes for what feels like half the night, I am brimming with confidence that the room will be filled with sunlight, but when I look at the bedside clock all hope is sucked right out of me. *How have I only been laying here for an hour?!*

Turning onto my back forcefully, I slam my head into the pillow and punch at the sides of it as if fluffing the damn thing will soothe my need to be in the next room. I lie still, watching the trees sway in the breeze outside the window and listen to the gentle howling from the wind sweeping over the sides of the house, but nothing can steal my mind away.

I race through thoughts, eager to find something to cling to that will help me fall asleep; anything. After searching over plays from old football games, an essay that needs to be written and blueprints from the jobsite my mind lands on my conversation the other night with Alex.

"Our love started out fast." His words echo in my mind, reminding me of how my relationship with Alyssa started out. Once we met, we could not spend a moment apart. It's as if I've lost a limb of my own body when she isn't near. I close my eyes and focus. Alex's face and words move aside and my mom settles into the back of my mind; a conversation we had a year before the darkness of ALS slowly started to steal her away, starting with the function of her body and finally the ability for us to even hear her beautiful voice.

I squeeze my eyes tighter, grasping at the sound of her voice now replaying in my mind. The sound isn't clear and I'm not even sure it belongs to her or if at this point, it's a creation that I've dreamt up over time.

"I want you to promise me something," her words slur and she pauses, aware of it herself.

I sit still on the edge of her bed, wanting to hear anything she has to say. Jake shuffles against my knee as he kneels on the floor with his elbows resting on the bed.

Mom takes a deep breath and smiles.

"Mom, are you ok?" I look over at Tristan quickly, irritated by his question. Of course she's not ok, I want to yell.

She nods, moving her hand to grab up one of his.

"I need you to be strong for your brothers, ok?"

My mind repeats the same thing over and over, knowing this could be the end. It could be, it might be but it might not. We may have to watch her suffer longer, we don't know. There is no way to know; no alarm that will go off to signify, "Hey, make sure you tell your mom goodbye today because she won't be here tomorrow. There's nothing, just today and the potential for tomorrow. And it sucks!

"Ok, Mom ... I will. Just don't worry about that right now," Tristan urges her to save her strength.

Days have been getting harder for her lately and although Tristan keeps the door shut most days, we all make a point to come in and spend time with her. As the days go by and as her speech slowly starts to get worse the family meetings become more and more common. I fear when I won't be able to come in and listen to her. What will life be like when her voice is gone, when all she can do is exist? A torturous pain slices across my chest, capturing my heart and slowly crushing it.

She nods, letting him know she is ok to go on. Opening her mouth, her lips quiver, but she pushes on.

"Promise you will all stick together and be there for each other when ..." she trails off and I'm not sure if it's from pain, irritation at her difficulty in speaking or if her heart is hurting like ours right now. Her eyes fog with tears and I know it's the latter. "Live."

It's a single word and she stops, pushing her head into the pillow.

"Ok, that's enough. Mom needs to rest. Let's go." Tristan stands up motioning for us to leave and although I want to yell at him to stop being so protective because she is our mom too, I don't. I'm too focused on the word she said. She's dying, I know she is, yet she says "live." Live, live, live ... it echoes though my mind on the way out the door as I wave at Mom.

I repeat the word in my mind; Live. I smile, where as back then I couldn't. *That was what she wanted us to promise ... that we would live.* It didn't make a whole lot of sense back then, but it does now. I stopped living after she died, we all did, but the second I saw Alyssa, that's when I felt life again. I could breathe and smile again; I could laugh.

"I promise," I whisper up to the ceiling as I jump to my feet and glide across the floor, trying my best to miss the floor boards that I already noticed creak.

Quietly opening my door, I glance down the hall to Abby's room, a bit of awkwardness rising into my chest at the thought that I am sneaking through someone else's house. *I feel like a total creeper!* I smoothly step into the hall and glance over the edge of the railing to the living room and can barely see the door to Alex and Angela's room. *No lights.* I let out a relieved sigh and proceed to Alyssa's room.

Her door is still wedged open so I barely nudge it, swinging it open with ease. Alyssa bounces up in her bed immediately as if she had been waiting for me; staying awake until I came to her side.

Three large strides and I fall onto her bed, sliding over her. My hand runs the length of her body, over her hip, feeling a sliver of skin at her waist and landing on her ribcage as I taste her beautiful, full lips. Knowing this is not a good idea, I roll to the side and pull her against me, feeling all is right in the world now.

She shuffles backwards, molding her back to my chest and bending her legs to match my own. She fits me like a puzzle piece that was cut and shaped for me alone.

We lay there in the silence of the room, no words spoken between the two of us. There isn't anything that needs to be said. My heart thumps and slams in my chest against her back and I know she can feel my love. It vibrates through every inch of my body; pouring out of me and pulling her into its grasp.

She threads her fingers through mine and rests them against her chest; allowing me to feel the pounding of her own heart. It's like our very own symphony and the chorus is right on key. Her heart beats with mine; each thud calling out to the next in a beautiful harmony of love and promise. I listen to each beat, pulling her so close that I know no one could ever pull us apart.

At last, my eyes grow heavy as I listen to Alyssa's soft breaths and I know I am home; she is my home.

Caught

MY EYES PEEL OPEN to a room full of sunlight and I find that neither Alyssa nor I moved an inch all night. She still holds my hands to her chest and we are still glued to one another like sculpted pieces of art.

Carefully unclasping my hand from hers, I run it down her body, stopping at the exposed flesh at her waist. Nuzzling my face into her hair, I pull in a deep breath of strawberries while my fingertips smooth back and forth over her delicate skin. She stirs from my touch, wiggling her body against mine on a small sigh.

I press a small kiss to the tender area of skin behind her ear that has been calling my name for the past few minutes, and trail my hand under her tank. Moving it forward onto her stomach, I spread my fingers apart, letting my pinky skim the waist band of her shorts.

Tensing up from a sudden movement near the doorway, I calmly pull my hand out of her shirt and straighten the fabric down over her skin. I avoid looking over out of fear it may be her parents out in the hall, but then the clicking of her doorknob has me glancing.

"I'm sorry," her mother whispers.

How long has she been standing there? Suddenly, I'm a little fifteen year old getting caught sneaking through the window of a girlfriend's house. I flash her an apologetic smile and flick my gaze over to Alyssa, still sleeping soundly.

"Are you hungry?"

The mention of food gets my attention fast. Nodding my head, I carefully slide my arm out from under her pillow. As soon as my weight shifts, the mattress creaks below me and my head snaps over to Alyssa, then back to Angela. She laughs and waves her hand to urge me to hurry up. I slip off the bed and scoot across the floor, a part of me hoping Alyssa wakes up, yet another part wanting to let her rest.

Craning my neck to see around the door one more time, I smile at her peacefully sleeping with a spray of blonde hair across the white sheets and her gripping the comforter to her chest as if she is missing something; me.

"I have some bacon and eggs made downstairs," Angela's soft tone barely reaches my ears as she walks a little ways in front of me.

I turn and join her on the way down to the kitchen.

"I'm so sorry if I woke you up." Her apology takes me by surprise.

"No, I was already awake. I'm pretty used to waking up at the crack of dawn. I worked on a farm for years, so I guess those early hours stuck with me," I say as we step off the last stair and make our way to the kitchen. "Listen, I'm sorry I was in Alyssa's room. I just …" I stumble trying to find an explanation that will suffice.

"Oh …" she laughs, waving it off, "honey, I remember being your age. Besides …" she glances over at me, taking in my attire as she walks up to the counter and proceeds to pour two cups of coffee. "You still have yesterday's clothes on, so I'm not worried." Her smile lights up her entire face just like Alyssa's as she hands me a cup.

My face is frozen, mouth drawn open and my eyebrows pulled up to my forehead from her assessment of my clothing. *This is where Abby gets her feistiness.*

Slipping past me, she dishes up two plates then heads to the table, motioning me over as she takes her seat.

"Grab a plate and come sit."

I slowly walk over to the table with my plate and cup in hand. Sitting across from her, I fidget with my fork, a whole nest of nerves finding a home in the pit of my stomach.

"Judd, relax. You know … actually, you and Alyssa remind me of myself and Alex when we were your age. We actually met not too far away from where you two met. Oh, we could not stay away from each other," she tells me, completely lost in thought.

I scoop up a bite full of fluffy eggs and look up at her while shoving them in my mouth. She looks as if she is thinking of a specific memory and with what she said, I'm not sure I want the details.

Looking back at me, she laughs, "You're looking at me just like my daughters do. Don't worry, I won't tell you about any of that. Now if you were them right now, I'd give a little extra information just to see them squirm in their seat."

I quirk my lips to the side, smiling as I savor the buttery flavor of the eggs mixed with the sweet maple tang of crispy bacon. It melts on my tongue, right along with a bit of my heart, as I notice Angela glancing over to her bedroom door where Alex is sleeping. Here I am thinking about how long it's been since my mom made me breakfast, and she is thinking about how there will come a day when she may never make one for him again.

With a vice grip on my heart, I clear my throat hoping to subtly get her attention and distract her from where her thoughts may be leading her.

"I don't mind. My mom used to tell me stories all the time." I gulp down a colossal amount of emotions that keeps making a reappearance "It's one of my favorite memories of her ... how she would find a story of hers to relate to anything I was going through."

Her lips rise into a sympathetic smile and it's apparent that Alex may have filled her in.

Tipping my head towards their bedroom, I add, "He was telling me a little about how you met outside a diner or store a little ways from here."

With that, her face breaks wide open into a child-like grin and I'm relieved that her mind is on happier thoughts. I toss back the rest of my breakfast and coffee as Angela reiterates a bit of the same tale that Alex told me the other night. The more she talks, the more I see my mom, in her positivity and her overall outlook on life.

After I finish up my second plate which Angela very generously dished up for me, she snatches both of them and deposits them in the sink.

"Well I feel like I have talked your ear off."

I laugh, remembering how Alex said the same thing, only I don't see it that way at all. I'm usually not a big talker and I'm usually never open. That's my little brother's department. I tend to bottle up my emotions, except with Alyssa; with her I totally wear my heart on my sleeve.

"I enjoyed it," I assure her as I walk up behind her with my empty coffee cup in hand. "It's been a long time since I've had a mom to talk to."

I don't even think before I say it, but as soon as the words are out of my mouth I realize how expectant it may sound; practically calling her mom. She has the opposite reaction, though, spinning around with a proud-as-can-be-mom-smile then tossing her arms around me to squish me in a warm hug.

"Judd, I'm so happy you came to stay this weekend. I can't even tell you what it means to me and my husband that she has you."

Keeping my arms slack at my side, I widen my eyes, a little surprised by her gesture. She pulls away, leaving her hands gently on my shoulders and standing at arm's length.

"I can tell such a difference in her this weekend. There is a lightness about her that wasn't there a couple weeks ago. She has taken the news about her father so hard and well … I know it will only get harder, but knowing she has you is a relief."

I let out a shaky breath with her statement, emotions bubbling to the surface of my heart; gratefulness for being here, heartache for what I know Alyssa will go through, fear of not being able to help her through it, worry of whether I will be able to hold it together myself and absolute love for this family that I've only just begun to get to know.

"Don't be a stranger. Make sure you come with her when she comes and visits … not that I have to say that. I can tell you two are pretty much joined at the hip." The corners of her eyes crinkle as she winks and slowly drops her arms to her sides.

I chuckle, liking the sound of being around Alyssa as much as possible.

"Thanks for having me. I guess I'm going to go see if Alyssa is awake yet." I turn, ready to head upstairs so I can cradle her back in my arms.

Angela sputters a laugh from behind me, "Don't get your hopes up. She's the sleeper in this family. I wouldn't expect her up any sooner than noon." Laughing she looks at her wrist as if there is an imaginary watch telling her the time.

That's one thing I've always loved about her. All the mornings we have woken up side-by-side, I've been the one that is fortunate enough to wake up first, allowing me to marvel at her beauty as she sleeps, listen to the sounds of her breath and watch the flicker of her eyelids as she wanders through dream after dream.

I nod my head and make my way out of the kitchen, but turn to add one more thing, "Thanks for breakfast, too."

Rubbing her hands on a towel that is draped over the edge of the sink, she swings around with a huge smile.

"My pleasure, honey."

My heartstrings tug and tighten every time she says a little thing like that and it makes me realize how much the little everyday things can mean to you once they are taken away; seemingly insignificant things such as hearing words like "honey" or "sweetie."

I offer my brightest, most appreciative smile and race upstairs to join Alyssa back in bed, which is exactly where Angela said she would be. Collapsing down beside her, I worm one arm back under her pillow and the other around her waist, pulling her warm, slender frame flush against me.

The day goes by faster than either of us would like and soon we are back in Rosemore. I'll have to admit, I loved being at her parent's and getting to know them, but nothing compares to being alone with her.

We spend Sunday evening completely tucked away from everyone. Luckily, her apartment is Bethany-free for a couple nights so we choose her place over mine.

Monday morning comes and it is back to reality; morning classes for us both along with her work schedule.

Reluctantly crawling out of bed and sliding on the same clothes from yesterday, I decide I better get over to my apartment to shower and change before I make us both late for class.

"I won't be long." Placing a long, sultry kiss on Alyssa's lips, I contemplate not even leaving the comfort of her bed or her body.

Her fingers clamp onto my shirt as I lean across the bed with each of my fists sunk into the soft, mattress on either side of her.

"Don't leave yet," she whines and I'm half temped to give in.

"Okay …" Grinning against her lips, I press the full weight of my body onto the bed, carefully hanging my feet over the edge as I scoot on my knees closer to her. "We'll just skip class and work."

Her eyes shift to the clock and the excitement quickly fades. Laughing at her sudden realization that we are running late, I sit back on my heels and study her as she lets out a mournful groan.

"Do we have to go to class?"

Yep, she and I are on the exact same page. "I'm afraid so. Otherwise, I would have never stepped out of this bed."

Knowing I barely have enough time to shower now, I offer her another kiss then slip out the doors to race home. My usual twenty minute trip to her apartment takes me twelve minutes flat. As I jet to my room to get clothes, the rattling of a dresser drawer from Evan's room tells me that he must be running late as well. I waste no time gathering a fresh shirt and jeans from my closet then hurry into the shower.

Stepping beneath the warm, relaxing stream of water and bearing in mind that showers are not near as fun without Alyssa, I scrub up quickly, anxious to get back to her apartment. Once my feet hit the cold linoleum floor, I nearly second guess jumping back in to knock off the chill, but instead I hastily pull my shirt and jeans onto my still damp body, struggling a bit like I did the other night. As I hop on one foot to pull on my last sock, the door snaps open and like a vacuum all the steamy, humid air is sucked out as Evan walks in.

"When did you get home? I thought you had class this morning," he says, glancing at his wrist watch.

I breeze past him into the living room, scoop up my shoes and collapse onto the couch with a thump. He follows me. Pulling and prying without wasting the time of untying my laces, I shove my foot into my sneakers.

"I didn't grab an extra pair of clothes before going to Fairview this weekend, so I just came by real quick to get changed and cleaned up. I'm running late. Aren't you supposed to be at work?"

Evan flashes me a smartass smirk, "Oh yeah. How did meeting the ol' fam go? You tell them you've been bumping uglies with their daughter?" he laughs, standing at the island with a glass of orange juice in hand.

Rolling my eyes, I grab my keys and ignore his remark.

"Oh and grandpa is at the site. He needs me to do some runs and pick up a few things for him," he adds in a drab tone.

Scrambling to the front door, my hand grips the door knob and I pull it open, in too much of a frenzy to register the conversation at hand.

"I have to go. I'm going to be late. By the way, I'm staying at Alyssa's again tonight," I shout out as I tread through the door and begin to close it behind me.

"Aww, honey, are we breaking up?!" Evan calls out igniting a burst of laughter from me.

Nodding my head, I snicker, snap the door shut behind me and yell out, "Bye, Evan!"

In no time, I pick Alyssa up and we speed to class, barely making it. Fortunately, our classes line up fairly well on Monday, allowing me time to drop her off at work before I have to be at my two afternoon classes then back to pick her up after work.

Pulling into the back parking lot of the dentist office after a long day, I shut off the engine and slouch down in my seat. One thing I have put off all weekend is calling my brother or going and seeing him like he had suggested. *I should have put that at the top of my list.* Looking down at the blank screen on my phone now, I know I should call him. After all, I do believe that was his effort of trying, for once. Clutching the phone nervously, I press the hard surface to my ear and wait … one ring … two rings … three …

"Hello," Tristan's voice comes on the line, sounding groggy and half asleep.

I pause, not really sure what to say. "Hey," is all I manage to get out.

"Hey, I thought you were coming by this past weekend?"

His assumption makes me feel like an ass. Usually it is Tristan leaving me and Jake hanging, not the other way around.

"Yeah, I'm sorry about that. I ummm …" *I really don't want to talk to him about Alyssa.* Last time either of us talked about her and Abby, it resulted in both of us spending a significant amount of one-on-one time in a hospital bed. "I sort of got hung up and couldn't make it. That's why I wanted to call."

"Aaah … what was so important?" he spits out like a spiteful little kid.

"Listen, I just felt bad for not coming by and wanted to see if I could come by later this week. Tristan, talking to you isn't the easiest thing. I mean, I've been trying the last few months but you were always mysteriously gone or busy."

"Easy?! This sure in the hell isn't easy for me, either. I feel like I have wronged everyone in my life and now I'm being punished for it. Oh and FYI, I wasn't mysteriously gone … I was probably at the hospital. I am still there half of my damn week." The level of his voice rises with each word and it's as if we are right back in that car, preparing to speed right over the embankment again.

I have no idea how to talk to him. We are both so damn stubborn that we end up talking in circles each time we try.

"Tristan, I don't even know all the details of what happened to you. Jake told me you have therapy a couple times a week and he said you have a lot that you may never recover from, but when I ask him what is wrong, he says it would be better if I ask you. Yet, all my attempts have gone unanswered."

"Damn, Judd … I almost killed you. I almost killed us both, because of my bitterness and anger. I didn't want to face you all this time. I didn't know what to say. What?! Sorry!?" he pauses to take a breath, both of us getting way too worked up over something that should be so easy for other families. "… I don't think that would be good enough. I haven't wanted to see you and the truth is I'd rather no one ever see me like this, but I figured …" he lets out a long winded, frustrated sigh and stops mid-sentence.

A movement from the corner of my eye catches my attention and I flick my eyes to the side to see Alyssa coming my way.

"I'll come by, okay?" I ask, feeling ashamed for not reaching out to him more.

"I have to go to therapy. We'll talk. Later."

The phone clicks in my ear right as Alyssa hops up into the window of my truck. *Perfect timing.* Dropping the phone into my lap, I twist, catching her face in my hands and covering her lips with mine, thankful that the day flew by, but still troubled by the conversation with Tristan.

"Hey you," she breathes out as our lips part.

I keep my hands on both sides of her face, savoring the smoothness of her skin and the sweetness of her warm breath. "Hey," I say pressing my forehead to hers as she teeters at the waist on the window ledge. "I missed you."

That ignites a giggle out of her and has her wrapping her arms around my neck as she climbs through the window. I crack up, my lungs burning and a spark of pain tingling in my shoulder as I pull her through as if the door is welded shut.

Later that night, we wind up in bed early and in a serious discussion about her dad.

"How did you handle it?" she asks hesitantly, with a pained expression in her eyes.

The turn in conversation takes me by surprise. I know this isn't something that is easy for her to ask me. Alyssa always shies away from bringing it up and I am truly grateful for her respect over my lack of communication on the subject, even though I really need to fill her in on more of my life if we are going to have a future together. I guess I just assume I will receive some grand sign from above when it is time to share everything with her. I'm not ready to unload it all on her now, but if my pain could help her just a little, then it is worth ripping open an old wound. I'm just not sure how I dealt with Mom's death would help her.

"I didn't really. I just went from one day to the next; moving on because I had to," I take a deep breath to gather my courage on this subject and tighten my grip on her hand, "… until I met you." That is the honest truth, too. She is what saved me from the pain. The day I saw her made me realize so much. "That was the first time I felt real happiness since she passed away. I didn't remember what truly laughing was until you came along."

I chuckle over a few forgotten memories of Evan trying to make me laugh the summer we had first met; the summer following my mom's death. He was having an equally difficult time in his life and though neither of us would talk about our troubles, we both could sense that we needed a friend. He needed one and I desperately needed someone to keep me from becoming an irresponsible, careless idiot; Tristan was already shaping up to take on that role.

"Sure, Evan could always manage to make me laugh but you … with you … I really laugh. With you, I see a happy future for the first time in my life," I pause, seeing a flicker of understanding in her eyes. My story may not help her near as much as hearing about what I see when I look at hers. "You know, I think your dad is more worried about how everyone he loves will be affected by all this rather than scared of what will happen to him. I think he has made peace with it and he truly is grateful for the time he has had. He knows there is no promise as to how long each of our lives are going to be or how each of our ends will come, but he knows he has lived the best he could. I truly believe he is ok with that. He just worries about if you all will be able to let him go when the time comes."

Her eyes fill with tears bringing forth an ache in my heart as well. She already knows all that, but sometimes hearing the obvious said out loud can shed new light on how you view a situation. Nuzzling into my chest, her breath sweeps over my skin in a soft laugh before she pulls away.

"You learned all that from one weekend with my dad?" her voice quivers as a few more tears slip down her cheek.

Clearing my throat to push back the surge of emotion that is threatening to break free inside of me, I smile, thankful for the conversation between Alex and me.

"Well, I have to admit, you have some pretty awesome parents and your dad is one of a kind. I wish my …" I stop talking, thinking carefully about what I wish for. *My dad chose to leave and never came back. No, I don't think I do want someone like that in my life.* "He loves you so much," I tell her, because that, I know without a doubt.

Pulling her against me, her lips meet mine and buzzes of electricity tingle through my body as her fingertips trail up both sides of my rib cage and over the tissue at my scar. She focuses her attention on that one area, tracing the deep groove and the sensitivity is about to drive me insane.

Trailing a steaming path down her chin to her neck with my lips, I lift her sweater over her head and toss it to the floor before concentrating on the clasp of her bra. Wouldn't you know it, when a guy finally masters unhooking the back clasp of a bra they go and switch it up to a crazy front one. Twisting and gently tugging at the contraption, a content breath escapes me as she spills out and I pitch the bra down to the floor alongside her sweater.

Sliding back over her body, our skin melts together as I look into her eyes and let my lips hover only a breath away from hers.

"I love you, Alyssa," I whisper, my heart raging out of control.

A slamming from the next room has Alyssa panicking beneath me and in a hurried frenzy to get up. I jump as well and land with my knees dug into the mattress. Reaching to the floor where her discarded clothes rest, I scoop them up and toss them her way, knowing full well what she is freaked about. Bethany must have come home early and we are caught with our pants down.

Locked out

I WATCH ALYSSA, MORE amused than concerned. She scans the room anxiously, looking from beneath the bed, to the closet, to the bathroom, then landing on the window with a determined expression on her face.

"Oh, no no …" *Hell no.* I chuckle at what she must be thinking. "I'm not climbing out the window. If that's what you're thinking, you can forget about it."

She spits out a quiet breath of laughter and covers her mouth, waving her hand back and forth to keep me from making her laugh anymore. Once her clothes are back on, I walk to the closed bedroom door, her hand grasped in mine.

"I guess it's time you talk to her. You want me to wait in here or come out with you?"

I'm half tempted to go out regardless. I really don't want her facing Bethany alone. I've never trusted Bethany and I wouldn't put it past her to make Alyssa feel like crap.

Squeezing my hand, she places her other one on my chest and leans up to whisper in my ear, "No, I better do this alone. She is going to freak as it is, but if she sees you here she's liable to tackle me."

Her words make me want to hang back even less, but I respect her wishes and watch as she gives me a brief smile before slipping into the living room and closing the door behind her. My ear is automatically

335

magnetized to the door as I listen to their muffled voices, barely able to catch all that Alyssa says over Bethany's shrill, enraged tone.

"… you're damn right … .How could you!?" Bethany screeches, nearly making me fly out of the room, but Alyssa stays calm and stands her ground, trying to explain.

"Let me …"

"I thought you were my friend …." Bethany's voice carries through the door as if she is standing in the room with me.

Alyssa says something in response, but I cannot make out the words. All of a sudden, Bethany's voice levels to a firm, commanding tone as she admits to Alyssa that she saw us Thursday night in my truck and had hoped we would be here tonight so she could see for herself. *What a conniving little brat!* My hand makes contact with the doorknob and I am ten seconds from busting in on their chat, but I finally hear Alyssa get through to her by demanding that she sit down and listen. Their voices get quieter, and I assume that the storm may have passed so I twist the knob, barely opening the door so that I can hear better; that's when I hear my cue.

"It's stupid for him to hide in there! Just tell him to come out!"

Sure thing, because I sure as shit have had enough of you talking to Alyssa like a piece of dirt. I pull the door all the way open, both of them so fired up that they do not even register my movement.

"He's not hiding! I told him to wait …"

Bethany cuts Alyssa off mid sentence, "You should have told me, but just don't flaunt it in my face!"

With that, I am fully pissed off and have had enough of letting my girlfriend stand alone in this. "Bethany, I was always straight forward with you. I told you I was not over my ex and Alyssa was who I was talking about. I just didn't want to discuss anything with anyone until I understood, myself, what had happened between us."

My bitter tone sparks a look of shock across her face as Alyssa turns to look at me, her shoulders tense and rigid from the interaction.

"Be honest! Did you use me to get close to her?"

She asks me a question that I can't quite figure out how to answer right off the bat. *I didn't use her, but I did take advantage of the situation in a way, especially when I wanted to leave a gift for Alyssa, but I never made her believe there was anything between us. Never.*

"No, because I told you from that very first day that I was only interested in being friends with you, and I never gave you any indication that that would change. You were the one that was always texting and calling me to come over, not the other way around. The only thing either of us is guilty of is not being honest about knowing each other, but I am in no way sorry for being with her now."

With this, Bethany retracts her claws and simmers down.

Feeling a bit unwelcome and uncomfortable, and also at Bethany's request, Alyssa and I hustle to my apartment for the night with a week's worth of her clothes in tow. Shaken and guilt ridden for no reason at all in my mind, she quickly falls asleep with her head nestled in the dip between my shoulder and neck.

The next few days we juggle hectic schedules, with peaceful evenings hanging with Evan and warm nights curled up together. Unfortunately, Evan's relentless moans and groans about seeing Piper in one of his classes starts to wear on our personal time, when he gives us only a three second warning a couple nights in a row before coming in to vent. Caught in a precarious position on the last bust in, I decide to take matters into my own hands and make sure there will be no more interruptions.

"Hey, I have to run. You got everything squared away?" I announce as I race to the door of the work trailer. "Alyssa gets off at 6:00 and I need to make a run to the hardware store before picking her up."

"Hardware store? What for?" Evan asks, leaning against his desk as he looks over some invoices.

I feel a little awkward answering Evan's question, because I know he'll have some sort of smartass comment, but I figure what the hell. "We've been together for a week, so there is something I wanted to get for her ... a surprise."

Evan scrunches up his face in confusion, "At the hardware store?" His eyes glimmer like a dog that just spotted a long, lost bone and I know, *here it comes.* "Ahhh, a hardware store ..." he air quotes with his fingers, flicking his eyebrows up and down, *"Nice."*

I shake my head at his insinuation, "Aaaa, not that kind of hardware store. Get your mind out of the gutter."

His eyes widen in surprise. "Me!? Oh ... Oh, my mind is the one in the gutter?" he tosses the paperwork to the desk and clutches his stomach. "You two are the ones that are constantly humping like a pair of crazed rabbits. Seriously, do you ever sleep?" he widens his eyes and takes on a serious tone, "Are you vampires? Horny vampires?"

I roll my eyes, craning my neck to look at the clock above the door. *5:35, shit, I'm going to be late.*

"Shut up, Evan. We're not rabbits and we're not vampires; we get plenty of sleep, we're just enjoying each other. You get it and don't act like you don't." I say, pointing at him with an I-dare-you-to-challenge-me-on-this-one expression on my face.

"Oh yeah, I get it. I just don't have it … at this time, so I have to bust your balls a little until that time comes." He waves his hands and laughs. *I know he is thinking of Piper.* "Go on. Get out of here. I'll close up." I wave and begin to shut the door as Evan call out, always wanting the last word, "whatever you're picking up, try to keep the screwing down. Nail her a little quieter, if possible. The late night hammering has to be getting hard. Oh and make sure you keep your drill bit …"

I shut the door on his ramblings and jet to a small 'mom and pop' hardware store around the corner from her work. *I hope they have a good selection.* Racing through the aisle, I find exactly what I'm looking for then turn into the next aisle and race up to the counter.

"Can I help you?"

"Yeah …" struggling with my key, I wiggle it off my keychain and hand it to the man behind the counter. He watches me through thick small oval framed glasses. "I need just one copy."

Nodding his head, he grabs the key and moves to the grinder, instantly firing it up with a sharp piercing noise that climbs straight to my eardrums and has me begging for earplugs. My nerves screech right along with the machine as I think about what I have planned. With a deep breath, I put it out of my mind and wait for him to finish.

"Anything else?"

"Can I pay for this back here, too?" I throw my other item onto the counter.

He quickly snatches it up and scans it in answer to my question.

After throwing him a twenty and some change, I offer a polite nod and take off for my truck with only five minutes before I need to pick her up. Pulling up right as she is stepping out of the back door with several other co-workers, I sigh and shove the small bag to the back seat before she gets in.

As we walk through the door of the apartment, I glance at the under counter blue tooth player in the kitchen and see it is only a quarter after six. Evan should be getting home a bit after 7:00; we'll have to hurry, otherwise he'll throw a conniption fit.

"You hungry?" I ask, heading into the kitchen and placing the bag on the counter.

"Starving," her soft, gentle voice answers and suddenly it isn't food I'm hungry for.

Clearly sensing my thoughts, she crosses the room and wraps her arms around my waist. Resting my head on the top of hers, I run my hands up her back, over the plush, fuzzy sweater that hugs her small body and think about how perfect every moment with her seems. *Is this really the life I'm going to have? How could I be this lucky; this blessed?*

"Hey, I have a present for you. Well actually it's something for both of us."

She looks up with a gasp and wide eyes. "Really!?" she says excitedly.

Tossing my head back on a laugh, I look down at her, wondering if I am screwing up the whole gift giving experience for her. I doubt a girl would consider this significant enough to be called a gift, but this is Alyssa. I mean, she finds the beauty in two by fours and a sheet of ply board. You give most girls a piece of wood and they would either light it on fire or stand back and wait for you to build them a house. Not Alyssa, she'd be the first to go grab the cordless drill and screws and join the work crew. Not to mention, I'm pretty pumped over it.

"It's not the typical present so I didn't wrap it." I grin, a little embarrassed. *Maybe this was stupid; too late now.* "Go open the bag and I'll warm up some left over pizza. Sound okay?"

Alyssa shoots me a breathtaking smile and rushes over to the counter, swooping the heavy bag up with a quizzical look on her face.

Reaching my hand into the ice cold refrigerator, I feel around for the pizza box, my gaze transfixed on Alyssa peeking into the bag. I watch as she giggles, a smile instantly forming on my face as if her laughter has remote access to my happiness. She glances my way just as my hand finds the box and pulls it out.

"Have I told you I love you yet today?" she says, tugging the new key lock door knob out of the bag. *Yep, she gets the significance.*

Tossing the pizza box onto the counter by her side, I wrap my arms around her and scrunch down to her height.

"Maybe, but you can always tell me again."

She bursts out laughing, clutching the plastic container surrounding the new door knob in both her hands.

"I love you Judd Michaels."

After planting a gentle kiss on my lips that doesn't last near long enough she then pulls back and levels me with a mischievous grin that is usually reserved for Evan.

"We'll eat cold pizza then you get the screwdriver and we'll lock that perv out once and for all!"

We both break into hysterics then get busy changing out my non-locking door knob with the new one while nibbling on bites of pizza, and each other, soon after it is installed.

The next morning, neither of us has to work and with it being a Saturday, the only plans we have are to go to her parent's house for a visit. With that in mind, we didn't set a single alarm, yet I woke up as usual at the crack of dawn.

Making subtle movements so that I don't wake her, I shift onto my side, gently nudging her with me so that I can watch her sleep. Her face lies hidden under a mass of blonde wavy locks, but as I lightly graze my fingers over her skin to brush away her hair she begins to stir. Her bottom lip puckers out as she tries to wake and I can't help but swoop in for a taste.

Nipping at her lips, she opens her mouth and draws me in, molding her bare chest to mine and sending a wave of heat through me. That little whimper of hers slips out from between our joined mouths and my body is instantly crazed with desire and need. Her breathing picks up as I dive down further to suck on the creamy flesh of her neck, my heart thumping wildly. I look up at Alyssa and all hope of proceeding is deflated as I realize Evan is awake.

"Hey, you got a second?"

The door rattles and immediately she and I stare at each other, frozen with sneaky smirks rising across both our faces. *There will be no interrupting today.*

"What the hell, man! When did you change the knob? I hope you know that my lease specified I could not make any changes or alter anything about the appearance of the place."

I laugh quietly, my chest shaking as Alyssa's eyes fill with amusement and mischief.

"Your butt is locked out," she whispers in a sassy tone with her finger pointed to the door.

Thud … Thud … Thud.

Evan pounds on the door again, bringing forth even more laughter from us both. Well this sure isn't sexy and no way are we going to be able to get the mood back with him pounding on the door, but I don't care. Grinning, I stare at Alyssa's beautiful smile. *I swear this is the most I've ever smiled; the most I've ever laughed.*

Evan's aggravated tone pierces the door, "Great! No way am I getting my deposit back now. Are you gonna answer me?"

I have to bite down on my lip to keep from busting up.

Knock … knock … knock.

His fist has to be getting sore.

"Are you going to answer him?"

I look at Alyssa and press my lips together to keep from laughing. I'm not sure what's more funny now, the fact that it is complete torture for him that I am not answering or the fact that it is driving him crazy that he cannot just barge in. Evan has dished out his fair share of tormenting me; *no I don't think I will answer him.*

Grabbing my phone, I raise my eyebrows and hold it up to signal to Alyssa that I have an idea. I carefully dig my elbows on either side of her, practically pinning her down beneath me as I hold the phone in front of my face and type out a message.

Me: Who's there?????

Hopefully he has his phone nearby.

His phone instantly buzzes on the other side of the door, signifying that he does indeed have it on him.

"Ha-ha! Real funny! Yeah ok, I'll play along." He goes silent.

I lay the phone back down on the nightstand, hoping for some playtime now, but then my phone chimes with an incoming text. *Of course, Evan always has to have the last word.*

Reaching across Alyssa, I pull my phone off the table to glance at it.

Evan: Evan

Laughter bursts from my chest as I think over the first summer we met, how we would sit for hours on the dock fishing and Evan would bore me to tears telling me knock-knock joke after knock-knock joke. He would just make them up as he went along, most of them lame as hell, but he'd still keep it up. They got so over the top ridiculous that I would end up cracking up at the mere effort Evan put into dreaming them up.

I shouldn't bite, but curiosity always seems to tug and pull me into relenting just so I can hear the punch line he has shoved up his sleeve. Of course this time is no exception, I take the bait.

Me: Evan who?

A rattling sounds from the door and I shake my head, still gripping my phone in my hand. Alyssa tilts the phone in her direction so she can read his messages.

"He can't get that door open can he?"

I lower my brows wondering if he actually can. The scraping rattling sound keeps up.

"He shouldn't be able ..."

Alyssa and I both snap our heads around as the door flings open and my phone chimes in my hand, all at the same time.

"Ha!" he belts out, with a smirk on his face and a bent up hanger twirling around his fingers.

Shuffling around with a spit of laughter, I tug the sheet down to make sure our bodies are covered then look down at my phone.

Evan: Evan a lock won't keep me out. :P

I look up at him, lowering my head to the sheet that is draped over

Alyssa's chest and close my eyes. *That's the worst one yet.*

"Am I going to have to replace all the hangers with plastic ones now?"

Evan's smirk grows as he looks at his bent up make shift key. "Nah, I'll just find something else."

I roll my eyes, knowing he will. *He's killing me.*

"Oh and by the way, that was the lamest one yet. Evan a lock won't keep me out?!" I huff out, grinning. *Where does he come up with this shit?*

He plasters on a shocked expression, eyes wide and his mouth gaped open. "What?! It worked. Oh and you get to explain to the land-lord about this," he says, twisting the doorknob.

"Already done. I ran down and talked to him earlier this week. He said he knows you and he fully understands." I smile and I hear a small giggle from Alyssa, reminding me that we were in the middle of something. "So, no worries ... now, do you mind closing the door? Oh and lock it, too." I add, grinning from ear-to-ear.

Evan shakes his head, "Damn Wabbits ..." he mumbles, finally locking himself out before he shuts the door.

Angel

THE NEXT WEEK SAILS by smoothly with a new lock for privacy, Evan no longer masterfully finding ways to barge in and Alyssa even hashing out things with Bethany, however, I'm still not comfortable being around her. The subtle gestures she gives when Alyssa isn't looking has me second guessing whether them making up is a smart idea. Unfortunately, every advance that Bethany has made could easily be her word against mine so I just hope Alyssa catches on to her conniving ways. Last thing I want is for someone to hurt her.

Friday comes the same as the week before, and I find myself counting each day we have been together. Today marks two weeks that we have been back in each other's lives, which is the same amount of time we were together this summer, yet it seems like such a longer stretch of time this go round as we juggle school, jobs, family, friends and our relationship. It makes our time at the lake seem like a fairy tale.

Sitting on the hard, cold surface of the metal bleachers at the Rosemore South football field, all feels right with the world as Alyssa snuggles up beside me and we watch Jake race down the field in possibly the last play of the night.

"Go long, Go long, Jake," I yell out as I bolt to my feet and cup my hands around my mouth.

Alyssa shouts and cheers beside me, jumping up and down just as the ball lands in Jake's hands.

"Go, go, go … Yeah!" I holler out with everyone around me going nuts, bouncing out of their seats. My body can barely contain itself as he runs hard, crossing the goal line and pushing the score over the top in the last ten seconds of the game. "Way to go!" I throw out towards the field, knowing Jake won't hear me, but just so proud of my brother and school.

The entire crowd goes crazy, jumping to their feet all around me and I do the same, Alyssa right at my side. Waving my arm in the air, I watch as Jake and the team rejoices before heading off the field.

"Come on; let's get out of here before traffic gets backed up. Jake said he'd meet us there."

I grab Alyssa's hand in mine, pushing my way through a mass of people thinking the same thing as me. She grips my bicep, staying close to me as we slither our way to the parking lot and race to hop into my truck.

"That was insane. I really didn't think they were going to win." Excitement shines through in her voice and I love how she gets into the game as much as I do.

"I knew they'd win. Jake is a beast out there. That other team knew they were going to lose as soon as he stepped onto the field." I smile confidently, remembering all the times we played together.

"He's amazing. Does he know what college he wants to go to yet?"

I crinkle up my brows on this question. "You know, he should be talking about that but he never does." I relax a little, remembering how nervous I was during my senior year, constant anxiety over getting the scholarship I was working my ass off to earn. "He's probably getting pressured by the coach and team with this being his last season, not to mention Tristan and I have never helped in the pressuring to succeed department." I swallow, steering the truck down the road. "Ever since he was in Junior High, we've pushed him to train and focus on the game. I guess it just came natural with us all going in the same direction and in love with the same thing."

"Do you miss it?" I glance at her and catch her shaking her head with her eyes closed. "Ok, you know what, scratch that question. Of course you miss it."

Reaching my hand over, she naturally scoots in closer to me as I clasp my hand in hers, gently threading my fingers through them.

"It's ok ... I don't mind you asking that."

"I know ... it's just ... it's no secret you love football and this isn't exactly a choice you made yourself."

Steering onto Water Street and scanning for a parking spot, I squeeze her hand.

"Trust me, this ..." I raise her hand up in mine and softly touch my lips to her knuckle. "... is the best trade off I could have asked for."

She crinkles her nose and casts me a skeptical, closed-mouthed grin.

"Trust me. This is better than playing football." *And it is.*

Pulling the truck up alongside a blue convertible, I throw it into reverse to parallel park as I think over my past. Football never filled that void in my heart. Before Dad left, I carried that normal child-like innocence, thinking my parents would be around forever. Assuming that dads never left and viewing death as something that only struck when your hair had turned snow-white, your skin was filled with wrinkles and your children were grown. Of course, I also always thought I would live at home forever. Some of my first memories were playing football in the backyard with Dad, going to water parks with both Mom and Dad in the summers, Christmases at my Grandma and Grandpa's house, Easter egg hunts at church and game nights in the living room with all five of us.

After Dad left, half of my heart flew out the window and left along with him. Life changed so much the next day that there was no way we could have possibly prepared for it. Not only did we deal with one less parent and the financial burden of one parent supporting a family of four, but then the doctors finally figured out what was happening to Mom.

Once she was diagnosed and all us boys found odd jobs to help out with putting food on the table, we then settled into a comfortable groove and adjusted. When my grandparents passed a couple years later, we kept going with yet another vacancy in our hearts and, surprisingly, things turned around. We somehow managed to find a house that I have no idea how we could afford and an in-home nurse was hired to come in and take care of Mom so Tristan could finish out high school. As always though, that run of good luck ran out. With only a few months until I turned sixteen, I found myself in a whirlwind of responsibility that ended with us laying Mom to rest and my heart chipped away to a barren, lifeless organ that I thought would never be filled.

Funny thing is I always envisioned myself staying strong for the sake of Jake when Mom died, but I completely went in the opposite direction. It wasn't Tristan that fell off the deep end right off the bat, it was me. When I came to my senses, I buckled down and made my main priority Jake and football, but I still felt empty every day.

"You ready?" Alyssa pulls me back to the present where I quickly smell the delectable aroma of grilled onions and peppers drifting through the air.

Slamming the truck into park, my stomach picks up on the same scent as my nose as I shove my door open and follow Alyssa inside. We take a seat in a cozy corner booth alongside a large group of people all dressed in red and black and sporting a picture of our schools mascot across the front of their sweatshirts.

Sliding onto the slick leather surface of the red cushioned seats, I settle up beside Alyssa and look around. Enthusiastic chatter fills the air as table after table buzzes over our fourth straight win this season. Last year we were undefeated and went on to beat Fairview at districts. Crazy now, considering I am sitting right beside someone that cheered for the opposing team at that game.

Glancing around at a sea of my schools colors, my eyes sweep around and land on Alyssa.

"Do you feel like a traitor or what?"

Her eyes follow my lips into a smile of their own as she answers, "Not really. I was a cheerleader, but I wasn't all into the whole our-school-is-better-than-yours aspect of it. I just loved the thrill of the game and the atmosphere," she says with a smile like that is just an ordinary comment for a girl.

I arch my brows and try to steady my heart. *Holy crap, Jake was right when he said if you don't marry her, I will.*

Opening my mouth to answer, the table jostles across from me and I look up.

"Hey, you guys haven't had to wait long, have you?" Jake leans forward onto the table with an ordinary look on his face as if he didn't just run in the winning touchdown.

Throwing my hand across the table, I grip my brother's arm and give him a firm handshake followed by a fist bump.

"Hey, man ... that play was crazy. You were like an animal out there," I say in amazement, so damn proud of him. "No one stood a chance. Keep playing like that and I think a scholarship is in the bag. Damn, you're fast."

Jake shifts back against his seat, still with a bland look on his face. "Yeah, I guess so. The team is pumped that we won. I think most of them are going out to celebrate."

"Well, get out of here, then. Go join them. You deserve to celebrate that victory. I mean that last play was sick." I'm practically jumping out of my seat with excitement, feeling as if I just won a game.

Shrugging his shoulders, Jake glances at Alyssa who has quietly been following along with the conversation, laughing and nodding her head.

"Nahh, there's better company here. Besides, it's been a while since we've been able to catch up." Jake adds smiling between me and Alyssa, yet his mood seems off for some reason.

"Everything ok?" I ask, hoping I'm reading too much into his behavior.

Jake has always been a little on the shy side and a whole lot more reserved than Tristan or myself; that is until he steps onto a football field. All shyness goes out the window at that point and he unleashes nine kinds of hell on his opponents. Honestly, I've always been a bit envious of his talent and speed. Tristan and I were good, but Jake even broke Dad's 40 time by two tenths of a second, which is astounding. Our dad's high school football career made him famous in school and here his youngest son blows his record out of the water. Jake can burn through every defensive back in the state and he can catch anything that is thrown at him, yet lately he seems to be losing interest in the game.

Shaking his head, he frowns and grabs a menu. "I'm fine ... just hungry."

I snatch it out of his hand and lay it face down on the table with my palm over it. "Nice shift in the topic. Man, you just played the shit out of that game and look around ..." I motion my hand around the room, notating all the chaotic excitement. "Everyone is on cloud nine with the prospect of making it to state for six years in a row. I mean, we won every single year that I played, nearly every year Tristan played and now every year you've played. Just look at what kind of legacy we are leaving behind," I lecture him, slowly noticing his face melting into a scowl.

"Can we just drop it with the talk of football? My world just doesn't revolve around it like you and Tristan's did. I just want to eat," he hesitantly says, grabbing the menu and opening it up so that he blocks me from looking at him.

I know from experience what kind of pressure he already has on him from the team, the coach and most of all me. Besides, how can I get onto him for not joining in on the celebration when I never did myself? Through Tristan's and my football careers, Jake saw me come home every night and help out at the house. He watched Tristan jet home after each practice and each game to take care of Mom and now I just expect for him to switch gears and enjoy a normal high school existence to make up for our lack of one.

Alyssa, clearly sensing the tension, shifts the subject, "You know what? I'm starved! Who wants to eat?" She grabs up a menu and flips it open as I catch my brother lower his, looking at her with a slight smile.

Subject closed. I shouldn't pressure him so much. "Sounds good. Let's eat," I state as a waitress swings by our table.

We all order and as a creature of habit, I end up ordering the same as usual. The plates make it to the table in a record speed and we each dig in. Between hearty bites of my cheeseburger and seasoned fries, Jake, Alyssa and I keep the mood mellow and less demanding.

After the restaurant starts to clear out, I bring up another strained topic right before heading out. "You think it'll be ok if I come by the house for a bit tonight before we head back to the apartment?"

"Aaaa ... I don't think tonight is a good night. He had a bad day at therapy," he says glancing at his phone nervously. "He's got a lot going on and he has not been up to seeing anyone."

This sends my frustration through the roof. "Not up to seeing anyone?! I haven't so much as seen his face since the day we wrecked … not once. I've come by … he's not there. I've called … voicemail. Then when he finally calls me, I don't know what to think. Neither of you will tell me anything that happened. I have no idea how bad he's hurt. I assume it's bad, but let's face it, at this point I'm not sure whether he is paralyzed for life or if he's missing an arm or what."

Jake puts his hands up, patting it in the air to motion me to calm down right as Alyssa's hand runs the length of my back in a soothing gesture.

"I know … I know, this hasn't been fair to you, but I just think he should talk to you about everything. He's pretty depressed and asked me to keep quiet. I told him he needs to talk to you and he did … he called finally. It's just …" He pauses and looks away with a heavy hearted sigh. " …he doesn't know how to talk to anyone anymore. He stopped caring a long time ago and so, give him time … as long as it takes, you know?" Jakes pleading eyes are all it takes for the vice of frustration to loosen and set me at ease.

I nod my head, searching for Alyssa's hand under the table. She quickly grips it, intertwining her fingers in mine then I'm able to breathe. *How did everything between he and I get so messed up? And when did we start putting Jake right in the middle? Maybe we always did and I never noticed.* It seems as one part of my life is finally falling into place, the other parts are falling apart. My family's relationship has been tattered and torn for a while; I guess all the pieces are just now beginning to chip away.

All three of us walk out to the curb where Jake's truck is parked.

"It was good to see you again," Alyssa says sweetly, giving my brother a surprise hug.

His forehead draws up as his eyes widen and he stares over her shoulder to me with a wide smile.

"It's getting cold so I'm jumping in the truck while you two say your goodbyes."

She lets go of Jake and turns to me, a message in her eyes as if she is nudging me to stop pressuring him; be nice; get along; all the stuff Mom would more than likely say.

"Bye, Alyssa. Maybe we can all go to dinner again soon," Jake suggests and I notice how much this time meant to him. I tend to forget that as I draw closer to Alyssa and her family, Jake still only has himself and I've been more than MIA the last two weeks, caught up with my love for Alyssa.

She moves past me and grabs the keys I have dangling from my fingertips. Keeping my ears perked up, I hear my door slam shut a few cars up and move forward toward Jake.

"So if Tristan is too busy to see me tonight, when is a good time to come by?"

"Let me talk to him, ok? He's been in and out a lot and I'm usually the one taking him to therapy. He's not able to work at the garage anymore so I'm supposed to meet up with someone and talk to them about a job."

Stepping forward with a deep urge to smother him in a death grip hug, my heart drops, heavy with all that he has experienced in this life, some of which I am realizing only tonight. He lived the same challenges as me growing up and now with me giving up the task of swooping in to save Tristan's ass, here he has taken on the feat. Plus, he has the pressures of getting into a good college, keeping up his grades, pressures of winning every game and who knows what else.

"I'm sorry about coming down on you about football," I say quietly as my arms wrap around him and I crush him in a brotherly hug. "I just want the best for you. You deserve the best, you now."

Jake grips me back, slapping my back twice before we pull away. He stares at me with a close lipped smile, relaying complete understanding and appreciation. That's Jake; never an angry bone in his body. I'd be in shock if I ever saw him lose his temper and if he did, I'd hate to be on the receiving end.

"I know you do. I'll give you a call later this week and maybe we can have dinner some night. I guess I better go … Tristan wants me to go check on his car tonight and set up that interview."

Drawing my eyebrows down in puzzlement, I question his comment, "What car?" The only car to my knowledge that Tristan has ever owned is his red 1969 Camaro that Grandpa gifted him for his sixteenth birthday.

"His Camaro," Jake says in a tone that says I should already know this. *His Camaro?!*

"I thought it was totaled? You mean it is salvageable?" Considering it is the size of a casket itself, I really figured it would have been toast after how hard we hit.

Jake chuckles while leaning back against the passenger side of his truck and slipping his hands into his jacket pocket.

"Somewhat … if it was in the right hands." He raises his brows and goes on, "He has it over at S & P salvage and garage. I'm supposed to go talk to the owner tonight. Apparently, one of his employees has been tinkering with it since it was towed in and they want to show him some things that they've done."

Jake shifts, moving away from the curb and slowly walking around to the driver's side. I remain still, generally interested in the fact that the car survived. My brother has always loved that car. He got it from my father's dad, who had always been into restoring classics. Even though we never saw my dad, our grandparents tried their best to stay in our lives, sending us cards and gifts, but never once contacting us or lending a hand to my mom as she got sicker. The day after Tristan received it, Grandpa had an aneurism, dying immediately. My brother took it hard, mainly because I think he saw the gift as one of the last pieces of our dad.

"Well, let me know how it goes. I'm actually pretty interested to see if it can be brought back to life. I haven't even seen it since before the wreck," I say, throwing my hand up in the air to wave him off.

Jake opens the door to his truck and jumps in, hollering out, "I'll keep you posted. See ya."

A couple steps towards my vehicle and my phone buzzes, announcing a new text. I shimmy my phone out of my pocket and look down at the screen, seeing a picture of the car.

Jake: I wasn't sure if you would ever want to see this, but I can tell from tonight that you are in a better place than you have been in months. The wrecker sent it to me while you two were still in the hospital.

I stare down at the picture and gasp, a sudden weightlessness in my chest as if I am back in that moment, flying through the air. All of the windows are in shambles with glass strewn all over the dash. The front of the car is compacted with metal digging into the tires and the hood crunched as if it is a simple piece of plastic. While the door on my side looks damaged, the driver's side has me thanking the Lord that my brother is still with us.

His side sustained the most damage. The tree that we smashed into at the bottom of the embankment must have slammed right into the driver's door, crushing it like a tin can. Even the base of the frame near the wheel well is completely compressed, leaving nearly no room for a driver to be. I can't believe my brother was in there and still lived. The roof of the car is torn free above the seat like a sardine can; I assume that is where they had to cut him out. *Wow ... and Jake says it may be salvageable?*

Looking up at my truck, I catch a glimpse of Alyssa in the rear-view mirror looking at me; probably wondering what has me stopped on the sidewalk on a surprisingly cold fall night. I look back at my phone once more before clicking the screen off and moving my feet forward. As I stare back at her, I can't help but be thankful that Tristan and I had an angel looking over us that day; an angel that I believe has been watching over us every day for the past several years. Even after she left, she's still taking care of us.

My refuge

THUMP, THUMP, THUMP, I pound my fist to the door of Tristan's room for the third time.

"Come on, Tristan … I texted you an hour ago and told you I was swinging by."

I glance down, shimmying my phone out of my pocket so I can look over the text I sent to make sure there is no mistake in what I typed. Pressing my fingertip onto the hard, cool surface, my phone lights up and I move my finger to pull up my text.

Me: Hey

Tristan: What's up?

Me: Not much. I'm at work. What are you up to?

Tristan: Same as always. At home. Not doing a damn thing.

Me: I had a free afternoon and thought I'd run by before I have to meet Alyssa. I thought we could hang for a bit.

My heart pumps with the same anxiety I felt when I sent it, wondering if some pissy ass comment would come back or if my phone would ring to him shouting. I swipe my finger to read more, studying every word of our conversation.

Tristan: Yeah … ok. I'll be here.

Me: Cool. See you in thirty.

No further response; nothing. It took him forever to answer if it was ok to swing by, but all he had to do was say no if it wasn't. I slam my fist into the door again, hastily twisting the doorknob in my other hand until my fingers are stiff and practically formed to the knob. "Come on, man! I know your door didn't lock itself! If you don't want to see me, just say so!" I shove the bottom of my boot into the door igniting a loud thud and making the door vibrate beneath my hand that is resting flat against it. "Tristan, come on. Just answer me." I wait and hear nothing. "Dammit I'm sick of this! I'm sick of it!"

My heart thunders in my chest and up into my eardrums while my body quakes in anger. Squeezing my eyes shut, I toss my head forward in to the door with a clunk, quietly going over each detail of the past several years, starting with how nearly each and every time I came to Mom's bedroom door near the end, he would have some excuse for why I couldn't sit with her. The front door rattles a ways behind me and I instantly snap out of my trance and turn.

"Hey," Jake says, looking uneasy and nervous. "What are you doing here?"

I find the question odd and I honestly have no clue what the hell is going on, but I am suddenly flooded with an unwelcome feeling from them both; like I now don't belong in this family, in the home where Mom last lived.

Jake stands at the edge of the living room with his book bag flung over his shoulder and an expectant expression on his face. I step forward, glancing to the room next to Tristan's, Mom's old room. The door has remained shut since the day she left. We never even got rid of her stuff, just sealed the room like a tomb. I take another step forward and grip the doorknob for the first time in ages, fear rising within me at the surge of heartache that may pull me under once I step inside.

"What are you doing?"

I don't answer Jake's first question and I don't even answer this one. I can't; I can't think right now, I just act, twisting the knob and pushing the door open. I expect to hear a gasp from Jake or watch as a ghost brushes by, but I'm greeted with a soft glow of sun light sprayed across the bed where she once used to sleep. I blink my eyes and re-member how quickly the medical supply company was to come and pick up the hospital bed and other equipment. Maybe Tristan called them, who knows; maybe he was even the one that moved her bed back to the center of the room, across from the window. He'd never tell us something so personal.

Glancing around, I move past her vanity in the corner with little bottles of lotions and makeup scattered about still. A couple dresses lie draped over her bench at the end of the bed, along with a dark navy blue one that has been forever abandoned on the floor. Moving my eyes up to look at the bed, I blink rapidly when a flash of her lying there with a fogged up respirator and her beautiful brown hair strewn about on the pillow, appears in my mind. My eyes glaze over as a hand falls onto my shoulder.

Jake remains silent behind me, but the weight of his loss is felt just as strong as mine. It rolls off of him like a tidal wave, hitting me hard and bringing up something I thought I had buried.

"Don't you blame him in a way?" The tears in my eyes spill over one drop at a time as I stare at the bed wishing more than anything that she was there one more time.

"What?" his voice comes out shocked and disbelieving, but he knows what I'm talking about.

"Don't you just wish we could have said goodbye that morning?"

His grip on my shoulder tightens and he moves closer to me, but I don't want to be comforted right now. I want to feel the pain, I want the anger to surge through me and explode until I have the courage to storm into Tristan's room and get it all out. Moving forward and out of Jake's grasp, I gravitate to the bed and sit along the edge, much as I did back when she was here. I smooth my hand over the maroon comforter, the skin of my palm catching on the fabric.

"I wish a lot of things, but I don't ..." I look over at Jake as he pauses, shifting his face back and forth across the floor at his feet. He looks up, his forehead creased in the same pain I saw the day he collapsed against the wall of this bedroom. "I think Tristan did the best he could. He was protecting us." Jake throws his best effort forth in defending Tristan's actions during a time when we should have been there every second.

"Yeah but he shut us out in the process." Hanging my head down, I close my eyes, an ocean of sorrow and confusion pours through my veins like lava. I brace myself with both my hands, the plushness of her comforter hugging them softly as the memories engulf me.

Lightly pushing the door open only a sliver, I shift with the strap of my bag digging into my shoulder with about fifty pounds of books weighing it down.

"Come on, Judd." Tristan races through the kitchen and to the front door with his bag in hand. "There's not time this morning. Jake, let's go."

"But ..." I point to Mom's door, desperately wanting to give her a hug and kiss before going to school. It used to be the last thing I'd do every morning before he took us to school, but lately those visits are becoming rare; obsolete from me and Jake's life, almost as if she's already gone and that hurts.

"Come on!" He urges, budging the front door open with a harsh look in his eyes. Jake follows behind him, but I don't move. "I'm serious, Judd. Besides, the Hospice nurse is already in there and I have a Chem test I have to make up after dropping you both off. We have to go!" His eyebrows dip down lower as he scowls at me.

Looking back at Jake for affirmation of how this is not fair, I am met with a shrug of his shoulders before he walks around Tristan and out the door.

"Tristan, I just wanted to ..."

"I know what you want, but now is not a good time."

That is all I ever hear from him anymore. "Is there ever a good time, Tristan?!" I spit out, getting frustrated that I cannot visit my mom in my own home.

"Judd, I'm serious ..." he pauses, an unrecognizable look flashing through his eyes, "Now let's go. You can go in today when you get home."

I glance back to her room before relenting. As I walk past him, I swing my eyes over to her barely cracked open door and have the per-

fect view of her angelic face lying still on the pillow while she sleeps.
"Bye, Mom. I love you," I whisper then shut the door.

My phone chimes, pulling me out of my daydream and I look down, still holding it in my hand with a white knuckled grip. I glance at the message, immediately being ripped from the spiraling darkness of grief.

Alyssa: You up for watching me try on some costumes. I'll make it worth your while. ;)

My mouth crooks to the side, even though I don't feel the smile in my heart right at this moment.

"Judd, he tried his best. We all handled it the best we could, but if you're holding that in … if that's the hang up that has been coming between you and Tristan, then you need to talk to him."

Clicking my fingers across the small keyboard on my phone to answer Alyssa back, I come to an abrupt stop and snap my head up to Jake, a little taken aback by what he said.

"I can't talk to him." I fling my hand in the air, motioning to his room. "You've seen and don't even tell me he isn't home, because I'm not stupid. He pushes me away at every turn. How am I supposed to talk to him, huh?" I spit out with more venom than I mean. I don't ever talk to Jake like this. A flicker of guilt bolts through me. "I'm sorry. I'm not mad at you."

Quickly typing out a reply to Alyssa, a little ease falls over my shoulders, knowing I'll be with her in just a bit and away from all this.

Me: Yeah, Babe. I'll head over in just a bit. I'm with Jake now. Call you in a sec.

Alyssa: K Can't wait to see you. Mmmmmwa … love you!

I breathe out, my shoulders falling and my body relaxing with her last words.

Me: I can't wait to see you, too. I love you so much.
Alyssa: <3

The bed dips as Jake takes a seat beside me.

"I'm glad you have her."

I look over and see his eyes on my phone. I stare down at our conversation and smile, the pain and loss that this room holds, dissolving with the thought of being with her. My phone screen falls black and Jake looks up at me.

"Mom would have liked her." It's the first time someone else has made a reference to Mom and Alyssa in the same sentence. "Have you taken her to the wishing well, yet?" He asks it like that's just a regular every day thing; like it's not something sacred.

I shake my head, slowly, looking down at my phone and reminding myself just how precious she is to me.

"Judd, you need to let some of this out. You can't always bottle it all up. You and Tristan are so much alike and I really fear ..." he stops, his face creased into a frown as he studies me.

"What?"

He blinks and takes a slow gasp of air. "I'm afraid you both are going to explode eventually if you don't talk." He glances at the doorway then turns, lowering his voice. "Call me next week and I'll find out a day when I know he'll be home. Only don't tell him you're coming by, just show up and try to be calm. Believe it or not, he's carrying a lot on his shoulders right now."

I nod my head, thankful for his words and encouragement as he leans my way, patting me across the back.

"Thanks, Jake. When did you become the big brother?" The words come out of my mouth as a painful reminder of how each of us was forced to grow up so much faster than we should have, and honestly, it's no one's fault. It's just the way the cards fell.

He crooks an easy grin, but says nothing.

"I'll call you next week and we'll figure it out." I fling my arm around him in a hug then look around, about to question if we should go through Mom's stuff eventually, but then I decide not to. Jake stares around as well and I wonder if he's thinking the same. "I better go."

"Ok ..." I stand and Jake hops to his feet with me. "Love you," he mumbles, something us three don't often say. It surprises me, but the subtle extra pulse in my heart as if it's been given an extra life, tells me that it's something I've needed to hear for a long time; and maybe he does, too.

"I love you, too, Jake."

We part ways and I race to meet up with Alyssa for a somewhat exciting night of picking out costumes along with the dreaded agony over Bethany being the third wheel.

Sitting on a somewhat stiff, velvety lounge chair outside the portable dressing rooms they have installed at the back of the store, I watch Alyssa step out in a sexy as hell outfit. My eyes catch on her pushed up chest, showing so much cleavage that it should be illegal. *She could cause a wreck in this outfit.* Moving down, my eyes take in the golden belt cinching her small waist then to the full length of her legs showing off miles of smooth, milky white skin interrupted only by a few strands of ribbon laced up to her knee.

Stretching my eyes open in awe, I smile. "That's the one," I breathe out with a wink. *I just don't want everyone else seeing her looking like this.*

Pulling her hand out from behind her back as if she has a hidden treasure, she nonchalantly dangles a matching male costume from her fingers. I immediately look at her in surprise. *Does she want me to wear that to the party?*

My eyes widen as I take in the picture on the front of the package. "No way …" I sputter, half panicked and part amused. "I'm not wearing that unless it is late at night and we are doing role play or some shit like that."

We both crack up, me with a vision of her and I acting out some roman seduction scene in full on attire as she walks backwards, swinging her hips and beckoning me into the room. No further invitation is needed than the alluring way she crooks her finger and wisps her eyes open and closed in a sensual manner.

In the tiny dressing room, she giggles as I clumsily slide the garment up my legs, feeling very unmanly in what is basically a dress. I sling the gathered fabric sash over my shoulder then Alyssa throws her hands up to my neck to clip on the long fabric cape, despite my reservations. Looking down at her as she snaps it, the hint of a smile flickers as she tries her best to hide it. I'm having a hard time keeping my laughter at bay as well.

She takes one stride back and looks me up and down, while I

stand there with a draft crawling up the skirt of the costume. *I cannot believe I'm in a dress.* Her eyes sparkle as they move across my chest and land back on my face. *I know that look. Maybe the dress isn't such a bad thing, after all.*

In one swift motion, I take her by the hand and pull her to me, engulfing her in my arms. Bethany's face pops into the room right as my lips descend on Alyssa's, killing the moment and completely annoying me.

"Hey girl, you rea …" she stops talking as Alyssa swings her head around. "Ooolala …" her voice grates over every nerve in my body and making me want to shudder.

Alyssa's hands clamp onto my chest in a territorial way and she stays positioned in front of me, keeping Bethany's wandering eyes away. That single act makes my ego swell, knowing I belong to her and her alone.

"We're just about ready," Alyssa tells her, turning her head back my way and focusing on the sash over my torso.

Looking over her head, I catch Bethany's gaze as she arches her eyebrows up and down while licking her lip in a way I'd rather not even think about. Drawing my brows down into a get-the-hell-out glare, she giggles and sweeps the curtain shut.

"So are you going to wear this to the party or what?" Alyssa runs her fingertips down the center of my chest, but all I can think about is how I wish she would have caught Bethany's obvious attempt at flirting.

After playfully helping each other out of our costumes, we make a stop for wings before heading back to her apartment so she can grab some clothes and spend the night.

"I'll be right back. I'm just going to grab my stuff," Alyssa calls out as she disappears into her bedroom with me not too far behind.

Just as I get to the threshold, my foot catches on something near the side of the couch. Stopping to look at what I kicked, Bethany lets out a small gasp at the mess at my feet.

"My fault. I forgot to pick that up earlier," she yells out, running from the kitchen to the living room with a wad of paper towels in hand.

Soda seeps into the carpet all around my foot which is presently weighing down a crushed 32 ounce foam cup. *Great.* Just as Bethany rounds the corner, I lower myself onto the edge of the couch and hold my hand out for the towels.

"Sorry," I tell her sincerely as she bends to clean the mess I made. "I can get it."

I look over her head as she kneels on the ground in front of me in a pattern of pushing and patting the folded towels. Snapping her head up, her face is suddenly inches from mine. Before I can make a move to dart back to the safety of the couch cushions, she has my face in her hands and her lips on mine.

With wide eyes, I instantly shove at her shoulders and push away from her. *What the hell is she thinking?* Cabinets opening and closing in the room beside me rings in my ears, but I cannot even move my mouth to speak.

Placing her hand over her mouth, I swear I see a touch of a smile as Bethany gasps. "Oh my gosh … I am so sorry. I think I read that wrong," she says blandly like she's instructing someone how to open a web browser. "It's just … Kyle acted the same way until he finally gave in and we …"

I'm not sure if my tongue even works any longer. I stare at her; shocked, confused. *What the hell is she saying? Why is she telling me this?*

Waving her hand to dismiss what she was attempting to confess to me, she gets up and bounces down onto the couch beside me.

"You know what, never mind. I read that wrong." She slouches back in the most ordinary way.

Bolting to my feet, I'm prepared to call her out on what just happened, but my speech gets lodged in my throat.

"You ready?" Alyssa's voice knocks me out of my daze and has me darting to her side as if I have something to be guilty over. *What on earth just happened?*

I don't say a word. My mind cannot even wrap around it, and what the hell was she talking about with Kyle. Suddenly, my mind shoots over conversations with Alyssa. *It was Bethany; she was the one at the party. Holy shit!* I dart my eyes over at Bethany whose mouth is moving but I don't hear a word. Her eyes meet mine and heat flares through my face in anger. She does things in a manner that makes it hard for me to blame her for any wrong doing. Just then, she kissed me; I mean she was the one that kissed me, yet I was leaning over her. I was so preoccupied with watching what she was doing in hopes that she would let me take on the task of cleaning up the spilled soda that I put myself in a bad position; close to Bethany with my guard down.

The whole drive back to my place, I analyze the hell out of what happened and what she said. All I can think about is what will happen if I accuse Bethany of wrong doing. She's so manipulative and sneaky that I have no doubt in her skill to be able to flip the tables on me. I also have no uncertainty of whether Alyssa would believe me; I know she would, but does she need this drama?

After a phenomenal distraction, my mind ponders over all the scenarios and worries. Lying in bed next to Alyssa, my heart still pounding from our bedtime acrobats and my breaths still heavy, I run through a mental check list of what she told me about the night her ex cheated and gently quiz her in hopes that she may put two and two together; or at least get curious.

It doesn't take long before she seems to be done with the lineup I have going on and she's ready to take this conversation to a new level, and that doesn't take much enticing. Slowly creeping her fingers up my chest, as if they are a stick figure walking up the street, she easily switches the mood and closes the conversation with her lips sealed to mine.

Flipping her over, I take my time; kissing and touching her until we are both desperate and crazed to be as close as possible. With one shift of my body, I put us both out of our misery and the currents that immediately spiral through my core upon contact nearly send me over the edge. Her hands clasp to my side, pushing into my flesh and pulling me forward with each movement. My mind is fogged over with all thoughts of Bethany thrown overboard.

After a heated night and all that was on the tip of my tongue being wiped clean, I wake up revived and ready for the day; for today. I've never been the type to get hung up on holidays and anniversaries, but with Alyssa each day is a moment closer to our forever.

As of today, she has been back in my life for a month. A measly thirty days may not be much to some, but for me time is a precious thing. I still remember counting down each day after my dad left;

adding day after day until he had been gone a month, a year, five years. Then that countdown soon turned into counting the days until my mom would leave us; subtracting each day as if the world would end when I got to zero.

It's funny how time goes so slow when there is pain and torment surrounding your life. It's as if it's a lingering presence sucking all the air from your soul; suffocating you slowly, yet when joy and happiness presents itself, time flies.

Slowly sliding out from beneath the sheets and from the comfort of her beautiful body curled up to mine, I quickly dress, scribble down a small note and head to the supermarket down the street. I'm only praying she doesn't wake up; I'd love to surprise her. She's had so much going on lately and I want so desperately to give her a day to smile. I want to give her a little piece of me; a part of me that I've never shared with anyone.

After tossing a ten to the cashier and pocketing my change, I grab the brown paper sack and race back to my truck. My feet soar over the pavement and land firmly on the floorboard. I push down on the gas pedal and hurry to my apartment so I can see her face light up. Reaching into the bag the cashier handed me, my hand quickly finds the small black box I found in the gift wrap aisle. It only takes me a second to find the brand new key I had placed on my keychain with all my others. The freshly ground steel shines, making all my other keys look weathered and old. Twisting and fumbling with it, I finally work it off of the ring and nestle it down into the bottom of the box and close the lid.

All is still quiet when I return, so Evan must be sleeping in. I noticed Skylar's car in the driveway so I'm sure she graced him with another of her late night visits, but I'm sure to hear him tell it, it's because we kept him awake all night. My lips slowly curl into a smile at that thought. *I really need my own place.*

Turning the door knob to my bedroom, my ears catch the sounds of sheets rustling and a slight creak of the bed, but as soon as I have her in full sight, there is no movement. *Pretending to be asleep, huh?* I close the door behind me quietly, knowing I'm not going to wake anyone, but still wanting to build on the suspense.

Sneaking over to the bed, I stop and take in all her beautiful features. The sheet lays draped over her small frame with part of her bare back peeking out, almost as an invitation for me to get back in bed. Her shoulders tense up and I can tell she senses my presence. I slowly slink down onto the mattress, making careful movement so she can continue in on her escapade of pretending to be asleep.

As I stare down at her with the roses clutched in my hand, she turns her head smoothly and lets out a sleepy sigh. I hold back my snickers at her effort. *Doesn't she know that I have memorized every breath she takes while she is peacefully sleeping?* I know exactly how her breathing slows only minutes before sleep captures her, and I know the low, steady rhythm of her breathes once she is floating from dream to dream. I've stayed awake so many nights listening to her soft inhales and exhales, committing each one to my memory.

Sliding my knee onto the mattress, I slowly sink down and slide onto the bed beside her. My smile widens as I see her body shake as if she is quietly laughing. The smooth clear sheet of plastic that surrounds the satiny pink roses crinkle as I move to position the cluster of roses over her arm that is stretched cut beside her. With the center rose jutting out just a bit further than the others, I set it against her elbow and trail it gradually up her arm towards her shoulder while leaning down to her ear.

"I know you're awake," I whisper with a wide smile.

Her face is positioned away from me, but I can see her eyebrows are drawn down into a frown as if she is confused. For a moment, I think she may need some coercing to give up the game, but then a smile breaks open across her face and she turns to me with her lips only millimeters from mine. Just seeing her happiness does something to my heart and I have to fight the urge to toss the flowers to the side and bury myself back under the sheets with her.

The sheet is clasped in her hand between us, pulled over her chest, but still revealing so much skin that my heart is about to pound out of my chest. She makes a move as if she is just as desperate to feel me against her as well, but I quickly shove all my desires aside, suck in a deep breath through my over-anxious smile and pull the roses up between us.

Her eyes widen and I know my attempt in surprising her has worked. It's the first time I've bought her flowers and it's way overdue. My brothers and I used to pepper my mother with gifts. Even if it was only a silly little drawing that we had made, we still made sure she always had something new to display on her nightstand each day; a new memento of how much she was loved to brighten her room.

"Happy one month anniversary," I announce, igniting a look of shock from her.

Her mouth drops open and she glances back and forth from the roses to me as my grin grows and my heart thuds.

"Has it really been a month," she squeaks, but I can tell she is desperately trying to calculate my estimation of the date of this occasion.

I know I got this right; I'll never cease to count each and every single day that I have been blessed to have her by my side.

Grabbing the bouquet from my hand, she buries her face in the sweet fragrance and I realize just how much the pale shade of pink in the petals match the faint tint of blush in her cheeks.

"They're beautiful," she declares with a gentle smile that completely captivates me.

A flower, beautiful? It's not even comparable. "You're beautiful," I correct her and pull her closer, not even caring if I crush the flowers.

I slide my lips over hers, gently linking us in a moist kiss that will no doubt put my body into hyper drive in no time. Pulling away before I hit a point of no return, I look at her in utter happiness and satisfaction.

"I can't believe it's already a month," she pauses and I grin at the slight bit of embarrassment that emerges as the pink in her cheeks deepens to a light crimson. "Ummm ... I have to admit, I didn't remember."

My chest vibrates with held in laughter. "Well, I can't see why. It's not like you've had anything going on," I joke, pulling her tighter into my arms.

Her eyes sparkle with gratefulness, which only makes my heart swell with delight. We've been going to Fairview around the clock, visiting with her dad. The last thing I expect is for her to even know the day of the week, let alone the significance of today; I had actually hoped she would forget. I have a lot of myself to give today without being overwhelmed with her trying to dazzle me as well. What I have planned will more than likely make this day about us both, me offering up my whole self and refuge while she gains a whole chunk of my heart that I've always kept closed off from the world.

Pulling myself back into the moment, I gaze into her crystal blue eyes then briefly down to the plush bundle of roses.

"I couldn't decide whether you were a red rose kind of girl or a mixed arrangement or what, so I went with this color. It's the same color as the tank top you wore the day I first saw you." *I'll never forget the way she looked that day.*

Her look of surprise grows with this revelation and she springs to her knees, abandoning the sheet and crashing into me with her arms stretched around my neck. My face is buried in her hair and her chest is crushed against mine. *I can totally deal with this.*

"I love you so much, Judd," her trembling, muffled voice whispers against my skin. "How did I get so lucky?"

Tipping my head back, I look at her and place my fingertips along her chin to nudge her face down. She looks at me like no one has ever looked at me; as if I am the only safe haven she has ever known.

With a slow-motion shake of my head, I correct her, "No, I'm the lucky one." Then my lips are back on hers.

Twenty minutes later, after lounging on the bed while Alyssa gets dressed, we are finally in the truck and getting this day moving. The entire morning flies by with us hitting a few stores and picking up this and that for Bethany. Aside from being plagued with how badly I need to talk to Alyssa about her 'so called' friend, the day is beyond enjoyable and half the time she has me rolling with laughter. Her need to have extravagant platters comprised of mini sandwiches and tooth-picked finger-foods has me nearly doubling over into hysterics in the freezer section. I envision several students sporting eye patches come Monday from involuntarily stabbing their eye out with a toothpick during their drunken haze. That is sure to bring out the realism in a Halloween party.

Soon after we have everything loaded, we make the dreaded trek back to Alyssa's apartment to drop it all off. I help carry the bags inside, but then I make myself scarce. I have no desire to be around Bethany and I'm hoping I can shed some light on what a conniving, back stabbing friend she is when I have a chance to talk to Alyssa. I really should have just spit it out last night, but it breaks my heart that with everything that she already has on her plate and at a time when she needs her friends the most, that I'll have to be the bearer of news that will sever one of those ties.

No sooner than I am two steps back into the hallway my phones buzzes. Looking down, I see Tristan's name. I take a deep breath, squeeze my eyes shut and answer with apprehension gnawing at my insides.

"Hello," I say with a calm, yet unsteady pitch to my voice, remembering all that Jake said.

"Judd, hey. Are you busy?" His voice actually sounds livelier than it has since this summer.

I continue treading back to my truck, keeping my eyes focused down to the concrete as I walk.

"No, not really. I'm just with Alyssa today." I pause and Tristan remains silent. "Are you calling to explain where you were yesterday?"

My ears pick up on a deep sigh from the other end of the phone and a part of me desperately wants to be there for my brother; to help him through whatever he is struggling with, but I never can make myself. Maybe Jake was right; Tristan and I are a lot alike, we're both stubborn.

He doesn't reply and for a second I wonder if he is still there, "Tristan?"

"I'm here," he replies in a different tone that I can't exactly pinpoint. "I'm sorry. I was here … I just had a hard day and thought I'd be ok when you texted but then I just …"

"Yeah?"

"I just got tired and fell asleep."

I spit out an insincere laugh, "Bullshit, Tristan. I was knocking loud enough to wake the dead." I stop talking abruptly, ashamed of the phrase I chose to use.

"I'm sorry. So what are you doing tonight?"

Does he want me to come over? The urge to jump into my truck and race over shoots through me, but then I shake my head, perturbed by our last supposed visit.

"I'm with Alyssa. I'm taking her somewhere special and then there is a party at her house."

"A party, huh? Sounds like fun. Well, hey … I won't keep you. I just thought I would say hi." His somewhat upbeat tone from only minutes ago suddenly is filled with sadness and bitterness.

"No, it's ok. I'm actually outside waiting for Alyssa. Are you at home?" I ask, partly worried. Jake mentioned how depressed he has been and I'm really hoping he isn't alone.

He lets out a huff of air that sounds like a laugh, but not at all sincere. "Yeah, I'm at home. Where else?! There are only two places I could be at this point … the hospital or here."

Squeezing my eyes closed for a brief moment, I press the phone harder to my ear and pinch the bridge of my nose between my thumb and index finger. I slowly settle back against my truck and let go of it all. This is ridiculous. He is my brother and he may not want to see me, but it's obvious that he needs me. What are all these calls about anyways, if he doesn't want to fix what's left of our family?

"Tristan, we need to talk," I pause, the wreck surfacing in my mind. "What happened? I mean, I know it's something serious, but all Jake tells me is that you need to be the one to tell me. I keep waiting, but you never do. I'm your brother, I'm here and I will help …"

He cuts me off, sounding completely pissed that I even breached the subject of the wreck. "Hey, well I guess I better go. I'd hate to make you late for your party or date or whatever the hell you have going on."

A part of me wants to lash out and scream, what the hell is your deal or tell him how ashamed Mom would be with how he is acting, but the other side of me knows he is just pushing me away; locking all the pain inside of himself until he explodes, like Jake said.

"Did I do something? I mean, are you pissed at me because we wrecked or maybe something else?" *I'm trying here … I'm taking Jake's advice and really trying, but it's just like it always is.*

He gasps and it's apparent that I hit a nerve, but not the one that makes him explosive; not the one I've hit so many times before; I got to him.

"I need to go. I can't do this. I have enough going on. Sorry I called," he says, his voice laced with sadness and regret.

The phone goes silent with a click and I stand there dumbfounded; almost angry with myself.

"Whatever," I whisper mostly to myself then shove the phone in my pocket as Alyssa walks towards me with Bethany by her side. *Wonderful!*

Tossing all my worry and confusion over Tristan to the back of my mind, I take a few steps to be by her side, doing my best to ignore our company, but of course, that is always impossible.

"So what are you two up to that is so pressing that you can't help me?" Bethany's shrill voice speaks up and I roll my eyes without even thinking.

How is it possible for someone's voice to grate so harshly on your nerves that you'd like nothing more than to rip your freaking ears off?

I keep my eyes locked on Alyssa as she fills me in with a tone that soothes my anxiety, "I told her we had something planned and that we would come back early to help."

Pulling Alyssa's hand into mine, I hold it firmly and smile. Any problem, stress or worry that has been weighing on my mind vanishes as I look into her eyes.

"Absolutely," I tell her lovingly, because I'll do anything for her.

Suddenly, all the warm and fuzzies I'm feeling being near Alyssa manages to get sucked dry with the single annoying sound of Bethany clearing her throat. I turn to face her and take in the defiant stance, her perturbed expression and the way she has her arms crossed like we've thoroughly pissed her off. Immediately, I'm on the defense and remembering all too well what she did and said last night.

"It's been a month since we have been together so I figured I would take *my girlfriend* somewhere special this afternoon."

I make sure to enunciate the fact that Alyssa is my girlfriend so that there is no mistaking that it is not alright to kiss me and it is not alright to treat my girlfriend like shit. The whole time, I can feel Alyssa watching me, no doubt confused, but Bethany's glare is something I do not miss. I definitely struck a chord there.

"Judd, is everything ok?" Alyssa's quiet voice knocks me out of my thoughts.

Not wanting to worry her or bring it up right now, I divert the whole situation back to my call. "Yeah, just a bad conversation with Tristan, that's all." It's not a lie, but it is also not what I should be telling her.

Staring into her eyes, I think about how much sadness she has felt lately. She is walking down such a painful path these days as she watches her father get sicker and weaker. This walk may very well end in complete annihilation of her heart and the last thing she needs is more loss or more pain. I can't tell her now, even though Bethany deserves for me to call her out right to her face.

No doubt, Bethany stays true to her selfishness and interrupts my attempt at being forgiving and not saying anything. *She knows I could.*

"I'm in a foul mood, too," she casts a glance to Alyssa then to me, "The guy I told you I was chasing after keeps blowing me off and I'm just about done with this whole cat and mouse chase." Her words are like a damn shotgun blast, completely taking me by surprise. She keeps her eyes on me as Alyssa offers words of comfort and encouragement. *Is she freaking talking about me? Cat and Mouse? Don't even tell me she thinks I have been leading her on!*

I don't offer a goodbye, good riddance, piss off, go to hell, nothing; I turn and walk to my truck with Alyssa close behind. After dodging a few questions of why I was snippy with Bethany and a pit stop at her favorite café so I can pick up lunch, we pull into the parking lot that I've ended up at so many times in my life. My stomach is wound tight with nervousness and my mind is frantically whirling with all the things I want to tell her today; all the things I want to show her.

I tumble and file through all the words I want to say to Alyssa as we wind along the walkway back to my brothers and my personal heaven on earth. It's where we come anytime we need Mom's advice or don't quite know where to go. Needless to say, I've ended up here a lot over the years. I have no doubt that Tristan has made many of stops here over the last few months.

As soon as we step out from beneath the canopy of trees that lead to Mom's fountain, Alyssa's eyes light up just as I expected. I stand there clutching the sack of food, which I already slipped my surprise into, as she carefully inspects the beauty of this place. My heart floods with emotion as I watch each of her footfalls and realize that Alyssa's feet are stepping along the same pathway that my mom's feet once fell upon. It's the same thought I have when I walk the perimeter of the fountain. The presence of my mother lingers here so strongly, even more so today. The sting of emotion overwhelms my heart and surges upward through my body until it spills over, moistening my cheeks with a few tears. I quickly wipe them away and continue watching Alyssa.

The second her eyes land on all of our initials in the carefully constructed pathway, my heart and soul overflow with love and the desire to give her every held back portion of my heart.

Her eyes go wide as she snaps her head up, looking completely awe-struck. "Is this you and your brother's initials?"

My heart sets sail on a never ending voyage of being in love with her at the fact that in two seconds flat she knew. I offer her a small smile as a reply, too weighted down with sentiment to answer. With careful movements, I walk towards her, gazing down at the mural of Mom so that I don't step on a single piece of it.

For a second, my mind flickers back to the day it was built.

"Tristan, I don't know where to put this piece. I need Mom here. I need her to show me where it goes," I plead with him through an avalanche of tears that has already soaked through my shirt today.

My brother cocks his head to the side and studies me for a minute as I stare helplessly at him. I don't know how to do this without her here. How does he?

"Judd, you can do it ... just like Mom taught us, remember. Here." He takes the sparkly brown square-shaped jewel from my hand and places it parallel to the one he had just laid down in the grout. "Now, grab another one and just line them up."

I sigh and look over at Jake who is slowly placing small gold gems side-by-side, forming the outline of a halo. His body trembles and periodically I hear a sniffle as I watch a small drop of moisture splash to the ground below his face.

Looking back to Tristan, I carefully study how he works, appearing completely unaffected. He looks up to me with a touch of a smile, silently urging me to keep working and to continue in our tribute to Mom.

As I kneel down beside Alyssa, I let it all out, spilling through the day we came across this place on a simple adventure to clear our minds from the heartache of losing Dad, to how Mom made arrangements with the city to revamp and make it our own.

Slowly winding my hand across the pebbly texture of the mosaic,

I think of my mom and how she could turn the smallest things into something extraordinary.

"Mom was really artistic. She could do anything with her hands. So she brought us here week after week with scrap pieces of craft supplies she got from work and all four of us made this," I say with a sharp sensation piercing my heart.

I glance over to Alyssa, dipping my head down as she mocks my motions by running her hand tenderly over the image.

"And this is her?"

I can tell she already knows the answer, but I nod anyways and move my hand closer to hers. My hand barely grazes the edge of hers and it reminds me of the first night we met; how I was so eager to hold her hand or kiss her; anything. I just wanted to be as close as possible to her. I wonder if my mom watched over me that night; if she has gotten to see me fall in love for the first time. I sigh before moving my thoughts back to the day we made this.

"My brothers and I came out here and finished this part after she died. We swore this would always be our place where we could be closer to her."

My heart swells as I think over how this place has become more than our sanctuary. In our eyes, it is our mom. It is a place of beauty and tranquility. It engulfs us in love and support when we need it, just like she would have. I lower my brows and take a deep breath to steer off the impending tears as Alyssa's hand runs the length of my jaw to my cheek.

"I love you. Thank you so much for sharing this with me," Alyssa says in a low tone with her lips only millimeters from mine.

I run my hand over her softly blushed cheeks up into her hair as a gentle breeze blows and sends a hint of strawberries into the air. Breathing her in, I pull her closer and whisper against her lips.

"I want to share everything with you … always," because I do. She is everything to me. Never would I have imagined bringing someone here. This place is a part of my soul; it's more than a fountain, it's my second home. Giving this part of me to her is equivalent to personally placing my heart in her hands. It is giving a part of my mother to her, and I do it with complete clarity, because Alyssa is the same thing to me. She is now my home, my refuge.

Advice

WE CUDDLE UP CLOSER and I lean my back against the hard cement bench that sits alongside my mom's mural. She clasps my hand in hers and I get the feeling that she is lending me a sense of strength because she knows what this place means to me. I wrap my free arm around her waist as she sits between my bent knees, leaning onto my chest.

"So how does the fountain keep running? Does the city pay for it or do you guys?"

Her question catches me off guard because honestly I never thought about it. We were always struggling to make ends meet after Dad left, which is why Jake and I spent nearly every weekend working at a dairy farm while Tristan took a part-time job as a mechanic, working nights. He was adamant about being there for Mom every second as soon as he got home from school or practice, yet he tried his best to shelter Jake and me from seeing too much of her sickness. We knew he was protecting us. Somehow he arranged for a private nurse to come stay with her through the night while he spent the evening, clear up until 1:00 am, working on cars. Then he would be up and at school bright and early the next day, but every extra penny we could earn we put towards bills, food and taking care of Mom.

She glances back at me and I frown. "You know, I never thought to question that. I mean, Mom worked it out with the city and got the deed to the land, but I'm not sure how we afforded it. When she first called the city, they had to dig to find out that the land belonged to an older couple who had passed away and who also had no living relatives interested in taking it over. From there, I'm not sure. Mom never really talked about finances with me. I think Tristan handled most of it."

"Strange. Perhaps the city thought you were restoring it as part of the park."

I laugh, "Maybe." As soon as the words are out of my mouth, her stomach lets out a monstrous rumble, reminding me that we have food that is more than likely ice cold by this point. "I think that is our cue to eat, not to mention it may be getting cold by now." I stretch around to nudge the sack in her direction as she moves out from between my legs to my other side. "I wasn't sure what you wanted so I got a little of everything," I half lie, knowing exactly what she likes from there, but rather wanting her to dig in and find my surprise. "Go ahead and pull it all out."

After anxiously watching her pull each item out, chuckling at her reaction then seeing the delight in her eyes as she spots her favorite soup, she finally reaches the bottom of the bag. Her eyes widen as she looks inside and her hand immediately slaps over her mouth in shock.

Oh no! What the hell was I thinking? I knew the box was the size of a ring box and although a part of me wanted to gauge her reaction, I honestly didn't even take into consideration that it may make her bolt.

I hold my hand out as if I'm trying to keep an attack dog at bay. "Ok, don't run away, freak out, cry or any of those things girls do. It isn't what it looks like at all. It's just something I wanted you to have."

Her face instantly turns the color of a bouquet of red roses I passed up just this morning. *I am an ass! Who does this to a girl?!*

"Oh, shit. Are you disappointed? Now I feel bad." *I didn't even consider that she may feel let down. I need to smooth this over.* Holding her hands securely in mine so she cannot hide, I move closer to her, ready to devour her lips instead of the food. "Let me take you on a couple more dates before we get to that point. Deal?"

My mouth mends to hers automatically as I place my top lip perfectly between her moist, luscious lips and gently nibbling at it. She was excited when she thought I was going to propose. It's way too soon, but my heart pounds with the thought of making her mine some-day, and the look in her eyes just now gives me just a glimpse at what that day may be like. It also gives me the perfect plan.

Pulling away, she softly agrees to my terms then I encourage her to open the box. By now, my gifts to her may be bordering on lame or she may be thinking I don't know what an actual gift is, but when I look at her, ordinary just isn't good enough. She deserves more than a simple shirt wrapped in a gift box or some fancy perfume. Besides, I want to keep her guessing.

She slides the box open carefully as if a spider may jump out to greet her, but as soon as she clasps the keys between her fingertips, her face lights up. Swiping it from her hand, I quickly hold it up between us, focusing on the bright metallic finish before my sights land back on her beautiful face.

"This may not seem like much, but it is the key to my apartment. This is a symbol of the fact that I want you with me all the time; every day; every minute; every second; I want you by my side. This leaves no barriers between us." As the words fall from my mouth, one thing repeats through my head: *All except for me telling you about Bethany*, but not now, not here. Right now is for us.

After scarfing down our lukewarm soup and sandwiches, we clean up our mess and I show her around.

"This was our first one and basically Mom did it by herself. Jake and I kept pretending the jewels were race cars." I laugh as I look down at the picture of a woman holding a baby securely in her arms. "I remember Mom telling us how the instant that she became a moth-er was the moment she knew everything in her life had meaning, no matter how hard or how sad." I let out another chuckle, thinking about Tristan's resistance to joining in on the artwork. "I think Tristan just wanted to leave. Every time Mom would put a stone in his hand, he would get this look on his face like he had just bit into something sour and he would say, 'Mom, stuff like this is for girls.'"

I look over at Alyssa laughing then glance over to the next image in front of us. It's one of my favorites. Staring at a perfect stair-step image of Mom, Tristan, me then Jake, I release a little more of my heart, slowly letting it all out, one story at a time.

"This one we attempted to make a couple times, but the weather got cold and the grout kept hardening too fast. Finally, we waited until the following summer when I was almost twelve. By then we all pretty much had the hang of it. After she had drawn up the design, me, Jake and Tristan took over. We were so proud of it once we got it done. It was fun, too. I mean, frustrating but fun." I chuckle at the memory. "All three of our hands were crammed into this small area, trying to create something magnificent that we could dazzle Mom with, so every once in a while I'd shove at Jake, then he'd smack at my hand, then Tristan would bump my shoulder and make me drop my jewel and so on until we were laughing ... just laughing and forgetting everything that was going on around us." I crinkle my brows and look up at Alyssa intently listening to everything I'm saying with a look of amazement and longing. She doesn't ask for details or more of an explanation of my mom's sickness; she just listens.

Crouched down by her side over the current picture, I look over to the next one and rise up, taking her hand in mine. I go over a few more stories, describing the tedious details that went into each of them. Looking to one of the last images of our four hands overlapping one another, I take three small steps and stand over it, squeezing Alyssa's hand in mine with the memory of how sick Mom was at that point.

"This one we did when I was almost fourteen. Mom had gotten pretty sick by then." Alyssa's head snaps up at the mention of sickness and although I know I should tell her about my mom's battle with ALS, for now it's not something I want to dive into. I will tell her, but no matter the time, the pain is just too real right now. "Tristan wheeled her back here in a wheelchair and she sat snuggled up with an old blanket and pillow while we worked. Mom couldn't draw up the elaborate images that she had in the past anymore, so Tristan had come up with something that we could do ourselves. He spent hours in the garage sanding down jewels to make sure they would fit perfectly. The whole time we worked, Mom watched us and…"

My eyes sting and a tidal wave of emotion washes over me suddenly, causing me to stop. I clear my throat and look up at Alyssa with a small forced smile. Her eyes sparkle with sympathy and love, instantly absorbing all the pain from my heart and replacing it with a calming I've never felt. Stretching my lips up further, I immediately notice her eyes flash to my cheek before she looks back into my eyes with a gorgeous smile.

"Hey, you know what? I have an idea before we go." I dig into my pocket, my hand quickly finding several coins. "My brothers and I used to always cast off two wishes each before we'd leave here." I hand Alyssa two coins, holding firmly to my two as she takes them from my hand.

"Are you going to make a wish too?" she asks sweetly, holding one coin up towards the fountain.

Raising my eyebrows, I smile and hold both my coins up so she can see that I'm already prepared for my wishes. She turns with a childlike grin on her face, closes her eyes and barely moves her lips in a silent whisper. I watch her closely, trying to zoom in on what her wish is, but no sooner than the coin is flipped through the air and lands with a splash, she then has the other coin ready.

Still holding tight to my coins, I let one go, tossing it lightly without taking my eyes off her.

Don't let this ever end.

Her coin plummets into the water soon after mine then she swings her gaze to mine as I toss my last coin over my shoulder. *I don't need any wishes. I have everything I need right here.*

After a short drive back to my apartment while I shamelessly pester her about what her wishes were, we manage to get cleaned up in a hurry, get a rather unexpected greeting from Evan then escape to the solitude of my bedroom for some alone time.

Coming out of my room with satisfaction over an absolutely perfect day, I nearly trip, my foot catching on a cord as I clutch onto the doorframe to keep from going face first.

"You're an ass! A heads up that you were here while we were showering would have been nice, and what's up with all the stereo equipment?" I ask, stepping out from my room while Alyssa changes. The floor is littered with strung-out cords and a huge prehistoric CD player that used to be out at his grandfather's cabin.

He shrugs with a grin, "I figured I would move stuff around and try to drown out the huffing and puffing coming from your room. It's pretty distracting, dude." His smile widens and I'm hoping he is not remembering the accidental glimpse he got of Alyssa as I had her flung over my shoulder. "And why am I an ass? You're the one that slammed me with a view I'm not likely to forget anytime soon."

Evan cracks up, kicking his foot against the floor as my eyes widen. I know he's messing with me, but it sure doesn't dispute the fact that he did see her bare ass if not more. This will probably be one of those topics that you lock up and never breach again; at least he better lock it up.

Squinting my eyes, I cast him a warning glare, "I don't even want to hear about what you saw." I shake my head to force that thought away as well. "I seriously need to invest in a siren or air horn that goes off as soon as you enter the apartment."

"Hey, wait a minute. You moved in with me, remember? I mean, you're just as likely to walk in on me getting my freak on."

I roll my eyes and give him a sideways glance. "Yeah, right! You just seem to time your walk-ins at precisely the moment when it will shoot me down the most."

"What?" Evan spits out in disbelief, but cracks a grin beneath his overly dramatic seriousness. "In fact, your running in and out this morning interrupted some midmorning happenings for me. Here I was planning to take a page from your book and haul Skylar into the shower when you came traipsing in the door, roses in hand and a pathetic sappy smile on your face. So in a way, my little interruption today was sweet revenge." He raises his eyebrows with a chuckle and I can't help but laugh.

"I was right; you are an ass." I shake my head with a laugh while leaning back in my chair and balancing on two legs with my feet braced against the base of the kitchen island. "So are you two dating now or what? I've been seeing her car parked in front of the apartment off and on for a while now."

He lets out a frustrated sigh and slouches down on the barstool. "I have no clue. I like her and all, but I just can't manage to ..." He pauses before going on. "I just don't know. I'm good with Skylar, I mean she's fun and definitely pretty, but her being friends with Piper is kind of weird, plus it's just a reminder of what I can't have."

"So call Piper."

He looks at me like I just said the craziest thing, his eyes wide and wild. "Yeah, ok! Whatever ... that doesn't work for us all. I just wish she ... I don't know." He stops talking as if the mention of her name just tore a bandage off an agonizing, unhealed wound.

I take a quick turn from the topic of his relationship, all too familiar with the look in his eyes. Besides, maybe he could help me with this Bethany issue.

"Hey, I sort of have a problem and could use your advice," I say in a low tone so Alyssa doesn't hear in the other room. I have every intention of telling her but I need to know the right way to go about it. Evan nods, urging me to go on.

"So, I haven't told Alyssa this yet and I know I need to, but I'm not sure how or when to approach the subject. She's going through so much lately and the last thing I want is to create more for her to deal with on top of what's happening with her dad."

"Ok, spit it out. What's going on?" Evan impatiently nudges me to the main source of my question.

"Bethany kissed me the other night and told me some things that she has kept from Alyssa," I spit it out and squeeze my eyes shut, a truckload of guilt punching me right in the gut for having not told her this yet. I go on to clarify the words 'some things.' "And I mean, she told me something that had it been you that kept this from me … we definitely would no longer be friends."

Evan's eyebrows are drawn up in shock and he sits there silently, stunned by my confession. "Ahhh, first off … Holy shit, wow!"

I quickly flag my hands around to signal for him to lower his voice. *Holy crap, I feel like a horrible boyfriend! I shouldn't have brought this up.*

"Ok, so yeah, you really need to tell her. When did it happen?"

I blow out a regretful sigh and answer with a knot in my stomach, "Yesterday evening."

Evan looks at me, crooking his lips to the side as if he's thinking or analyzing my answer. *Wait, Evan doesn't analyze shit before speaking … he must be confused.*

"So why haven't you told her?" he asks in a perplexed tone with his hand held out in front of him as if he's waiting for a tip.

Same question I keep asking myself. "I should have, but at first I was in shock then I wanted to see if maybe she knew this crappy little secret that Bethany has been keeping from her and then, well …" I bite the inside of my lips remembering the turn that last night's discussion took. "I got distracted. Then today I took her to Mom's wishing well." I glance his way as his face lights up with recognition of what today meant to me.

"Oh yeah, wow … you took her there. Well, then today definitely would not have been a good time to tell her. That kind of drama doesn't need to be brought up there and that had to be a big step for you, so that is completely understandable. So, what is the secret that she has been keeping?"

Pressing my lips together in a subtle frown, I look over to him before speaking.

"You know, actually I'd rather not say. I mean, I think it is something she should know. Honestly, I shouldn't even know this and the fact that Bethany just casually threw it out there has me all sorts of confused." *Why the hell did she tell me anyway?* "I know for a fact, that this information will hurt Alyssa when she finds out, but others knowing before her will only make her feel like a fool."

"Ahh, understood." Evan stretches his arms above his head, looking at the ceiling before and back to me. "Well, listen … I know it's weighing on your mind, but she's in there getting ready," he says, pointing to my bedroom door. "She's getting all jazzed up so she can have fun tonight, so my advice …" he pauses as if he is waiting to see if I stop him. Nudging my chin in his direction, I urge him to go on and he does, "I'd say you've held it in this long. You guys go to the party, have fun, get all wild and crazy," he widens his eyes, drumming his fingers in the air. "Then tell her in the morning. You didn't do anything wrong. After you tell her, stand back and watch Alyssa lay twinkle-toes flat on her ass. Oh and get it on video so I can watch."

Evan grins and I smile back, appreciative for the advice. Now if only I can sit on this for a day, because it is eating me up.

Bury the Hatchet

NOT WANTING TO THINK about this any longer, or chance Alyssa hearing it and think I was the one that deceived her, I change the subject.

"So, you wanna come with us tonight? I have a super snazzy Greek God or gladiator costume you could borrow." I roll my eyes and laugh, igniting a look of skepticism from him.

"Are you dressing up tonight?"

I shake my head immediately, "No way. I'll leave the dressing up to Alyssa." Just as the words leave my mouth, out steps Alyssa in her short white costume with a golden belt strapped tightly beneath her breast and showing off way more cleavage than anyone needs to see.

A piercing whistle from Evan bounces me out of my daydream as she gracefully spins in a circle with her skirt floating around. I catch a glimpse of some very skimpy undergarments beneath the skirt and sneak a quick look at Evan from the corner of my eyes, then back to her. The sight of her makes my mouth water and now I really don't want to go to this party.

"Holy shit, you look good," I breathe out, slowly licking my lips before saliva starts to drip down my chin.

"I second that, although the first view I had today even tops this outfit," Evan boldly says while ogling my girlfriend.

I smack at his arm, nearly sending him off his chair. "I'm telling you now, you better wipe that image out of your mind."

Evan laughs while keeping his eyes on Alyssa, "Yeah, I'll work on that. Seriously though, you look smoking in that outfit."

Her face lights up at his words, making my heart pound fiercely with any ounce of happiness that anyone can bring her. It takes no time at all for us to convince Evan to join us then we are off. The whole way to the party the subject of Bethany burns on the tip of my tongue, threatening to be spit out, despite Evan's advice. Once we're parked and ready to head in, the guilt of knowing about Kyle and her roommate is flooding out all my decision making skills on whether she should know now or later. When Evan knocks on the window, interrupting our conversation, it takes only one glare from him when Alyssa isn't looking, to know that he is trying to save me from a drama-filled wreck of a night with Bethany as the team captain.

Fifteen minutes into the party and the drama I was trying to avoid swooshes clear past me, landing face first into Evan's lap.

"I'm outta here! I am not going to stay here and let her punish me for something I can't change! See ya later, Alyssa." Evan storms out and I have no clue what just happened.

I glance over to Piper, clearly pissed off herself, then back to Alyssa.

"I'll be right back," I say, racing through the door on Evan's heels. "Hey wait a minute. What happened?"

He spins around with his arms folded over his chest as the door snaps shut behind me. His nostrils are flared and his brows are drawn down, crinkling the skin above his nose as he casts me a look I've only seen when he has to deal with his brother.

"The same thing that always happens. I screwed up one time ... one time and she is fully prepared to punish me for it for life. I just wish she knew ..."

He throws his arm out, flinging his hand in the direction of the door. The pain in his eyes is evident; he's not pissed at her. I know to not even bother asking about what happened in their past, he won't budge on that topic.

"Just go in the opposite direction as her tonight," I suggest, knowing good and well that there is no way he will come back inside.

This summer was torture enough for him seeing her for two

weeks. The only reason he didn't bolt then is because he was on a job and his grandfather was depending on him.

"No way!" He shakes his head rapidly enough that he may give himself whiplash, but then goes on, "She hates me. I know she hates me and I can't do a damn thing about it." His expression turns pained as he throws his hands to his sides and looks down to the ground. With a heavy sigh, he looks back up in an angry glare. "I just … I mean, this is killing …"

My whole body tenses, watching him struggle with this. I've rarely ever seen Evan get emotional over anything. I open my mouth to talk, but he quickly holds his hand up.

"Just go have fun and I'm going to head home. I'll see ya later." With that, he shoves his hands in his pocket and walks away, looking defeated in every way.

"See ya," I say quietly.

I want to stop him and find out what on earth she has over him, but in the end I understand. Knowing that Alyssa's ex slept with Bethany is something I don't dare tell a soul before she finds out herself. Some things are better left unsaid.

Sliding back through the door into a sea of sweaty vampires, slutty nurses and extremely under-dressed super heroes, I immediately spot Alyssa in the middle of the chaos looking around as the music slows down.

A dozen steps or so and my chest is pressed against her back with my hands resting on her hips. Using my chin, I nudge her hair to the side so that I don't have to let go of her then slide my face up to her neck. Her skin is moist with the fragrance of strawberries mixed with the slight scent of sweat, which has never smelled sweeter.

"Were you leaving before I could dance with you?" I whisper, my lips barely grazing the smooth flesh of her ear.

I pull her tighter, my arms crisscrossed around her with my palms resting on the slick surface of her belt. Her body goes slack in my arms and with a deep breath, the weight of her breasts fall upon my wrists before she flips around to look into my eyes.

"More like, I was going to find you and drag your butt out here with me." She lets out a laugh, casually snaking her arms around my neck and melting into me as I pull her closer.

The curve of her body pieced perfectly with mine, detonates a scorching flame deep inside me and rouses every limb and nerve within me.

"So, how much more of an appearance do we need to make before we can turn this into a private party?" Alyssa giggles, her body shaking against mine and sending my insides into a frenzy.

Biting the edge of her lip, she looks upward through thick coal black eyelashes as if she's contemplating my words. *Please let her say we can leave.* Looking back into my eyes and moving in closer to my lips as the music switches to a fast-paced song, I can already tell from her body language that I've lost this battle.

"Let's stay a little while longer and I'll make it worth your while later."

Her eyes sparkle and glimmer as she speaks, having the opposite effect on me that I believe she is hoping for. Saying something like that is not going to calm my racing pulse and hammering heartbeat.

"Mmmhmm … You said that yesterday, too." I raise my eyebrows and flick my head to the side, giving her a sideways glance and trying to hide my ridiculous smile.

"And didn't I make it worth your while last night?"

Well worth my while, I think wiggling my eyebrows. Throwing her head back into a fit of laughter, I am presented with the perfect opportunity to dive in and feast on her neck, and I do. I don't care who's around. She giggles and squeals as I nibble on her skin and sway to the music.

Bass thumps through the floorboards beneath our feet and a steady vibration of loud music fills our eardrums, but we still never break away or quicken the pace of our movement. We are the only two on the dance floor.

After three more songs and once my body seems as if it's glued to hers from the intense body heat encompassing us, I'm suddenly unhitched from Alyssa by Abby's small frame slamming into me. She giddily slides over, shifting her shoulders and hips to create a good-sized gap between us. I drop one arm to allow the interruption, although I really don't want to break away from the secluded trance Alyssa and I have been in for the past ten to fifteen minutes.

"Get your ass over here and dance with me," Abby stumbles over her words as she speaks.

I lean back a little more still keeping one hand on Alyssa's elbow as she raises her arms in the air and starts to bounce to the beat with her sister.

"You dance and I'll go get us another drink," I holler over the music, leaning over Abby into Alyssa's ear.

"I'll take care of her," Abby slurs to me as I back away, dazzled by Alyssa as she lets loose and has fun.

Abby shoots me a wink with her words and I laugh. I don't think she is on the same wave-length as us, deciding not to drink, but it's good to see them both be able to enjoy themselves after months of worry and fear. They aren't out of the woods yet and my heart pinches at the thought of how this year could end for them. *I hope I'm wrong.*

Spinning around, I bump into the kitchen bar which is draped in a black table cloth and littered with knocked over cups, half empty liquor bottles, plastic spiders and of course, the high maintenance party platters that look like they were recently involved in a hit and run. *So much for the beauty of finger food.* Scooping up one of the empty plastic cups, my eyes scan the counter in search of something mild that Alyssa would like.

"Judd, hey," a voice calls out from across the room and has me halting in my search.

Craning my neck around with my hands planted on the bar, I find a couple guys sitting at the kitchen table looking at me expectantly; one of them is Alyssa's ex. *Great!* Now knowing that not only did he cheat on Alyssa but he had the audacity to screw her best friend then not fess up when she was deciding to move in with her, has me infuriated.

"Come over here," some beefed up looking jock sitting across from him waves me over.

Not particularly fond of having a one-on-one with Alyssa's ex, yet still curious with what they want, I turn and walk over to the table.

"Hey," the 'supposed boyfriend' from this summer says, "I'm Kyle." He puts his hand out to shake, but I just stare at it, gritting my teeth.

"I know who you are." Tossing the cup onto the table, I take a seat. If he wants to talk, we'll talk, but he should not expect for me to be polite and gracious for the invite.

Clearing his throat, he slowly lowers his hand and glances at his friend.

"Oh yeah, I'm Hayden." He holds his hand over the table, but this time I reciprocate, grasping his hand in a firm hand-shake while glaring at Kyle.

Kyle flinches slightly, obviously perturbed by my blatant disrespect, but then goes on to explain why they called me over.

"So our coach had us sit through two hours of old football videos yesterday. One game was Rosemore High's final game that sent them to state this past year. I hear you were the quarterback." He raises his eyebrows in question, but I remain silent. "Well, coach had some great things to say about you and was not happy that you have thrown in the towel."

Now I flinch, squeezing my eyes shut for only a second as an image of blurred trees flying past me and the sounds of crunching metal flickers through my mind.

"You were hard-core out on the field, man," Hayden joins in, bringing my attention over to him.

"Yeah, correct me if I'm wrong but I believe that was the game after we kicked Fairview's ass," I say, looking back at Kyle with a stone cold serious face and wanting desperately to treat him like the low-life he truly is. "Hey, weren't you the quarterback that year?" I add with a bit of a smirk as I say the last part, hoping he catches my not-so-chummy tone.

I really have no desire to be friends with him. He stole my entire summer from me. If being cocky about how I kicked his ass in every game the last three years is the only way I can take him down a notch or two, then so be it.

Kyle lets out a low chuckle and looks me right in the eye. "Yeah, that's right," he says slowly and for a second I think he isn't going to retaliate. "So, why did you quit playing? That's got to suck." He casts me a smirk on his last words. *Well played, asshole.*

"Yeah, it does suck," I reply in a low tone. *Even with a bum shoulder, I could still kick your ass.*

"I had a wreck this summer that basically crushed any hopes of me ever playing again."

Surprisingly enough, all humor fades from his face at my words. "That's too bad, man. Heard you were one hell of a player. Could have gone pro from the way it sounds. Sorry to hear about the wreck ... I had no idea."

I want to holler out, *"Yeah, asshole ... that wreck happened days before you declared to me that you were her boyfriend ... that's when I needed her by my side and she needed me by hers, but thanks to you, it didn't happen."* I want to so bad, but I don't, instead I keep it civil, yet keep an underlying message behind my words.

"Yeah, well it worked out for the best." I say, fully talking about getting Alyssa back.

He shrugs, his eyes wandering over to Alyssa. A sting of jealousy bolts through me and I really want to slam him to the ground and warn him that he is never getting her back, because I don't intend on throwing it away like he did.

"So you and Alyssa, huh?"

I have no idea where he wants this conversation to go with that remark, but he is skating on thin ice.

"Yeah me and Alyssa," I say through a tensed jaw while glaring at him.

Obviously uncomfortable with our turn of subject, Hayden stands to leave. "I'm going to go get a drink."

"Listen, since you brought it up, I have a question."

Kyle's face immediately flashes with the look of guilt and remorse as if he knows exactly what I'm about to ask. He's probably right, too. There's only one thing I've ever cared to discuss with him, until recently at least.

"You want to explain to me why the hell you thought you could lie about being with her when I called this summer?"

He doesn't try to avoid the conversation like the coward I thought he was, instead he looks me dead in the eye and doesn't look away.

"Yeah that was a jerk thing for me to do and honestly, I hate that I screwed you over like that and hurt her in the process, but ..." He looks back at her out on the dance floor.

She's huddled up between Abby and Piper, swinging her arms in the air and flipping her hair around wildly. Any other time, I would be consumed with desire and longing when I look at her, but right now all

I can think about is how her chest is bubbling out of her dresses, how her skirt is raised up on her sweaty thigh and how he is soaking it all in, one eyeful at a time.

His voice bounces me out of my thoughts as he finishes his sentence, "… wouldn't you have done the same thing in my shoes? I mean, it's Alyssa." He looks back at me and I'm truly about to lose it. "I know how amazing she is and I felt threatened. Most people would have done the same."

Leaning forward towards Kyle, I lower my voice, "First off Kyle, keep the stares to a minimum. Second, no I would not have done the same. *None of it*, because I do know how amazing she is, so I wouldn't have screwed someone else behind her back and when she finally found happiness I wouldn't have tried to snatch it away. Finally, if I finally found myself lucky enough to call myself her friend, I'd come clean and tell her the one piece of the puzzle that she doesn't know." I stare him down and for once, he squirms in his seat, looking uneasy and guilty. *He knows what I'm talking about.*

Clearing his throat, he gives me a conquered look with a sadness to his eyes, his brows creases at the center and his lips shift back and forth as if he's nervously biting the inside of his lip.

"Ok, I know I screwed up any chance of us getting off on the right foot. I also know I screwed up with her." He points to Alyssa, which is now over by the counter with Abby and Piper. "But I'm not so much of an asshole that I can't appreciate the fact that she seems to be truly happy. I do care about her and that's all I really want. Obviously you make her happy and I'm good with that. Let's just bury the hatchet. Is that possible?"

He makes no attempt to explain why he never told Alyssa about Bethany, but he also did not try to deny that he is in the wrong. I continue to glare at him, trying to figure out what to say. Honestly, I'm half convinced he was sincere, but still not ready to go pick out friendship bracelets. I'll 'bury the hatchet' so long as he keeps his distance.

Dreams

HAYDEN RETURNED, SCOOTING OUT the chair adjacent from Kyle and scraping the legs over the floor in a sharp sound.

"So what are we doing? We should get a drinking game going."

Kyle nods his head and then looks to me with a small grin.

"Judd, you in for quarters?"

"I really don't know if I should. We agreed not to drink too much tonight in case we would need to leave suddenly," I explain as Alyssa walks up and slides into my lap.

A spark of pride in the fact that she so easily made a claim for me in front of him settles into the pit of my stomach as I pull her as close as possible. For a minute, Kyle looks at my arms clasped around her waist and a flicker of jealousy flashes in his eyes, but then it's gone. He nods his head in understanding.

"Gotcha," he answers, catching Alyssa's attention.

"What were you two talking about?"

I begin to answer on only part of the conversation, but Kyle beats me to it, obviously having the same plan in mind.

"Football, then I challenged him to a game of quarters." He casts me a look and I nod in agreement.

Abby settles up beside us along with a couple others and, after reassurance that it's ok to drink, we quickly get neck deep in a game of quarters. Unfortunately, I've never indulged much in party drinking games, so I hit a losing streak from the get go. At first, I'm tossing the shots back one after another with very little effect, but by the sixth one it's as if all the alcohol moves from my throat like a lead weight into my chest, making me sway slowly in my chair. Alyssa manages to sail through with very little drinks.

Little by little, everyone disappears, leaving Alyssa and I side-by-side with a full bottle of vodka and a new made up game surfacing in my mind.

"We each have to think up a statement that is true about ourselves, but the catch is that we try to come up with something we've never told each other. If the statement you throw out is in fact something I don't know, I drink, but if it is something I do know, you drink. Kind of a get-to-know-each-other-even-better type of game. Sound easy enough?" I explain.

"Kind of like truth or dare?" Alyssa looks a little confused or, maybe, she's staring at me with her forehead crinkled up because my words are all starting to slur together.

My mood is upbeat and my mind seems clear, yet it is swirling around like dust in a sandstorm. I note how steady my hand seems as I pour a small amount of vodka in each of our shot glasses.

Looking back at her, I try my best to clear up her confusion, "Yeah, but without the dare." *Although, this could get interesting if we added a dare, more so if there wasn't anyone else here.* "I'll go first. I was so drunk when I lost my virginity that I didn't remember anything about it the next morning."

I know without a doubt that I never told her this critical detail of my first time.

"I knew you were drunk when you lost it, but I didn't know that you didn't remember it. So, like you didn't even know who the girl was the next day?"

I laugh at her shock, though if my mind wasn't spinning, I would be embarrassed. "Ah ah … no questions during this game just random facts. You drink."

She quickly throws back a shot back like it's water then paints on a mischievous grin that I've never seen before. *I may be in trouble.*

"I've fantasized about you on more than one occasion," she delivers while leaning forward so that I can have perfect view down her dress. *Oh geez ... I think this party needs to be ending very soon.*

Her words come out matter-of-factly, gaining an immediate reaction from my body. *Holy shit!* My chest tightens, my heart thuds loudly, and my nearly numb limbs suddenly feel very capable and eager.

"You mean you ... you ..." I cannot even form the words through the extremely vivid image I have floating through my head. I drink without hesitation. Now I have a whole new dream to keep me company when we are not together.

For my turn, I decide to answer her initial question and keep it simple. I'll save the more shocking confessions for later.

"No, I did not know who she was the next day, but she did show up at my house and discussed with Tristan about how good I was. *Most* humiliating moment of my life."

She spits out a giggle and swallows another shot before slamming the glass back down to the table.

"No doubt, on account of how smooth you are," she winks with a huge grin.

I join in her laughter and pour us both another shot. Alyssa stares at the table in a blank expression and for a minute I wonder what she's doing. Looking up to me in confusion, I snicker. *Let's make this fun.*

Glancing around, I spot the kitchen clock above the counter and tap at my wrist.

"You're running out of time. You better go or you're going to have to drink," I inform her, causing her mouth to drop open.

"Wait. You never said there was a time limit. I'm thinking here," she squeals, but I try my best to keep a straight face.

"Ten more seconds," I can barely hold back my laughter.

"You can't do that. That's cheating. You made that up!"

I make a loud buzzing sound and point my finger towards her. "That's true. I did make it up. It's my game and I already knew that." I lean forward and steal a quick kiss, grinning from ear-to-ear with how riled up she got. Her feistiness dissolves as soon as my lips meet hers. Pulling away, I smile and whisper, "Your drink."

She shakes her head and complies with an amused roll of her eyes as I gear up for my next fact so that we can continue the game.

"I never wanted to fall in love, ever ... until the day I saw you."

Seeing Dad walk out on my mom when she needed him the most had a negative effect on my outlook on love, but when I saw her, it didn't matter what the end result would be. I had to give it a shot.

"I'll gladly drink to that." She gives me a warm, sincere smile with absolute love showing in her eyes as she slowly lifts the shot glass to her lips. Placing it gently to the table, she twirls it beneath her fingertips and quirks one eyebrow, telling me I'm in for another bombshell. "I can tie a cherry stem with my tongue."

I arch my eyebrows, my mouth immediately salivating with this new detail. *That's sexy as hell.*

"Like with no hands."

She shrugs with a small smile.

"Show me," I ask, desperately needing to see this.

Casually she slides off her chair, stands and walks up to the bar where there is an array of half devoured party snacks. She sneaks a quick grin over her shoulder and I can't help but slide my gaze down her body and take in her small waist, the way her dress sticks to the back of her thighs and the way her hips swing as she walks. Once at the bar, she pops the cherry in her mouth and strolls back my way.

Half ready to fall out of the chair from the way she's making me feel, and half because the alcohol is slowly winning the battle over my bodily functions, I steady myself as she grabs my hand and turns it palm up inside of hers. I stare hard at her lips, which every once in a while morphs into two. Watching in fascination, she slips the stem out of her mouth and places it in my hand. Squinting, I can barely make out a small knot in the center of the stem. I cock my head back and grin. *Wow.*

"Ok … so, I'm not sure I can top that, but …" I look at her, trying to decide whether to go with shocking like I've had to escape for alone time with fantasies of my own or tell her something that will completely capture her heart and make her know just how much I love her. I go with the latter, already knowing I'll have to drink for this. With my best seductive expression, trying to mock the same look she gave me, I lean forward, lick my lips and whisper, "I love you."

She shifts and wiggles in her seat, then throws her arms around me. *Yes, party is over.* No sooner than my arms snake around her waist, she pulls back, still giggling.

"Drink. My turn."

I sigh as my mouth drops along with my eagerness, igniting a new eruption of laughter from her. *She's torturing me on purpose.*

"Oooo … I got a good one," she clears her throat and wipes the smirk off her face. "I took three years of gymnastics when I was a kid and to this day, I can still put my leg behind my head."

The smirk returns to her face as my mouth drops open. This I have to see, but definitely not here.

"Are we done with this party, yet?" My heart is going full throttle and I may very well implode if I don't have her to myself soon.

Crooking her index finger side-to-side in front of her, she swallows up all my hopes of escaping to the bedroom with her, in an instant.

"Your turn."

I take yet another drink, the warmth of the vodka stinging my tongue and heating up my chest as it joins the colossal amount of liquor whirling in my stomach. *Time to step up my game.*

"Someday, I'd like to have three kids; two girls and one boy." It's totally true and I've actually had dreams of Alyssa holding our first baby in her arms, her face lit with a beauty that is beyond any description.

"But you never wanted to get married," she points out.

I crack up, not at all knowing where the outburst comes from, but my head is spinning so fast that everything seems either hilarious or manages to turn me on at this point.

Holding my hand up, I stick a finger in the air to correct her.

"Up until I met you, I didn't want to."

She gasps, holding her breath for a second as she takes a drink without another word. I'm hoping her level of surprise will end in me hauling her to the bedroom, but then she throws out another fact about herself.

"I told Mom all about our two weeks together at the lake."

A tiny groan slips out of my mouth as I squeeze my eyes shut from embarrassment and take a drink. *That, I was not expecting.* Images of me meeting her parents surface in my mind and I think back to how her mom hugged me for the first time, saying how she had heard so much about me. *Oh God!*

"Wait, how much did you tell her and was this before I went home with you the first time?" I spit out with a lump in my throat as I pour more shots. Horniness and humor are not the only things I'm feeling now.

"Ah ah ... I thought there were no questions?" *Now she's just being ornery.* Looking at her with my mouth half gaped open, this time I don't give in to the rules of this game. Luckily, she caves in to my charm or at least my stunned helplessness.

"Well, if you want the truth, maybe you should just take another shot or..." she giggles, "...maybe even two shots."

Oh shit! I bring the shot glass to my mouth and drink it down, swaying forward and widening my eyes partly from her confession as well as the alcohol.

"If it makes you feel any better, the first time she met you she gave me a thumbs-up when she hugged you," she goes on, bringing on a whole new level of mortification.

I toss another back, knowing at this rate, I may not be able to stand in the next few minutes. *I need something good that will make her ready to end this game.* I look over at her, studying her for minute. My eyes go in and out of focus, but I see the hint of her beautiful smile on her face as she looks at me waiting, and one image comes to mind.

"Ok, so ..." Bringing this up isn't the easiest, but I want her to know this regardless of the game. "You were the last thing I saw when I wrecked," I pause, watching her face change to astonishment laced with longing and love. I go on as if it were yesterday, "I had an image of you in my mind. You were sitting in that old fishing boat out on the lake. It was the day we went fishing and the sun was shining down on you while you talked about your dad."

I can barely think, hardly sit upright, but one thing I can do is see that image plain as day and also how much it means to her. She confirms my thoughts by jumping out of her seat and smoothly sliding into my lap. The heat from her skin moves over my legs as I instinctively wrap my hands around her waist and hold her as tight as I can. Before I can add my last bit of information, her lips are on mine and I nearly say the hell with it all. *I so want to take her to the bedroom right now.* Sliding my hands up to cradle her face, I move my mouth in sync with hers until she pulls away. She stares back at me, so I move in for the kill with the last bit of information that I never got around to telling her, but something that I am ready to share with her now.

"Do you know that the day I got out of the hospital, my first trip was to my mom's wishing well? I sat down on that bench and relived every single second of our two weeks together. So I guess both of our moms know everything." My heart swells with love for her as I say the words.

Her arms close in around my neck, steadying me then she says the words I've waited all night to hear.

"Let's go to my bedroom. I think it's time to turn this into a party for two, don't you?"

Finally!

She gets up first, giggling as she side-steps then regains her footing. I watch her, knowing it may be a losing battle for me to attempt to walk. Clearly reading my mind, she grabs my arm and places it over her shoulder, helping me to my feet. Halfway up, I feel a little silly and foolish for drinking so much.

"I think I got it," I say as we get to the living room.

"You sure?" She looks over to me and I nod. "Ok, well, we might as well stay here tonight so I'm going to tell Abby that we are going to bed and make sure everyone stays out."

After she slips away, I spot Bethany in the middle of the floor dancing between a couple of guys. She makes eye contact with me, winking before she looks away. *What the hell. I really cannot stand her.* Taking a page from her book, I disappear into Alyssa's room, grab up a fuzzy scarf that is lying on her nightstand and tie it to the door knob. Not that this makes a difference to her intrusive ass, but maybe eventually she will get the point that she doesn't stand a chance. Holding steady at the door, I wait for Alyssa to return, casually making eye contact with Bethany then down to the scarf. *Shove that in her conniving ass face.* I sway and grin as she curls up her lips, looking pissed.

The minutes click by until Alyssa returns, and my mind gets hazier as the night treads on. My eyes are weighted down as if someone is slowly soldering them closed, my head is sunk into the pillow and Alyssa's fragile petite naked body is molded to mine. My hand traces a pattern back and forth from her waist to her shoulder with a million goose bumps forming beneath my touch. I'm aware that my mouth is moving and I can even hear the quiet murmur of my voice, but I'm unable to muster up the brain power to figure out what is spilling from it. She moves away suddenly, barely unhitching our bodies, but I pull her in tighter. *I don't want her to move. I need her close.*

Opening my mouth, I try to relay to her how much I love her, but it sounds as if I'm underwater and I'm not even sure words are coming out. Her body suddenly slides against mine with her legs falling to each side of my waist. No sooner that her lips and tongue join mine, I am fully awake and aroused. All amounts of drowsiness and fogginess are pushed to the wayside, as I pull her flush against me.

"I thought you were tired," she breaths out as my mouth slides over the skin of her jaw like there is a candy coating over her body that I am determined to devour.

"I'm not *that* tired," I inform her as I alternate between quick breaths and tasting her skin.

In one swift motion, I flip her over, a dizzy sensation bouncing through my head as I move further down her body with my tongue. My arms and mouth damn near feel numb, but as she whimpers, every fiber in my body catches fire and sends my heart into overdrive along with a rush of blood to my lower half.

She breathes out a loud moan as I grind against her. "I need to put the scarf on the door."

"I already did," I gasp out over her skin as I work my way back to her mouth, sliding my hands slowly over the curve of her waist across to her stomach and down until her whimpers slowly become pleasure-full cries the more my fingers move.

Just listening to her breath speed up and watching her chest heave in and out beneath me has alarms screaming inside my head ... *Now ... Now ... Now.*

I can't wait. Pulling my hand up to her waist, I slide it behind her as she arcs her back up and brings her body closer to me in an effort to have my lips back on hers; so I do. One shift and shock waves barrel through me as her mouth opens and her head slams back into the pillow. I watch her, enamored with every movement she makes, every moan, and with the way her eyebrows dip down as if it feels so good that it hurts.

Her mouth remains open, letting out a sharp breathy whimper

with each thrust, but I can no longer just watch. I capture her breaths with my lips, slipping my tongue into her mouth in a crushing kiss that makes me crave even more of her. Her breathing speeds up as I move faster and as she trails her hands to my hips, pulling me against her with an excitable force. I arch my back, dipping my head down to her chest and slowly running my tongue over her nipple. She trembles beneath me and lets out a loud moan but I don't stop.

Her body melts for a moment as I keep moving, a fiery sizzling burst of sensations gradually building within my core. It heightens and heightens making me squeeze my eyes shut and clasp the sheet beside her waist in my fist. Every inch of my body tenses as Alyssa wiggles against me, bringing on more sensations that I can barely handle before my body is quivering in delight and a loud groan ruptures from within me. My arms simultaneously give out as I crash on top of her with my face in her neck, breathing in strawberries and the salty scent of her sweat. My skin is aware of every movement, every single brush of her skin against mine as my tremors slow.

I gently slide to her side, kissing her shoulder, and pulling her with me so that we can remain close the whole night. My eyes get heavier and all I can hear is steady puffs of air as my chest rises and falls along with Alyssa's soft, subtle breaths. Gradually, my body slips as if I am falling into a blanket of darkness further and further with no end.

I have no idea how long I sleep when hands roam up my chest and around my neck, locking our bodies together again. I keep my eyes closed and enjoy the explosive currents coursing through me. At this point, I'm not even sure I'm awake, but I can hear Alyssa's whimpers and I can smell her skin. My hands smooth over the rose petal softness of her thighs and I can feel her on me, moving slowly.

Suddenly twisting my body, Alyssa is beneath me and she lets out another loud moan as I pull her so tight against me that I swear we are one body.

"You feel so good," I barely make out my own words. "I'm not going to stop."

And I don't.

I keep us sealed together, basking in the most incredible and over-powering feelings, yet as my heart verges on explosive, my mind remains hazy with my eyes welded shut. *Am I dreaming?*

Time slips by in a storm of blurry images of Alyssa against me, beneath me and on top of me and every second I devour her, taste her and indulge in the warmth of our body's closeness. I whisper things I've never said before to her all through the night, wanting her to know how she makes me feel and just as I begin to slip into the fogginess of sleep, the heat from her skin rouses me again.

After what seems like a marathon, my heartbeat begins to slow and my breathing calms as I settle back into the softness of the mattress with her still clasped in my arms. I don't think I've separated from her since I crawled into this bed. Stretching my eyebrows up, I struggle to open my eyes, to sober up and stay awake. I've never been this drunk.

"I'll be back..." I think I say; at least the vibrations of words move over my tongue.

With a good deal of effort and with a heavy weight still tugging at my eyelids, my feet manage to find solid ground, yet my legs are rubbery and unstable. I brace my hand on a hard surface nearby and push up, my knees nearly buckling beneath me before I gain control. *I got this.*

After the difficult task of using the restroom while turned on, plus being unable to clearly see anything within a six inch radius, I stumble back into the bedroom, bumping my shoulder on the door frame and my feet catching on something crunchy.

"I'm so tired ... I think I'm still drunk too," I say aloud as my head spins and my legs shake.

My shins finally hit the side of the mattress and I know I've made it back to bed.

"Over here," her sweet voice calls out from behind me. "You're going to fall if you don't open your eyes."

Forcing them open, I take in Bethany's sloppy side of the room. I glance down and barely make out the shape of a soda cup hanging onto my foot. *What the hell is up with cups always being on the damn floor?* I snicker, shake the nasty cup from my foot and turn the other way.

"You need to switch beds with her. Going back and forth between our apartments, I can't keep this straight," I mumble quietly, ready to lie back down.

I slink down between the sheets and naturally pull her to me, the silky tender flesh of her breasts brushing over my chest and molding to me.

"I keep having these wild dreams about you. Then I'll feel you beside me and I can't control myself. I'm not complaining about the dreams or waking up at all hours of the night with you, but don't ever let me drink that much again."

As soon as the words are out of my mouth, sleep reaches out and tugs me under into complete darkness and silence, until a new dream interrupts my peaceful slumber.

She's gone

ALYSSA SUDDENLY STIRS BESIDE me and I want her more than I've ever wanted anything in my life. It's as if my heart will stop beating if I am not joined to her in some physical way. Her soft touch moves across my abs then two thighs slide to either side of my hips. I'm instantly turned on at the thought of being so close to her again.

I move my hands to grip her waist and guide her, trying to will my exhausted eyes open. A slight moan fills my eardrums and has me wide awake in an instant. My eyes shoot open just as I hear a gasp over my shoulder. Bethany's naked body is straddling me and she looks just as shocked as I am. I waste no time shoving her off.

"What the hell!" I yell before realizing the gasp from the doorway is Alyssa.

I'm in utter shock. *What the hell happened! How?!* One minute I was dreaming of Alyssa on me and the next overly-obsessed Bethany is putting in motion her plan to destroy my life. *Where the hell was Alyssa? I thought she was in bed with me.* Instantly, my mind starts running through the entire night, panicked.

I jump to my feet, ripping the sheet off the bed and tearing my jeans up from the floor.

"This isn't what it looks like!" I plead pointing to Bethany lying in her bed. I flinch my head back to look at the bed then over to Alyssa's bed. *What the hell! Why am I in Bethany's bed? Did I sleep walk?*

"Alyssa, I'm so sorry. He got into bed with me after you … one thing led to another. It all happened … and then we just got carried away. I'm so sorry!"

Her words ignite a fury inside of me that verges on destructive. I angrily toss my head from side-to-side, my glands about ready to pop from the amount of adrenaline raging through them.

"I did not! Don't even make up some bullshit like that!" I point to Bethany, who has a whiney-ass-fake-as-hell-wounded look on her face that I am not falling for. *She knew what she was doing.* Turning to Alyssa still in the doorway, I plead for her to believe me and not her psychotic roommate, "God no, Alyssa … this is not what it looks like. I did not do anything with her."

She stares at me in utter disbelief and shock and for a minute I want to yell at her that her friend is a complete liar, a cheat and a complete fraud, but all I care about is her looking me in the eyes right now; to really look at me. She knows I would never do this to her.

"Alyssa, you have to believe me, please. I was asleep and I just woke up and she was …"

She looks back and forth between her bed and Bethany's and I know without a doubt what she wants to know, but she already knows the answer. It's not the first time I've mistakenly turned the wrong direction in mid-sleep. My bed's on that side at my apartment so naturally, when I'm not thinking or semi-unconscious I tend to go with old habits. I look back at her bed, my heart aching that I have to defend myself from this. *There is no way I could have … could I?* It crosses my mind for only a second but I dismiss it.

"What was going on? Did you two …"

I don't even let her finish, "Hell no, we did not! I would never do that to you!" I yell louder than I should as she turns to look at Bethany.

"Bethany?" her soft voice is thick with sadness and pain.

Bethany doesn't answer right away, but I cannot even bring myself to look at her. My mind flies through the night of all the dreams I had and how half the time, I swear I was making love to Alyssa, but then the other half I could hardly tell whether I was awake. *God, there is no way I could have mistaken …*

"I am so sorry. I didn't mean for it to happen. It just did," Bethany starts, jerking me out of my spiraling thoughts.

"You're lying! I didn't touch you!" I holler out as she remains situated in her bed with the sheet clasped around her body. Just the sight of her makes me sick.

She goes on as if I'm not hell bent on proving her wrong, "As soon as you left, I came in to sleep in my bed of course, and Judd walked over and got in beside me. It wasn't like me and Kyle, he initiated this, I promise. You have to believe me."

I drop my head into my palms and squeeze my eyes shut, anger and regret surging through my veins, into my heart and dragging me into a pool of shame.

"There it is," I whisper to myself, shaking my head in disbelief.

This was her plan, all along. How could I be so stupid and not just tell Alyssa from the start? I grit my teeth as she goes on, a throbbing sensation shooting through my jaw and down my neck.

"The night you walked in on me and Kyle. I assumed you always knew. I was just jealous and we both got drunk and it just happened. That was my fault, but this time is different. He got into my bed. I thought he wanted me and so …"

No way is she twisting this around.

"I do not want her and I did not crawl into her bed to be with her. I was half asleep and half drunk and just got into the wrong bed," I shout while glaring at Bethany then back to Alyssa. *She is not winning here! I will not lose Alyssa! I can't!*

She backs away a bit, taking on a defiant stance that I haven't seen since the night we got back together. *No, please, no.* Her eyes are bloodshot, but her facial features are etched in sadness.

"You did crawl into her bed though!"

"Yeah, but I …" I try to justify my actions that I was half asleep and it was a simple mix up, but Bethany's shrill voice interrupts.

"He got in and I had no idea .. "

I refuse to let her play the victim here.

"You're a liar! I would never touch you!" I shout out until the blood vessels in my neck and face may burst. Holding my trembling hand up, I beg Alyssa to listen. "Alyssa, please. If you would just listen to me …"

She looks down at the floor, not even willing to look me in the eyes. It crushes me; destroys me.

"Have you been screwing her this whole time? Is that what was so urgent that you needed to talk to me about last night? What, you needed to get it off your chest?"

What the hell! The simple fact that she would ask something like that infuriates me and tells me I've already lost this battle. *Why didn't I tell her when I had the chance?!* I'm not giving up, though.

Stumbling all over myself for the right words and still in sheer shock, my voice comes out harsh, "No! Why would you ask that?! You know I love you!" That is the one thing I know with absolute certainty through this whole crazy mix-up. I love her!

She steps away, ripping my heart right out of my chest with the distance. Glancing up, she looks over to Bethany with pleading eyes.

"We only had sex this one time. Other than that all we have done is kiss. He kissed me the other night after we went shopping for costumes but that's it."

God no! This was it the whole time! I played right into her hands by not saying anything!

"No! Wait! That is not true! She's lying! I did not ..."

Her voice clips me off and I swear I've never had the urge to hit a girl before, until now.

"I told him that I was the one that slept with Kyle and that I would not hurt you like that again. That's when he ..."

That was her plan and she made damn sure to beat me to the punch so that I wouldn't be able to defend myself.

"Wait a minute! I did not ..."

"Did you kiss her? Did you know that about her and Kyle? Answer me!" she yells, cutting me off before I can explain, and technically I can't explain because I screwed up.

I should have told her. I should have known Bethany would pull something like this if she was bold enough to kiss me, with Alyssa just in the other room.

"It's not like that. Please, this is all getting blown out of proportion," I plead with her, determined to make her understand, plus frantic to understand everything that happened this morning myself.

I barely get to finish before an outraged Alyssa bolts out of the bedroom, into the kitchen and towards the front door. My bare feet pound against the carpet behind her, hitting wet spots periodically where someone has soaked it with alcohol. This seems too familiar and a place I never thought I'd be again.

"Would you wait? This is not how it looks!"

She gives me an angry glare with her eyebrows drawn down right before she slams the door in my face. Reaching for it, I quickly halt, nearly colliding into it. Slamming my hand to the door knob, I hear one sound and I nearly come unglued.

"Judd, wait," Bethany calls out from behind me.

My whole body tenses as I rip the door open, not even caring if I detach it from the hinges at this point. *She would be best to stay the hell away from me.*

Snapping my head around, I see Piper stirring on the couch and Bethany standing in the doorway to the bedroom only covered by her sheet.

"You're a damn liar!" My jaw is concrete and my teeth grind so hard I'm sure I may break a tooth. I don't even wait for her to reply.

Speeding through the door and out of the complex I catch up with Alyssa in a mad dash to get in her car. *I can't let her go! What the hell do I do? I can't lose her!* Right on her heels, every nerve in my body is in a panic. *Where is she going? Don't go, don't go … I'll do anything.* My mind races and swerves over things to say, but all I want to do is hold her and beg her to stay.

She bends to get into the car and my arms function completely on their own by surrounding her waist in an urgent and terrified grip.

"Lyssa, please let me explain. This is all wrong," I say, burying my face in her hair.

She flinches at my touch, retracting her stomach away from my fingertips and making my heart shatter into oblivion as she spins around out of my grasp.

Her beautiful blue eyes are ice cold and I know, without a doubt she is not going to listen to anything I have to say. I'm helpless to everything but watching her go, and that kills me.

"Then, explain!" she screams with so much animosity that I find myself flinching from the pain this whole situation is causing my heart. Her voice softens and her eyes fill with tears, pooling until they slip out one by one in a steady stream. "You were in her bed; you were naked and she was naked on top of you." Her voice holds so much sorrow that it impels my soul and, my chest wall closes in slowly and irreversibly. "I could see, Judd. You were turned on while she was on you."

I shake my head slowly; my own eyes stinging with pending tears. I want to deny it all, but the part that hurts the most, aside from seeing her pain, is that I don't know what is true and what isn't. Everything she is saying is correct, yet I cannot and will not believe for a second that I had sex with Bethany. I would have known it wasn't Alyssa, despite how drunk or sleepy I was. There is no amount of unconsciousness that could make me hurt her like that.

She goes on, her cheeks soaked with tears, "She said you two kissed the other night. She said you knew about her and Kyle."

I don't know what to say. My mouth won't cooperate to explain that this is exactly what I have tried to tell her the last two days; this is what was so urgent. Words leave me and I stand there stunned and silent, reaching for her until my hands fall back against her waist. I want to beg her to stay, to plead with her but all I manage to do is shake my head in denial; denial that this is happening, denial of how such a beautiful night with her could take such a miserable turn.

Her delicate features flare into a heated glare as she shoves me away.

"So please, explain all that!"

I can't stay silent; she has to listen to me. My mind is a hurricane of horror as I imagine her walking away and never coming back to me.

"Alyssa, I was going to. Please, you know me. Let's just go inside and talk about this? I would never hurt you ... I love you," I say calm, knowing this may be my last chance as she inches back towards the doorframe of the car.

My left hand still clutches to the fabric at her waist, holding on for dear life as if I will cease to breathe if this last cord is clipped. She glances down at my hand then back at my face with a look of hatred. My body goes numb and what's left of my heart crumbles to dust.

Jerking backwards out of my reach, the fabric slips from my fingers as my eyes mist over.

"Save it! I refuse to be played for a fool anymore! I can't do this!" she spits out as she jumps into the car, pulling the door closed as a barrier between us.

My hands fall to the window frame and I grip it with a force I didn't even realize I had in me. Just as my mouth opens to implore her to stay and to hear me out, she looks up into my eyes with a look of loss and heartbreak; a pain I know I'm the cause of. *I did this. I was so determined to keep her from any extra amount of hurt that me not saying anything brought us both right here; to this.*

"Goodbye, Judd. Just let me go ..." she says so softly, the pleading in her tone shooting through me until all I can do is slowly and hesitantly respect her request.

My hand falls to my side at the same time as the tears slowly seep from my eyes, dripping down my cheeks.

"Lyssa, please ..." I begin in one last effort to make her stay, but as the engine revs and her car pulls away, I know there is no effort good enough. *I've lost her and it's all my fault.*

The car gets further and further away, shredding every ounce of happiness in my soul into nothing.

I have nothing without her.

I want to shout out and beg her to come back.

I want to run after her until my feet can't hold me up.

I want to pound my fist into the brick wall of her complex, hoping the pain in my hand will lessen the ache in my heart.

But instead of giving into my anger and hurt, I look at the window of their apartment and know there is only one thing I can do at this point; get to the bottom of this bullshit. Storming up to her apartment, I try to focus on controlling my temper instead of thinking about the fact that I may have lost her forever. If I think about that then there is no doubt that I will lose it and unleash all my fury on Bethany.

I twist the door knob and walk back in, immediately coming eye-to-eye with her exiting her bedroom, fully clothed with a content look on her face like she just won a major victory. *What a bitch!* My forehead creases, my lips are curled and my brows dip so low that the hairs come into my line of sight. Opening my mouth, I am fully prepared to go off, but then she quietly points to Piper asleep on the couch, shushes me with her fingers over her mouth and turns to go back in her room. *That's the last place I want to be with her!*

Letting out a strained sigh, because right now it is tough to breathe with this vice clamped down on my heart, I move my feet forward knowing I need to still get my shirt and shoes. I also have no intention of leaving without confronting her even though I doubt she'll be honest. There isn't much that will convince me that she didn't plan this.

I pass by the couch, glancing at Piper curled into a ball and sleeping soundly as if all hell didn't just break loose only minutes ago. Walking through the threshold of the bedroom that has held painful memories as well as absolutely amazing moments, all the rage and fury from this morning amplifies as I hear her whiney voice.

"Judd, I am so sorry for what happened. I don't know how it happened. Just one minute I was in my bed and the next …"

Widening my eyes, I cut her off with a sudden added rush of ferocity brewing inside me, "Don't give me that crap. You knew exactly what you were doing. Was this your grand master plan?" I spit out as I tear my shirt up off the ground and throw it over my head quickly.

"What?!" Bethany jumps off Alyssa's bed where she has been perched and for some reason seeing her near that bed makes my anger blaze. "Like I had any control over you crawling into bed with me. Remember, you were in my bed?" she slowly, raises one eyebrow and places her hands firmly on her hips, as if her sternness will have some sort of power over convincing me.

"You know that was an accident. I wouldn't have gotten into your bed on purpose, especially if I knew you were in it. I'm with Alyssa and I love her. I don't feel a damn thing for you!"

"Well you've gotten into my bed before … on your own." She crosses her arms, eyeing me and making my skin crawl with just the thought of …

"Yeah, again … I was drunk off my ass and trust me, it wasn't on my own accord. If I had full mobility at that moment, I would have run far away from your crazy ass."

She huffs out a laugh and I take a deep breath, trying my best to not let her rile me up any further. Grabbing my phone off the nightstand and shoving it in my back pocket, I glance at it briefly to see if maybe Alyssa has called. Completely irritated, but with a bit of renewed calm, I try to get to the bottom of this whole situation so I can go find Alyssa.

"Listen, Bethany, I don't know what your angle is here. Bottom line, I love Alyssa and I'll tell you right now, even if you and I were the last two humans left on Earth and the weight of the human race fell upon our shoulders to rebuild the population, personally, I think I'd prefer all of mankind to die out, all together …" shrugging, I stare at her, "… but that's just me."

She squints her eyes as I speak and her innocent expression turns darker with a hint of hostility and hatred. *It's about damn time.*

I go on a little further, needing some answers, "With that said and with you now understanding that you will never stand a chance, because I love Alyssa and Alyssa only … I need to know, what happened?"

She opens her mouth, quick to answer me and all I see waiting in her eyes is lies. I hold my hand up to halt her, before she goes over all the same crap she spewed in front of Alyssa.

"And I repeat, even if you are hell bent on lying about everything, even that won't make me want you, but tell me honestly what happened and at least you can spare yourself the humiliation of everyone knowing what a conniving, manipulative person you are." I grit my teeth as I spit out the word 'person', because there are far more impolite terms I could use for her at this point.

Her lips snarl and for the first time, I swear I see something different in her eyes as she looks at me; animosity and fear.

She continues standing between the beds with her hands tightly folded over her chest and her hands clinched into fists. My brows, mouth and jaw are all permanently locked into an enraged grimace with my own fists balled so forcefully that my knuckles have turned white as I unhitch them to grab up my shoes and socks.

Bethany remains silent as I stand back up, fixing my glare back on her.

"Well?"

Clearing her throat, I brace myself to hear the truth; to actually know that I did not touch her. Anxiety climbs into my throat and my eyebrows quiver with the thought that this whole morning was some sick joke.

Her expression softens and hope leaps through me as she finally speaks up, "What I said was true."

My entire world takes a nose dive with her words, crashing in an explosion of astonishment, anguish and shame. I grip my shoes in my hand with such force that it could nearly break my fingers in two.

"The truth!" I spit out, still not believing her. "I think I would know if we had …" nausea barrels through me.

"It is the truth. We were together. We had …"

I am not going to listen to this, "Together? I've never been *together* with you! Stop saying we did! There is no way! I would know if we had!" My mind races through any sort of blurred, alcohol generated delusions that I can find, but I find nothing. "I did not touch you. I wouldn't have! Quit lying!"

My head throbs and my body quakes in horror like some cruel nightmare that I cannot force myself to wake up from. *We didn't! We couldn't have!*

"Judd, we did. It was only for a little while, but we did … we had sex."

That single word shoots right through my heart, slaughtering any hope I had for getting Alyssa back. *I've lost her. She's gone.*

Believe

I DON'T DARE GIVE Bethany any more of my time. If what she said is true, if I did touch her while I was asleep and still half intoxicated, then I do deserve to lose Alyssa, but I just cannot believe I did. My mind developed a case of black-out-drunk-amnesia right in the most crucial moment for me to remember every detail, not that I would want to if what she said is true. I could punch myself for drinking at all last night.

Slamming the door of my truck, I sink into the seat and push back hard against the headrest with my eyes held closed and my mind on a constant cycle of replaying everything that I can remember from last night until this morning.

The buzz from an incoming text message has my eyes springing open and my whole body rocketing forward to get it out of my pocket and see if it is her. *Please let it be her, wanting to talk.* Finally getting it out of my back pocket, my eyes focus on the message that lights up my lock screen and my heart sinks.

Evan: Hey, when you decide to join the living give me a shout. I'm running into work today to get a few things done and wanted to see if you were up for some overtime?

My hand tightens and I stare at it with absolutely no motivation to answer him right now. I'm not even sure if I could think about work at this point. A movement flickers from the corner of my eyes and I turn my head to look over to the sidewalk in front of the complex. Kyle stands near the doorway in a deep discussion with Piper, who must have finally woke up.

Looking back at my phone, I decide to hell with waiting. She may hang up but I have to try.

After tapping on her name at the top of my recent call list, I shove the hard face of my phone to my ear and wait, silently counting each ring until I hear her voicemail message.

"Hi, this is Alyssa. Leave a message."

I have no clue what to say, but with no particular thought in mind, my mouth opens and everything I thought I didn't know to say, spills out.

"Lyssa … I know you're not going to pick up and I know you need time, but please know that I am so confused about all of this. I have no memory of anything and I have no idea how this could've happened. I know you are hurt and you have every right, but please call me back. Please don't end it like this! Let's talk about it all and try to figure it out together. I … I know saying sorry isn't good enough, but I will do anything and everything to fix this. You have to …"

… If you are satisfied with your message, press two…

The automated voice cuts me off and I hang up out of frustration, immediately pressing her name to call her back.

"Hi, this is Alyssa. Leave a message."

My heart aches as I listen to her sweet voice. *God, I wish she was in my arms.* Starting to leave another message, I catch a movement near my window and turn instantly to see Piper, smiling right outside my truck door. Holding my finger in the air, I signal for her to wait one second as I begin to speak.

"Sorry. I guess I better make this a little shorter. Please call me, Lyssa. I love you. You have to know that! I know you need time and I know you are hurt so I will wait as long as I have to, but please call me. I can't lose you. I love you. Bye."

After hanging up, I swing my door open and step out to see what Piper was wanting. She stands patiently by the bed of my truck, her hands dangling at her sides, her hair a wild slept in mess and still outfitted in her costume from last night. Aware of me walking up behind her, she spins around with a gloomy look on her face and my heart flips with the thought of her going off on me for the sake of her best friend's sister.

"Hey," I say quietly, shoving my hands in my pockets and looking down to the ground. *Damn, I need to remember what happened.* "Listen, I know Alyssa is hurt and she has every right to be, but I swear I don't think I …"

Piper cuts me off quickly, moving forward and grabbing my arm in a tender gesture, "Judd, I'm not going to pry into the whole ordeal that happened this morning. That's between you and her."

I look at her dumbfounded, probably with my mouth hung open. She immediately reads into my reaction.

"Yes, I heard dang near all of it. Kind of hard not to with all the shouting and doors slamming, but hey, it doesn't concern me. Besides, I was half awake/half asleep so I could have heard some things wrong."

She offers me a gentle smile then folds her arms over her chest, looking down as I stare at her in surprise. I've barely said a word to Piper since I've met her, but just this small interaction tells me so much more than I've ever known about her. Something about her expression suddenly seems lost, sad and lonely; nearly the same look I see on Tristan's face from time to time.

"I wanted to tell you that Abby left me a note that says they went to the hospital."

My heart slams to the ground as if it's been ripped from my chest. "What happened? Is it her dad?" I ask in a panic, ten seconds from bolting to the hospital without a single thought of whether Alyssa wants to see me or not.

"Yeah, it is. I don't know all the details. I just texted Abby briefly and they don't know everything, yet."

I turn to get in my truck, before she finishes, but her hand once again falls on my shoulder.

"Wait," she calls out as I turn to look at her. Not too far behind her I catch sight of Kyle coming out of the apartment complex, straining to carry the empty keg and struggling to talk on his phone with his head bent to the side, pressing the phone into his shoulder.

Piper's voice knocks me out of my daze along with all the questions I wish I could ask Kyle about the night Bethany sank her teeth into him. "I know you want to race over there, but let them face this as a family first. Maybe at least call her later," she sighs, looking at me as if it is hard for her to advise me to spare Alyssa's feelings right now. "I just think if Alyssa is dealing with this, maybe she won't be able to handle much else. You know …" she crinkles her nose up and stops talking.

I smile, grateful for the advice, but still desperate to go to Alyssa. *What can I do? Piper's right.* I can't put more on her right now. Last thing Alyssa needs to deal with is what happened this morning when she could be facing the toughest moment in her life. My heart squeezes as if someone's fist is sunk into my chest, crushing it to nothing. Not only do I want to be there for her, but her father filled a piece of my heart that has been empty for so long. I can't stay away. I've never had the opportunity to say goodbye to anyone I loved before. I know this isn't about me, but I need to thank Alex.

Piper looks at me with a questioning expression as if she's fearful that she hurt my feelings.

"No, I agree. You're right, but is there any way that maybe I could get Abby's number?" It's a long shot that Abby will be very happy to hear from me, and ultimately it will be putting added stress on her as well if she feels the need to defend her sister's honor, but I'm hoping I can at least have a civil conversation with her about her dad. Piper sidesteps uneasily, studying my face as if she's contemplating what to do. I give her a strained smile and finally, she smiles back.

"Ok … but if she's pissed off, you didn't get it from me." She holds her hand out and I immediately hand her my phone so she can enter the number in.

I watch as she carefully adds Abby's name and number as a new contact. Handing it back, I peer down and am ready to call right this second.

"Just wait until later today maybe, ok?" I snap my head up and want to disagree totally, but I don't. Instead, I nod, agreeing to her terms. "And don't upset her," she adds sternly.

A scraping sound pierces my ears and I turn my head to see Kyle situating the keg in the back of his truck before slamming the tailgate shut.

"Ok, I'll see you around." Piper darts off with a warm smile and jumps in a car a couple spaces over from mine.

Slowly turning to leave, my mind swims with questions that I have no answers for, my heart is heavy with worry for Alyssa and her family and my entire body vibrates with an unsettled feeling that I cannot pinpoint. Searching the ground as I move to the door of my truck, I look up and catch a subtle nod from Kyle as he jumps in his truck. *What the hell.*

Lifting my hand, I holler out in his direction, "Hey, wait up."

He looks surprised, still grasping the door handle of his vehicle as I take long strides to join him and hopefully gain some comprehension on what could have possibly transpired in those few unconscious moments that were robbed from me this morning.

"Hey, man. How are you feeling today? You were pretty wasted last night," Kyle pipes up as I walk towards him, but I'm in no mood for pleasantries. I just want to get to the bottom of this whole Bethany situation.

"I'm fine. I have some questions for you," I say, getting right to the point as I automatically fold my hands across my chest.

He puts his hand up between us as if he's prepared to hold me back, like I may attack him. This amuses me, but the emotions swirling in my heart and head hold back any ounce of laughter I could possibly have left.

"Listen, about that call this summer ... I really am sorry. I was in a bad place and I ...."

Lowering my brows, I quickly correct him so we can move on, "No, it has nothing to do with that," I pause, watching him slowly nod in understanding. "I actually wanted to know about the night you slept with Bethany." I put it out there plain as day and wait, staring at him as his face shifts from shocked to uncomfortable and nervous.

"Man, did you tell Alyssa? She is going to hate me."

"No, I didn't. The other participant from that night broke it to her in a rather blunt and shitty way this morning." I really don't want to dive into what happened between me and her out of fear that he may view her as being back on the market, but I don't see how I can avoid it.

"Ahhh, shit! What the hell. She's the last person I thought …"

"Kyle, I don't really care about whether my girlfriend hates you or not and the last thing I want to discuss with her is what went down that night, but I really need some answers so I can straighten something out." He has no reason to answer my questions as bitter as I'm being, but after all he stole from me this summer it's hard to pretend to be buddies.

"What do you want to know?"

His simple remark surprises me, but I go for it and make it as uncomplicated as possible, "Did you actually sleep with her." He looks at me, baffled, so I rephrase my question, "Do you remember everything that happened?"

He takes a deep breath, staring me down, obviously hesitant to be so open with me.

"Listen, that night was the biggest mistake I've ever made. I've stood by knowing my dad has cheated on my mom for as long as I can remember, so that," he raises his eyebrows and although I want to stop all the get-to-know-me bullshit, I let him go on, "… it is not something I'm proud of. I'll always regret it happening, but yes, I remember it and wish I didn't."

He stops talking but I still need to know more. I just cannot believe that I slept with Bethany. There is no way. I don't care what she says; I don't believe it. Kyle shifts uneasily, clearly as uncomfortable as me.

Just as I'm about to urge him to go on, he opens his mouth to elaborate, "All night I kept texting Alyssa to come to the party, but she insisted that she had plans with her family. I had no idea about her father's heath at that time." He looks at me, defeated and beat down and my heart drops to my stomach, knowing that Alyssa may be facing the tail end of that pain-stricken journey right now as we speak.

"After being shot down for the twentieth time, I drug myself to bed, frustrated and barely able to form a thought. I have no idea how long I was in bed, but I woke up with someone on me and we were already … you know. I was so wasted that nothing really registered until I heard someone else walk in … that's pretty much when I realized the person in bed with me was not Alyssa, the person who walked in, was her."

He looks over to Alyssa's bedroom window which faces the parking lot and a bolt of jealousy slices through me with the thought that he is probably thinking about her right now and how he wishes that night had never happened. I can't say that I blame him, considering that is exactly the feeling that is engulfing me at this very moment, but I still would rather not have the knowledge of when of he is strolling down memory lane. It's bad enough that he told me he went to bed frustrated after texting Alyssa that night. I know exactly what that means and why he wanted her there. My jaw tightens and my stomach knots, but I remain quiet, hoping to gain some insight into Bethany's manipulative ways.

"When I came back up to my room that is when I was finally sober enough to recognize all that had happened and that's when I got slammed with the drunken fact that I had not only cheated, but that it was with her best friend. I was so ashamed..." He looks over at me and I shift my feet, a truck load of trepidation washing over me. "... but the kicker was when I told her to get out and that what happened shouldn't have ... her response ..." staring right at me with his jaw clamped tight in what looks like anger, he goes on in a bitter tone, "If I can't have you, neither can she." He sighs and glances back at her window. "After that, she called me, bugged the shit out of me and would not give it a rest. I knew Alyssa would hate me for life if she knew, so I stayed quiet. I should have told her," he shrugs.

With a deep sigh, I relent and do something I shouldn't, but something that is weighing so heavily on my heart at this moment that I fear I may explode. I tell Kyle about what happened, about my absence of memory, about waking up much as he did and finding out I may have done something unforgivable. Dread slowly slithers over me with each word that flows from my mouth as I wonder if he will see this as a window of opportunity.

After starting from the beginning and ending with my discussion with Piper, he studies my face with a confused, almost thoughtful expression; much different from what I expected.

"Do you think you did?"

I look down at my feet and subtly kick a pebble with the tip of my shoe. Flexing my jaw muscles in frustration, I hold back the desire to catapult that stone clear across the parking lot with the amount of disappointment and irritation that is surging through my veins.

"No!" I snap then fling the stone a good five feet in front of me. "I don't know. She said we did, but that's like trusting Satan with your soul."

Folding his arms across his chest, Kyle lets out a breathy chuckle, "Isn't that the truth. I wouldn't trust anything she says. I'd go with your gut instinct on this one. Man, and here I thought she was determined to ruin my life and all along it's Alyssa that she is hell bent on annihilating."

Nodding my head slowly, I let his words sink in. "Yeah, it was real weird how she told Alyssa about you two. I mean completely cornering me, like she planned this whole morning out. Like she sat down and strategized it as if she was going off to war or something."

He and I both stare dead ahead, possibly thinking over the same fact. *How the hell did we not see through her?!*

"Who the hell needs enemies, when your girlfriend has a friend like her?" Kyle says in a bland tone. I don't see how he held this in for so long. I have no proof of the fact that I did not sleep with her, but I am about to burst with the need to get the truth out of her. *I refuse to believe what she says.*

Day by Day

AFTER A QUICK SEE-YA-LATER, Kyle and I part ways and I head towards the office. My head is whirling with everything that has happened and although I'm only a block away from the site of the new mall, my heart and soul are actually a couple miles away, beating in despair for Alyssa.

Once I pull into the lot, relief floods every ounce of my body when I see Evan and Mr. Jansen making their rounds over the site. Frankly, the last thing I feel like doing is rehashing the details of my morning to Evan, even though he is my best friend. For now, I'd rather just hide in the office. Once inside, I bury myself in work, unable to shove the ache in my heart aside, but sinking my mind into blue prints, work orders and contracts.

Looking up at the clock, I note that it has barely moved since the last time I glanced at it. *Only 11:30; the clock hates me!* Slouching down in the uncomfortable office chair with my elbows pressed into the rock-hard surface of the desk, my eyes linger to my phone which is conveniently placed face up right by the laptop so that I will have an immediate view of any incoming calls and texts. *As if she would call me after what I may have done.*

My chest retracts and my shoulders drop as a strangled, desolate sigh creeps up my throat and out my mouth, not giving me any relief from my misery. I want to call her so bad. *Screw this! I'm not going to be any good today.*

Pushing myself away from the desk, my chair rolls back until I jump up and bolt out the door to my truck, to do who knows what. I honestly have no clue where to go or what to do. My heart tells me to go to the hospital so I can be there for Alyssa, for them all, yet my mind is screaming for me not to put her through the pain of seeing me when she already has a heart wrenching road ahead. God, I'll never forgive myself if something would happen to Alex during this time; if I was unable to say goodbye. He's been the closest thing I've had to a father in a good ten years. I, at least, want the opportunity to thank him for that.

"Hey, whoa, wait up!" Evan yells, just as my hand falls upon the handle of my truck door. I squeeze it tightly, releasing some of the energy and pain of this day into it.

He jogs up behind me with a grin on his face and I'm sure some sort of wisecrack on the tip of his tongue. Looking at him with what I can only imagine as an expression that relays all my emotions for the world to see, his smile fades and his eyes widen in alarm.

"Hey, what's wrong, what happened?" Evan immediately looks around, panic taking over his features. "Oh shit, where's Alyssa? Her dad didn't …"

I shake my head instantly to stop that train of thought.

"No, as far as I know he's ok for now, besides, why would I bring Alyssa to work with me?"

The fact that we seem to be a package deal, joined together all the time in most people minds, makes me smile.

"Oh yeah. Well, either way, you look like shit. Did you guys get in a fight? Because the last time I saw that look on your face, her ex said he was taking a big bite of your cupcake."

I drop my head and look at the ground, my headache amplified. Avoiding talking to anyone else about this will be impossible. I definitely do not have a poker face.

We end up heading for lunch however my appetite is nowhere to be found. Evan chomps down on his wings without a care in the world. Barbeque sauce decorates his top lip as he gives me his complete attention, listening to me ramble on endlessly until we are headed back to the office.

I feel helpless; I should be pacing the halls of the hospital or holding her hand or screaming at Bethany to tell the truth, anything but just sitting here. This isn't helping anybody.

Evan makes a pit stop at the contractor's supply store, but I don't budge from the seat.

"You want to wait out here or come help me get some supplies?"

"I'm good here."

I slouch back, defeated and miserable in the stone cold silence of my thoughts, before hastily ripping my phone out of my pocket. Bringing up Abby's name, my fingers tremble from the possibility of her tearing me into two, with words alone.

> **Me: Hey, this is Judd. I'm sorry for texting you with everything going on but I couldn't hold back any longer. I'm worried sick about your dad and I know you have no reason to talk to me after what supposedly happened, but can you at least tell me how he is doing? Please believe me when I say I care about your family and if it was at all possible, I would be there in a heartbeat.**

I pause before hitting send, the need to ask about Alyssa burning inside of me, but also knowing I may not even have the right to ask, so I hit send without adding to the message. The seconds tick by, but less than a minute later her reply comes through, gripping my heart with the chime that sounds from my phone.

> **Abby: He is in the intensive care unit right now. Andrea is in with him at the moment. I'm going in at 3:00 and sitting with him until 5:00. I know you love my dad and he knows that, too. You'd have to be blind to have not noticed that. I'm not sure if he can hear us at this point, but I'll still tell him that you are thinking about him.**
> **Ok, so now I want to know what the hell happened this morning. Please tell me that you did not sleep with Bethany.**

Letting out a deep sigh, I drop my eyebrows in anguish. I can't even answer that question.

Me: Honestly, I don't know what happened. I wasn't even awake. I wish I knew what happened, but I've racked my brain all day and cannot remember a single thing.

Abby: Come on, Judd, you're a guy. I think you would have a clear picture of what the aftermath of having sex is!! Did you feel like you had?

This question amplifies my anxiety because the dreams I was having all through the night were pretty well equivalent to an extremely vivid wet dream.

Me: I was drunk and having some very explicit dreams so all I can say is no one would have had to work to get me to that point. The first thing I remember is something felt different than the picture that was in my mind and when I opened my eyes, there was Bethany on top of me and Alyssa standing behind the bed. I was drunk, asleep and obviously Bethany found the perfect opportunity to swoop in and destroy my whole world.

Abby: Ok, again, do you feel like you had sex with her?!! This is a simple question. Quit analyzing it and answer the question.

I nearly want to chuckle from Abby's bluntness. She sure doesn't sugar coat things.

Me: No, I don't think I did. AT ALL!! I think Bethany lied to break us up.

Abby: Well, there is your answer then. Give me some time and I'll see if can get Alyssa to talk. She hasn't said a word to me so far.

The vice on my heart tightens and all I want to do is tread concrete to get to her side.

Me: How is she?

I hit send before I realize how stupid that question is. Shaking my head, I quickly follow it up with another text.

Me: I mean, I know you all have to be scared and worried, but is she ok? I mean …

What the hell do I mean? Part of me imagines her crying uncontrollably all by herself as I text back and forth to Abby. I guess I just want assurance that what happened this morning is not in the forefront of her mind. I'd hate to be a burden on her mind that is keeping her from giving every sliver of attention she has to the situation at hand. Just as I'm about to reword my message, my phone chimes and another text comes through from Abby, as if she picked up on my brain waves.

Abby: She's sitting across from me. She's a mess, we all are, but she is a tough cookie and she'll be fine. I'll talk to her as soon as I can. My nephews just got here so I'll chit chat with you later. I go to see Dad here in a bit too. ;)

Me: Thanks, Abby.

Abby: Thanks for checking on Dad, Judd! Stick to your guns. If you don't think you did it, then don't let Bethany make you think you did. TTYL

Evan hops in the truck not even two minutes later and we are back on our way to the office to pick up my truck; once again neither of us saying a word. He may have a wisecrack 99% of the time, but he knows when to keep quiet and hold back on the jokes.

"Man this is killing me."

Evan looks at me wide eyed as if my sudden outburst took him by surprise. He raises his eyes in question as guilt, anger and regret surges through me uncontrollably.

"Just thinking about what she is going through and I'm not there!

I should be there! Damnit, Bethany! What the hell!" I kick the floor board of the truck like a toddler acting out over not getting their way. "I should have told her! I should have told her that Bethany was a lying, back-stabbing fraud of a friend! She's never been her friend! I guarantee she set this whole damn thing up. She just waited for the perfect damn opportunity and wham! There it was at the most critical point in Alyssa's life when she needs me the most! God, why didn't I tell her?!"

I toss my head back into the head rest as my eyes sting with tears. I don't even care if Evan sees me crying like a little girl. *Screw it; this hurts and I'm not going to hide it!*

"Hey man, you can beat yourself up all you want but it isn't going to do any good. I know better than anyone that it won't change anything. Honestly, I don't believe for a second that you did anything with Ms. Psycho-bitch. I mean, how long was Alyssa gone anyways? I'll admit I'm no expert on your stamina, man, but I do have ears and lately, you've been keeping my ass up for hours with your grunts and her whiny little moans." Evan shakes his head as if he's trying to rid himself of a horrible image. Any other time I'd totally want to laugh, but this definitely is not funny.

I glare over at him, furious with myself for not even knowing how long she was gone.

"I don't know how long she was gone. I didn't know she left. I didn't even remember the point when I got up and accidently fell into the wrong bed," I snap out completely flustered. "Abby said it couldn't have been more than twenty minutes tops, but…." I pause, totally humiliated that I'm going to admit this to anyone, most of all someone that likes to give me shit.

"But what?"

I glance over at him, rolling my eyes out of disbelief that I'm going to say it.

"It's just that…" I look back at him, silently warning him not to screw with me after I admit this. "I was extremely turned on all night because I kept having these really vivid dreams of me and her. I really could have sworn she was on me right at that moment, but something didn't feel right and I opened my eyes. That's when I saw…"

"Yep…the bitch," Evan finishes off my sentence in a far more appropriate way than I would have.

"Yeah and Alyssa." I slam my hand over my face, feeling a splinter of pain from her words. "Man... she even said she could see that I was turned on." I squeeze my eyes shut hoping it will erase it all.

"Ok," Evan calls out abruptly, tightly winding both his hands over the steering wheel. "So, go to the hospital."

I flinch my head back with a slight shake as his preposterous words hit me.

"What?! I can't go to the hospital. Her dad is sick. I hurt her," my voice raises as I go on, as if I'm punishing myself by yelling the words. "I cheated on her. I was caught in someone else's bed, with her best friend on top of me and she got to see it all!"

Evan cocks his head to the side with a smirk and right now, his humor is not going to budge me one bit. *I deserve to feel miserable.*

"Come on ... you don't believe you slept with her? You were drunk off your ass that night I hauled your ass to her apartment and still, you kept it all in your pants. There is no way...no way you did the deed with her. You would have known!"

His words slam into my chest, making my heart crumble and slowly sink into my churning stomach.

"I don't know. I just wish I could remember something, because at this point, all I remember is Alyssa on me in my damn dream and it felt pretty damn real."

Evan turns the key in the ignition and shifts the truck into gear.

"Well, that's it. You're going to the hospital. Yes, she may want to split your lip in two, but if anything, at least go to see her dad. Do what comes natural to you, Judd. You're a good guy and I know you love her and her family. Don't give up. Try what you can to win her back, but for now just be there, because I know your dying to."

I look to the side with my mouth hung open. *Did Evan just say something without cracking a smile? Did he just give me advice and stay completely serious?*

He sneaks a quick glance at me from the corner of his eyes and chuckles.

"What?! I can be serious," he shrugs his shoulders and makes a right onto the interstate.

I don't even know what to say.

"Just don't tell anybody." He looks at me quickly as he shifts and smiles.

I smile back and shove his shoulder, completely code for 'thank God I have a friend like you.'

Thirty minutes later and after texting Abby, I'm slipping into the intensive care unit while frantically looking around for Alyssa. I make eye contact with Abby, standing beside the door to a room with a small smile on her face, but anything other than happiness misting her eyes. Walking up beside her, she slides her arm through mine as if we are on our way to prom then she pulls me closer, keeping her voice low as she speaks.

"Hey, I'm glad you took my hint and came by," she winks.

"Thanks, Abby. Are you sure it's ok for me to sit with him? I know this is precious time for you and I don't want to steal that away from you."

Smiling, she shrugs her shoulders. "My dad isn't going anywhere, so I'll have time with him. If a nurse asks, I'll just tell them that you are my brother. I'll stay nearby until you're done."

Giving me a gentle nudge-sort-of-hug, she then let's go of my arm and I give her a thankful smile before sliding the door open. As soon as I step inside my heart falls. Alex lies quietly on the hospital bed in the middle of the small drab room. An oxygen mask covers his face and the tone of his skin nearly matches the crisp white cotton sheets that are perfectly pulled to his chest.

I walk forward cautiously, as if any noise may wake him. Staring at his chest, I watch as it rises and falls in a slow, shallow tempo. A small metal folding chair is positioned beside the bed, so I quietly take a seat, barely knocking it backwards with a subtle scraping sound that makes me grit my teeth.

Once seated, I lean forward placing my elbows on the bed and fidgeting my hands to find a comfortable place for them without baring any weight of my arm on him. They find a home beside his arm, with my hand a few inches from his wrist. I stare down at the thin, frail structure of his arm, which seemed much stronger only a few weeks prior. My eyes travel to his face and I take in his sunken cheeks making his bones stand out, the wrinkles along the corners of his eyes and new sprouts of hair along the frame of his face.

Sucking in a deep breath, my mind leaves me and falls to a place I have long since left behind.

"One more lap guys and I'll let you shower up," my fifth hour gym coach yells out, then sticks his whistle back between his lips as if they are naked without it.

I breeze around the track easily, my lungs more than used to the brunt force of breathing and running and dodging obstacles. I round the track, not in any particular hurry and catch sight of the principal rushing up to coach with a panic stricken look on her face, while eyeing me. The air in my lungs leaves me and suddenly my legs slow to a stop as my eyes fill with water.

The coach looks at me, motioning me in his direction with his hand, but I don't need to be told what happened. The sorrow in their eyes is crippling. I race off the field, into the school without looking back. I don't bother to change my clothes or go to my locker, all I can think of besides going home, is getting to Jake, but as I round the corner of C hall, my feet are suddenly cemented to the ground as I see my little brother crouched on the floor, his arms pulling his legs to his torso and his face buried in the gap between his knees and chest. His entire body shakes and suddenly my own tears feel selfish. We didn't get to see her one more time. We didn't get to say goodbye.

As I slide down the wall beside him with the rough surface scraping my bare back, my mind floods with thoughts, worries and words that I should have said; things I would give anything to say one more time. I struggle to conjure up her voice, her laugh, but I cannot even pinpoint the sounds; all I know is that they were the most beautiful sounds I had ever heard and that I'll never hear again.

Drifting back to the present, I look down at Alex's hands and figure to hell with it; he is the closest I've had to a parent in years. I scoop up his fragile bony hand, pressing it between the two of mine as I spill my heart with tears fogging my eyes.

"Alex, I'm not sure if you can hear me or not, but I wanted to thank you. Thank you for being the father I didn't have. Thank you for allowing me to be part of your family when I'd forgotten what a family was and thank you so much for letting me be in Alyssa's life; for letting me love her. Even if it was only for a little while, I loved every second of it."

With that, the dam of tears break free and I welcome them. I let them flow down my face with each and every word that I whisper to him. Not only has Alex become someone I look up to as a father figure, but he has become my friend; a friend that I'm not quite ready to say goodbye to, so I don't. Instead I tell him more about my mom and my past, things that I've never shared with anyone, because that is what friends do.

A good forty-five minutes race by, when I finally convince myself to stop talking and let Abby make use of this precious time. I know she feels she has all the time in the world, but time is a precious thing and not a single second should be taken for granted.

After giving her a small hug and a full-hearted thank you, I drag myself back down the long corridor and past the waiting area, where I catch a glimpse of Alyssa sitting silently in a tan, stiff-looking chair. Her eyes seem vacant as she stares down at her hands, and a part of my heart chips away, thinking about how part of her sorrow today is partly my fault.

Pulling my phone out quietly as I sneakily hide behind the wall separating the hall from the room, I pull up her name and shoot her a simple text just so I can gauge her reaction.

Me: Hey …

I hit send and wait. She doesn't budge and although I have my phone on silent, I find it odd that I hear no noise or she makes no effort to see who it is. Maybe she doesn't have it with her. That one thought keeps me from running over to her and begging her to forgive me.

Her hair falls over her shoulders and surrounds her face as she hangs it down. I can't make out her eyes from here, but I can tell without a doubt that she has been crying. She's right there, yet I can't touch her, kiss her, hold her or even ease her pain; it's killing me. My heart clutches as if it is being compressed in someone's bare hands, about ready to be ripped from my chest and all I want is to race over to her side.

"Sir, can I help you?"

Swinging my head around, I jump at the sound of the nurse's voice. She stands behind me, glancing back and forth from me to the waiting room. I more than likely seem like some creeper, sneaking looks around the corner.

Stepping to the side, fully out of Alyssa's view, I decide it may be time to leave. Besides, Evan was nice enough to wait out in the truck for me.

"No thank you. I thought I saw someone I knew," I say in a quiet tone before slipping away and out of the intensive care wing.

My mind reels and my heart tugs as I step out of the hospital, moving further and further away from Alyssa and her family; the few people in this world that I consider family. I want to camp out right outside the waiting room. I want nothing more than to run up to her, drop to my knees and beg for her forgiveness, even though there may be nothing to forgive. Every fiber of my soul is shouting that this is not the end; that it cannot end like this. I won't let it. I love her and I would do anything to be with her and because of that, I will step aside and give her time. I'll wait and pray, day-by-day, that this horrible nightmare unfolds into a horrible mix up with a happy end.

Running

T HE DAYS GO BY in a blur and with each passing second my heart breaks a bit more until some days it seems as if there is not enough oxygen to fill my lungs. Every night I make sure to send her a message to let her know that I will not, what so ever, fail on my promise to be here for her. I told her I would be here through this battle that her dad is facing and I don't intend to break it, no matter whether we are together or apart. If text messages are the only thing I have, then so be it.

Abby makes sure to keep me up to speed, sending me random text messages with updates on her dad's health and assuring me that Alyssa is doing fine. I don't know why but to hear she is carrying on as usual sends a swirl of mixed emotions right through me, followed by guilt. I don't want her to hurt, but despite that, knowing she may not be missing me like I miss her, makes my heart ache.

So far today, I've received only one text from Abby informing me that Alex is being moved to a "real room." That news lessened the dull throbbing pain that had been splintering through my heart all week just a bit, and although it may be a bad idea, I decide to go visit again.

"I'll probably only stay a few minutes," I call out to Evan as I fling the truck door open with a loud creak and jump to the pavement.

"No problem. Take your time."

He doesn't even look up from his phone as he frantically goes between flipping through his newsfeed to answering the non-stop chirps that has been going off since we left the office. I stand there frozen for a second just staring at him, not sure if this is a good idea.

Looking up, Evan's brows lower. "Hey, seriously, you don't have to hurry." His voice is laced in compassion and takes me by surprise. "Listen, I really doubt she is going to give you much of a chewing if she sees you're there to visit her dad. Besides, it's been three days. Surely she knows this has been killing you."

I look over my shoulder at the sliding doors to the lobby of the hospital. They stand wide open, mocking me; teasing me to come inside like I've been invited; only I haven't. Letting out a sigh, I push aside all my doubts and hesitations If my mom had one more day on this Earth, I wouldn't let anything hold me back from seeing her.

"You're right. I'll be back in a bit."

Evan gives me a small smile as I slam the door and turn to go inside.

Not even five minutes later, and after asking the front desk for Alex Mason's room number, I casually walk down the hallway of the cancer center, extremely alert to my surroundings and nearly jumping each time someone walks up behind me. My heart is drumming in my chest and my hands don't quite want to sit still as I nervously shove them in my pockets to keep them at bay.

I find his room easily, tapping lightly on the door as it slowly swings open from the vibrations of my knock. Peaking around the corner, I find a pair of pale blue eyes immediately looking up at me.

"I'm sorry. The door was open. I'll just …" anxiety suddenly takes root and I want to bolt.

Just as I turn my back to dart away, Angela's carefree laughter fills the room.

"Oh non-sense. Get back in here, Judd. You should know you are perfectly welcome," she says in a playful tone, while pointing her finger to the smooth beige ceramic tile floor.

Turning slowly back around, the tension and worry from coming here melts away with her easy smile that reminds me so much of her daughter. I smile and look around the room, wondering where Alex is.

"They are actually wheeling him down as we speak," she says, crossing the room. Her arms fall over my shoulders and she immediately crushes me with a motherly hug that always seems to warm my heart and fill me with nostalgia. "I'm so glad you came to visit. Alex will be so happy to see you. Oh and speaking of the devil …" she laughs and I swing around as a commotion sounds behind us.

A tall nurse and gentleman push Alex through the doorway, careful to clear the frame and lugging an IV line on rollers behind them. His eyes are open and he is sitting up, although he still appears weak and frail. *I'd trade places with him in a heartbeat if I could.* What I definitely don't miss is how his face lights up when he sees me. That's all the confirmation I needed to know this was a good idea.

"Hey kiddo," he says in a low, groggy tone.

I lift my hand and wave, my lips curving into a huge grin with the skin over my cheeks stretching uncontrollably from how happy I am to see him awake and talking.

It takes no time at all for the nurses to hook him up and set up his new temporary home. As soon as they shuffle out, Angela busies herself finishing up with arranging a slew of balloons, teddy bears, flower arrangements and ceramic angels that I assume have been sent in by friends and family.

"So you ready to jump ship yet and escape this place?" I joke as I take a seat in a wide chair next to his bed.

"Did you bring me a file?"

I laugh at Alex's reference; that is how I felt when I was strapped to a bed for weeks on end.

"Nah … I just planned to come back later and sneak you out when everyone was sleeping," I snicker as the corners of his lips twitch into the hint of a smile.

Leaning in towards his bed, I clasp my hands together onto the mattress with my elbows supported onto my knees. Alex subtly moves and the coolness of his hand falls over my wrist. My eyes flicker down to his bony fingers for a moment and back to his face. He looks at me, quiet, still and composed, yet I can read the sadness in his eyes as if he is silently saying his goodbyes to me in this very instance. I stare back at him, transfixed into this unspoken conversation and unable to speak from the lump that suddenly has formed in my throat. *Don't give up … please don't give up the fight.*

Rustling sounds behind us and breaks the trance as Angela moves things back and forth across the counter as if she is nervously trying to kill time or preoccupy her mind.

With a slow blink of his eyes, Alex speaks up in a barely recognizable pitch, "Thank you for coming to see me. I was hoping I would see you again."

His words have me glancing back at Angela as I sense her stillness with his suggestion that he is nearing the end.

"Of course, I would come to see you. You're like a …" my brows furrow with the thought of what this family means to me and the possibility of one of them no longer being in this world. My heart crashes to the floor and a wave of emotion collides with the good sense I have to stay strong for him and Angela's sake.

His cool, clammy hand pats at my wrist. "I know. So Judd, man to man … are you going to take care of my baby girl?"

His words throw me off guard. Normally this would be a typical-I'm-breaking-out-the-shot-gun kind of introduction, but we have already passed that point so I know this is his way of assuring himself that Alyssa will have someone to lean on; someone to protect her when he is no longer here.

My throat wobbles as I gulp and try to form a sentence, "Always."

The walls close in on me and the air thins, but I keep going because he is the one that needs the support and assurance right now. His tomorrows are numbered and if this conversation can make him rest easy, then I will suck it up and forever hold true to anything I promise him.

"With your permission and her acceptance, I'll always take care of her." I think back to the conversation he and I shared the first weekend I met him and how he told me the story of him and Angela meeting. "I'll love her like you've always loved Angela."

This ignites a quivering giggle from behind us and Alex's eyes instantly sparkle with a glimmer I've only seen when he looks at his wife. It's a look I hope to always exhibit when I look at Alyssa.

"I think we have ears," Alex informs me, sneaking a quick look over to her.

She doesn't even turn, still acting as if she isn't listening in on our conversation.

I laugh and look back to Alex. "Shoot. I shouldn't have said that out loud." I grin and he chuckles. "Lay all your cards on the table and she'll never let anything slide."

He erupts with a healthy, yet soft laugh and I instantly catch sight of Angela beaming over by the counter. Their love shines bright even through their darkest days, and I know it will live on even when he is gone.

Before the hour draws near, I lean down and hug Alex with a vengeance; vengeance for this horrific disease that has robbed him of a long life with his loved ones. I hold tight and tears well up in my eyes as my hand falls over the back of his neck, feeling each and every indentation of his spine. Squeezing my eyes shut, a tear escapes as a small overwhelming feeling slithers through my chest and into my heart with the thought that this may be the last time I see him. With that, I know without a doubt that I have to say the one thing I was never able to tell my mother in those final moment.

My voice quivers and another tear slides down my face as I whisper into his ear while still clutching his head to my shoulder. "Goodbye, Alex," I hesitate before saying it even though I've told him he makes me feel as though I have a father again. In the end I let it slip out, knowing I have to tell him. He has to know what he means and I have to know I said it before it was too late. "I love you, Dad."

A surge of energy and strength must suddenly spiral through him as his grip on me tightens and I hear him chuckle. "I love you, too, son. Proud to call you that."

That's all it takes to open the flood gates. A loud gasp escapes my lips as I slowly pull away and sniffle back my tears. Angela is by my side in a second and Alex continues to hold tight to my hand just as a father does when they are guiding their child through a life lesson that is hard to endure.

"Thank you so much for coming by." Her hug is fierce and relentless giving me a taste of how fragile she is on the inside even though she is holding it together on the outside. I hug her back, trying my best to lend her my strength and courage before leaving.

Dragging out of the hospital, a whole different pain fills my heart, a feeling I know so well, yet one you never get used to. My body shakes with each trembling tear and all I can manage to do on the way home is stare out the window in silence. I watch every tree and every car pass by with a new emptiness that somehow makes me feel grateful. Not grateful for losing another person in my life, but for the opportunity to have him in my life. I've spent so many hours of my life wondering, why me, thinking life isn't fair; feeling sorry for myself, but now I see a whole light. How blessed was I to get the opportunity to know what it's like to have a dad again; to know the love of a dad. *He called me son.*

With tear-streaked eyes, I get back to the apartment, drained and unable to carry a single thought. Evan stays quiet and gives me my privacy as I slip away to my room, shooting Alyssa my nightly text.

Me: Another day without you and you're all I think about! I'm here if you need me, I hope you know that! I love you!

As soon as I hit send and toss my phone to the nightstand, my head hits the pillow. Normally, sleep escapes me as I lay in bed thinking of Alyssa and trying to figure out how I can get her back, but not tonight. Tonight I sleep.

Groggy and barely able to focus in on what the ringing sound is in my ear, I slowly start to wake, then bolt forward when I register the sounds of my phone. My eyes swing to the clock on my nightstand and my heart stops. It grows eerily quiet in the room. I don't hear the slight hum as I inhale; the beating of my heart is absent, even the shuffling of my legs under the sheets stills. All I hear is the ringing and all I see is Abby's name across my screen not far below the time. The time on my phone reads 2:00 a.m.; my heart sinks.

Without any signal from my brain to reach out and grab it, my hand acts, snatching up my phone and bringing it to my ear. *Please, God, no! Please no ... no ... no!*

"Abby, what's wrong?!"

Shaky breathes sound on the other side of the phone before she gathers the strength to speak. "Alyssa just ran out! I'm not sure where she is going but I'm hoping she is headed there!"

The second the words are free from her mouth, the front door snaps in the other room, followed by another click as if it is being closed. Given the fact that Evan hit the hay before me, I know Alyssa is here.

"Don't hurt her, Judd. She can't handle that now," she says then breaks into tears. Others are crying in the background and I know without a doubt that I have to do anything to be here for Alyssa.

"I would never hurt her," I assure her, an ache in my heart amplifying as I think of what this call truly means.

"You already did, don't do it again."

I sigh, knowing I'll never forgive myself for how I have already hurt her. I'll turn the world upside down to make it right.

"I won't. I promise. Let me know if you need anything," I tell her right as my bedroom door opens.

"Thank you."

"Bye," I whisper before hitting the end button without even looking down.

I carefully lay my phone back on the nightstand never taking my eyes off of her. She stands in the doorway and even with only the lights from the street filtering in through the blinds, I can see she has been crying. I remain completely still, as though she is a stray cat that may bolt if I make any sudden movements. She eyes my phone on the nightstand and although I should explain that it was only her sister on the other end, I just want to hold her. My heart yearns for her; aches to take all this ugly pain from her shoulders. If she would run to me right this second, it still would not be soon enough to feel her in my arms.

I move my hand to my comforter and flip the soft pillowy fabric back as an invitation for her to crawl in beside me. She doesn't hesitate and a grateful breath slides over my lips as soon as her legs slip between the sheets. Her skin sliding against my own ignites an electric current inside of me as her beautiful body hugs to mine like it was custom made to fit me. Wrapping my arms around her, I pull her closer. Her head lies still on my chest but her soft sobs are like a beacon to my heart. Moisture from her tears gathers on my skin as I run my hand across her back up into her hair.

God, it feels so good to hold her. I don't want to be selfish at a moment like this but I want to beg her to stay, to tell her I'm sorry, to plead with her that I have no idea how something like that could have ever happened. I love her and I can't lose her, but in the end I keep my mouth shut about my own needs.

"I wish I could take your pain away. I would do anything to shoulder this instead of you," I say to her while holding her as tightly as I possibly can.

She moves her body a little and looks up at my face. The lights from the street reflect off her angelic features highlighting her puffy eyes and the small streaks down her cheeks that make her even more beautiful in my eyes; vulnerable and in need of my shoulder. Just the sight of her in pain is enough to rip my heart wide open.

I want to steal her away and hide her from all this pain and loss, just like she has done for me. When Alyssa came into my life, I was lost, I was running and she found me; she saved me from a spiraling cycle of grief, heartbreak and bitterness and showed me that I was still alive. I would take all of her pain on my shoulders in an instant if I could, because when she is by my side, I can handle anything.

She pulls her face up level with mine and I place my hand behind her ear, gently stroking her cheek with my thumb.

"I'd do anything to make this go away. I just wish I could stop it for you. What can I do to make it hurt less," I whisper, knowing full well there is nothing I can do to stop it.

She searches my face then slowly her lips descend on mine. She needs comfort and I know that is what she is here for, but a part of me wants to hear her say she loves me still; to know that she still wants me in every way.

Moving my mouth with hers, I taste her every breath. I grip her waist as she lies on top of me and as my fingers graze over bare skin, invisible sparks ignite in a sizzling trail. My whole body comes alive when she is near. I only feel whole when I am with her; all the pain, loss and emptiness from my life seem to dissipate with the simple sound of her voice.

"Judd … please … just for a moment, help me forget." Her voice comes out in a gentle and fragile, pain-stricken tone that pierces my soul and knocks the wind right out of me.

Her lips fall back to mine and although this is where I want to stay, slowly mending each fragment of her shattered heart with a kiss or touch, I know deep inside this isn't what she needs.

Nudging her back with my fingertips while softly tracing the smooth skin of her cheek, I desperately try to change the path of this night, "Baby, I don't think that is a good idea. Trust me, I know. All that pain and heartache will just be waiting for you afterwards and I don't want you regretting it later."

I remember all too well about wanting to run from this sort of agony. It engulfs you; eats you up from the inside out and at times the blanket of grief is so thick that it swallows every drop of life within you.

"Please, I need you," she pleads, looking straight into my eyes and slowly unraveling all my will power.

I don't want to bring it up at a time like this, but I have to. "Lyssa, we really need to talk about things if we are going to …"

The soft touch of her fingertip silences me and I know there is no way I'm going to win this battle. Even with her falling apart at this very moment, she is still stronger than I have the courage to be; I'm at her mercy.

"I don't want to talk. I need you. Please,"

My breathing kicks up with those words, with the overwhelming thought of touching her, tasting her and being with her, although guilt clutches every fiber of my being. A blast of the sweet strawberry fragrance of her skin hits me and all my restraint is lost. Flipping her onto her back, my mouth instantly drops to her lips, tasting, sucking and drinking her in. Inching my way down her neck, I nibble at the creamy, delicate flesh above her collarbone while I tug at the hem of her shirt. I dip lower, continuing to look up at her in case she changes her mind. It takes no time at all to have all our clothes off.

Guiding my lips back up to hers, the heat from her body sends a surge of tingles rippling over the surface of my skin as my torso slides back over all her delicate curves. I lean in, ready to devour her lips and join us, but pause. She looks into my eyes, pleading, begging for me to go on.

"Are you sure?" Everything inside of me wants her, yet there's this sliver of will power still holding on, screaming at me that this is exactly what I did; I ran from the pain, seeking any amount of escape in any way possible. "I'll hold you all night. I'll never let go … I promise," I assure her, even though a part of me wants the comfort of her body against mine as well.

Her voice is soft and garbled with the pain of her loss as she answers me, "I want you; I need you."

I don't wait for any other words. She didn't run to just anyone for comfort, she ran to me. She wants me and I want her; forever.

With one slow, gentle push, electric pulses course through my body making my heart drum and igniting an immediate groan to barrel up from my chest. A surge of emotion nearly overwhelms me, but I never take my eyes off of her. Her hair splays across the pillow around her head as her back comes off the bed and a breathy whimper fills my ear drums.

Softly sliding one arm beneath her shoulder blade and the other around her body, I pull her closer, concentrating on not rushing this moment. Her head falls back over and over, side to side as breathy sighs and moans move over her lips. I capture a few with my mouth, tasting and never getting enough. Slowly trailing my lips over the fine, tantalizing line of her jaw, I can't hold back any longer. My heart may rupture if I don't tell her now.

"I love you, Alyssa. I love you so much."

As soon as the words are out of my mouth, the fire between us blazes, pulling me under until shockwaves are vibrating throughout my body; down my legs, up my torso and then centralizing. My neck dips forward and I suck in the sweet perfume of her skin as I gasp out loud with a final shift of my body. A few loud whimpers sound in my ear as she clings to me.

The soft touch of her skin against mine and the tingling sensations that still rage inside of me strangle my breathing as I lean against her, still gasping for air. Never has there been a time that we have been like this and not said I love you to each other. It makes my heart ache and honestly, it scares me.

"Tell me you love me, please," I whisper softly over the tender skin of her earlobe as I work to catch my breath.

Instantly, I lean up to gauge her reaction and like a magnet her hands find my face as she stares back at me. I look straight into her eyes, waiting, nearly wanting to beg for the words. Her eyes shift and her fingertips slowly descend from my cheek, down the side of my face and land right where I suspected it would. Now she waits and watches, almost studying me. I don't have to ask; I don't have to think about it. Quickly running my tongue over my lips to moisten them, I press my lips together in a sort-of-smile and feel the familiar dip in my cheek. Her eyes sparkle as she looks at me, glancing from my eyes to my cheek with a hint of a smile that fills me with gratitude and hope. Then I hear it; the words that make my heart sail.

"I love you, Judd."

I don't sweep her up and kiss her with all the passion that is spilling from my heart like I want to, instead I stay calm and slide off of her, knowing more than anything that she needs my arms tonight; my strength.

"Come here. I want to hold you."

And that is exactly what I do, but as soon as a few tears start to dampen my chest, she sits up with her thighs on either side of my hips and pulls me up to her. Slightly moving her hips around, I immediately know what her intensions are. I've been here before and it doesn't wipe away the pain; it only delays it and holds it off until it is crashing down on you again.

Running my hand down to her hip then encircling her small waist, I stop her while gently running my other hand over her cheek, in a calming caress.

"Alyssa, baby, no. You can't run from this. You can't hide. You have to face this. I know it's hard, baby … believe me I know. We'll face this together. If you will let me, I will hold your hand through it all, I promise, but you have to face this. Otherwise, all that pain and hurt is going to come crashing down on you. You have to figure out a way to cope with it now while it's fresh."

My heart shatters as I stare into her eyes and all I want to do is steal her away from all the pain and suffering that has burrowed deep into her heart. I'm trying desperately to be strong for her, to not cave to my own feelings of loss, because I truly did love her father as if he were my own, but as soon as she speaks, it's nearly my undoing.

"I don't know if I can," she whispers in a broken, almost inaudible tone that damn near rips my heart out.

"You can. I know you can."

She collapses against me, letting the crushing weight of losing her dad drag her down. I can see it; every ripple of pain that runs through her, I feel it too. I pull her tight to my side with my arm fully around her so that maybe I can shield some of the grief from swallowing her up.

All through the night, tidal waves of hurt and agony attack her, but I don't let go. What once was filled with laughter and the sweet sounds of our love when we lay in this bed, my bedroom now is filled with traumatic sobs that have my own eyes shedding tears and my insides screaming to stay strong. She shakes and shudders against me as I gently shush her and whisper all that my heart holds.

A river of tears dampens the sheet beneath us and my abdomen, but I don't move. After nearly an hour or so, her body stills and she only lets out a painful whine every few minutes. Exhaustion soon takes over, but I still refuse to close my eyes even though sleep is clawing its way through me.

Nearly an hour later, all is silent and I still force myself from falling asleep, but it becomes more and more impossible.

"Shhhhh," I murmur, my eyes weighted down and my breathing deepening. "Shhhhh," I barely get out before darkness surrounds me.

A tender touch dances over my lips and starts to rouse me, although sleep keeps a firm grip, holding me down and under the warmth of darkness. I can't see her face, but my ears barely pick up on Alyssa's soft voice as if she is speaking through a tunnel.

"I love you …" Her words bring a sense of serenity over me that I've never felt, but then I pick up on more moving further away. "… bye, Judd," I flinch with the desire and need to wake, but unable to pull myself out of the veil of exhaustion.

Don't go … don't run … not from me. I call out a desperate silent plea before more garbled noise from a distance finally forces me from the hands of sleep. Slowly peeling my eyes open, sunlight bleeds through the blinds and has me squinting to look around.

The bed beside me is vacant and the room is silent. Instantly my heart rate kicks up as I remember a dream or a memory of Alyssa saying goodbye. Swinging my head to the left so fast that a slicing pain shoots down my neck, I see that it is already well into the morning hours. *Shit!*

Without a single thought or care in the world for whether anyone is here or not, I bolt up out of bed, spring to my feet and race out my door with only the sheet clutched around my waist. Evan's face snaps up from the couch as I search the room, but come up empty. *She's gone.*

"Where is she?" I ask panicked.

"Ahhh, can you put some clothes on?"

I jerk my head to the side, instantly aggravated at his nonchalant tone. "Where is she!?"

"Calm down. She's fine," Evan says with his hands raised in surrender as he slowly rises from the couch.

I can't calm down. I can't do anything. I need to find her.

"Where is she?" I say again, this time raising my voice with so much panic and adrenaline racing through me that I'm about to run for my truck and comb the street with only the security of a thin white sheet.

"Ok … I … don't…know …" he drags out his words softly, moving in front of me with his hands held out as if I'm a dog foaming at the mouth. His expression switches from alert to surprise and I realize my eyebrows are drawn down to the point of making my head hurt and the skin on my forehead feeling tight and strained. "Wait … ok, I don't know where she went but I assumed that her dad …" he stops talking and looks at me with a question in his eyes.

"What about her dad? I thought …" my heart stops. *Did I misunderstand everything?*

He sighs and puts his hands down, now standing directly in front of me, all while I still stand here in only a sheet.

"She said she was going to say goodbye to her dad so I assumed that he might have passed …" he says the last part with hesitation.

I breathe out a heart wrenching breath, partly for the awareness that Alex is no longer on this Earth today and also because I hate that I can't be with her.

"When did she leave?" my voice cracks and all I want to do is run after her, because I know that is what she is doing. She is running; running from the pain, running from any source of added torture and running from us, because to stay would only hurt more.

I'll do anything

THE DAY GOES BY torturously slow and it's a struggle to function; to not fall apart. All that runs through my head is how I've lost everything all over again. I just found my place in life and now it's gone. I'm not quite sure where to go from here; what to do.

Fortunately, Evan conveniently decides to hang out at the apartment all day and keep me preoccupied with useless conversation. Although my mood is as foul as they come, I welcome the distraction and let loose a couple brief smiles. Without him, I'd be wallowing or possibly even racing to her doorstep to plead my side, when really, all she needs right now is to be with her family no matter how brutal the pain is.

Returning to my room earlier today, I found a note she left for me on my phone. I screen captured the image, prepared to save it forever. For now, I study every last word with my insides closing in on me at the absence of her signature 'I love you' at the end of the message.

Judd … I'm sorry I came here last night. I really shouldn't have, but thank you for being here when I needed you most. I know there is so much that needs to be said, but I just need time. I can't deal with everything right now.

After reading over it for the hundredth time, I decide to send her a message. A small inner voice has been gnawing at me to call or text her all day; that she needs me.

Me: I know you said you need time, but I just want you to know you have been on my mind all day. You all have been. Alyssa, I love you so much!

As expected, I don't hear back from her, and cannot manage to get a good night's sleep. This all feels way too familiar, and the fact that I can't be there to hold her is slowly killing me. *I promised Alex.*

Work and school drag by and all I can imagine is Alyssa sitting in her room crying. Each day is another day without her and another day that the happiness that I found with her is drained from my life, leaving me lost and wondering if this will be my forever.

Standing in the snack aisle of the grocery store, I lean back against the cool metal shelving that houses the peanuts while Evan takes a decade to pick out a simple bag of chips.

"Hurry up, will ya," I say impatiently, because today is Alex's viewing.

"Chill out. These things take time," Evan pipes up, reaching for a gigantic bag of plain wavy chips and a jar of dip. "Hey, did you use my shampoo? I went to use some and ..."

With my hand drawn up in front of me, his voice tunes out as I stare at the conversation between Abby and I from earlier today; the clamps on my heart tighten.

Me: Hey. How are you holding up? I've been thinking about you all and I hope you know, if there is anything I can do, I'm here ...

Abby: Hey. As good as expected. It's funny ... I hated Dad's workshop a couple summer's ago when I was forced to help Alyssa with a birdhouse, but now I just can't seem to leave it. I feel like he is still here as long as I am sitting on his old stool I sometimes even think I can hear the faint sounds of his drill running. Lol! Silly, I know.

Me: It's not silly, at all! It's absolutely normal to feel all that and to feel their presence. I'm sure he is watching over you every second you are sitting at that bench. You should make something ... shock the hell out of him. Lol!

Abby: Hahaha! It would! And he would be cracking up the whole time wishing he could explain to me the correct way to hold a hammer. "Don't hold it so far down, honey and don't tap the nail ... swing at it." Lmao! I can actually hear him now.

My heart tugs as I read where she typed 'lmao', because I know laughter isn't easy at this point; it won't be for a while, but I have no doubt that Alex is in that garage with her.

Me: Lol!

Abby: Btw, his viewing is at 4-8 today, downtown at Ripply's Funeral Home. I think you should be there. Dad would want you there.

Me: Are you sure? I want to come ... to be there, but I don't want to upset Alyssa more.

Abby: She will be fine and besides, you were family ... she knows that. You should be there. If you are afraid to upset her, just stay on the other side of the room. Seriously though, I think she would be happy to see you. I've caught her gawking at your name on her phone a couple times. My bet is that she misses you.

Me: Thanks for telling me that. I miss her, too. And thanks for asking me to come. Yes, I will be there.

Abby: C-ya then. :)

"Are you listening to me?"

I look up and notice Evan halfway down the aisle with a few things balanced between his arms.

"They have carts for a reason."

"No way, those things are lame. Besides, I start lugging one of those around with me, people might get the wrong idea about us, and assume you're my girlfriend," he chuckles.

"Hey, why am I the girlfriend?"

"A, because you keep staring at your phone like you're gabbing with your Bff. B, because you're the one that suggested for me to get a cart and C, because no way I'd be the chick."

Shaking my head and letting out a genuine snicker at his logic, I give up arguing. All that would do is fuel him to take a jab at my clothing or how I need to get a haircut.

I quickly shove my phone back into my pocket and tread behind him to the shampoo aisle, watching as he grazes over the varieties, even though each and every time he ends up getting the same stuff.

"Oh … get on with it already," I urge him with a deep sigh as my eyes flick over the shelf to the side of him and catch on a familiar looking bottle.

"As I said before these things take time. When do you need to leave for the viewing anyways? You have a couple hours, right?" Evan asks as he carefully wedges another item in his arms.

"Mmmhmmm," I answer, completely zoned in on the shampoo sitting eye level, across from me.

A pitcher of cream being poured over an overflowing mess of strawberries adorns the cover of the plastic bottle and I have no doubt that it's the same shampoo I've seen Alyssa use a dozen or more times. *I miss her.*

"Hey, you ready?"

"Oh yeah …"

Turning to follow him, I take one more glance at the bottle then swing my head around to see if anyone else is in the aisle before I slip my hand out and snatch it up. Quickly flipping up the snap-top cap, I bring it to my nose and inhale, immediately hit with a wave of strawberries and cream that smells just like Alyssa's hair and skin. My eyes seal shut instantly and my heart drums as if she is in my arms; as if my face is buried in her neck with handfuls of her hair tickling my nose.

"Geez ... what are you doing?! See, I told you you'd be the chick."

Opening my eyes and spinning my head around, Evan stands only steps away looking at me like I've lost it. *Maybe I am the chick.*

"What?" I spit out in an innocent tone. *I'm totally turning into a girl, but he doesn't have to know I think that.* "It's the shampoo that Alyssa uses. It just reminds me of her, so I was ... What?!"

Evan stares at me, his mouth gaped open and I just know ... just know it's only a matter of time until he ...

"Were we having a moment?" his sarcastic, amused tone interrupts my train of thought.

I glare at him, tucking the shampoo bottle under my arm and perfectly confident in purchasing it. He keeps an eye on my hand as I slip it back to the shelf and scoop up a matching conditioner to file under my bicep beside the other bottle. I snicker at his bored expression as he turns and walks out of the aisle.

"Come on, Sally. We'll swing by the tampon aisle before we leave so you can grab some of those, too. You need a cart?"

And there it is ...

My lips curl into a smile and we both laugh out loud as I look over, knowing he's another blessing that God sent into my life after Mom died. I would have never survived without his friendship.

Three o'clock rolls around and I'm already fixed up in a black dress jacket, black slacks, a crisp white button down that I bought after we left the grocery store and a new tie. Running into the bathroom, I do my best to tame my mess of hair that is in bad need of a cut then race back to the living room.

"Ok, I'm going to leave. I can't handle just sitting here. It's going to make me a nervous wreck."

I swipe my sweaty palms across my slacks then hastily shove them into my pockets as Evan watches with a smirk.

"You'll be fine," he mumbles between crunching on a chip.

My chest expands on a deep inhale as I flip around and grab my keys and phone off the island before walking to the door, scared to death to do this. It's been years since I've stepped inside a funeral home and my heart is lodged into my throat with the anxiety that all of it will come crashing back down on me, every memory of the day my mom was laid to rest. Sliding my hand around the hard metal surface of the door knob, Evan stops me in my tracks.

"You want me to come with? You know, for moral support."

I look back and smile; proud that he is my friend. "Thanks, but I think I should do this alone."

He nods in understanding with a tight-lipped smile as I slip away, wracked with fear, apprehension and trepidation.

I can do this ... I can do this, I chant over and over as I drive to the funeral home and park, sitting quietly in my truck as Alyssa's family drives up. She gets out of the back seat and I truly need all the will power in the world to hold me back from stopping her. She tugs at the bottom of her black dress then her arms automatically wrap around her waist, making me envious of them. *I wish I were those arms right now.* Tipping her head back before she walks inside the building, her hair dips down her back in a meticulously woven braid, and I wonder for an instant if she is saying a prayer or perhaps talking to her dad.

I want to text her or run after her to be by her side as she faces this day, but I wait, keeping my hand steady on my knee so that I don't vibrate my way right out of the truck with the way I'm shaking.

Nearly an hour later, when I've worked up some courage and after I've seen dozens of unknown faces enter the building, I slowly step out of my truck and walk towards the funeral home with one driving thought ... *I promised Alex and I promised Alyssa.*

She may not want to see me, but I made a promise to her that night we got back together, to be here for her every step of the way. We may have hit a very huge roadblock, in the form of her overly-obsessive and scheming roommate, but I just don't buy what Bethany is selling. Unless she caught it on video, I'm done believing for even a second that I could have done that to Alyssa, drunk or not. I'm going to be here for her and I plan to be there tomorrow when she has to see her father laid into the ground. That's the worst part of it; seeing that casket lowered into the ground is like having them ripped away from you all over again. I squeeze my eyes shut with that thought and take a calming breath before opening the door to the funeral home.

The sounds of chatter greet my ears and the whole place is already swarming with most likely family, friends and coworkers of Alex's. My head goes fuzzy, replaying sounds I heard years ago. Shaking my head to rid myself of that memory, I scan the room, looking for faces

I know, but I don't see anyone familiar.

One foot after the next, I walk quietly towards the front room, where I finally catch a glimpse of Alyssa through the crowd. She looks run down and exhausted. Her eyes are a pale, glassy blue and her cheeks are lightly blushed, beautiful. I suck in a breath and wish above all that I could somehow toss her a rope, a life preserver, anything to hold her up because right now I know she is drowning. I know it all too well.

Body after body crashes into her, wrapping their arms around her in a compassion-filled, genuinely concerned hug, but it won't be enough. Keeping my eyes locked on her, déjà vu creeps up and gives me a slap in the face as I remember Tristan doing the same thing. Jake and I sat silently in the pews, staring off into space. The place wasn't packed, but there were a few people mingling through. I couldn't even look up at the casket, but Tristan never took his eyes off it. It was as if he was a guard dog defending her. I never realized until now how worn down he was that day; how defeated and empty he looked.

"Hey stranger."

Flipping around, Abby throws herself to me and I instinctively give her a firm hug.

"Hey. Are you hanging in there?" I whisper with my chin braced against her forehead.

"I guess," she sniffles then slides back out of my grasp. "I'm just tired and just …"

As she blows out a heavy breath, the hair hanging over her forehead breezes outward before fluffing back down.

"I know," I say softly. *There is nothing I can say or do to help them.* "How is your mom?" It's a silly question, but basically like everything that is said at a funeral, I say it anyway. "Is she holding it together ok?"

Abby lets out a sarcastic laugh, "Oh, she seems great and it scares me. She has seriously been like a rock, like concrete; she is not breaking. We are all falling apart every five seconds and there she is, smiling, greeting everyone, thanking them for coming."

Her eyes fill with tears as she goes over her mom's behavior like it's wrong or possibly because she knows it's just a wall that will eventually come crashing down, crumbling and potentially burying her alive. I've always thought that is how Tristan dealt the day Mom died. He held it together. He was a tower of strength, but then a couple weeks later he went MIA, off the grid and I haven't ever seen my brother again; not the Tristan he was before she died. That Tristan died as well and I'm not sure if I'll ever see him again.

"I don't think Alyssa will be able to go up and say goodbye to Dad."

My heart hurts as I look back at her, still lost in a sea of people wanting to comfort her.

"It's important to say goodbye, but that's not him up there. She was there with him when it mattered." I stop talking and think about what I just said, then glance back in the direction of Alex's casket, seeing an entirely different scene. *The time you have leading up to a death is what matters; all those little moments that seem so insignificant at that time.* Suddenly, a weight I've carried around for years seems lighter, easier to tolerate. "Abby, your dad was always so graceful in a conversation. He always knew what to say and how to put it so that everyone could empathize with what he meant. I think …" a smile ticks within me as I say aloud something I am just now discovering to be true for my own life. "I think he used that same grace when he left this world. If he could have chose … I don't think he would have chosen to leave while you were watching, so you all would have had to see that. He waited. He left this earth in peace."

Abby's eyes bubble over with water until they slowly drip down her face in a stream of tears. She smiles with a small shaky laugh.

"He left while Mom laid by his side. That's how he would have wanted it." She frantically wipes the tears away with her hand and then throws her arms around my shoulders as hard as any linebacker I've ever been up against.

"Whoa," I laugh quietly, crushing her in a strong embrace.

"Thank you, Judd. I hope you know how much he loved you." She moves away and looks at me with warm eyes and a grateful heart. "He was always talking about you with Mom," she pauses, looking at me intently, as if she's just discovered something. "Give her time, she'll come around. She has to."

With a deep breath, I smile, feeling renewed for so many reasons. After a few minutes I take off, ready to say my own goodbyes if I can.

I walk slowly, barely able to put one foot in front of the next until he is in sight. Not even two feet away from the casket, sitting at the front of the room surrounded by a monstrous menagerie of over-powering fragrant flowers, and my heart is hammering. I don't step completely up; I stop as if my feet are welded to the floor.

Alex doesn't look like himself. His kind, loving, sometime mischievous smile that always brightened his face is no longer present. The twinkle that sparkled in his eyes when he would look at his daughters and wife is also long gone with his eyes being sealed shut for eternity. I glance down to his hand, still and silent across his waist. I remember how when he would talk, his hands were just as loud, motioning back and forth along with his stories.

As if a volcano just exploded, my heart tears open and I can't hold back the tears any longer. I step forward two more steps and my hands find his joined, warmth-deprived hands as I softly rest mine above his.

"Goodbye, Alex. I promise, I'll take care of her and love her forever just you loved Angela," I whisper to myself as I hear a few people shuffle behind me.

Taking in a large breath, I pull my hand away and quickly move across the room with my eyes planted on the tiled floor. I count square after square in a desperate need to escape, even though I need to stay. The weight of it all is falling onto me and I'm struggling to stay upright. My shoulder hits something and I glance up.

"Hey, Judd."

Looking up, I stare right into the face of someone I not too long ago loathed, but yet today his face is a welcoming sight. He glances over his shoulder and I see Alyssa slumped down into a pew. He stares at her, as do I, then he turns back to me with a shadow of guilt in his eyes.

"Ummm, have you talked to Alyssa?" he asks uncomfortably. He knows the situation.

"No. I'm afraid it will only make things harder today." He nods, both of us throwing a look in her direction. "Hey, listen …" *I cannot believe I'm going to ask this of the one person that could potentially steal her away from me.* "Ummm … ahhh …" *Just spit it out.* "Would you maybe go sit with her? I want to, but I just think it may cause her more grief at this point. I mean, just make sure she's alright," I say it even though my head is yelling out what a fool I am.

"Sure." Kyle slaps his hand against my shoulder and crinkles his eyebrows. "Are you sure you don't want to give it a shot and go talk to her. She may surprise you."

I glance back over and watch as she nervously fidgets her hands along the hem of her skirt while staring down to the floor.

"I know, but I don't want to chance upsetting her. I'm not leaving …" I make sure to add this just in case he gets any ideas.

"I will." He nods with a look in his eyes that tells me that I can trust him with this. "I'll go sit with her and try to keep her mind off of everything," he pauses before going on. "I hope you get this Bethany crap straightened out. Hang in there. You'll get her back. She needs you."

With that, he heads over to the pew she is slouched down in, gives me one more glance with a heartfelt smile and slowly sits beside her. She doesn't look back or pay too much attention as he talks to her, but I can tell that she is welcoming the distraction. Tipping my chin up so that I can get a look at their hands, my heart eases as I see he is keeping his hands to himself. *I may trust him with this, but I'll always be leery.*

Instead of going home, I stay in my truck parked a little ways down from the funeral home. It's as if I'm back to the day I got out of the hospital, sitting outside her house and waiting to see if she pulls up.

Staring down at my phone as I toss around the idea of calling Tristan, I catch movement from the corner of my eyes. My head snaps up and I see her. She looks lost, exhausted and barely still standing. I don't waste a moment pulling out my phone. I may not be in the position to hold her when I want to, but I can work around that and still be there for her.

Me: Just Breathe! Close your eyes and feel my arms around you! I'm here if you need me. I love you! ( )

"Just breathe" is something I overheard my mom tell Tristan many times when they were unaware of me and Jake's eavesdropping.

"Just breathe when you think the pain is too much."

"When you're unsure of what to do or where to go, just breathe."

I watch from afar, marveling over her beauty as she looks down at her phone and sucks in a breath. She doesn't look around and it's then that I am grateful that I chose to remain unnoticed.

I don't leave, I don't move, I just stay in my truck until night falls, thinking over everything from the morning after the Halloween party, to the night Alex passed, to what will happen tomorrow and whether I will be able to handle watching another person I love fall beneath the surface of our world. All the while my heart keeps beating and my lungs keep refilling with new air as time goes on. Somehow, I always thought the Earth would stop spinning once you were enveloped in pain and grief. I guess Mom was right when she told me "God never gives you too much to handle." And just like back then, I know I will keep moving and keep breathing, for Alyssa, I'll do anything.

Catch my breath

THE NEXT DAY, I climb out of my truck parked nearly in the same place Tristan parked years ago. Walking across the dried out, slowly dying grass littered with fallen leaves, I stare at each of my footfalls wondering if they are landing in the same spots they did back then.

"Just keep walking, Judd. If I can do it, you two can too." My brother's words echo through my mind, sounding emotionless and already leaning towards the point of the Tristan I know today.

Slowly pulling my chin upright, I look out towards the black canopy set up over Alex's grave spot and I instantly see Alyssa, Andrea, Angela and Abby all huddled together as a pastor speaks kind, praise-filled words.

Smoothing my hand over my white button down shirt to the waist of my slacks, I straighten out the fabric, grateful that I arrived undetected. I come to a stop under a large leafless maple tree about fifteen yards away and watch, still unable to hear all the words that are being spoken. In the distance, as if a voice is calling to me, I look over to my mom's plot, a place I barely visit, yet I'm in this area nearly every week. I guess, in a way I view her grave as her death, whereas the wishing well I see as her life. When I go there, I feel her all around. Looking at her headstone and the words that were delicately engraved on it, I'm overwhelmed with the dark finality of her life.

It doesn't take long for the entire mournful ritual to wind down and people slowly start to trickle off to their cars. At last, my eyes fall back to the five people that remain. Angela is crouched on the ground near the grave and that impenetrable wall that Abby saw in her mom is at last falling to bits, piece-by-piece.

Moving my feet at a hurried pace to get to them, Andrea and Abby fall to the ground to support Angela while Alyssa stands back, frozen. As soon as I see her sway and begin to fall back, my feet blaze over the ground to catch her. She lands in my arms with her back to my chest as I easily wind my hands around her small frame to pull her closer, as close as I can.

"I got you," I whisper as she looks up at me through tear streaked eyes. *I'll always catch you.* "Let's help your mom, ok?"

She nods, using my arms to support herself as we both move forward and squat down by Angela. For an immeasurable time I stay close, afraid to let go of Alyssa. I trail my hand over her back, up then down again in a loving attempt to let her know I'm close by. All four of the girls shake and quiver as their sobs fill the air. Alyssa's arms wrap around her mom's waist much like mine did hers as I stand, moving back to give them room to grieve as a family. Greg, Andrea's husband, moves back with me and we both stand side-by-side, helpless and heart-sick for the ones we love.

I look past the girls as they weep to see the casket make its descent into the crumbly ground with the soft humming sound of the lowering device to serenade it, along with the ocean of tears from the girls that loved him. A few roll down my cheeks and drip from my chin, dampening my shirt, but I don't try to hide it. Greg's hand lands on my shoulder in a tight grip and I look over.

Nodding his head, he presses his lips into a straight line with a barely-there smile. "Thanks for coming."

I clear my throat and nod back to him, unable to speak just yet. My head is whirling and my heart is on a roller coaster of emotions. Alyssa stands and slowly walks backward until, she gently and purposely bumps into me. I don't even think about what I'm doing before her hand is already clasped in mine, with our fingers woven together like they were meant to be sealed together for eternity. Time clicks away as I hold tight to her and keep a watchful eye on her mom and sisters. Eventually, everyone begins to compose themselves and make peace with the fact that Alex will not be leaving with us. It hurts my heart to think of that because it seems like only yesterday that I stood crumpled on the ground by a gravesite myself, yelling out for Mom to please come back. I couldn't scream loud enough and my brother's were the only thing that kept me from diving in after her.

After waving goodbye to everyone, I take a profound breath about to let her completely into my soul, somewhere I've let very few people, but in the end I love her and was being honest when I told her I want to share everything with her.

"Do you feel up to taking a walk with me?"

She's hesitant at first, but agrees. We walk hand-in-hand, with her clinging to my arm as she always has, but I can tell she's preoccupied and so am I. Two people I love now live here. A part of that gives me comfort, thinking maybe Mom and Alex could become friends or watch out for us together. A silly thought, but it still brings me peace.

At the edge of the cemetery and only about fifteen yards from Alex's grave, I come to a stop with Alyssa gently thudding against my body as she stares in the opposite direction. I don't look over at her, instead I stare straight forward, the recognizable emptiness of loss burrowing into my heart.

I clutch Alyssa's hand tighter in my grasp and she squeezes back, hugging closer to me possibly to hold herself up or maybe to hold me steady.

The sunshine was brighter because you were here. The corner of my lips tick as I silently read the inscription that we had etched on Mom's stone. I glance up and note the clouds in the sky, carefully hiding the sun as if all happiness has been drained from the air today, and just like the day she was buried.

"Mom, please ... please ... Mom, don't go," the echoes of my voice ring in my mind, taking me back.

Jake sobs beside me with my jacket wound up in his hand for security. He gasps and squeals at times, trying to catch his breath, but I can't help him.

Suddenly, when I am two seconds away from dragging the casket away and refusing to accept that she is gone, another set of arms find me. For a minute, I close my eyes and pretend they are Mom's; her arms before she lost mobility, back when she gave fierce hugs that made everything better.

"Jake, Judd, let's go and let her finally rest," Tristan's voice chimes in my ear, cool and calm as if it's just any other day.

I know she had a long battle and was sick for so long. "We can't leave her by herself," I huff, craning my neck over my shoulder to look at him through foggy eyes.

"Just come with me, I have a surprise for you both," he smiles, making Jake and me both quiet our cries and stare at him completely curious.

Shaking my head out of my daydream, I look around remembering how that day through all the misery and grief, it didn't even dawn on me where we were; so many details from that day have been lost, maybe even blocked out until now. I smile, thinking over one single significant detail, before looking back at Alyssa.

"Come on." I pull her with me towards the fence that rises up at the edge of the cemetery.

She doesn't question my motives or stop me, just follows along, looking around much as I did back then. Once we move past the small park, recognition sparkles in her eyes and a bit of happiness emerges that makes the hole in my heart mend a bit. She holds to me tighter as we step onto the beautiful pathway that my brothers, Mom and I created around the fountain and remains against me as we sit at the bench.

I'm not sure what is in her head as we sit here, and I'm not even positive that she understands why I'm bringing her to this place today, but a part of me thinks she gets it. Staring over, her eyes glisten with held back tears and understanding as she looks at the angel at our feet.

I know how her heart hurts and the fears she has that her life will be forever altered by the single moment when Alex took his last breath.

But I want her to see that life moves forward, it goes on whether we want it to or not, we carry on day-by-day, step-by-step and little-by-little the pain lessens. It's always there, but then one day you look up and you see sunlight again.

I did, when I saw her.

I thought the clouds that blanketed the sky the day Mom died would always fog my life, but when I least expected it, there it was again; the sun, another angel sent into my life.

Even if we don't move past all the lies and deceit that Bethany has shoved our way, I'll always be grateful. Alyssa taught me that I can move forward and I hope in some small way, I'm showing her the same thing today. *I still don't intend on giving her up without a fight.*

After a quiet drive home followed by the solitude of her and I sitting silently in my truck for what seemed like the entire night, she retreats back inside and I watch her go. Pounding fiercely like an animal running for its life, my heart pleads with my mind to speak up; to make her stay, and although I breach the subject, I still hold back and let her have her space. This time is sacred and today the weight of the world has fallen upon her, so I head home. As always though, I send one more message to let her know I am here and will remain nearby.

Me: Every second I'm without you only makes me fall more in love with you. I love you more than you will ever know. When you are ready, I will be here. I'm not going anywhere. I love you, Alyssa.

The next day drags on and on. My head may very well explode from lack of sleep, I have no desire to even go to class and my heart is hyperaware of the emptiness that has taken root since she's been gone. The one good thing is that when I make it to work, Evan and Mr. Jansen keep my mind busy. They send me on every silly odd errand they can dream up then proceed to take me to dinner after our shift. But nighttime eventually falls, and the side of the bed that became accustomed to her body seems more and more empty.

Me: You're on my mind, in my heart, in my dreams and a part of me. I miss you and love you.

And that becomes our routine. I have no doubt that Alyssa loves me but she is in the midst of fighting a battle, a war with her heart and head. I waged that same one, years ago, and have been struggling for air, to catch my breath ever since; up until she came into my life. I love her, so I am more than willing to step back and let her breathe; let her find her way. When the time is right, I'll know when to take her hand

and help her up.

Today, thankfully I'm off work and decided once again not to go to class. Instead, I find it is finally time to put some things in the past. Tossing my phone to the passenger seat, I drive, ready to see where this road will take me. I'm hopeful for the first time, because now I am armed with new information. Things I was unable to remember for so long. My mind stays busy drawing up each and every moment from the days leading up to Mom's death as I drive home. I go over the look in Tristan's eye each time he told me and Jake we couldn't sit with Mom, over the expression on his face the day of her funeral as he struggled to hold it together. He struggled to hold it together for us.

Walking inside the house, I'm greeted by silence and Tristan's closed door once again, but fortunately I called Jake on the way over and he assured me that Tristan was here. He even managed to sneak the key to his room off his keychain. Slipping around the kitchen bar, I reach under the wire basket that holds a few apples and oranges. I slide the metal key over the tile and pick it up.

"Thanks, Jake," I say under my breath with a whole new outlook on everything, yet a swarming fear in my gut that Tristan may not be in the same place as I am.

Closing my eyes, I send a prayer up and hope that if at all possible, that maybe Mom can give me some advice. She knew Tristan better than anyone. Once I'm to the door, I slide the key in, turn the knob and push it open. I slip inside, quietly while Tristan lies asleep in bed. Glancing around, I immediately find a wheelchair beside the bed along with a dresser adorned with a collection of pill bottles. My mouth goes dry as I glance back at the wheel chair, then to his legs stretched out buried under a pile of blankets.

"Hey …"

His voice startles me, but I continue to stare at the blankets.

"Did you find the key Jake left for you ok?"

This gets my attention.

"What?!" My eyes widen in astonishment that he possibly knew I was coming and breaking into his room, no less. "You knew he took your key?" *Shit! If he didn't, he does now.* Suddenly, I feel like a kid getting ready for their punishment.

He chuckles, pulling himself up with his arms and throwing a pillow behind his back.

"Well, yeah.." he smiles, crinkling his brows as he situates himself, smoothing the sheet up to his ribcage, which sports all sorts of healed gashes, but he never moves the blankets. "I may have been a shitty choice for a guardian, but I did learn some tricks from Mom. Besides, Jake is too honest … it's written all over his face when he's being sneaky. He must have repeated the same thing twelve times when he was grabbing my keys."

"But why …"

He doesn't even let me finish before he starts laughing and I fear his asshole ways are about to emerge and dig into me until we are in some hellacious fight.

"Judd, honestly, I figured it was time we talked. I've been trying to for a while now, but it just seemed there was always something standing in the way, either with you or with me."

This shocks me; practically knocks me down. "And now?"

"You tell me."

I look at him, not sure of what to say. *Is this it?* Here I came to him, ready to get it all out and resolve all that has stood between us for so long and now I'm scared to death. This bitterness between us has gone on for so long that I don't remember what life would be like without it. It's been so long since I've known normal; since we both have. Looking back to the blanket, I ignore his question and decide we need to start somewhere.

"Tristan, what happened?" I pause, afraid my intrusive question may open up a window to a storm, but I go on, "Your legs … are you?"

He cuts me off quickly, shaking his head with a frown etched across his face.

"Listen, don't worry about me. I can take care of myself … I need to take care of myself and this …" he points down to his legs, with a breathy chuckle that sounds anything other than funny. "This is no big deal. It's nothing I can't handle."

"But are …"

"Judd, I've put a lot on you for a while now and I should never have done that. I forced you to grow up fast, because that's what I had to do. I couldn't see past my selfishness and I'm sorry."

He looks down, shame and remorse shadowing every feature of

his face, but I can't say a word. *That came out of nowhere. I came to apologize and here he is doing it before I can even find the courage.*

I draw my head back, stunned. Deep down I want to rush across the room and hug him. I want to rejoice at seeing my brother again; the brother I grew up with. Tears sting my eyes as I remember who he used to be.

"Tristan, push me," I yell, knowing I can do it myself, but also loving how he runs under the swing on a big push just like Dad used to.

"Hang on."

Jake laughs as Tristan gives him a big shove on the merry-go-round. He races my way, gripping the chain at my sides.

"You ready?" He pulls me back as far as he can reach. "One more push and then I have to go check on Mom back at the fountain. Deal?"

"Deal!" I yell, looking around to make sure there are no other kids in sight to see my big brother push me like I'm some sort of baby. I'm almost ten, definitely not a baby.

"Here you go bud," he says on a strained voice as he runs forward on a heavy push then runs under the swing at the last minute, boosting me high in the air.

My belly jumps with a tickle and he races off into the woods to go find Mom.

"I'll be back," I hear as he disappears.

I stare at Tristan, my mouth unable to form words. My heart gapes open on the thought of how he was constantly running to help Mom, to make us dinner, to get us to school when she got sicker, in his room studying late at night, working midnights at the garage, helping us with our homework. He became our mother and father for years.

A tear slips down my face and I wipe it away quickly, with more guilt flooding my soul. I came here to talk to him, to apologize to him, so why is it so hard now.

"Can I ask you something?" I don't know why I want to ask or why all of sudden that I feel defiant on something I felt so clearly just a bit ago. I know now that Tristan had the cards stacked against him, but I need to know.

"Sure …" his voice cracks as he looks up at me then back down to the hem of the comforter, which he keeps fiddling with in a nervous manner.

"Why did you shove that same life at me as soon as Mom died?" I cringe with the last words I speak, and I see him flinch as well.

He threw adulthood at me before I was even old enough to drive. I want an answer, yet suddenly, I no longer see him as the selfish, greedy screw off that he has been; with only a few words between us today, I now view him as lost and in a desperate search for the happiness we all knew before Dad left and Mom got sick. Not much different than me.

"Hey, you remember when we were kids and we lived in that house on the corner with that huge ass hill?"

I nod my head, unsure of where he's going with this, but eager to listen. This is the first civil discussion we've had in forever.

"You, me and Jake would line our bikes up at the top and speed down that hill going a hundred miles an hour it seemed." He laughs and I can see him lost in the memory. "We'd fly and fly, but we always hit that bottom turn going too fast and you and I would inevitably go flying off our bikes into that cluster of bushes."

I laugh out loud, unable to control myself at the carefree child-hood memories. *I had forgotten about that.*

He looks up at me, all amusement and happiness drained from his face. "Every single time, you would jump up and get right back on your bike and keep going. You remember?"

I lower my brows, still confused, but I nod anyways.

"Sometimes, it just takes some of us longer to get back on the bike. Jake, he always managed to slow down before he hit that turn. I swear he never fell off." He pauses and smiles, yet it's an unhappy expression. "Me … I ended up walking home with a busted lip once, a broken arm one time and even needed stitches in my chin another time." His eyes mist over as his voice cracks on a chuckle that makes my insides hurt. "I wasn't ever able to figure out how you and Jake kept going. I've been trying to get up for four years, Judd. I'm not telling you that I found a way up yet, but I want you to know that I have my eyes open now." He looks down, playing with the edge of the comforter again. Shaking his head, all emotion drops from his voice.

I stare at him, ready to stop him from talking, to tell him I understand, but he ends the sentiment.

"Listen, I need to get some rest," he clears his throat as if pushing away a deeper emotion than he is letting on. "I'm taking some heavy duty pain pills that knock my ass out."

"Ok ..."I say, my heart lodged in my throat.

Turning toward the door, I grip the handle and make my way into the hall, glancing at Mom's door. A sudden sensation climbs through me, an urge, a nudge filled with hope. *This is the beginning.* I swing around so fast, a light headedness overcomes me and I grab the door to steady myself.

"Tristan ..."

He smiles. Not a shitty grin like he's about to pummel me with some smartass comment and not even a frown which I've seen more than anything; he smiles, a genuine look that reminded me of when he was a teenager.

"Yeah?"

"So, there were a lot of things I wanted to say also. Things I now realize, that I didn't before. Things I've been mad at you for, when I had no right to be." He nods, crooking his mouth to the side slightly.

"Maybe another day?"

His eyes droop as he stretches his brows up in an effort to keep them open. *He looks exhausted.* Glancing back at the assortment of bottles on his dresser, I nod my head in agreement.

"Yeah, sounds good."

I leave the house and drive back to my apartment with a few tears in my eyes over me being blind for so long, yet having a small bit of the load lifted from my shoulders even though everything didn't get discussed or resolved. I cling to that one thought. *It's a start.* It's words that I swear Mom gave me at the exact moment I needed them. Walking in the apartment, I shove my keys into my pocket along with my phone out of habit then think of Alyssa, wishing I could share this with her. There is so much I need to tell her and I'm ready now. I want to screw the cap off the bottle once and for all and let it all spill out.

Knock, knock, knock.

The noise at the door is a surprise, but immediately puts my heart on alert as I hear the dainty taps, unlike the heavy pounds that come when Tyler or Jake come by. My heart speeds at even the smallest inkling that it could be her. I race to the door and swing it open, an instant fit of rage boiling in my veins with what is waiting there.

"What the hell do you want?!" I spit out as Bethany stands only a few feet in front of me, her hair a wild mess and makeup smeared beneath her left eye; or wait, is that a black eye? "What the hell happened to your face and how did you know where I live?"

"Ummm, I brought you home one time, remember?"

I forgot about that. Great! I snarl my lip and step back a couple paces, uncomfortable with how close she is.

"Well you can leave … I have nothing to say to you!" I spit out, ten seconds from slamming the door in her face.

"Wait," she yells frantically, slamming her hand flat against the door as I am swinging it closed.

Sighing, I look back at her face and although the sight of her pretty well makes me ill, I study her. Her left eye is framed in faint hues of purple, black and blue marks that look like bruising.

"Fine! What happened to you anyways?"

Quickly folding her arms across her baggy, wrinkled tee, she lets out a heavy breath and looks at the ground. "Alyssa hit me," she mumbles, but I catch every word.

My eyes widen and a bolt of delight and amusement ripples through me. *Alyssa hit her? Good for her. Frankly, I'm surprised I've never been the recipient of my own black eye or worse yet, a swift kick to the balls.* I chuckle at the feisty image of Alyssa that flashes through my mind. Bethany looks up at me, but I don't hide my smile.

"So since you didn't know, I guess she's not here?"

This surprises me.

"Why would she be here?" I spit out, excited that she presumed that Alyssa would be with me.

Bethany's eyes instantly fill with tears and I step back some more. *Oh hell!*

"Judd, I lied! About everything! We never slept together! You knew it was me immediately and shoved me away! I had just snuck into bed and you were saying her name in your sleep and I tried to take advantage of the situation just like I did with Kyle. Only you knew it wasn't her and stopped me right away! I just told her all this just now and assumed she would come …."

My eyes cannot open any wider as she rambles on and my heart has already exploded, along with a mountain of anger that I have held back for Bethany. *I knew it!*

Bolting past her, I slam the apartment door and bump my shoulder against hers in a hurry to leave. I definitely don't need to hear anything else. *I didn't sleep with Bethany...I didn't betray Alyssa! I have to find her. Did she go home? Why would she not come find me? Have I lost her already?*

"Hey, wait ..." Bethany yells out behind me, but I don't stop.

All the pieces of my life feel as if they are finally falling into place. So much has been lost that will never be recovered, but I'm seeing what is in front of me now; that my life is not sucked dry, it's just starting. Each loss has brought me closer to another blessing in my life, things that have been strategically placed in the road, and most I didn't notice right off the bat or still may not see, but I'm looking now, and I'm grateful.

A half hour later and after a quick pit stop at the store for something that is probably completely ridiculous, I am sitting outside the cemetery, a distance away, assuming she would have come to visit her dad. My phone rings and I'm hoping it is Alyssa, but her home number comes up instead of her cell.

My insides are bouncing with the hope that it is her.

"Hello,"

"Judd, is Alyssa with you," Angela's voice sounds a little worried, yet hopeful just like I feel.

At least I'm not the only one thinking she should be with me right now. Apparently, everyone is on the same page as me, but as I glance up, I still do not see her anywhere around. I thought for sure she might have come here.

"No, why did you think she was with me?" I honestly do not know if Angela knows about what happened or not, and I'm not about to tell her that I was mistakenly in someone else's bed, even though I now know nothing happened.

"Well, Bethany called for her earlier, but I thought she was getting her stuff from there, so it confused me. I had talked to her about you before she left and I thought maybe ..." she pauses and I can almost hear her mind clicking away, thinking. "Anyways, she's not answering her phone and I need her to stop and get something at the store. Bethany mentioned before she hung up that maybe Alyssa was on her way to see you."

I sigh, confused on where she could be. As soon as Bethany's confession spilled from her mouth, I had a thought tugging at me, pulling me, urging me to come here.

"No, she didn't come see me, but I'll find her. I'm actually looking for her now. Want me to have her call you?"

"You know what? I have a pretty good idea where she is. I'll just give her some time and call her a little later, unless you find her before that. You know it is none of my business, but I know you two are having some sort of issues. I hope I'm not overstepping my boundaries but when life hands us a struggle, some of us don't know how to react right off the bat. Some of us face it head on and move forward, but most of us run, some of us fall and refuse to get up, but it's the people around us that can help us back up. When Alex and I met, we had to make so many sacrifices in our lives to move forward, but we eventually found our way and we got past those struggles. That's not to say that life doesn't keep throwing struggles our way, but I think once we finally find it, we always can. Alex was the love of my life and I will miss him every day, but some day I hope to see the meaning behind his loss."

Her words are like a throttle to my heart, like she stepped right into my mind and I know, I have to find Alyssa and I have to hold on tight. She was meant to come into my life and I can't ever walk away. She brought air and the sun back into my life, she showed me what family was and her loss showed me a way to break through a wall of anger and hurt that had held me and my brother apart for years.

"I really think right now, Alyssa just needs to be found. Whatever was between you two, you'll work it out … just find her … the rest will fall into place."

My eyes softly close and I grip the phone to my ear tightly, a surge of emotion and reassurance coursing through me. *It's not only Alyssa that needs to be found.*

Opening my eyes, I push away the lump in my throat, "So you think she's ready?"

Angela has no idea what our situation is, but I ask it anyways.

Maybe all the times I wanted to just walk up and fall to my knees and beg her forgiveness, maybe that's exactly what I should have done; over and over.

"I do, Judd, and if you know her well enough and love her, like I know you do … you'll know exactly where to find her, too." The pain in her heart from her loss is evident, yet there is still a smile in her voice as she speaks of the love I hold for her daughter.

"I know exactly where to find her. I'll bring her home later. Thank you for calling me," I say staring ahead as Alyssa hops the fence and makes her way past my mom's grave, pausing to look at it then slowly trailing to kneel in front of her father's headstone.

She didn't come here first. My eyes fill with tears over the fact that I came to her dad's resting place to find her, yet all the while she was only a breath away at my mom's place.

Remaining in my truck, parked behind the big oak tree, I watch as she sits in the grass, running her fingers through the dirt. Her lips move as she talks to her dad, looking ahead at the newly placed granite stone. I desperately want to race over and scoop her up into my arms but it is as if someone is quietly and gently holding me back, I wait and watch with a happiness in my heart once again. *This is their time.*

A little while goes by, and the hands that were holding me in place slowly start to nudge me out of my truck and toward her and Alex. My feet carry me as if they have a mind of their own and my arms can almost already feel her within them.

Coming to a complete stop, only steps away from her with only Alex's plot and stone separating us. I watch as she speaks to him in a hushed tone with tears sliding down both her cheeks.

"Please come back, Daddy. I just need to hug you one last time. I need to tell you goodbye…" she sobs and my heart rips open for her. "I need to tell you so much. You said you'd be here."

Her chest heaves in and out, and although I should feel as though I am invading on a private moment, I move forward a few more steps as if a barrier of gravity is pulling me to her. She sucks in a breath and runs the back of her hand across her face, slowly lifting her head to look up. I stop and hold my breath, in complete awe. Her face is streaked in tears, her eyes are bloodshot and a bright aqua blue, but she is absolutely breathtaking.

Silence captivates us both for a few moments before she breaks the spell, "How did you find me?"

Stepping around to the side of Alex's plot, I walk towards her wanting nothing more than to grab her up into my arms, but again I stop and guide my hand to cup her chin between my fingertips. Her beautiful pain-filled eyes look back at me and I can see all signs of what happened between us are gone. I only see love and longing there.

Opening my mouth I begin to answer her question with 'I have no idea how I found you' but different words pop into my mouth.

"I'll always find you," I whisper and it suddenly dawns on me that I will. I don't know how or why she was brought into my life, but it was for a reason. She found me and brought me back to life. It doesn't matter what happens between us or in the future; I'm here and I'll never leave her. "I know nothing happened that morning and I know for a fact that you know that now, too," I tell her so that there are no walls left between us.

The little crook between her brows that she always gets when she is confused or upset appears and she sucks in a panicked breath.

"I didn't trust you. I'm so sorry I didn't believe you. How can you still want me when I was able to believe her instead of you?"

I want to laugh at how silly she is for thinking that I could not forgive her. There was never anything to forgive.

"Of course I want you. Didn't you hear me? I'll always want you. Alyssa, you take my breath away. When we are together, I have to remind myself to breathe, because you make my heart beat so fast. When we're apart, I'm constantly trying to catch my breath, because I can't breathe without you. You're my life, my air, my whole world. You're it for me, Alyssa. I love you and I can't live without you. I'm lost without you, baby."

No sooner than the words flow from my lips, she is in my arms and her mouth is on mine. I pull her off the ground, up level with me and I swear I cannot get her close enough. Her arm grazes the back of my neck igniting a shiver that runs through my body and her hair gently blows over my cheek, but I cannot stop tasting the sweetness of her lips.

Finally sitting her down, I look into her eyes with my heart bursting. *She's everything.* I take a quick glance to Alex's stone, grateful and forever indebted to him for trusting me to love his daughter, for asking me to take care of her and for in some way leading me to her.

"I'll always find you … I promise, because you found me."

She found me when I was once again ready to run; run to California and leave everything behind.

She pulled me up when I didn't even realize the pain of the past was still eating me alive.

She saved me, brought me back to life and if I can show her just a trace of that amount of love, then that will be more than most people experience in a lifetime.

After our lips are once again accustomed to each other, we step forward in the direction of my truck and I slip my hand down to grab the sack that slipped from my hand when I picked her up. I was so happy to hold her again everything else on my mind was forgotten.

"Let me take you to your mom and dad's house. I'm not much of a cook, but I thought I could make these for you girls," I chuckle as she peers inside the bag that I have held open.

Her face breaks open into a wide grin. "I think we would all like that," she giggles with a small escaped tear of joy as we make our way back to my truck.

Unwilling to separate for even a second, we abandon her car at the playground and choose to make our way back to her parents together. I have no extra set of clothes and no toothbrush, I have to work tomorrow, but all I know is I am not leaving her side. I grip her hand tightly as I sit beside her in the small cab of my truck, feeling the weight of the world being released from my shoulders as the welded shut gates to my heart swing free and open.

I squeeze her hand tighter, knowing there is one more thing that has been left unsaid; one piece of myself that I have held back.

"Alyssa," I clear my throat, prepared to shove down every ounce of hesitation that I've always felt on this subject, but there is none. I sigh and go on, "My mom started getting sick around my ninth birthday." I see her head turn as her other hand falls across my forearm. "She wasn't real sick at first, just stumbling, losing her balance." I pause, seeing it like it was yesterday, yet having a rush of confidence in going on and letting it all out. "Me and Jake didn't really think anything of it for the longest time, but eventually after Dad left, Mom got a diagnosis." I gulp, still not looking over at her. "The doctors told her she had ALS and that the life expectancy is usually less than five years." I turn my head and finally glance at Alyssa.

Her eyes are glazed over with love and tenderness, hope and happiness and just like that, I know without a doubt that Mom is right here with me; that Alex never left Alyssa's side. They are both with us and will walk through life with us and always, always give us guidance and a nudge to face the hardest things in life. It's because of them that we can stare down unbearable tragedies such as losing a parent, and still keep our head above water; still breathe.

"She showed them, because she hung in there for five full years after that diagnosis." I smile, gripping the steering wheel with a sudden lightness in my heart over how brave my mom was until the very end. *God, she fought; she fought for us.*

On the drive, we continue to talk and hold each other close, but this time there are no tears because we have one another. She leans into me and I stroke my thumb over the back of her hand, tingles racing over my skin. My heart kicks up and, although I shouldn't be thinking it, flickers of us making love fly through my mind. The way her heart pounds at the same rhythm as mine; the way when I am lying above her, I can feel the drumming of it blended with my own to create the most beautiful music I've ever known. Our breaths, however fast and ragged that they become, they're in sync; she breathes, I breathe. Her body melts into mine with her head securely resting against my shoulder and one of her legs draped over mine. If the stars had eyes, I know they would look down and see only one figure.

As we pull up to her house, I casually lean forward and sneak a kiss before we head inside. As her lips touch mine, my heart floods with love and I'm reminded of the first time I kissed her. It was as if I had blasted off to the moon. My feet no longer stood on solid ground because at that very moment, I was lost in her forever.

It's truly as though we were once one single block of clay that was molded, shaped and carved into existence. Once that one piece was perfected, we were separated into two bodies with air breathed into our lungs then cast down from the heavens to someday find each other again. Our lives were intertwined in the most exceptional way that we would have searched the globe if it meant finding one another.

Her losses have brought new light into my life and my heartache and love will pull her through hers.

I know she is mine and I never intend on letting her go. I'll forever keep that promise to Alex. She is my life; my reason for wandering this earth.

I've never known happiness like this until she walked into my life. She found me, simple as that. It only took a second, a fraction of a moment in the strand of time, but when her eyes met mine, I could breathe. It was then and only then, that I could finally catch my breath.

Epilogue

I WALK INTO ALYSSA'S bedroom, instantly admiring her petite figure all sprawled out on the bed. My eyes roam up the length of her legs to her tight shorts up to the sliver of skin peeking out from beneath her shirt then over the peaks of her breasts and last to her beautiful face. She stirs and I can't help the ridiculous smile that pulls at my lips. This is a nice opportunity to surprise her.

Walking silently over to the side of her bed, I gently slide on top of her, being careful to not bear the full weight of my body on her. My face hovers above hers and she immediately opens her sleepy eyes. Once she focuses on me her face lights up and her eyes beam with adoration.

Glancing down to my lips, her eyes sparkle and I know she wants me to kiss her, so I do. She worms around beneath me and it takes all my will power to not get carried away like we always do. However, I have an agenda to keep, so I pull away. As my lips leave hers she lets out a small whimper and I have to chuckle. *I completely understand.*

"Are you packed for the lake, yet?" She nods. "Why are you napping now? We have a four hour ride that you can sleep during."

She laughs at my question. "Oh I have no intention of sleeping on the drive." Her mischievous tone makes me laugh but she quickly informs me of her plans. "It just so happens that I have the perfect view of your dimple from the passenger seat." I crack up as she moves in to plant a kiss on my right cheek. *She is so obsessed with that.*

"Well you just so happen to see it more than anyone else in my life ever has." It's the complete truth. No one has ever made me smile like Alyssa does. I should just have surgery to make it permanent.

"That's just because I make you so happy," she giggles, but I don't even laugh.

I continue to smile at her knowing it is the complete truth. Instead of telling her, I decide to show her and kiss her deeply. Slowly the edge of her heels slide around the backs of my thighs then further up to clasp around my hips. Once she lets out her little noise that I love so much, I decide play time might have to wait. Pushing up to sit, I slide to the edge of the bed and settle down beside her. The look she gives me has me grabbing my stomach to hold back laughter.

"Sit up; I have something I want to give you."

"But Christmas is not for another three days," she says looking excited.

"I know, but there will be tons of people there and I want this to be something just between you and me."

Her eyes light up and she quickly sits up sliding her hand beneath mine. Instinctively, I thread my fingers through hers while reaching my other hand into my pocket. I pull out a small black box and waste no time informing her exactly what it is not.

"Hey, it's not a ring."

We both laugh remembering the last time I gave her a black box. I have another little black box to give her for Christmas. That one is also not a ring, but I figure if I give her several of these, by the time I give her the one that actually has the ring in it, it will be completely unexpected. At least that's the plan.

She giggles and squeals like a little kid and I am immediately on top of the world. Taking the box in her hands, she unties the delicate, satiny, pink ribbon and opens it slowly. Once she sees the contents she falls forward into my lap laughing hysterically. *Not exactly what I was expecting.*

"Judd, I already have a key to your apartment. Besides we are always together so there is no need for two, let alone three keys."

I smile happy that I have stumped her; I thought for sure she would figure it out.

"You don't have a key to my *new* apartment," I say as I gulp down a ball nerves in order to say the next part, "Our apartment actually."

Her eyes widen.

I better explain my reasons pretty fast. "I know we only discussed the topic of moving in together as a joke to get away from Evan barging in, but I was looking around my room the other day and…"

I look at her and her face is blank. She has a hint of a smile, but not near what I was hoping for. *Damn, I hope I didn't rush this.*

I go on with my explanation,"… what I saw wasn't what I wanted to see. When I look on my dresser I want to see your stuff. When I open my medicine cabinet I want to see your tooth brush beside mine. I want to see all your clothes beside mine in the closet. And I always…" I pull her against me and look into her eyes with a smile. "I always want you by my side."

I know more than likely no one will approve. They will think we are rushing this and moving too fast and maybe we are, but this whole thing between us started out fast from the get go so why change things up now. I smile thinking back on Alex's words the day we sat on the back patio grilling. He said the same thing.

With my last words she breaks into a fit of giggles and lunges at me nearly knocking me off the bed. I throw my arms around her and breathe in a sigh of relief.

"Yes, yes! I will move in with you," she hollers through a thunder of laughter. Moving back only a bit, she looks me in the eyes with a worried expression. "I mean if that's what you're asking, then yes."

I laugh, "Of course, that's what I'm asking you. Move in with me."

With no more words between us, she attacks my lips and jumps into my lap pushing me back into the bed. Straddling me, she raises my hands above my head and wiggles around. I chuckle at her aggressiveness. *I could get used to this. If this is her reaction to a key I can't wait til I do give her a ring.*

She leans into me and kisses my neck while letting her hands roam over my chest. I take in a deep breath, my jeans instantly tightening and not a fiber of my body wanting to put the brakes on even though we are in her parent's house. *I really do not want to stop this!* She raises my shirt, her hands tickling across my abdomen and making me shiver beneath her touch. *Oh good God!* One last fraction of self control makes my hand fly out and grab hers before we are down to only a few articles of clothing between us.

"Your mom is down in the kitchen." I glance over to the door, indicating that it is also wide open.

She bends down into my ear, whispering, "We can be quiet and I can shut the door."

I laugh at her suggestion.

"You're never quiet and neither am I." If we were quiet we would probably be able to make it through one night without Evan calling out that he hears us or listening to his sarcastic remarks the next morning. "Get dressed and I'll show you the apartment."

She looks at me in shock then places both her hands on my face, her soft skin making a scratching sound as it scrapes over my five-o-clock shadow.

"It's already ours?" she asks in disbelief and I crack up at the tone of her voice.

"Of course it is ours. How do you think we have keys already?"

She jumps off me, bouncing into the air like a cheerleader cheering at a winning game. I stand up, placing my hands lightly on her hips so I don't go and get excited all over again.

"Get dressed and grab your bag while you're at it. We'll leave for the lake from there."

She looks at me quizzically, probably wondering why we wouldn't just swing back by here. I'd bet money that she thinks the apartment is in Rosemore. Thankfully, I found a place perfectly positioned between school, both our jobs and her parents house. I want her to be close to home.

It takes no time at all for her to slip out of her shorts and shirt and to slip into jeans and a hoodie. Once clothes go a flying, I decide to make myself scarce. My will power can only go so far around her. Instead I go down to visit with her mom.

Fifteen minutes later we are in my truck, driving to the place we will soon call home. *I cannot believe we are taking this step together.*

Glancing over at her in the passenger seat, I flash her a smile, unable to hold back my own giddiness as she excitedly bounces up and down like a little kid waiting for Santa Claus. That's all it takes for her to slide across the seat and snuggle into my side. My hand falls to hers and I have no intentions of letting it go anytime soon.

Pulling into the private driveway, I kill the engine, open my door to step out and look over at her. *Ok, maybe I lied about the apartment part but a duplex is somewhat of an apartment.* Lucky for us, we only have listening ears to the left of us and our bedroom is clear on the right side of the house. Her eyes widen and she jumps up in her seat.

"Judd, oh my gosh!!! Can we afford this? Wait! We're only 15 minutes from Moms house!" she yells excitedly.

She tears her hand from mine and slaps them both across her mouth, tears filling her eyes as she looks at me. Standing right outside the driver's door, I lean against the seat and pull her closer.

"Twelve minutes from your moms house actually," I say proudly.

I timed it after I saw the for rent sign. I was pretty pleased when I found it; it was like it was destined. I never believed in that kind of stuff before Alyssa but now it seems like the universe is throwing fateful things at me by the handful, her being the most amazing of them all.

"… and yes we can afford it and still afford both of our tuitions," I finish telling her. "Let's go inside."

Gripping her by the waist, I help her out of the truck through the driver's side then pull her hand into mine again. We stroll up the walkway with her making a spectacle of peeking inside the mailbox, looking in the window of the garage and giggling as she runs her foot across the landscaping timbers that line the front flower bed. *I knew she would love this.* I grab my own key and unlock the door, carefully swinging it open.

"Wait!" I point at her before she can step inside. She pauses her footing and eyes me. "I have to carry you across the threshold." I grin at her fully prepared to lift her into my arms.

She gives my arm a nudge and laughs. "That's your wedding night silly. But I'll settle for a piggy back ride." She laughs as she jumps onto my back.

I step through the doorway of our new apartment with her clung to me and turn in a circle so she can take it all in. Her hand leaves my shoulder and from the corner of my eyes I can now see that it is covering her mouth as she looks around.

"It's beautiful!"

I rush over to the breakfast bar and set her down. I have to look at her because yes it is wonderful but beautiful, no; she is beautiful.

I pull her hand away from her mouth and look into her eyes. "You're beautiful, Alyssa. I love you."

Her eyes fill with tears as she grasps my face, pulling me closer. I think she's going to kiss me but instead, she just holds me close, pressing her forehead to mine. Her eyes are closed and tears rush down her face. If it wasn't for the unbelievably beautiful smile I would think she was sad. I stare at her with a bit of concern, wondering if I should say something, but then she finally opens her eyes. She pulls her forehead away but still keeps me close.

"I love you so much, Judd. I have to pinch myself every single day to make sure you're real; that this is real. I can't believe that I found you. How did I find someone that is so amazing and that loves me so completely? Someone that has been there for me at every turn and that knows me better than I know myself most days."

I smile at her and feel an overwhelming surge through my heart that has my pulse racing. When my eyes glaze over, I know there will never be anything that will compare to the love I feel for her; a love that literally brings tears to my eyes. I wrap my hands behind her backside and slide her to the edge of the bar with her legs on both sides of my hips.

Once her body is flush against my own, I cover her lips with mine. I lick and taste her mouth with such tenderness and passion while running my hands back into her hair. Her hands glides around my neck and her breathing speeds up. I slowly lay her back on the bar and brace my knee into the barstool to step up with her. She breaks our kiss and giggles as soon as my body is pressed against hers, pushing back into the counter.

"Is there a bed in here yet?"

I shake my head with a trace of mischievousness in my smile. "No bed."

She gives me a quizzical look and looks back at the bar we are currently laying on as I quirk my brows.

She then looks around while I add, "no couch."

She looks back to me and raises her eyebrows, tapping her fingertips against the granite top. In one swift motion, she pulls me all the way against her body; we both laugh.

"The way I figure it, this is our house now so it's only fitting for us to break in each … and every room … properly." I wiggle my eyebrows up and down and add, "… starting with the kitchen."

And that is exactly what we do.

Releasing Spring 2016:

Breathe With Me
Book Three in **The Breathe Series**

Evan's Story

Acknowledgements

First off, I have to give a huge thanks to everyone who has messaged me, supported me, posted reviews and purchased my first book, Take My Breath Away. Going into this, I mainly wanted to publish a book for myself because it was a long time dream of mine. To my surprise, over the past few months I have been flooded with people telling me how much they love my book, how it has touched their lives in some way and even how it has helped some cope with a tragedy of their own. I can truly say that I hold each and every email, Facebook post, text, private message and kind words that you all have said to me and locked them in my heart. Thank you so much.

Thank you to two exceptional supporters, my husband and Karrie Zschille who promote the heck out of me and help me more than I could ever imagine. You both go above and beyond and I don't know how I would get through this journey without you two.

Thank you to my editor, Jeremy Thompson. Not only are you always spot on with your advice and suggestions for my books, but some days you double as my therapist. I'm so thankful to call you a friend!!!!!

Also thank you to Karen for the added help on editing. You're awesome as always.

Thank you to a wonderful group of beta readers: Karrie Zschille, Tara Dameron, Ashley Shoen, Heather Cavanaugh, Lisa Icard, Cori Wray and Jaclyn Keller as well as Deanna Richardson, Laura Liley, Billy Wilson, Morgan Swinford, Billie Jo Sadler, Debbie Lands, Jesica Schultz, Laura Estes and Angela Patterson. I'd like to give a special shout out to Karrie and Lisa, whose in depth edits were invaluable to this book. It would have never reached the potential I had hoped for had it not been for you two.

Thank you to Daniela with DCP Designs who is fabulously talented beyond words, exhibits exceptional one-on-one communication with her clients and always manages to blow me away with her work.

Thank you to Julio and Mandy. You two definitely knocked another one out of the park with the stunning pictures and as always, you captured the exact emotion I was looking for to bring Judd and Alyssa to life for the cover.

Thank you to Kari with Cover to Cover Designs. The cover for book one was so beyond gorgeous that I feared we'd never come close to matching its beauty, but I was wrong. This cover is unbelievable and surpassed all my expectations and hopes.

Thank you to Stacey Blake with Champagne Formats for matching the beauty of my story, cover and characters with an absolutely stunning interior. Your talent always impresses me and perfectly caps off the entire process leading up to publishing.

Last but not least, thank you to all the readers and fans of this series. You all make me want to keep writing and writing with no end. Also, I'd like to give a big shout out to all my fans in my childhood town of Jackson, Missouri and my now hometown of Chaffee, Missouri. You have amazed me with all the support and faith you have in me. I love you all, especially my "super fans" (you know who you are.)

About the Author

Wendy Wilson is an independent author. As a little girl on through adulthood, she has dreamt of writing and is finally able to indulge in that dream with the release of her first books in *The Breathe Series.* She enjoys spending time with her family, hanging with her friends and reading. She also has a passion for running and has found it is the perfect time to create and think up more exciting plots and characters to add into her books. She currently lives in Chaffee, Missouri with her husband, two adorable sons and two cats.

Visit my website at:
www.wendylwilsonauthor.com
https://www.facebook.com/wendylwilsonauthor

www.ingramcontent.com/pod-product-compliance
Lightning Source LLC
Chambersburg PA
CBHW020247030726
47499CB00001B/91